AMERICAN SUPERNATURAL TALES

It takes an unusual caliber of writer to deliver readers into the terrifying beyond—to conjure tales that are not only unsettling, but unnatural, with elements and characters that are all the more disturbing for their impossibility. From Edgar Allan Poe to Stephen King, American authors have excelled at journeying into the supernatural. You'll find them here, including H. P. Lovecraft, Shirley Jackson, Ray Bradbury, Nathaniel Hawthorne, and others. An unprecedented anthology of phantasmagoric, spectral, and demonic writing, *American Supernatural Tales* celebrates our enduring need to be spooked and horrified.

𝔓enguin 𝕳orror

Penguin Horror is a collection of novels, stories, and poems by masters of the genre, curated by filmmaker and lifelong horror literature reader Guillermo del Toro. Included in the series are some of his favorites: *Frankenstein* by Mary Shelley, *The Raven: Tales and Poems* by Edgar Allan Poe, *The Thing on the Doorstep and Other Weird Stories* by H. P. Lovecraft, *The Haunting of Hill House* by Shirley Jackson, *Haunted Castles: The Complete Gothic Stories* by Ray Russell, and *American Supernatural Tales*, edited by S. T. Joshi and featuring stories from Ray Bradbury, Joyce Carol Oates, Robert E. Howard, and Stephen King, alongside many others. Penguin Horror reminds us what del Toro writes in his series introduction: "To learn what we fear is to learn who we are."

PENGUIN BOOKS

AMERICAN SUPERNATURAL TALES

S. T. JOSHI is a freelance writer and editor. He has edited Penguin Classics editions of H. P. Lovecraft's *The Call of Cthulhu and Other Weird Stories* and *The Thing on the Doorstep and Other Weird Stories*, as well as Algernon Blackwood's *Ancient Sorceries and Other Strange Stories*, Arthur Machen's *The White People and Other Weird Stories*, and *American Supernatural Tales*. He has also written critical studies on Lord Dunsany and H. P. Lovecraft; edited works by Ambrose Bierce, Clark Ashton Smith, and H. L. Mencken; and has completed a two-volume history of supernatural fiction entitled *Unutterable Horror*.

GUILLERMO DEL TORO is a Mexican director, producer, screenwriter, novelist, and designer. He cofounded the Guadalajara International Film Festival, and formed his own production company—the Tequila Gang. However, he is most recognized for his Academy Award–winning film, *Pan's Labyrinth*, and the Hellboy film franchise. He has received Nebula and Hugo awards, was nominated for a Bram Stoker Award, and is an avid collector and student of arcane memorabilia and weird fiction.

AMERICAN SUPERNATURAL TALES

Edited with an Introduction
by S. T. Joshi

✝

PENGUIN HORROR

Series Editor Guillermo del Toro

PENGUIN BOOKS

PENGUIN BOOKS

Published by the Penguin Group
Penguin Group (USA) LLC
375 Hudson Street
New York, New York 10014

USA | Canada | UK | Ireland | Australia | New Zealand | India | South Africa | China
penguin.com
A Penguin Random House Company

First published in Penguin Books 2007
This edition with a series introduction by Guillermo del Toro published 2013

Library of Congress Cataloging-in-Publication Data

American Supernatural Tales / edited with an introduction by S.T. Joshi ;
series editor Guillermo del Toro.
   p. cm
   ISBN 978-0-14-3122371 (hardback)
   1. Horror tales, American.   2. Paranormal fiction, American.   I. Joshi, S.T., 1958– editor of
compilation.   II. Toro, Guillermo del, 1964–
   PS648.H6A49 2013
   813' .0873808—dc23 2013027157

Printed in Italy
10 9 8 7 6 5

Set in ITC New Baskerville Std Roman
Designed by Spring Hoteling

ACKNOWLEDGMENTS

The author and publisher are grateful for the following parties for permission to reprint the following copyrighted works:

H. P. Lovecraft, "The Call of Cthulhu." Copyright © 1928 by Popular Fiction Publishing Company. Reprinted by permission of Lovecraft Properties LLC.

Clark Ashton Smith, "The Vaults of Yoh-Vombis." Copyright © 1932 by Popular Fiction Publishing Company. Reprinted by permission of Arkham House Publishers, Inc. and its agents, JABberwocky Literary Agency Inc., 24-16 Queens Plaza South, Suite 505, Long Island City, NY 11101.

Robert E. Howard, "Old Garfield's Heart." Copyright © 1933 by Popular Fiction Publishing Company. Reprinted from *The Black Stranger and Other American Tales* by Robert E. Howard, edited and with an introduction by Steven Tompkins, by permission of the University of Nebraska Press. Copyright © 2005 by Robert E. Howard Properties, LLC.

Robert Bloch, "Black Bargain." Copyright © 1942 by Popular Fiction Publishing Company. Reprinted by permission of the Estate of Robert Bloch by arrangement with Richard Henshaw Group LLC.

August Derleth, "The Lonesome Place." Copyright © 1948. Reprinted by permission of Arkham House Publishers, Inc. and its agents, JABberwocky Literary Agency Inc., 24-16 Queens Plaza South, Suite 505, Long Island City, NY 11101.

Fritz Leiber, "The Girl with the Hungry Eyes." Copyright © 1949 by Avon Books, Inc. Reprinted by permission of Richard Curtis Associates.

CONTENTS

HAUNTED CASTLES, DARK MIRRORS

ON THE PENGUIN HORROR SERIES

There is no god but this mirror that thou seest, for this is the Mirror of Wisdom. And it reflecteth all things that are in heaven and on earth, save only the face of him who looketh into it. This it reflecteth not, so that he who looketh into it may be wise.

—Oscar Wilde, "The Fisherman and His Soul"

To learn what we fear is to learn who we are. Horror defines our boundaries and illuminates our souls. In that, it is no different, or less controversial, than humor, and no less intimate than sex. Our rejection or acceptance of a particular type of horror fiction can be as rarefied or kinky as any other phobia or fetish.

Horror is made of such base material—so easily rejected or dismissed—that it may be hard to accept my postulate that within the genre lies one of the last refuges of spirituality in this, our materialistic world.

But it is a fact that, through the ages, most storytellers have had to resort to the fantastic in order to elevate their discourse to the level of parable. Stevenson, Wilde, Victor Hugo, Henry James, Marcel Schwob, Kipling, Borges, and many others. Borges, in fact, defended the fantastic quite openly and acknowledged fable and parable as elemental forms of narrative that would always outlive the much younger forms, which are preoccupied with realism.

At a primal level, we crave parables, because they allow us to grasp the impossibly large concepts and to understand our universe without and within. These tales can "make flesh" what would otherwise be metaphor or allegory. More important, the horror tale becomes imprinted in us at an emotional level: Shiver by shiver, we gain insight.

But, at its root, the frisson is a crucial element of this form of storytelling—because all spiritual experience requires faith, and faith requires abandonment: the humility to fully surrender to a tide of truths and wills infinitely larger than ourselves.

It is in this abandonment that we are allowed to witness phenomena that go beyond our nature and that reveal the spiritual side of our existence.

We dislocate, for a moment, the rules of our universe, the laws that bind the rational and diminish the cosmos to our scale. And when the world becomes a vast, unruly place, a place where anything can happen, then—and only then—we allow for miracles and angels, no matter how dark they may be.

Penguin has a particularly important place in my own relationship with the fantastic. When I was a child—roughly seven years old—I started purchasing and collecting fantastic literature. My first purchases were paperbacks, and the two main purveyors of my collection were, almost inevitably, Editorial Bruguera in Spanish and Penguin Books in English. As a kid, I was so grateful to have these short story collections and novels in an affordable—albeit fragile—format. Reading these tales at such an early age most definitely shaped me into whatever manner of creature I am today.

The discovery of the horror tale at such an early age was fortuitous for me. This sort of tale serves, in many ways, the very same purpose as fairy tales did in our childhood: It operates as a theater of the mind in which internal conflicts are played out. In these tales we can parade the most reprehensible aspects of our being: cannibalism, incest, parricide. It allows us to discuss our anxieties and even to contemplate the experience of death in absolute safety.

And again, like a fairy tale, horror can serve as a liberating or repressive social tool, and it is always an accurate reflection of the social climate of its time and the place where it gets birthed.

In the eighteenth century, Romanticism—and with it, the Gothic tale—surged as a reaction against the suffocating dogmas of the Enlightenment. Empiricism weighed heavily upon our souls so, as the age of reason went to sleep, it produced monsters. Reason and science were being enthroned when the Gothic Romance exploded full of emotion and thrills. "The great art of life is sensation, to feel that we exist, even in pain," said Lord Byron, enunciating a basic Romantic idea and, perhaps, hoping that goblins, ghosts, and demons provided some necessary release to a puritanical society.

The Gothic has its sights planted firmly in the past because it is there that ghosts reside. Romanesque ruins evoke, with their incomplete grandeur, the will that built them and the echoes they left behind. The innate necrophilia subjacent in the Gothic spirit is made manifest as a tribute to the eternal notion of love.

The enormous popularity of this genre produced a deluge of inferior titles and sub–Minerva Press imitations; its elements became so well-known as to be somewhat parodied in Jane Austen's *Northanger Abbey* (created in direct response to Ann Radcliffe's Gothic novels) or, more obliquely, in the *Don Quixote* of the Gothic genre: *The Monk*, by Matthew G. Lewis.

Toward the end of its run, the Gothic's resistance to modernity gave way to a new set of devices—it began to utilize the shiny artifices of science, psychology, and other avant-garde tools to lend plausibility to its phantoms.

And it is at this point that the modern horror tale, in the hand of young, skillful, and powerful writers, starts evolving from its Gothic roots and delivers bold, very experimental works that shape the language in exciting and innovative ways.

Much like Matthew G. Lewis, who was twenty years old when he wrote *The Monk*, Mary Shelley was painfully young—a teenager, in fact—when she first published *Frankenstein, or the Modern*

Prometheus and into the monster and his tale she was able to pour all her contradictions and her questions—her essential pleas and her feelings of disfranchisement and inadequacy. The tale spoke about such profound, particular feelings that, irremediably, it became universal.

While reading the novel as a child, I was arrested by the epistolary form Shelley had chosen (and which *Dracula* would use to good effect many decades later), because it felt so immediate. I was overtaken by the Miltonian sense of abandonment, the absolute horror of a life without a reason. The tragedy of the tale was not dependent on evil. That's the supreme pain of the novel—tragedy requires no villain.

Just as Poe will prefigure the ambiguities of psychiatry, Shelley utilizes the most cutting-edge science and philosophy to drive her existential discourse home. Galvanism, chemistry, and surgery provide the alibi for the monster to gain life and to arise and question all of us.

The Faust-like thirst for knowledge and the arrogance of science are embodied in the character of Victor. He becomes an uncaring god who can force dead flesh to be reanimated but cannot calculate the consequences of his creation. This leads to the infinite sorrow of his creation, who will experience the hunger, the loneliness, and the burden of existence, far removed from its creator.

And the Creature, like the wolf of St. Francis, wanders through the world, encounters mostly evil and hatred, and learns of rage and pain. He becomes hardened and lonely. And I, at age ten, in a comfortable house in a suburb, felt exactly the same way. Shelley goes deeper than many authors by refusing to impose a pattern of good and evil only as discourse (like Stevenson's "Markheim" or Poe in "William Wilson"), but by actually weaving it into the plot.

The unnatural essence of the Creature is defined by his origins—by the god that gave him life—because Victor usurps not only the divine function of God, but also that of intercourse. Victor is barren and alone when he creates the Creature, and their final encounter brings it all full circle—they finally meet in a desolate, frozen landscape, which provides the perfect theater for the colloquy between the arid God and the abandoned Man.

In usurping the role of God, Victor is also faced with questions and reproach that far exceed his paternal capabilities and ultimately allow the Creature to see him, too, as just a man. Another abandoned man. So, as the tale ends, and as his god dies a simple man, the Creature will fade into the cold limbo with the sole desire to die himself. To be no more. Remote as Victor may have been, he was the only thing that gave sense to the Creature's life, and with him gone, only oblivion remains.

Frankenstein is the purest of parables—working both as a straight narrative and as a symbolic one. Shelley utilizes the Gothic model to tell a story not about the loss of a paradise but rather about the absence of one.

The novel is so articulate and vibrant that it often surprises those who approach it for the first time. No adaptation—and there are some masterful ones—has ever captured it whole.

Taking its rightful place among the essential characters in any narrative form, Frankenstein's Creature will go beyond literature and will join Tarzan, Sherlock Holmes, Pinocchio, and Monte Cristo in embodying a concept, even in the minds of those who have never read the actual books.

Clearly, the horror tale deals with the essential duality of mankind, a topic that has proved irresistible to philosophers, prophets, and saints. The Adamites, the Dulcinians, and other savage orders advocated salvation through Bosch-like excess and violence—and they all situated the root of all evil in the soul. It is not until Poe that the seat of evil is transferred back to its proper place: the human mind.

It is in Poe that we first find the sketches of modern horror while being able to enjoy the traditional trappings of the Gothic tale. He speaks of plagues and castles and ancient curses, but he is also morbidly attracted to the aberrant intellect, the mind of the outsider.

Poe grappled with the darker side of mankind, with the demons that reside within us: our mind, a crumbling edifice, sinking slowly in a swamp of decadence and madness. He knew that a rational, good-hearted man could, when ridden by demons, sink a knife in the eye of a beloved cat and gouge it out. He could strangle an old man or burn alive his enemies. He knew that those dark impulses can shape us, overtake us, make us snap—and yet, we would still be able to function, we would still presume to possess the power of rational thought.

Why would anyone say we are mad?

In Poe, the legend weighs heavily upon his readers. Partly because of the singular misfortune of his life, but also due to one outstanding fact: The portrait of Poe as a dissolute, intoxicated wretch comes chiefly from the biased chronicling and ruthless eulogizing of one Rufus Wilmot Griswold. Griswold had the singular duty of being an enemy of Poe and guardian of the writer's legacy. So, quite early after the writer's death, the misinterpretation of Poe starts in earnest. Griswold publishes a most ruthless epitaph and a distorted biography that will, to this day, define Poe in the popular imagination.

One of the most surprising aspects of Poe is how remarkably uninterested he is in the supernatural. He is interested in figures of uncanny origin, and—much like the medieval artists—is capable of giving the plague a body and a voice, but he is not compelled toward the ghostly or physically monstrous; he is a rationalist (it should come as no surprise that he pioneered the detective novel) repulsed by and attracted to madness and loss.

Like every good writer of horror fiction, there is a large degree of autobiography in Poe's work. The imprinting of death and love, the almost Dickensian nature of his childhood and the fact that his savage muse did not endear him to the mainstream of American literature all cooperated to create the sense of isolation in his fiction. This remarkable characteristic—which he will share with another accursed American writer, Howard Phillips Lovecraft—is of the foremost importance in understanding Poe. Most of his protagonists are outsiders. They stand alone, trapped, confined within themselves.

But it is here that two thoroughly modern demons make their appearance: perversity and arrogance. Part of the fundament of the horror tale is that it exists in a regimented social reality. The inner monologue of a Poe character becomes more effective when juxtaposed against minute social detail and quaint norm. The desires that pulse within are deemed irrational or perverse by the outside world and lay these characters on a disastrous route that suffuses each story and poem with a driving sense of doom.

His poems and stories, such as those in *The Raven: Tales and Poems*, have a passion for the abnormal and the hopeless that makes clear his ambivalence toward "normalcy." He can only paint normalcy as a saintly virtue, a quiet, enraging sounding board for the drumming of madness. And little by little, as his tales unfold, that quaintness will become unsustainable, repugnant even, and it must be extinguished. It is in this arrogance that Poe's characters reveal their true nature: They are not victims but executioners. Wolves in a land of sheep. In this, Poe hints at the psychopathy and sociopathy that will shape the criminology of centuries to come. Standing above moral judgment, he gives us a true glimpse into the criminal mind.

Poe is enraptured by the loss of all that was noble and grand and good. The tragedy in Poe's world is not the darkness in which we wallow but the fact that we once contemplated heaven. The warm, bright kingdom of the smile has fallen, and it has given way to a valley of despair and demented laughter.

Poe instilled polarized reactions and remains, to this day, a writer often misinterpreted and even reviled. To an obstinate few, the exquisite, precise nature of his prose remains invisible, asphyxiated by the effect it provokes. But his work is without a doubt the fundamental stepping-stone between the legacy of Gothic horror and the threshold of its modern incarnations.

Poe redefines the Gothic edifice as a haunted castle of the mind, but it will have to wait until the end of the nineteenth century to be fully inhabited, when Henry James creates *The Turn of the Screw*.

The ghost story is perhaps the most venerable and accepted part of horror literature. Just as monsters can be found as far back as *Beowulf*, *The Ramayana*, or *The Iliad*, so can ghosts be traced to the very origins of the consigned narrative.

The ghost story has had many great practitioners, but, justly, two names stand above them all: M. R. James and Joseph Sheridan Le Fanu. In their hands, the ghost story acquires such solidity and conviction as to become fact. Their distinct styles achieve this result through varied means, which I will discuss succinctly. In James, horror comes as much by the punctilious nature of the detail and background provided for the story as it comes from the obstinate omission of such details in a capricious manner by the story's narrator. This lends the story the patina of truth. It is no secret that, in describing his horrors, James is evoking his own intimate phobias and, it is said, the echoes of a single ghostly encounter he had at a very early age.

Le Fanu's case is entirely another matter. Even when James drinks from the same stylistic resources—which he absorbed as a student and scholar of Le Fanu's legacy—it is the innate connection that Le Fanu feels with the supernatural that dominates his work and separates it from the rest.

The tenuous but precise way in which Le Fanu builds up the supernatural elements is akin to the pervasive effects of mildew on a solid wall. It is not by force but by accumulation that he demolishes disbelief and tears down the barrier that separates us from fear. The relentless but delicate construction of atmosphere and dread that Le Fanu creates comes partly from a calculated and precise style of writing and partly from the lifelong relationship he has with the darkest folktales of his native Ireland.

The tenets of ghost story fiction are quite varied but almost invariably require the rooting of a haunting within an edifice, a patch of land, or an ancient object. The ghost must be "tethered" to a host of some kind. A haunted castle.

Henry James was fascinated by ghost stories—which he defined as fairy tales for adults—and studied them carefully. He devoted considerable time to the creation and contemplation of such tales and, in my opinion, devised one of the most moving and tenuous of all ghost tales in "The Way It Came."

In *The Turn of the Screw*, James utilizes many a traditional Gothic story element (a haunted edifice, a manuscript, a secret from the past, and the element of innocence at the center of the tale) but creates a breathtaking exercise in ambiguity and duality—the house and the mind of the governess seem to be equally infested with darkness and ghosts.

Through the ages, it has been a tradition in Great Britain to have a great ghost story for Christmas. This tradition gave us *A Christmas Carol* by Dickens, and it extends into the twentieth and twenty-first centuries through the gorgeous productions the BBC has done through the decades at the yuletide season.

Henry James utilizes this device to start *The Turn of the Screw*. He also utilizes, obliquely, a most popular framing device: the club story.

The club story, along with the ghost story, is a cherished tradition that can be found in settings as varied as *The Dinner Club* stories by Sapper, *Tales from the White Hart* by Arthur C. Clarke, assorted stories by M. R. James, or even "The Body Snatcher" by Robert Louis Stevenson, to name but a few. In the typical club story, a varied assortment of characters gathers in a supper club, a tavern, or a smoking room and, after describing the settings—the quality of the brandy, the gentle glow of the fireplace—stories of one sort or another are shared. This device often produces in the reader a sense of comfort and allows for a colloquial narrative that gives the most outlandish tales the patina of reality. Often a manuscript is quoted. The epistolary nature of the tale within the tale also lends credence to the events narrated, even if they unfold through a most unreliable narrator. The reader may now be in the wrong hands.

James then proceeds to weave a brisk but dense tale that engages the heart and the mind of the reader. We are at once as fascinated by the chilling nature of the tale as we are by the bifurcating possibilities of the haunting. We are either seeing the chronicle of the most tragic, relentless mental abuse of two children, or we are witnessing a chilling story of spiritual infestation. James himself has left some scattered evidence as to where his loyalties lay, and while there is some indication of his belief in the reality of the haunting, this has been disputed ardently through decades of literary analysis by some of the great minds of our century.

At the heart of the tale lies a most English virtue: repression.

Regardless of the factual reality of the proceedings, the constant pulse of repressed desire gives the characters a susceptibility, a proclivity to heightened emotion, to hysterical reaction. James maintains the children as chillingly ambiguous, manipulative, and strong willed. This alone would have unsettled a governess at the time, but particularly one who can only define her subjects in the most anodyne and antiseptic terms: "charming," "beautiful," "beatific," or "radiant." The governess seems uncomfortable at the hint of any complexity in the children and at great unease with almost any demonstration of flattery or physical affection. That is why James is so brilliant in constructing his two ghosts around the very thing that would frighten his main character: carnal desire.

The origins of Quint and Miss Jessup (the former governess) are not an Anglo-Saxon myth or an ancient tale of revenge but the carnal story of two lovers consumed by physical passion. It is, in a way, a different sort of possession that also scares and bewilders our heroine/villain, quite in the same way that native lust would shock goodwilled missionaries across the South Seas.

The duality in the tale lies also within James. The English streak in him supports one side of the story—the one permeated by ghost tales and moral colonialism. His empirical, liberal American streak supports the other side. And even structurally, the pacing of the piece—which can be defined as a long novella or a short novel—throughout its compact chapters is entirely American while its coruscated prose and internal pacing are decidedly Old World.

A sophisticated mind still has, hardwired in it, the trigger of pareidolia—the human tendency to organize any random pattern into a system or a shape—and James lays before us an inkblot test of a tale. Whether we believe the haunting to be real or not speaks volumes about our nature as well as the nature of the tale's characters. Our experience reading the novella mirrors the experience of the governess trying to assemble the tale. After all, James said that the reader should rely on "his own experience, his own imagination" to complete the haunting.

The haunted castle is now officially our mind and the ghost is desire.

Which brings us to Howard Phillips Lovecraft. There is so much to say about him and such illuminating texts have been written by brilliant scholars (above all else my kind accomplice S. T. Joshi), colleagues (L. Sprague de Camp's Lovecraft biography), or fellow authors (*H. P. Lovecraft: Against the World, Against Life*, Michel Houellebecq) that I feel at a disadvantage trying to scribble a few thoughts.

I will then speak about my personal relationship to his work. One hot summer afternoon (I must have been eleven or twelve years old) I stumbled upon the text of the Lovecraft story "The Outsider." I was riding in the family car, and the text was included in Spanish in an anthology for my older brother's lit class. I started to read, and almost an hour later, I was left behind in the car, still reading, oblivious to the inclement heat, mesmerized and moved by this story.

In it, an entity emerges from the depths of the earth and ascends painfully, seeking, lost. And he encounters a horrifying entity at the end of a corridor. A loathsome creature, pale and deformed—who is it? And why does he stand there, looking directly at him? What is that frame that surrounds the door where the wretch stands? In the final paragraphs of the story, the narrator extends his hand and the horror hits the reader full force. The story provoked such strong emotions in me. "The monster was I . . ." And, as I closed that book, I felt transmogrified. I had become an acolyte of Lovecraft.

Starting that afternoon, and for the rest of my life, I have devoted more time to Lovecraft than virtually any other author in the genre. His mannered, convulse prose, so antiquated and yet so full of new ideas, is very compelling to a young writer for the same reason that Bradbury's is—it *seems* easy to forge. It is so clear, so full of evident quirks, that you long to imitate it, and it is then that you find out how full of secrets his prose can be.

Many a time the term "visionary" is used to describe a particular type of artist, one with such conviction about the worlds that he or she is building that he seems to be transcribing rather than creating. I wrote about this in my introduction to a Penguin Classics edition of Arthur Machen's work. Well, Lovecraft is that type of artist. His phobias and inadequacies do dictate in him the compulsive worlds and characters he creates. He speaks of what he knows—corrupt lineages in old Eastern Seaboard towns, bizarre forms of sea life that terrorize the pious white men with their undulating, soft folds of pale flesh, the fundamental loneliness of men trapped out of time in urban monstrosities that seem to shift and change around them—all of these things stem from the dark moments in his own life.

Lovecraft's biography rivals Poe's in bizarre occurrences and outrageous misfortune, but his is a quiet, isolated, phobic existence, whereas Poe's is marked by excess and adversity. The details of his misfortune are too many and too odd to enumerate here, and the best thing I can do is ask you to follow Mr. Joshi's notations and books and the few other titles I recommended earlier.

The stories included in this Penguin Horror volume of *The Thing on the Doorstep and Other Weird Stories* are an absolute treasure trove that will show you many of the thematic and stylistic aspects of HPL's work. He is a well-versed student of the weird tale and can metamorphose at will. He drinks from the wells of Poe, William Hope Hodgson, Algernon Blackwood, Lord Dunsany, Arthur Machen, and many others, but impresses all of his narratives with his own phobic, misanthropic seal. No one has ever created a more adverse and bizarre cosmos than Lovecraft. No one.

You'll be delighted with the lysergic "The Music of Erich Zann," the necrophiliac "The Tomb," the often imitated, multi-anthologized "Pickman's Model," the disturbing "The Dunwich Horror," and a few other masterpieces, including the titular story.

But the crown jewel in the collection is, in my opinion, "At the Mountains of Madness." A great admirer of Poe, Lovecraft sets out to riff on *The Narrative of Arthur Gordon Pym of Nantucket*, but then he stumbles into uncharted territory by hinting, through science and revelations, at the darkest possible origin of mankind. A group of scientists embarks on a fossil hunt to the frozen edges of the globe. Utilizing cutting-edge technology and tools, they attempt to catalog and decipher the evolutionary clues found in fossils and remains that are gradually revealed to them. They stumble upon the ruins of a cyclopean alien city. It is there that it is revealed that an ancient race of extraterrestrials created mankind as a cruel cosmic joke. They also created a race of slaves that can shape-shift at will, and that still lurk in the ruins of the city. The final encounter in the few final pages and lines of this story are so powerful, so primal as to render one speechless.

Reading this tale in my midteens was a revelation. I had never been exposed to any literature that so dwarfed our existence and hinted at the cold indifference of the cosmos. I became entirely enamored. Making a film of it became my quest.

For the last fifteen years or so, I have attempted repeatedly to make a film based on this story. From 2009 to 2011 I dedicated my every waking hour to sketching, sculpting, and writing about every detail in the adaptation of Lovecraft's difficult prose. Difficult to adapt, that is, since it is a superb tonal work, chock-full of erudite and minute scientific annotations and peppered with brief but shocking episodes of devastating power. The adaptation took necessary liberties but remained faithful to every landmark of the novel.

Needless to say, the film didn't happen, and for now I have to be content to share my home office with a life-size Lovecraft sculpture, many Cthulhu and HPL busts, a portrait by Michael Deas, hundreds of conceptual drawings, a visual effects test by Industrial Light and Magic, and the few eerie music tracks that Jónsi, from Sigur Rós, composed for us . . .

It is my hope to, one day, share my love for HPL with the world.

With *The Haunting of Hill House*, Shirley Jackson evolves the ghost story one step further by creating an equally fluid tale—one that will again test the relationship between the fantastic and the psychological.

Jackson is the perfect case of a writer associated with a genre that a substantial portion of her readers would avoid. Her prose and poise are obliquely reminiscent of E. B. White,

Thurber, or the spirit of *The New Yorker*, and yet her fierce grasp of the supernatural, her lapses into the Gothic Romance tone and trappings, and her undeniable attraction to the bizarre would have her equally at home in *Weird Tales*. So, much like James, she injects her own ambiguity into the tale. But whereas James brings a fin-de-siècle sensibility to the stories, Jackson brings forth a decidedly modern and American approach.

One of the most remarkable feats Jackson pulls off is to make the house a character. It is not the melancholic edifice that hosts the lamia. It is the lamia. Stephen King would later define this notion further by postulating that bad places attract bad things, but Jackson provides the foundation by asserting over and over again the presence of the house as a sentient, physical, spiritual entity of evil.

As an extension of the loneliness prefigured in Poe, Jackson continually speaks of that condition in most of her fiction. Hill House can only hold the truly lonely souls, reclaim them, invite them to belong. The symbiosis, the abandon that is needed for the house to possess the novel's heroine, Eleanor Vance, is a game changer—a tacit agreement that will be cashed in the final pages of Jackson's masterwork: "[S]ilence lay steadily against the wood and stone of Hill House, and whatever walked there, walked alone."

In its efficiency, Jackson's prose transmits modernity—she allows the novel to remain crisp and lean. She refuses to over-complicate her writing with unnecessary description or mannerisms and, therefore, when she delves into detail, she has the reader's complete attention.

And this is where one of the most genial touches of the novel comes into play. Jackson sets forth the entire endeavor as a scientific experiment, and therefore we are forced to accept the background and history (biography?) of Hill House as pure fact and the parameters of modernity as our safety net.

The experiment as background will again be put to good use by Richard Matheson in the magnificently unsubtle *Hell House*, but Matheson will choose to solve the novel as a dark riddle, whereas Jackson chooses to let it evolve like a collision course.

And it is here that the kinship with Henry James's work stops. Rather than maintaining the boundaries of the story as fluid as a question mark—Is it real? Is it not?—Jackson opts for an exclamation point—a fascinating piece of nature documentary: Hill House is the lion pouncing in slow motion on the smallest, weakest gazelle in the herd: Eleanor.

We are told that this is a house with "insistent hospitality; it seemingly dislikes letting its guests get away," and one that will disintegrate Eleanor's sanity and sense of self without ever defining the nature of the evil that animates it. But evil there is, undoubtedly—and this, too, is a characteristic that separates James and Jackson.

Jackson forces us to contemplate all the haunted occurrences through each of the participant's eyes and vulnerabilities. And by never denying the malevolence of the house: The haunting is real and everyone within it is alone, trapped in their own minds and circumstances, blind to the plight of the others.

This is perhaps one of the most veiled and pervasive horrors in Jackson's fiction: We are always alone.

If *Hill House* is a colloquy, then it is a colloquy between the different sides in Jackson's mind, the many "me's" that face the vast, hostile world alone. And in the end, Jackson's misanthropic, nihilistic view of the world seems to assert that, in the darkness, there is a refuge. That if Eleanor needs to belong and Hill House needs to possess, then, finally, in that coupling there might be hope.

The case of Ray Russell offers us a chance to talk about one of the most peculiar horror writers. Russell links postpulp literature and the Grand Guignol tradition with the modern sensibilities of America in the 1960s. Within him resides a neopaganistic streak that is passed from Algernon Blackwood and Sax Rohmer to him and other writers of unusual proclivities, such as Bernard J. Hurwood. A fascinating combination of the liberal and the heretic.

Russell was born in the early twentieth century and saw action during World War II. He held a variety of jobs and published in a variety of publications. He was part of the resurgence of fantastic literature in American letters. As executive fiction editor of *Playboy* in the magazine's infancy (1954–1960), Russell probably knew his share of excess and power, but he utilized this power to provide refuge to a host of valuable genre writers, among them the brilliant Richard Matheson and the precious Charles Beaumont, but also heralded the birth of adult fantastic fiction by publishing also Vonnegut, Bradbury, Fredric Brown, and many others.

Russell authored numerous short stories and seven novels—including his most famous one, *The Case Against Satan*, which pioneers and outlines the plights of *Rosemary's Baby* and *The Exorcist*. But, in spite of this and his continued collaborations with *Playboy* throughout the 1970s, Russell remains a forgotten writer. A sort of writer's writer, an acquired taste. This in spite of being a recipient of both a World Fantasy Award and the Bram Stoker Award for Lifetime Achievement.

In fact, in the last few decades, so little has been published about Russell that the only quote, oft repeated, is Stephen King's blurb, in which he enthrones *Sardonicus* as "perhaps the finest example of the modern gothic ever written."

But King, as always, is absolutely right. Russell has a savage streak in his prose, one that would today be considered inappropriate and even offensive and, to me, entirely reminiscent of the Grand Guignol Theatre. But in his best stories he also captures the tenuous atmosphere of the Gothic Romance. At a secondary level, Russell seems to wallow in a sadistic impulse akin to the *conte cruel* so aptly practiced by Auguste Villiers de l'Isle-Adam.

This tortuous vocation is never clearer than in his Gothic *S* trilogy. The tales *Sanguinarius*, *Sagittarius*, and *Sardonicus* are all surprisingly inventive stories, with shocking twist endings that are here reprinted in their entirety.

My favorite of the three, *Sagittarius*, may not be a perfect exercise in style, but it is a luscious, devoted repast of Gothic fiction. *Sagittarius* centers around the tale of two stage actors—the divine Sellig and the revulsive Laval, a freakishly deformed performer who shocks the Grand Guignol audience every night, and who embodies evil to perfection.

If you can guess the not too subtle wordplay hidden in the performers' names, then it will feel only natural that, in an inspired stroke, Russell links the pair with two more infamous figures of gaslight London: Jack the Ripper and Mr. Hyde. The connection is effortless and feels neither mannered nor insincere and, I guarantee this: It packs a powerful punch in its final pages.

"La vie est un corridor noir / D'impuissance et de désespoir!" cries Laval. "Life is a black corridor of impotence and despair." Indeed.

Sanguinarius retells—from an unorthodox perspective and with great macabre gusto—the story of Countess Elisabeth Báthory and her thirst for blood. Russell provokes and subverts the tale by adopting the Countess's point of view. He succeeds in this by infusing the story with period quirks and idioms that lend an air of authenticity to the macabre proceedings.

It is also remarkable to hear the tale told in this manner as we find empathy and reason behind the most atrocious actions. Báthory starts her journey as a virginal bride in her early teens and is swallowed by a vortex of depravity and bloodshed that is described, at times, with zealous excess. In this, *Sanguinarius* represents an aspect of Russell's fiction that will erupt in full in *Incubus*—the capacity of the author to get caught in his own compulsions as he attempts to titillate and shock the reader.

The most famous of his tales, and the only one that is frequently reprinted and discussed, is *Sardonicus*. First published in *Playboy* at the end of the 1950s, this is a tale of enormous originality that remains, at the same time, a grand homage and a reinvention of the Gothic. To the eyes of its seemingly straight protagonist, Sir Robert Cargrave, everything in Castle Sardonicus is askew and in decay. He has been called there to assist the husband of a former liaison of his—the man in question, the preternaturally pale Mr. Sardonicus, has the lower half of his face paralyzed in a horrid rictus, and the reason for this is too preposterous and delightful to consign in these few lines!

In my opinion, Ray Russell is the literary equivalent of the Italian filmmaker Mario Bava, a supersaturated neo-Gothicist who shines above the premises of his material based on style, conviction, and artistic flair. Sadly, most of Russell's work has remained unavailable, except for outrageously overpriced paperbacks and expensive collectors' editions. It is therefore that I take great pride in presenting a new edition of *Haunted Castles: The Complete Gothic Stories* as part of this Penguin Horror series.

And this brings us to the final title of the series, S. T. Joshi's edited volume of *American Supernatural Tales*.

Foremost among the modern scholars of the genre, Mr. Joshi has published many volumes dedicated to the study of the weird tale and has edited many volumes of horror fiction with unparalleled rigor and love. In every respect, he will be a more adept guide than I in taking you hand in hand through the amazing catalog of supernatural fiction he has curated.

So, there you have it. We have prepared a small collection of books that I hope will find their way into the hands of young, strange readers—like I was—curious about this deranged form of storytelling—seeking that late-night chill, that intimate shiver that happens when the lamia crosses the threshold of our room and whispers at us from the darkened corner.

When the certainty of seeing a monstrous thing takes ahold of us and forces us to gaze at the end of a corridor—there, an apparition stands, a thing of supreme horror. And, as we advance toward it—as in HPL's "The Outsider"—we are overwhelmed by the realization that the putrid flesh, the vacant eyes, the mad stare we see in that lonely figure is nothing but the reflection in a mirror. A dark mirror facing us.

May your nightmares be plentiful.

GUILLERMO DEL TORO
Thousand Oaks, California, 2013

INTRODUCTION

The supernatural in literature can be said to have its roots in the earliest specimens of Western literature, if we take cognizance of such monsters as the Cyclops, the Hydra, Circe, Cerberus, and others in Greek myth. There is, however, a question as to whether, prior to a few centuries ago, such entities would have been regarded as properly supernatural; for a given creature or event to be regarded as *supernatural*, one must have a clearly defined conception of the *natural*, from which the supernatural can be regarded as an aberration or departure. In Western culture, the parameters of the natural have been increasingly delimited by science, and it is therefore not surprising that the supernatural, as a distinct literary genre, first emerged in the eighteenth century, when scientific advance had reached a stage where certain phenomena could be recognized as manifestly beyond the bounds of the natural. H. P. Lovecraft, one of the leading theoreticians of the genre as well as one of its pioneering practitioners, emphasized this point somewhat flamboyantly in his essay "Supernatural Horror in Literature" (1927):

> The true weird tale has something more than secret murder, bloody bones, or a sheeted form clanking chains according to rule. A certain atmosphere of breathless and unexplainable dread of outer, unknown forces must be present; and there must be a hint, expressed with a seriousness and portentousness becoming its subject,

of that most terrible conception of the human brain—a malign and particular suspension or defeat of those fixed laws of Nature which are our only safeguard against the assaults of chaos and the daemons of unplumbed space.

What this means is that the supernatural tale, while adhering to the strictest canons of mimetic realism, must have its emotional and aesthetic focus upon the chosen avenue of departure from the natural—whether it be a creature such as the vampire, the ghost, or the werewolf, or a series of events such as might occur in a haunted house. If *all* the events of a tale are set in an imaginary realm, then we have crossed over into *fantasy,* because the contrast between the natural and the supernatural does not come into play. Conversely, the supernatural tale must be clearly distinguished from the tale of psychological horror, where the horror is generated by witnessing the aberrations of a diseased mind. Lovecraft, in discussing William Faulkner's tale of necrophilia, "A Rose for Emily" (1930), made clear this distinction, also pointing out the degree to which the supernatural tale is tied to developments in the sciences:

> Manifestly, this is a dark and horrible thing which *could happen,* whereas the crux of a *weird* tale is something which *could not possibly happen.* If any unexpected advance of physics, chemistry, or biology were to indicate the *possibility* of any phenomena related by the weird tale, that particular set of phenomena would cease to be *weird* in the ultimate sense because it would become surrounded by a different set of emotions. It would no longer represent imaginative liberation, because it would no longer indicate a suspension or violation of the natural laws against whose universal dominance our fancies rebel. (Letter to August Derleth, November 20, 1931)

Given the fact that the commencement of supernatural literature in the West is canonically dated to the publication of

Horace Walpole's *The Castle of Otranto* (1764), there is no intrinsic reason why Americans need feel any inferiority to Europe in regard to their contributions to the form; for it was just at this time that American literature was itself beginning to declare its own aesthetic independence from that of Great Britain. And yet, less than half a century after the United States became a distinct geopolitical entity, British critic William Hazlitt threw down the following gauntlet: "No ghost, we will venture to say, was ever seen in North America. They do not walk in broad day; and the night of ignorance and superstition which favours their appearance, was long past before the United States lifted up their head beyond the Atlantic wave" (*Edinburgh Review*, October 1829). Hazlitt may have been seeking merely to emphasize the new nation's continued cultural inferiority to the land that gave it birth, and he may also have been guilty of exaggerating the rationality that governed the founding of the American colonies, but in spite of all caveats he does appear to raise a valid point. Since so much of supernatural fiction appears to find the source of its terrors in the depths of the remote past, how can a nation that does not have much of a past express the supernatural in literature? The Gothic novels of the late eighteenth and early nineteenth centuries were predicated on horrors emerging from the "ignorance and superstition" of the British or European Dark Ages, but if a country did not experience the Dark Ages, how could those horrors be depicted plausibly? The authors represented in this volume, covering nearly the entirety of American history, sought to answer these questions in a multiplicity of ways, and their varying solutions shed considerable light on the development of the supernatural tale as an art form.

Although there is considerable evidence that the British Gothic novel was voraciously read in the United States, few Americans attempted their hand at it: the sole exponent of the form was Charles Brockden Brown (1771–1810), who chose to follow the model of Ann Radcliffe in making use of what has been termed the "explained supernatural," where the supernatural is suggested at the outset but ultimately explained away as the product of misconstrual or trickery. As a result,

Brockden Brown does not qualify as America's first *supernaturalist,* and that distinction remains with the unlikely figure of Washington Irving: unlikely because his writing as a whole—lighthearted, urbane, comic, even at times self-parodic—would seem as far removed from the flamboyant luridness of Matthew Gregory Lewis or the guilt-ridden intensity of Charles Robert Maturin as anything could possibly be. And yet, the supernatural comprised a persistent thread in Irving's work, notably in his two story collections, *The Sketch Book* (1820) and *Tales of a Traveller* (1824). That Irving was able to find inspiration in the Dutch legendry of New York and New England—a legendry already two centuries old by the time he began writing—suggests that even a "new" land (new, of course, only in terms of European settlement) could quickly gain a fund of superstition that had the potential of generating supernatural literature.

In the next generation, two towering figures—Edgar Allan Poe and Nathaniel Hawthorne—chose starkly different means to convey the supernatural. Hawthorne, plagued by an overriding sense of sin inspired by the religious fanaticism of the Puritan settlers of Massachusetts, found in the American seventeenth century—culminating in the real-life horror of the Salem witchcraft trials—a fitting analogue of the European Dark Ages, and his novels and tales, supernatural and otherwise, constantly draw upon the Puritan past as a source of evil that continues to cast its shadow over the present.

Poe, younger and more forward-looking, felt the need to found his horrors on the potentially hideous aberrations of the human mind, with the result that much of his best fiction falls into the category of psychological horror ("The Tell-Tale Heart," "The Man of the Crowd"). As he noted somewhat aggressively in the preface to *Tales of the Grotesque and Arabesque* (1840), in defending himself from accusations that many of his horrors were borrowed from European examples, "I maintain that terror is not of Germany, but of the soul." And yet, Poe rarely strayed from the supernatural; indeed, many of his most distinctive tales chart the progressive breakdown of the ratiocinative intellect when faced with the "suspension of natural laws." Poe also recognized that compression was a key element in producing the *frisson* of supernatural terror: in accordance with his strictures on the "unity of effect," he understood that an emotion so fleeting as that of fear could best be generated in short compass, and for a century or more his example compelled the great majority of literary supernaturalists to adhere to the short story as the preferred vehicle for the supernatural. Indeed, it could be said that "The Fall of the House of Usher" is a kind of rebuke to those countless British Gothicists who had dissipated the vital core of their supernatural conceptions by extending it over novel length: here, instead, was a "Gothic castle" every bit as terrifying as that of Otranto or Udolpho, but concentrated in a fraction of the space. Poe achieved this condensation by a particularly dense, frenetic prose style that could easily be mocked (and would in fact be mocked by such a fastidious writer as Henry James), but whose emotive power is difficult to gainsay.

Poe, then, is the central figure in the entire history of American—and, indeed, British and European—supernatural fiction; for his example, once established, raised the bar for all subsequent work. No longer could such entities as the vampire or the ghost—already becoming stale through overuse and, more signifiantly, through the advance of a science that was rendering them so implausible as to become aesthetically unusable—be manifested without proper emotional preparation or the provision of at least a quasilogical rationale; no longer could fear be displayed without an awareness of its psychological effect upon those who encounter it. And yet, over the next half-century or more after Poe's death, we can find no writer who focused singlemindedly upon either supernatural or psychological horror as Poe had done; indeed, excursions into the supernatural emerged almost at random from writers recognized for their work in the literary mainstream. This may indeed suggest that the supernatural was not, properly speaking, a genre clearly dissociated from general literature, but a mode into which writers of all stripes could descend when the logic of their conceptions required it.

And so we have the examples of F. Marion Crawford, popular historical novelist, writing the occasional short story, and even one or two novels, of the supernatural; it may or may not be significant that these short stories were collected only post-humously in the volume *Wandering Ghosts* (1911). Another popular writer, Robert W. Chambers, began his career writing a scintillating collection of the supernatural, *The King in Yellow* (1895), but lamentably failed to follow up this promising start, instead descending to the writing of shopgirl romances that filled his coffers but spelled his aesthetic ruination. Edward Lucas White, also better known for his historical novels, persistently recurred to the supernatural in his short stories, notably in two substantial collections, *The Song of the Sirens* (1919) and *Lukundoo* (1927).

If any figure can be said to have followed in Poe's footsteps, it is the sardonic journalist Ambrose Bierce. From the 1870s until his mysterious disappearance in 1914, his occasional "tales of soldiers and civilians" danced continually on either side of the borderline between supernatural and psychological horror. Bierce became the hub of a West Coast literary renaissance that featured other writers such as W. C. Morrow, Emma Frances Dawson, and even the young Jack London, all of whom dabbled in the supernatural. Short fiction comprised only a relatively minor proportion of Bierce's total literary output—he was best known in his time as a fearless, and feared, columnist, chiefly for the Hearst papers—and, while he may have derived inspiration both from Poe's example and from his theories on short fiction construction, the literary mode he evolved could not have been more different from Poe's: a prose style of stark simplicity and spare elegance, a detached, cynical, occasionally misanthropic portrayal of hapless protagonists in the grip of irrational fear, and a probing utilization of the topography of the West in contrast to the never-never lands of Poe's imagination. Indeed, Bierce successfully answered Hazlitt's old query by showing that even a land as raw and new (again, in terms of Anglo-Saxon settlement) as the West could be the source of terror: the abandoned shacks and deserted mining towns of rural California become the *mauvaises terres* of the Biercian imagination, lending a grim distinctiveness to tales whose relatively conventional ghosts and revenants might otherwise relegate them to second-class status. And of course Bierce followed Poe in the meticulous etching of the precise effects of the supernatural upon the sensitive consciousness of his fear-raddled protagonists.

If Bierce was the head of the West Coast school of weird writing in his time, Henry James was, perhaps by default, the leader of the East Coast school. Like so many other mainstream writers, he found the supernatural—manifested almost exclusively in the form of ghosts—a perennially useful mode for the expression of conceptions that could not be encompassed within the bounds of mimetic realism. And yet, James rarely tipped his hand unequivocally in the direction of the supernatural, instead mastering the technique of the ambiguous weird tale, where doubt is maintained to the end whether the supernatural has actually come into play or whether the apparently ghostly phenomena are merely the products of psychological disturbance on the part of the characters. Preeminent among James's contributions in this regard is *The Turn of the Screw* (1898), which has inspired an entire library of criticism debating whether the revenants at the focus of the tale are or are not genuinely manifested; clearly James did not wish the question to be answered definitively. In short stories written over an entire career he probed the same questions, and his final, fragmentary novel, *The Sense of the Past,* might have been his greatest contribution to weird literature had he lived to complete it. James's compatriot Edith Wharton manifestly followed in his footsteps—perhaps, indeed, at times a bit too closely. Nevertheless, there is enough originality and artistry in her dozen or so ghost stories to earn her a place in the supernatural canon.

H. P. Lovecraft joins Poe and Bierce in the triumvirate of towering American supernaturalists. In a career that spanned little more than two decades, Lovecraft transformed the horror tale in such radical ways that its ramifications are still being felt. Although an early devotee of Poe, Lovecraft was also a diligent student of the sciences and came to the realization that the standard tropes of supernatural fiction—the ghost, the vampire, the witch, the haunted house—had become so played out and so clearly in defiance of what was then known about the universe that alternate means had to be employed to convey supernatural dread. Lovecraft found it in the boundless realms of space and time, where entities of the most bizarre sort could plausibly be hypothesized to exist, well beyond the reach of even the most advanced human knowledge. This fusion of the supernatural tale with the emerging genre of science fiction (canonically dated to the founding of the magazine *Amazing Stories* in 1926) generated that unique amalgam known as the Lovecraftian tale. In such tales as "The Call of Cthulhu," "The Colour out of Space," "The Whisperer in Darkness," *At the Mountains of Madness,* and "The Shadow Out of Time" Lovecraft exponentially expanded the scope of supernatural fiction to encompass not just the world, but the cosmos.

Lovecraft fortuitously emerged as a literary figure at the exact time when supernatural horror could finally be said to have become a concretized genre, with the founding of the pulp magazine *Weird Tales* in 1923. This was in every sense a mixed blessing. It is now difficult to determine whether the establishment of *Weird Tales* (the first magazine exclusively devoted to horror fiction) and its analogues in the realms of mystery, science fiction, the Western, romance, and other genres actually precipitated the banishment of the supernatural (except by the most eminent mainstream authors or in suitably tame and conventional modes) from leading literary magazines, or whether their prior banishment led to the founding of the pulps; whatever the case, a manifest dichotomy was established, and those writers who chose to focus on the supernatural found themselves obliged to appear in the pulps for lack of other venues. Simultaneously—perhaps as a result of the literary Modernism that dominated the 1920s, with such writers as Theodore Dreiser, Sinclair Lewis, F. Scott Fitzgerald, and Ernest Hemingway—a prejudice developed among mainstream critics for any literary product that departed from strict social realism, so that virtually all ventures into fantasy or the supernatural were indiscriminately declared subliterary. This prejudice—based upon the very real fact that the great majority of material in the pulp magazines was indeed trite, hackneyed, and subliterary—took decades to dissipate, and in large part it caused Lovecraft's work to languish in the pulps, so that his friends had to band together after his death to publish his work in book form.

Nevertheless, during his lifetime Lovecraft attracted a wide cadre of like-minded writers who were determined to raise supernatural horror to the level of an art form, even if some of them perforce wrote to the narrow demands of *Weird Tales* and other pulps. Clark Ashton Smith, who had already established a reputation as a scintillatingly brilliant poet, produced more than a hundred tales that fused fantasy, science fiction, and horror in an indefinable amalgam, while Robert E. Howard, in his short career, definitively established the subgenre of sword and sorcery as a viable component of the supernatural or adventure tale.

Lovecraft's most valuable influence was exemplified in his patient and tireless tutoring of younger writers—August Derleth, Donald Wandrei, Frank Belknap Long, Robert Bloch, Fritz Leiber—into the finer points of literary artistry, and his laborious efforts paid dividends in the generation after his death. Other writers who had not had any direct contacts with Lovecraft, such as Ray Bradbury and Richard Matheson, nonetheless benefited from the example of his relatively small but extraordinarily rich output of weird work. Derleth and Wandrei established Arkham House as the leading publisher of supernatural work—another mixed blessing, as their publications tended in part to enhance the relegating of supernatural horror to a literary cul-de-sac. But such dynamic writers as Bloch, Bradbury, and Leiber followed Lovecraft in expanding the range of the supernatural by melding it with elements drawn from the mystery or suspense tale, the fantasy tale, and the science fiction tale.

This melding had, by the 1950s, become a necessity, because the pulp magazines were in their last throes. *Weird Tales* finally folded in 1954, and no replacement was in sight: the magazine *Unknown* (later *Unknown Worlds*) had had a short but influential run in the 1940s, but that was all. The pulps gave way to digest magazines, chiefly in the realms of fantasy and science fiction (whose readership was, and today remains, much larger than that for supernatural horror), while the paperback book generated potential markets for mystery, the Western, science fiction, and fantasy, but not for horror. Accordingly, such writers as Richard Matheson and Charles Beaumont were compelled to write supernatural tales under the guise of these other genres—perhaps a natural development in an era when the threat of atomic annihilation caused an entire society to ponder the mixed blessings and dangers of scientific and technological advance.

For writers of the 1950s, the Lovecraft influence manifested itself even in the way in which they consciously strove to battle against it. Writers such as Matheson, Bradbury, and Beaumont, while admiring Lovecraft, came to regard his work as too remote from everyday reality for credence in an age in which television, radio, and film were celebrating the nuclear family and the American way of life. They also protested against the occasional flamboyance of Lovecraft's prose, so contrary to the skeletonic syntax of a Hemingway or a Sherwood Anderson, and so easily parodied—especially, and unwittingly, by a host of self-styled disciples who sought to mimic Lovecraft's lush texture and elaborate upon his Cthulhu Mythos. Accordingly, Matheson and his compatriots fashioned tales emphatically, perhaps aggressively, set in a recognizable world of telephones, washing machines, and office jobs. This tendency had been anticipated by Fritz Leiber, who in "Smoke Ghost," "The Girl with the Hungry Eyes," and other tales of the 1940s nonetheless managed to fuse Lovecraftian cosmicism with mundane reality. That latter story was pioneering in a different way: in its baleful account of the dangers of sexual obsession, it had introduced a bold new element to a genre that had otherwise seemed almost prudishly chaste.

From a very different direction, the mainstream writer Shirley Jackson found in both supernatural and psychological horror a vital means for conveying her pungently cynical skepticism regarding human motives and actions. The fact that many of her tales appeared in *The New Yorker* and other prestigious venues helped to break down the resistance of magazine editors who had axiomatically banished the supernatural from their pages.

Well-paying men's magazines such as *Playboy* began specializing in mystery, horror, and science fiction, and the occasional supernatural tale even found its way into such staid organs of literary classicism as the *Atlantic Monthly* and *Harper's*.

Media, especially film and television, now began to cast an increasingly significant influence upon supernatural literature. The dominant figure in the field in the 1960s was a television personality, Rod Serling, whose *The Twilight Zone* (1959–64) immediately and permanently entered into the American collective psyche. While Serling was in fact a skilled writer, it was his aloof, sardonic commentary on his television show that rendered him an icon in his own time. At the same time, the crude B-movies of the 1950s—rightly condemned as pablum for the uncultured or as self-parodic camp—slowly improved in cinematic quality. Perhaps this fusion of literature and media laid the groundwork for what would become a three-decade "boom" in horror literature.

Such bestselling novels as Ira Levin's *Rosemary's Baby* (1967), William Peter Blatty's *The Exorcist* (1971), and Thomas Tryon's *The Other* (1971) were all adapted into successful films, especially the first two. Horror suddenly became a blockbuster genre, and Stephen King was the first to capitalize on it: such of his early books as *Carrie* (1974), *'Salem's Lot* (1975), and *The Dead Zone* (1979) all benefited from striking film adaptations, and King went on to become perhaps the most remarkable phenomenon in publishing history. It is, of course, naïve to think that the number of copies an author happens to sell has any correlation with his or her literary standing, and the majority of King's writing is indeed marred by clumsy prose; hackneyed conceptions derived from film, comics, and other media; and a rather dreary prolificity that does not bode well for the endurance of his work. King's success as a horror novelist also spelled, at long last, the downfall—at least as a publishing phenomenon—of the short story as the chosen venue for supernatural horror, even though the number of cases in which a supernatural plot can be said to be sufficiently rich and complex to be sustained over novel length is, in spite of the thousands of novels that have poured off the press in recent decades, disconcertingly small.

To be sure, not all the writers who strove to grab a residue of King's commercial success were hacks or tyros, although there certainly were, and are, a distressing number of these. Such a writer as Peter Straub (*Ghost Story,* 1979) may have indulged in a bit of self-congratulatory exaggeration when he declared that King was the Dickens of the horror tale while he himself was its Henry James, but there is no denying that his artistry as a prose stylist is substantially greater than King's. Although Anne Rice's first supernatural novel, *Interview with the Vampire,* dates to 1976, it took some time in becoming a bestseller; her following now may be even greater than King's, and some of her works (mostly her early novels) are far from contemptible on the purely literary scale. Dean R. Koontz, on the other hand, can take his place with Judith Krantz and Danielle Steel as bestsellers whose work will be deservedly forgotten in the next generation.

The current emphasis on the horror novel, whether supernatural or psychological, is largely a marketing phenomenon: in today's publishing environment, short stories are not seen as commercially viable. And yet, King himself had begun his career with some highly able short stories, collected in *Night Shift* (1978), and other writers of the 1970s continued to be devoted to the short form regardless of the slim pecuniary profits to be derived thereby. T. E. D. Klein, although the author of one novel, *The Ceremonies* (1984), that briefly reached the bestseller lists, has made an imperishable name for himself by excelling in that hybrid form, the novella, which allows for expansiveness in the conveyance of the supernatural manifestation while at the same time adhering to Poe's "unity of effect." Dennis Etchison, Karl Edward Wagner, and others may also find their short work surviving as literary contributions while the novels of their contemporaries— and, indeed, their own novels—lapse into oblivion. For these writers, the small press has become the haven for their weird work; pay is slight or perhaps nonexistent, but there is something to be said for writing that is largely divorced from market considerations.

In this regard, the most remarkable phenomenon in contemporary supernatural horror is Thomas Ligotti, whose eccentric output of short stories (he has admitted that he will not and cannot write a horror novel) has somehow managed to secure a following almost entirely through word-of-mouth. Uncompromising in his uniquely twisted vision of a universe of grotesque nightmare, Ligotti is content to offer his meticulously crafted tales to a relatively small audience capable of appreciating it; like Lovecraft, he scorns the notion of writing to a market. If Ligotti ever appears on the bestseller list, it will be an aberration more bizarre than anything depicted in his tales.

The 1990s were a period of ferment in the horror field. The "boom" that had begun in the 1970s seemed to be dying of inanition—and, perhaps, of an overdose of the mediocre, the shoddy, and the calculatingly commercial. Some writers and critics gleefully predicted the downfall of the supernatural and its replacement by either the serial-killer novel or other forms of psychological suspense, while still others, protesting against "dark fantasy"—a mode of writing that sought to convey its horrors by subtle implication rather than blood and gore—found a loud alternative in the subgenre labeled splatterpunk. This name—a variant of the avant-garde science fiction mode called cyberpunk—was coined by David J. Schow, who proved to be nearly the sole writer of this sort whose work has any hope of survival as a genuine contribution to literature. Melding references to slasher films, rock-and-roll music, and true crime, splatterpunk writers proclaimed their greater relevance to a society in which violence had become so prevalent as almost to be banal; but in the end, the sheer absence of talent exhibited by most such writers caused this movement to flare out almost as quickly as it had emerged.

Today, supernatural horror comes in as many forms as the imaginations of its diverse writers can envision. Once again—with the exception of Joyce Carol Oates, who has followed Shirley Jackson in repeatedly evoking the supernatural in the course of her mainstream work—the predominant venue is the small press, and in recent years the Internet has proven to be a welcome haven for much sound work. It is at this juncture difficult to determine which authors will survive the relentless winnowing of posterity: in my judgment, at least Caitlín R. Kiernan and Norman Partridge deserve tentative canonization, although others might wish to make a case for such writers as Brian Hodge, Douglas Clegg, Patrick McGrath (a leading figure in the "New Gothic" movement, which strives to return to the Gothic roots of the genre and bypass the excesses of both the old-time pulps and the recent bestsellers), Jack Cady, and any number of others.

As a literary mode, the supernatural has undergone as many permutations and variations in the past two hundred and fifty years as any other, and has left a rich legacy of literary substance that deserves to be chronicled and interpreted. For writers like Lovecraft, it may have chiefly represented "imaginative liberation"—liberation from the mundane, the everyday, the commonplace—but for others, like Shirley Jackson, it was a vehicle for the conveyance of conceptions about humanity and its relations to the cosmos beyond that offered by mimetic fiction. To the extent that it draws upon the past—in the form of myth, legend, and superstition that persistently suggests a world of shadow behind or beyond that of ordinary reality—it appears to represent a permanent phase of the human imagination, and as such it will remain perennially vital as a literary mode. Its emphasis upon fear, wonder, and terror may perhaps render it a cultivated taste, but the flickering light it casts upon these darker corners of the human psyche will bestow upon it a fascination, and a relevance, to those courageous enough to look upon its revelations with an unflinching gaze.

—S. T. Joshi

WASHINGTON IRVING

Washington Irving was born in New York City in 1783. Generally regarded as the first significant writer in the United States, Irving practiced law until 1803. After a two-year visit to Europe (1804–06) to improve his health, Irving began writing articles and sketches in magazines; his first book, *A History of New York* (1809), published under the pseudonym Diedrich Knickerbocker, brought him immediate fame. Shortly thereafter, Irving moved to England, where he remained for nearly twenty years. It was there that *The Sketch Book of Geoffrey Crayon, Gent.* (1820), including such celebrated tales as "Rip Van Winkle" and "The Legend of Sleepy Hollow," was published. *Tales of a Traveller* followed in 1824. Financial considerations led him to accept a position at the United States embassy in Madrid, where he wrote several works reflecting his interest in Spain, notably *The Legends of the Alhambra* (1832). Irving was minister to Spain in 1842–46. During his later years Irving worked on *Astoria* (1836), a history of the Astor family, and biographies of Oliver Goldsmith (1849) and George Washington (1855–59; 5 vols.). Irving died at Sunnyside, New York, in 1859.

Irving is distinctive in combining humor and satire with the supernatural. "The Legend of Sleepy Hollow," with its well-known image of the headless horseman, has been adapted for film or television at least seven times.

Many of Irving's best-known horror tales are included in *Tales of a Traveller,* among which are "The Adventure of My Uncle" and "The Adventure of My Aunt," about animated portraits; "The Devil and Tom Walker," a popular account of a bargain with the devil; and "The Bold Dragoon," which features both a ghost and animated furniture. "The Storm-Ship," a segment of the tale "Dolph Heyliger," in *Bracebridge Hall* (1822), is an engaging tale of the Flying Dutchman.

"The Adventure of the German Student," first published in *Tales of a Traveller,* is an unwontedly grim tale of a reanimated corpse and foreshadows the tightly knit work of Poe and his successors.

THE ADVENTURE OF THE GERMAN STUDENT

On a stormy night, in the tempestuous times of the French revolution, a young German was returning to his lodgings, at a late hour, across the old part of Paris. The lightning gleamed, and the loud claps of thunder rattled through the lofty, narrow streets—but I should first tell you something about this young German.

Gottfried Wolfgang was a young man of good family. He had studied for some time at Göttingen, but being of a visionary and enthusiastic character, he had wandered into those wild and speculative doctrines which have so often bewildered German students. His secluded life, his intense application, and the singular nature of his studies, had an effect on both mind and body. His health was impaired; his imagination diseased. He had been indulging in fanciful speculations on spiritual essences until, like Swedenborg, he had an ideal world of his own around him. He took up a notion, I do not know from what cause, that there was an evil influence hanging over him; an evil genius or spirit seeking to ensnare him and ensure his perdition. Such an idea working on his melancholy temperament produced the most gloomy effects. He became haggard and desponding. His friends discovered the mental malady preying upon him, and determined that the best cure was a change of scene; he was sent, therefore, to finish his studies amidst the splendours and gaieties of Paris.

Wolfgang arrived at Paris at the breaking out of the revolution. The popular delirium at first caught his enthusiastic mind, and he was captivated by the political and philosophical theories of the day: but the scenes of blood which followed shocked his sensitive nature; disgusted him with society and the world, and made him more than ever a recluse. He shut himself up in a solitary apartment in the *Pays Latin,* the quarter of students. There in a gloomy street not far from the monastic walls of the Sorbonne, he pursued his favourite speculations. Sometimes he spent hours together in the great libraries of Paris, those catacombs of departed authors, rummaging among their hoards of dusty and obsolete works in quest of food for his unhealthy appetite. He was, in a manner, a literary goul, feeding in the charnel house of decayed literature.

Wolfgang, though solitary and recluse, was of an ardent temperament, but for a time it operated merely upon his imagination. He was too shy and ignorant of the world to make any advances to the fair, but he was a passionate admirer of female beauty, and in his lonely chamber would often lose himself in reveries on forms and faces which he had seen, and his fancy would deck out images of loveliness far surpassing the reality.

While his mind was in this excited and sublimated state, a dream produced an extraordinary effect upon him. It was of a female face of transcendent beauty. So strong was the impression made, that he dreamt of it again and again. It haunted his thoughts by day, his slumbers by night; in fine, he became passionately enamoured of this shadow of a dream. This lasted so long, that it became one of those fixed ideas which haunt the minds of melancholy men, and are at times mistaken for madness.

Such was Gottfried Wolfgang, and such his situation at the time I mentioned. He was returning home late one stormy night, through some of the old and gloomy streets of the *Marais,* the ancient part of Paris. The loud claps of thunder rattled among the high houses of the narrow streets. He came to the Place de Grève, the square where public executions are performed. The lightning quivered about the pinnacles of the ancient Hôtel de Ville, and shed flickering gleams over the open space in front. As Wolfgang was crossing the square, he shrank back with horror at finding himself close by the guillotine. It was the height of the reign of terror, when this dreadful instrument of death stood ever ready, and its scaffold was continually running with the blood of the virtuous and the brave. It had that very day been actively employed in the work of carnage, and there it stood in grim array amidst a silent and sleeping city, waiting for fresh victims.

Wolfgang's heart sickened within him, and he was turning shuddering from the horrible engine, when he beheld a shadowy form cowering as it were at the foot of the steps which led up to the scaffold. A succession of vivid flashes of lightning revealed it more distinctly. It was a female figure, dressed in black. She was seated on one of the lower steps of the scaffold, leaning forward, her face hid in her lap, and her long dishevelled tresses hanging to the ground, streaming with the rain which fell in torrents. Wolfgang paused. There was something awful in this solitary monument of wo. The female had the appearance of being above the common order. He knew the times to be full of vicissitude, and that many a fair head, which had once been pillowed on down, now wandered houseless. Perhaps this was some poor mourner whom the dreadful axe had rendered desolate, and who sat here heartbroken on the strand of existence, from which all that was dear to her had been launched into eternity.

He approached, and addressed her in the accents of sympathy. She raised her head and gazed wildly at him. What was his astonishment at beholding, by the bright glare of the lightning, the very face which had haunted him in his dreams. It was pale and disconsolate, but ravishingly beautiful.

Trembling with violent and conflicting emotions, Wolfgang again accosted her. He spoke something of her being exposed at such an hour of the night, and to the fury of such a storm, and offered to conduct her to her friends. She pointed to the guillotine with a gesture of dreadful signification.

"I have no friend on earth!" said she.

"But you have a home," said Wolfgang.

"Yes—in the grave!"

The heart of the student melted at the words.

"If a stranger dare make an offer," said he, "without danger of being misunderstood, I would offer my humble dwelling as a shelter; myself as a devoted friend. I am friendless myself in Paris, and a stranger in the land; but if my life could be of service, it is at your disposal, and should be sacrificed before harm or indignity should come to you."

There was an honest earnestness in the young man's manner that had its effect. His foreign accent, too, was in his favour; it showed him not to be a hackneyed inhabitant of Paris. Indeed there is an eloquence in true enthusiasm that is not to be doubted. The homeless stranger confided herself implicitly to the protection of the student.

He supported her faltering steps across the Pont Neuf, and by the place where the statue of Henry the Fourth had been overthrown by the populace. The storm had abated, and the thunder rumbled at a distance. All Paris was quiet; that great volcano of human passion slumbered for a while, to gather fresh strength for the next day's eruption. The student conducted his charge through the ancient streets of the *Pays Latin,* and by the dusky walls of the Sorbonne to the great, dingy hotel which he inhabited. The old portress who admitted them stared with surprise at the unusual sight of the melancholy Wolfgang with a female companion.

On entering his apartment, the student, for the first time, blushed at the scantiness and indifference of his dwelling. He had but one chamber—an old fashioned saloon—heavily carved and fantastically furnished with the remains of former magnificence, for it was one of those hotels in the quarter of the Luxembourg palace which had once belonged to nobility. It was lumbered with books and papers, and all the usual apparatus of a student, and his bed stood in a recess at one end.

When lights were brought, and Wolfgang had a better opportunity of contemplating the stranger, he was more than ever intoxicated by her beauty. Her face was pale, but of a dazzling fairness, set off by a profusion of raven hair that hung clustering about it. Her eyes were large and brilliant, with a singular expression approaching almost to wildness. As far as her black dress permitted her shape to be seen, it was of perfect symmetry. Her whole appearance was highly striking, though she was dressed in the simplest style. The only thing approaching to an ornament which she wore was a broad, black band round her neck, clasped by diamonds.

The perplexity now commenced with the student how to dispose of the helpless being thus thrown upon his protection. He thought of abandoning his chamber to her, and seeking shelter for himself elsewhere. Still he was so fascinated by her charms, there seemed to be such a spell upon his thoughts and senses, that he could not tear himself from her presence. Her manner, too, was singular and unaccountable. She spoke no more of the guillotine. Her grief had abated. The attentions of the student had first won her confidence, and then, apparently, her heart. She was evidently an enthusiast like himself, and enthusiasts soon understand each other.

In the infatuation of the moment Wolfgang avowed his passion for her. He told her the story of his mysterious dream, and how she had possessed his heart before he had even seen her. She was strangely affected by his recital, and acknowledged to have felt an impulse towards him equally unaccountable. It was the time for wild theory and wild actions. Old prejudices and superstitions were done away; every thing was under the sway of the "Goddess of Reason." Among other rubbish of the old times, the forms and ceremonies of marriage began to be considered superfluous bonds for honourable minds. Social compacts were the vogue. Wolfgang was too much of a theorist not to be tainted by the liberal doctrines of the day.

"Why should we separate?" said he: "our hearts are united; in the eye of reason and honour we are as one. What need is there of sordid forms to bind high souls together?"

The stranger listened with emotion: she had evidently received illumination at the same school.

"You have no home nor family," continued he; "let me be every thing to you, or rather let us be every thing to one another. If form is necessary, form shall be observed—there is my hand. I pledge myself to you for ever."

"For ever?" said the stranger, solemnly.

"For ever!" repeated Wolfgang.

The stranger clasped the hand extended to her: "Then I am yours," murmured she, and sank upon his bosom.

The next morning the student left his bride sleeping, and sallied forth at an early hour to seek more spacious apartments, suitable to the change in his situation. When he returned, he found the stranger lying with her head hanging over the bed, and one arm thrown over it. He spoke to her, but received no reply. He advanced to awaken her from her uneasy posture. On taking her hand, it was cold—there was no pulsation—her face was pallid and ghastly.—In a word—she was a corpse.

Horrified and frantic, he alarmed the house. A scene of confusion ensued. The police was summoned. As the officer of police entered the room, he started back on beholding the corpse.

"Great heaven!" cried he, "how did this woman come here?"

"Do you know anything about her?" said Wolfgang, eagerly.

"Do I?" exclaimed the police officer: "she was guillotined yesterday!"

He stepped forward; undid the black collar round the neck of the corpse, and the head rolled on the floor!

The student burst into a frenzy. "The fiend! the fiend has gained possession of me!" shrieked he: "I am lost for ever!"

They tried to soothe him, but in vain. He was possessed with the frightful belief that an evil spirit had reanimated the dead body to ensnare him. He went distracted, and died in a madhouse.

Here the old gentleman with the haunted head finished his narrative.

"And is this really a fact?" said the inquisitive gentleman.

"A fact not to be doubted," replied the other. "I had it from the best authority. The student told it me himself. I saw him in a madhouse at Paris."

NATHANIEL HAWTHORNE

Nathaniel Hawthorne was born in 1804 in Salem, Massachusetts, and spent the bulk of his life there. One of his ancestors was a judge during the Salem witch trials. Ill health, along with a naturally solitary and bookish nature, kept him at home and limited his schooling for much of his youth, which alternated between his Salem home and a family home in Raymond, Maine. He graduated in 1825 from Bowdoin College, where he met Henry Wadsworth Longfellow and the future president Franklin Pierce. Over the next dozen years, spent largely in seclusion, Hawthorne published his first several books, including *Fanshawe* (1828) and *Twice-Told Tales* (1837). After marrying Sophia Peabody in 1842, Hawthorne published *Mosses from an Old Manse* (1846) and the two volumes for which he would be best remembered, *The Scarlet Letter* (1850) and *The House of the Seven Gables* (1851). For a time he worked in the Custom House in Salem; later, when Franklin Pierce became president, Hawthorne became United States consul at Liverpool, spending the years 1853–57 in England. His friendship with Herman Melville fostered both writers' careers. Among Hawthorne's later works are *The Blithedale Romance* (1852) and *The Marble Faun* (1860). Hawthorne died in Plymouth, New Hampshire, in 1864.

The supernatural was a lifelong concern for Hawthorne, and he used it in variegated ways to underscore the moral messages he sought to convey. The celebrated tale "Young Goodman Brown" (1835) is a haunting account of secret witchcraft, while "Rappacini's Daughter" (1844) is a story of science gone mad. Although not overtly supernatural, *The House of the Seven Gables* is a powerful rumination on an ancestral curse. Throughout his life, Hawthorne worked on several narratives about the elixir of life, including such works as *Septimius Felton* (1872) and *The Dolliver Romance* (1876). "Edward Randolph's Portrait" (first published in the *United States Magazine and Democratic Review*, July 1838, and included in the revised edition of *Twice-Told Tales*, 1842) embodies many of the central themes in Hawthorne's supernatural work, notably the powerful effect of the crimes and evils of the past upon the present.

EDWARD RANDOLPH'S PORTRAIT

The old legendary guest of the Province House abode in my remembrance from midsummer till January. One idle evening last winter, confident that he would be found in the snuggest corner of the bar-room, I resolved to pay him another visit, hoping to deserve well of my country by snatching from oblivion some else unheard-of fact of history. The night was chill and raw, and rendered boisterous by almost a gale of wind, which whistled along Washington Street, causing the gas-lights to flare and flicker within the lamps. As I hurried onward, my fancy was busy with a comparison between the present aspect of the street and that which it probably wore when the British governors inhabited the mansion whither I was now going. Brick edifices in those times were few, till a succession of destructive fires had swept, and swept again, the wooden dwellings and warehouses from the most populous quarters of the town. The buildings stood insulated and independent, not, as now, merging their separate existences into connected ranges, with a front of tiresome identity,—but each possessing features of its own, as if the owner's individual taste had shaped it,—and the whole presenting a picturesque irregularity, the absence of which is hardly compensated by any beauties of our modern architecture. Such a scene, dimly vanishing from the eye by the ray of here and there a tallow candle, glimmering through the small panes of scattered windows, would form a sombre contrast to the street as I beheld it, with the gas-lights blazing from corner to corner, flaming within the shops, and throwing a noonday brightness through the huge plates of glass.

But the black, lowering sky, as I turned my eyes upward, wore, doubtless, the same visage as when it frowned upon the ante-revolutionary New Englanders. The wintry blast had the same shriek that was familiar to their ears. The Old South Church, too, still pointed its antique spire into the darkness, and was lost between earth and heaven; and as I passed, its clock, which had warned so many generations how transitory was their lifetime, spoke heavily and slow the same unregarded moral to myself. "Only seven o'clock," thought I. "My old friend's legends will scarcely kill the hours 'twixt this and bedtime."

Passing through the narrow arch, I crossed the courtyard, the confined precincts of which were made visible by a lantern over the portal of the Province House. On entering the bar-room, I found, as I expected, the old tradition monger seated by a special good fire of anthracite, compelling clouds of smoke from a corpulent cigar. He recognized me with evident pleasure; for my rare properties as a patient listener invariably make me a favorite with elderly gentlemen and ladies of narrative propensities. Drawing a chair to the fire, I desired mine host to favor us with a glass apiece of whiskey punch, which was speedily prepared, steaming hot, with a slice of lemon at the bottom, a dark-red stratum of port wine upon the surface, and a sprinkling of nutmeg strewn over all. As we touched our glasses together, my legendary friend made himself known to me as Mr. Bela Tiffany; and I rejoiced at the oddity of the name, because it gave his image and character a sort of individuality in my conception. The old gentleman's draught acted as a solvent upon his memory, so that it overflowed with tales, traditions, anecdotes of famous dead people, and traits of ancient manners, some of which were childish as a nurse's lullaby, while others might have been worth the notice of the grave historian. Nothing impressed me more than a story of a black mysterious picture, which used to hang in one of the chambers of the Province House, directly above the room where we were now sitting. The following is as correct a version of the fact as the reader would be likely to obtain from any other source, although, assuredly, it has a tinge of romance approaching to the marvellous.

In one of the apartments of the Province House there was long preserved an ancient picture, the frame of which was as black as ebony, and the canvas itself so dark with age, damp, and smoke, that not a touch of the painter's art could be discerned. Time had thrown an impenetrable veil over it, and left to tradition and fable and conjecture to say what had once been there portrayed. During the rule of many successive governors, it had hung, by prescriptive and undisputed right, over the mantelpiece of the same chamber; and it still kept its place when Lieutenant-Governor Hutchinson assumed the administration of the province, on the departure of Sir Francis Bernard.

The Lieutenant-Governor sat, one afternoon, resting his head against the carved back of his stately armchair, and gazing up thoughtfully at the void blackness of the picture. It was scarcely a time for such inactive musing, when affairs of the deepest moment required the ruler's decision; for, within that very hour Hutchinson had received intelligence of the arrival of a British fleet, bringing three regiments from Halifax to overawe the insubordination of the people. These troops awaited his permission to occupy the fortress of Castle William, and the town itself. Yet, instead of affixing his signature to an official order, there sat the Lieutenant-Governor, so carefully scrutinizing the black waste of canvas that his demeanor attracted the notice of two young persons who attended him. One, wearing a military dress of buff, was his kinsman, Francis Lincoln, the Provincial Captain of Castle William; the other, who sat on a low stool beside his chair, was Alice Vane, his favorite niece.

She was clad entirely in white, a pale, ethereal creature, who, though a native of New England, had been educated abroad, and seemed not merely a stranger from another clime, but almost a being from another world. For several years, until left an orphan, she had dwelt with her father in sunny Italy, and there had acquired a taste and enthusiasm for sculpture and painting which she found few opportunities of gratifying in the undecorated dwellings of the colonial gentry. It was said that the early productions of her own pencil exhibited no inferior genius, though, perhaps, the rude atmosphere of New England had cramped her hand, and dimmed the glowing colors of her fancy. But observing her uncle's steadfast gaze, which appeared to search through the mist of years to discover the subject of the picture, her curiosity was excited.

"Is it known, my dear uncle," inquired she, "what this old picture once represented? Possibly, could it be made visible, it might prove a masterpiece of some great artist—else, why has it so long held such a conspicuous place?"

As her uncle, contrary to his usual custom (for he was as attentive to all the humors and caprices of Alice as if she had been his own best-beloved child), did not immediately reply, the young Captain of Castle William took that office upon himself.

"This dark old square of canvas, my fair cousin," said he, "has been an heirloom in the Province House from time immemorial. As to the painter, I can tell you nothing; but, if half the stories told of it be true, not one of the great Italian masters has ever produced so marvellous a piece of work as that before you."

Captain Lincoln proceeded to relate some of the strange fables and fantasies which, as it was impossible to refute them by ocular demonstration, had grown to be articles of popular belief, in reference to this old picture. One of the wildest, and at the same time the best accredited, accounts, stated it to be an original and authentic portrait of the Evil One, taken at a witch meeting near Salem; and that its strong and terrible resemblance had been confirmed by several of the confessing wizards and witches, at their trial, in open court. It was likewise affirmed that a familiar spirit or demon abode behind the blackness of the picture, and had shown himself, at seasons of public calamity, to more than one of the royal governors. Shirley, for instance, had beheld this ominous apparition, on the eve of General Abercrombie's shameful and bloody defeat under the walls of Ticonderoga. Many of the servants of the Province House had caught glimpses of a visage frowning down upon them, at morning or evening twilight,—or in the depths of night, while raking up the fire that glimmered on the hearth beneath; although, if any were bold enough to hold a torch before the picture, it would appear as black and undistinguishable as ever. The oldest inhabitant of Boston recollected that his father, in whose days the portrait had not wholly faded out of sight, had once looked upon it, but would never suffer himself to be questioned as to the face which was there represented. In connection with such stories, it was remarkable that over the top of the frame there were some ragged remnants of black silk, indicating that a veil had formerly hung down before the picture, until the duskiness of time had so effectually concealed it. But, after all, it was the most singular part of the affair that so many of the pompous governors of Massachusetts had allowed the obliterated picture to remain in the state chamber of the Province House.

"Some of these fables are really awful," observed Alice Vane, who had occasionally shuddered, as well as smiled, while her cousin spoke. "It would be almost worth while to wipe away the black surface of the canvas, since the original picture can hardly be so formidable as those which fancy paints instead of it."

"But would it be possible," inquired her cousin, "to restore this dark picture to its pristine hues?"

"Such arts are known in Italy," said Alice.

The Lieutenant-Governor had roused himself from his abstracted mood, and listened with a smile to the conversation of his young relatives. Yet his voice had something peculiar in its tones when he undertook the explanation of the mystery.

"I am sorry, Alice, to destroy your faith in the legends of which you are so fond," remarked he; "but my antiquarian researches have long since made me acquainted with the subject of this picture—if picture it can be called—which is no more visible, nor ever will be, than the face of the long buried man whom it once represented. It was the portrait of Edward Randolph, the founder of this house, a person famous in the history of New England."

"Of that Edward Randolph," exclaimed Captain Lincoln, "who obtained the repeal of the first provincial charter, under which our forefathers had enjoyed almost democratic privileges! He that was styled the arch-enemy of New England, and whose memory is still held in detestation as the destroyer of our liberties!"

"It was the same Randolph," answered Hutchinson, moving uneasily in his chair. "It was his lot to taste the bitterness of popular odium."

"Our annals tell us," continued the Captain of Castle William, "that the curse of the people followed this Randolph where he went, and wrought evil in all the subsequent events of his life, and that its effect was seen likewise in the manner of his death. They say, too, that the inward misery of that curse worked itself outward, and was visible on the wretched man's countenance, making it too horrible to be looked upon. If so, and if this picture truly represented his aspect, it was in mercy that the cloud of blackness has gathered over it."

"These traditions are folly to one who has proved, as I have, how little of historic truth lies at the bottom," said the Lieutenant-Governor. "As regards the life and character of Edward Randolph, too implicit credence has been given to Dr. Cotton Mather, who—I must say it, though some of his blood runs in my veins—has filled our early history with old women's tales, as fanciful and extravagant as those of Greece or Rome."

"And yet," whispered Alice Vane, "may not such fables have a moral? And, methinks, if the visage of this portrait be so dreadful, it is not without a cause that it has hung so long in a chamber of the Province House. When the rulers feel themselves irresponsible, it were well that they should be reminded of the awful weight of a people's curse."

The Lieutenant-Governor started, and gazed for a moment at his niece, as if her girlish fantasies had struck upon some feeling in his own breast, which all his policy or principles could not entirely subdue. He knew, indeed, that Alice, in spite of her foreign education, retained the native sympathies of a New England girl.

"Peace, silly child," cried he, at last, more harshly than he had ever before addressed the gentle Alice. "The rebuke of a king is more to be dreaded than the clamor of a wild, misguided multitude. Captain Lincoln, it is decided. The fortress of Castle William must be occupied by the royal troops. The two remaining regiments shall be billeted in the town, or encamped upon the Common. It is time, after years of tumult, and almost rebellion, that his majesty's government should have a wall of strength about it."

"Trust, sir—trust yet awhile to the loyalty of the people," said Captain Lincoln; "nor teach them that they can ever be on other terms with British soldiers than those of brotherhood, as when they fought side by side through the French War. Do not convert the streets of your native town into a camp. Think twice before you give up old Castle William, the key of the province, into other keeping than that of true-born New Englanders."

"Young man, it is decided," repeated Hutchinson, rising from his chair. "A British officer will be in attendance this evening, to receive the necessary instructions for the disposal of the troops. Your presence also will be required. Till then, farewell."

With these words the Lieutenant-Governor hastily left the room, while Alice and her cousin more slowly followed, whispering together, and once pausing to glance back at the mysterious picture. The Captain of Castle William fancied that the girl's air and mien were such as might have belonged to one of those spirits of fable—fairies, or creatures of a more antique mythology—who sometimes mingled their agency with mortal affairs, half in caprice, yet with a sensibility to human weal or woe. As he held the door for her to pass, Alice beckoned to the picture and smiled.

"Come forth, dark and evil Shape!" cried she. "It is thine hour!"

In the evening, Lieutenant-Governor Hutchinson sat in the same chamber where the foregoing scene had occurred, surrounded by several persons whose various interests had summoned them together. There were the Selectmen of Boston, plain, patriarchal fathers of the people, excellent representatives of the old puritanical founders, whose sombre strength had stamped so deep an impress upon the New England character. Contrasting with these were one or two members of Council, richly dressed in the white wigs, the embroidered waistcoats and other magnificence of the time, and making a somewhat ostentatious display of courtier-like ceremonial. In attendance, likewise, was a major of the British army, awaiting the Lieutenant-Governor's orders for the landing of the troops, which still remained on board the transports. The Captain of Castle William stood beside Hutchinson's chair with folded arms, glancing rather haughtily at the British officer, by whom he was soon to be superseded in his command. On a table, in the centre of the chamber, stood a branched silver candlestick, throwing down the glow of half a dozen wax-lights upon a paper apparently ready for the Lieutenant-Governor's signature.

Partly shrouded in the voluminous folds of one of the window curtains, which fell from the ceiling to the floor, was seen the white drapery of a lady's robe. It may appear strange that Alice Vane should have been there at such a time; but there was something so childlike, so wayward, in her singular character, so apart from ordinary rules, that her presence did not surprise the few who noticed it. Meantime, the chairman of the Selectmen was addressing to the Lieutenant-Governor a long and solemn protest against the reception of the British troops into the town.

"And if your Honor," concluded this excellent but somewhat prosy old gentleman, "shall see fit to persist in bringing these mercenary sworders and musketeers into our quiet streets, not on our heads be the responsibility. Think, sir, while there is yet time, that if one drop of blood be shed, that blood shall be an eternal stain upon your Honor's memory. You, sir, have written with an able pen the deeds of our forefathers. The more to be desired is it, therefore, that yourself should deserve honorable mention, as a true patriot and upright ruler, when your own doings shall be written down in history."

"I am not insensible, my good sir, to the natural desire to stand well in the annals of my country," replied Hutchinson, controlling his impatience into courtesy, "nor know I any better method of attaining that end than by withstanding the merely temporary spirit of mischief, which, with your pardon, seems to have infected elder men than myself. Would you have me wait till the mob shall sack the Province House, as they did my private mansion? Trust me, sir, the time may come when you will be glad to flee for protection to the king's banner, the raising of which is now so distasteful to you."

"Yes," said the British major, who was impatiently expecting the Lieutenant-Governor's orders. "The demagogues of this Province have raised the devil and cannot lay him again. We will exorcise him, in God's name and the king's."

"If you meddle with the devil, take care of his claws!" answered the Captain of Castle William, stirred by the taunt against his countrymen.

"Craving your pardon, young sir," said the venerable Selectman, "let not an evil spirit enter into your words. We will strive against the oppressor with prayer and fasting, as our forefathers would have done. Like them, moreover, we will submit to whatever lot a wise Providence may send us,—always, after our own best exertions to amend it."

"And there peep forth the devil's claws!" muttered Hutchinson, who well understood the nature of Puritan submission. "This matter shall be expedited forthwith. When there shall be a sentinel at every corner, and a court of guard before the town house, a loyal gentleman may venture to walk abroad. What to me is the outcry of a mob, in this remote province of the realm? The king is my master, and England is my country! Upheld by their armed strength, I set my foot upon the rabble, and defy them!"

He snatched a pen, and was about to affix his signature to the paper that lay on the table, when the Captain of Castle William placed his hand upon his shoulder. The freedom of the action, so contrary to the ceremonious respect which was then considered due to rank and dignity, awakened general surprise, and in none more than in the Lieutenant-Governor himself. Looking angrily up, he perceived that his young relative was pointing his finger to the opposite wall. Hutchinson's eye followed the signal; and he saw, what had hitherto been unobserved, that a black silk curtain was suspended before the mysterious picture, so as completely to conceal it. His thoughts immediately recurred to the scene of the preceding afternoon; and, in his surprise, confused by indistinct emotions, yet sensible that his niece must have had an agency in this phenomenon, he called loudly upon her.

"Alice!—come hither, Alice!"

No sooner had he spoken than Alice Vane glided from her

station, and pressing one hand across her eyes, with the other snatched away the sable curtain that concealed the portrait. An exclamation of surprise burst from every beholder; but the Lieutenant-Governor's voice had a tone of horror.

"By Heaven!" said he, in a low, inward murmur, speaking rather to himself than to those around him, "if the spirit of Edward Randolph were to appear among us from the place of torment, he could not wear more of the terrors of hell upon his face!"

"For some wise end," said the aged Selectman, solemnly, "hath Providence scattered away the mist of years that had so long hid this dreadful effigy. Until this hour no living man hath seen what we behold!"

Within the antique frame, which so recently had inclosed a sable waste of canvas, now appeared a visible picture, still dark, indeed, in its hues and shadings, but thrown forward in strong relief. It was a half-length figure of a gentleman in a rich but very old-fashioned dress of embroidered velvet, with a broad ruff and a beard, and wearing a hat, the brim of which overshadowed his forehead. Beneath this cloud the eyes had a peculiar glare, which was almost lifelike. The whole portrait started so distinctly out of the background, that it had the effect of a person looking down from the wall at the astonished and awe-stricken spectators. The expression of the face, if any words can convey an idea of it, was that of a wretch detected in some hideous guilt, and exposed to the bitter hatred and laughter and withering scorn of a vast surrounding multitude. There was the struggle of defiance, beaten down and overwhelmed by the crushing weight of ignominy. The torture of the soul had come forth upon the countenance. It seemed as if the picture, while hidden behind the cloud of immemorial years, had been all the time acquiring an intenser depth and darkness of expression, till now it gloomed forth again, and threw its evil omen over the present hour. Such, if the wild legend may be credited, was the portrait of Edward Randolph, as he appeared when a people's curse had wrought its influence upon his nature.

"'T would drive me mad—that awful face!" said Hutchinson, who seemed fascinated by the contemplation of it.

"Be warned, then!" whispered Alice. "He trampled on a people's rights. Behold his punishment—and avoid a crime like his!"

The Lieutenant-Governor actually trembled for an instant; but, exerting his energy—which was not, however, his most characteristic feature—he strove to shake off the spell of Randolph's countenance.

"Girl!" cried he, laughing bitterly as he turned to Alice, "have you brought hither your painter's art—your Italian spirit of intrigue—your tricks of stage effect—and think to influence the councils of rulers and the affairs of nations by such shallow contrivances? See here!"

"Stay yet a while," said the Selectman, as Hutchinson again snatched the pen; "for if ever mortal man received a warning from a tormented soul, your Honor is that man!"

"Away!" answered Hutchinson fiercely. "Though yonder senseless picture cried 'Forbear!'—it should not move me!"

Casting a scowl of defiance at the pictured face (which seemed at that moment to intensify the horror of its miserable and wicked look), he scrawled on the paper, in characters that betokened it a deed of desperation, the name of Thomas Hutchinson. Then, it is said, he shuddered, as if that signature had granted away his salvation.

"It is done," said he; and placed his hand upon his brow.

"May Heaven forgive the deed," said the soft, sad accents of Alice Vane, like the voice of a good spirit flitting away.

When morning came there was a stifled whisper through the household, and spreading thence about the town, that the dark, mysterious picture had started from the wall, and spoken face to face with Lieutenant-Governor Hutchinson. If such a miracle had been wrought, however, no traces of it remained behind, for within the antique frame nothing could be discerned save the impenetrable cloud, which had covered the canvas since the memory of man. If the figure had, indeed, stepped forth, it had fled back, spirit-like, at the daydawn, and hidden itself behind a century's obscurity. The truth probably was, that Alice Vane's secret for restoring the hues of the picture had merely effected a temporary renovation. But those who, in that brief interval, had beheld the awful visage of Edward Randolph, desired no second glance, and ever afterwards trembled at the recollection of the scene, as if an evil spirit had appeared visibly among them. And as for Hutchinson, when, far over the ocean, his dying hour drew on, he gasped for breath, and complained that he was choking with the blood of the Boston Massacre; and Francis Lincoln, the former Captain of Castle William, who was standing at his bedside, perceived a likeness in his frenzied look to that of Edward Randolph. Did his broken spirit feel, at that dread hour, the tremendous burden of a People's curse?

At the conclusion of this miraculous legend, I inquired of mine host whether the picture still remained in the chamber over our heads; but Mr. Tiffany informed me that it had long since been removed, and was supposed to be hidden in some out-of-the-way corner of the New England Museum. Perchance some curious antiquary may light upon it there, and, with the assistance of Mr. Howorth, the picture cleaner, may supply a not unnecessary proof of the authenticity of the facts here set down. During the progress of the story a storm had been gathering abroad, and raging and rattling so loudly in the upper regions of the Province House, that it seemed as if all the old governors and great men were running riot above stairs while Mr. Bela Tiffany babbled of them below. In the course of generations, when many people have lived and died in an ancient house, the whistling of the wind through its crannies, and the creaking of its beams and rafters, become strangely like the tones of the human voice, or thundering laughter, or heavy footsteps treading the deserted chambers. It is as if the echoes of half a century were revived. Such were the ghostly sounds that roared and murmured in our ears when I took leave of the circle round the fireside of the Province House, and plunging down the door steps, fought my way homeward against a drifting snow-storm.

EDGAR ALLAN POE

Edgar Allan Poe was born in Richmond in 1809. After the early death of his parents, Poe was taken into the family of John Allan, from whom his middle name derives. He spent the years 1815–20 in England, attending the academy at Stoke Newington. He later briefly attended the University of Virginia and West Point. Poe's earliest publications were volumes of poetry, including the extremely rare *Tamerlane and Other Poems* (1827), *Al Aaraaf, Tamerlane, and Minor Poems* (1829), and *Poems* (1831). By the early 1830s he had turned his attention to short fiction, and in the course of his short career he virtually invented the short story, the tale of detection (beginning with "The Murders in the Rue Morgue," 1841), and the tale of supernatural and psychological horror. Many of his earlier tales were gathered in the landmark volume *Tales of the Grotesque and Arabesque* (1840).

In 1835 Poe became editor of the *Southern Literary Messenger* in Richmond, where many of his tales were published. He later edited *Burton's Gentleman's Magazine* (1839–40), *Graham's Magazine* (1840–42), and the *Broadway Journal* (1845–46). During this period he produced such well-known tales as "Ligeia" (1838), "William Wilson" (1839), "The Masque of the Red Death" (1842), "The Tell-Tale Heart" (1843), and "The Black Cat" (1843). His sole novel, *The Narrative of Arthur Gordon Pym* (1838), is an ambiguous tale of physical horror and exploration of the unknown. His later stories were collected in *Tales* (1845). Late in life he produced an eccentric work of philosophy, *Eureka* (1848). Poe died under mysterious circumstances in Baltimore in 1849.

"The Fall of the House of Usher" (*Burton's Gentleman's Magazine*, September 1839, in *Tales of the Grotesque and Arabesque*) is emblematic of Poe's supernatural work, in such elements as the intense focus on psychological states, the inclusion of weird verse (in this case, "The Haunted Palace"), the setting in a never-never land of the imagination, and in the inexorable progression from beginning to cataclysmic end. It becomes evident that Roderick Usher, his sister Madeline, and the house itself all share a single soul, and that they all perish simultaneously.

THE FALL OF THE HOUSE OF USHER

Son cœur est un luth suspendu;
Sitôt qu'on le touche il résonne.

De Béranger

During the whole of a dull, dark, and soundless day in the autumn of the year, when the clouds hung oppressively low in the heavens, I had been passing alone, on horseback, through a singularly dreary tract of country; and at length found myself, as the shades of the evening drew on, within view of the melancholy House of Usher. I know not how it was—but, with the first glimpse of the building, a sense of insufferable gloom pervaded my spirit. I say insufferable; for the feeling was unrelieved by any of that half-pleasurable, because poetic, sentiment, with which the mind usually receives even the sternest natural images of the desolate or terrible. I looked upon the scene before me—upon the mere house, and the simple landscape features of the domain—upon the bleak walls—upon the vacant eye-like windows—upon a few rank sedges—and upon a few white trunks of decayed trees—with an utter depression of soul which I can compare to no earthly sensation more properly than to the after-dream of the reveller upon opium—the bitter lapse into everyday life—the hideous dropping off of the veil. There was an iciness, a sinking, a sickening of the heart—an unredeemed dreariness of thought which no goading of the imagination could torture into aught of the sublime. What was it—I paused to think—what was it that so unnerved me in the contemplation of the House of Usher? It was a mystery all insoluble; nor could I grapple with the shadowy fancies that crowded upon me as I pondered. I was forced to fall back upon the unsatisfactory conclusion, that while, beyond doubt, there *are* combinations of very simple natural objects which have the power of thus affecting us, still the analysis of this power lies among considerations beyond our depth. It was possible, I reflected, that a mere different arrangement of the particulars of the scene, of the details of the picture, would be sufficient to modify, or perhaps to annihilate its capacity for sorrowful impression; and, acting upon this idea, I reined my horse to the precipitous brink of a black and lurid tarn that lay in unruffled lustre by the dwelling, and gazed down—but with a shudder even more thrilling than before—upon the remodelled and inverted images of the gray sedge, and the ghastly tree-stems, and the vacant and eye-like windows.

Nevertheless, in this mansion of gloom I now proposed to myself a sojourn of some weeks. Its proprietor, Roderick Usher, had been one of my boon companions in boyhood; but many years had elapsed since our last meeting. A letter, however, had lately reached me in a distant part of the country—a letter from him—which, in its wildly importunate nature, had admitted of no other than a personal reply. The MS. gave evidence of nervous agitation. The writer spoke of acute bodily illness—of a mental disorder which oppressed him—and of an earnest desire to see me, as his best, and indeed his only personal friend, with a view of attempting, by the cheerfulness of my society, some alleviation of his malady. It was the manner in which all this, and much more, was said—it was the apparent *heart* that went with his request—which allowed me no room for hesitation; and I accordingly obeyed forthwith what I still considered a very singular summons.

Although, as boys, we had been even intimate associates, yet I really knew little of my friend. His reserve had been always excessive and habitual. I was aware, however, that his very ancient family had been noted, time out of mind, for a peculiar sensibility of temperament, displaying itself, through long ages, in many works of exalted art, and manifested, of late, in repeated deeds of munificent yet unobtrusive charity, as well as in a passionate devotion to the intricacies, perhaps even more than to the orthodox and easily recognisable beauties, of musical science. I had learned, too, the very remarkable fact, that the stem of the Usher race, all time-honoured as it was, had put forth, at no period, any enduring branch; in other words, that the entire family lay in the direct line of descent, and had always, with very trifling and very temporary variation, so lain. It was this deficiency, I considered, while running over in thought the perfect keeping of the character of the premises with the accredited character of the people, and while speculating upon the possible influence which the one, in the long lapse of centuries, might have exercised upon the other—it was this deficiency, perhaps, of collateral issue, and the consequent undeviating transmission, from sire to son, of the patrimony with the name, which had, at length, so identified the two as to merge the original title of the estate in the quaint and equivocal appellation of the "House of Usher"—an appellation which seemed to include, in the minds of the peasantry who used it, both the family and the family mansion.

I have said that the sole effect of my somewhat childish experiment—that of looking down within the tarn—had been to deepen the first singular impression. There can be no doubt that the consciousness of the rapid increase of my superstition—for why should I not so term it?—served mainly to accelerate the increase itself. Such, I have long known, is the paradoxical law of all sentiments having terror as a basis. And it might have been for this reason only, that, when I again uplifted my eyes to the house itself, from its image in the pool, there grew in my mind a strange fancy—a fancy so ridiculous, indeed, that I but mention it to show the vivid force of the sensations which oppressed me. I had so worked upon my imagination as really to believe that about the whole mansion and domain there hung an atmosphere peculiar to themselves and their immediate vicinity—an atmosphere which had no affinity with the air of heaven, but which had reeked up from the decayed trees, and the gray wall, and the silent tarn—a pestilent and mystic vapour, dull, sluggish, faintly discernible, and leaden-hued.

Shaking off from my spirit what *must* have been a dream, I scanned more narrowly the real aspect of the building. Its principal feature seemed to be that of an excessive antiquity. The discoloration of ages had been great. Minute fungi overspread the whole exterior, hanging in a fine tangled web-work from the eaves. Yet all this was apart from any extraordinary dilapidation. No portion of the masonry had fallen; and there appeared to be a wild inconsistency between its still perfect adaptation of parts, and the crumbling condition of the individual stones. In this there was much that reminded me of the specious totality of old wood-work which has rotted for long years in some neglected vault, with no disturbance from the breath of the external air. Beyond this indication of extensive decay, however, the fabric gave little token of instability. Perhaps the eye of a scrutinising observer might have discovered a barely perceptible fissure, which, extending from the roof of the building in front, made its way down the wall in a zigzag direction, until it became lost in the sullen waters of the tarn.

Noticing these things, I rode over a short causeway to the house. A servant in waiting took my horse, and I entered the Gothic archway of the hall. A valet, of stealthy step, thence conducted me, in silence, through many dark and intricate passages in my progress to the *studio* of his master. Much that I encountered on the way contributed, I know not how, to heighten the vague sentiments of which I have already spoken. While the objects around me—while the carvings of the ceilings, the sombre tapestries of the walls, the ebon blackness of the floors, and the phantasmagoric armorial trophies which rattled as I strode, were but matters to which, or to such as which, I had been accustomed from my infancy—while I hesitated not to acknowledge how familiar was all this—I still wondered to find how unfamiliar were the fancies which ordinary images were stirring up. On one of the staircases, I met the physician of the family. His countenance, I thought, wore a mingled expression of low cunning and perplexity. He accosted me with trepidation and passed on. The valet now threw open a door and ushered me into the presence of his master.

The room in which I found myself was very large and lofty. The windows were long, narrow, and pointed, and at so vast a distance from the black oaken floor as to be altogether inaccessible from within. Feeble gleams of encrimsoned light made their way through the trellised panes, and served to render sufficiently distinct the more prominent objects around; the eye, however, struggled in vain to reach the remoter angles of the chamber, or the recesses of the vaulted and fretted ceiling. Dark draperies hung upon the walls. The general furniture was profuse, comfortless, antique, and tattered. Many books and musical instruments lay scattered about, but failed to give any vitality to the scene. I felt that I breathed an atmosphere of sorrow. An air of stern, deep, and irredeemable gloom hung over and pervaded all.

Upon my entrance, Usher arose from a sofa on which he had been lying at full length, and greeted me with a vivacious warmth which had much in it, I at first thought, of an overdone cordiality—of the constrained effort of the *ennuyé* man of the world. A glance, however, at his countenance, convinced me of his perfect sincerity. We sat down; and for some moments, while he spoke not, I gazed upon him with a feeling half of pity, half of awe. Surely, man had never before so terribly altered, in so brief a period, as had Roderick Usher! It was with difficulty that I could bring myself to admit the identity of the wan being before me with the companion of my early boyhood. Yet the character of his face had been at all times remarkable. A cadaverousness of complexion; an eye large, liquid, and luminous beyond comparison; lips somewhat thin and very pallid, but of a surpassingly beautiful curve; a nose of a delicate Hebrew model, but with a breadth of nostril unusual in similar formations; a finely moulded chin, speaking, in its want of prominence, of a want of moral energy; hair of a more than web-like softness and tenuity; these features, with an inordinate expansion above the regions of the temple, made up altogether a countenance not easily to be forgotten. And now in the mere exaggeration of the prevailing character of these features, and of the expression they were wont to convey, lay so much of change that I doubted to whom I spoke. The now ghastly pallor of the skin, and the now miraculous lustre of the eye, above all things startled and even awed me. The silken hair, too, had been suffered to grow all unheeded, and as, in its wild gossamer texture, it floated rather than fell about the face, I could not, even with effort, connect its Arabesque expression with any idea of simple humanity.

In the manner of my friend I was at once struck with an incoherence—an inconsistency; and I soon found this to arise from a series of feeble and futile struggles to overcome an habitual trepidancy—an excessive nervous agitation. For something of this nature I had indeed been prepared, no less by his letter, than by reminiscences of certain boyish traits, and by conclusions deduced from peculiar physical conformation and temperament. His action was alternately vivacious and sullen. His voice varied rapidly from a tremulous indecision (when the animal spirits seemed utterly in abeyance) to that species of energetic concision—that abrupt, weighty, unhurried, and hollow-sounding enunciation—that leaden, self-balanced and perfectly modulated guttural utterance, which may be observed in the lost drunkard, or the irreclaimable eater of opium, during the periods of his most intense excitement.

It was thus that he spoke of the object of my visit, of his earnest desire to see me, and of the solace he expected me to afford him. He entered, at some length, into what he conceived to be the nature of his malady. It was, he said, a constitutional and a family evil, and one for which he despaired to find a remedy—a mere nervous affection, he immediately added, which would undoubtedly soon pass off. It displayed itself in a host of unnatural sensations. Some of these, as he detailed them, interested and bewildered me; although, perhaps, the terms, and the general manner of the narration had their weight. He suffered much from a morbid acuteness of the senses; the most insipid food was alone endurable; he could wear only garments of certain texture; the odours of all flowers were oppressive; his eyes were tortured by even a faint light; and there were but peculiar sounds, and these from stringed instruments, which did not inspire him with horror.

To an anomalous species of terror I found him a bounden slave. "I shall perish," said he, "I *must* perish in this deplorable folly. Thus, thus, and not otherwise, shall I be lost. I dread the events of the future, not in themselves, but in their results. I shudder at the thought of any, even the most trivial, incident, which may operate upon this intolerable agitation of soul. I have, indeed, no abhorrence of danger, except in its absolute effect—in terror. In this unnerved—in this pitiable condition—I feel that the period will sooner or later arrive when I must abandon life and reason together, in some struggle with the grim phantasm, Fear."

I learned, moreover, at intervals, and through broken and equivocal hints, another singular feature of his mental condition. He was enchained by certain superstitious impressions in regard to the dwelling which he tenanted, and whence, for many years, he had never ventured forth—in regard to an influence whose supposititious force was conveyed in terms too shadowy here to be re-stated—an influence which some peculiarities in the mere form and substance of his family mansion, had, by dint of long sufferance, he said, obtained over his spirit—an effect which the *physique* of the gray walls and turrets, and of the dim tarn into which they all looked down, had, at length, brought about upon the *morale* of his existence.

He admitted, however, although with hesitation, that much of the peculiar gloom which thus afflicted him could be traced to a more natural and far more palpable origin—to the severe and long-continued illness—indeed to the evidently approaching dissolution—of a tenderly beloved sister—his sole companion for long years—his last and only relative on earth. "Her decease," he said, with a bitterness which I can never forget, "would leave him (him the hopeless and the frail) the last of the ancient race of the Ushers." While he spoke, the lady Madeline (for so was she called) passed slowly through a remote portion of the apartment, and, without having noticed my presence, disappeared. I regarded her with an utter astonishment not unmingled with dread—and yet I found it impossible to account for such feelings. A sensation of stupor oppressed me, as my eyes followed her retreating steps. When a door, at length, closed upon her, my glance sought instinctively and eagerly the countenance of the brother—but he had buried his face in his hands, and I could only perceive that a far more than ordinary wanness had overspread the emaciated fingers through which trickled many passionate tears.

The disease of the lady Madeline had long baffled the skill of her physicians. A settled apathy, a gradual wasting away of the person, and frequent although transient affections of a partially cataleptical character, were the unusual diagnosis. Hitherto she had steadily borne up against the pressure of her malady, and had not betaken herself finally to bed; but, on the closing in of the evening of my arrival at the house, she succumbed (as her brother told me at night with inexpressible agitation) to the prostrating power of the destroyer; and I learned that the glimpse I had obtained of her person would thus probably be the last I should obtain—that the lady, at least while living, would be seen by me no more.

For several days ensuing, her name was unmentioned by either Usher or myself: and during this period I was busied in earnest endeavours to alleviate the melancholy of my friend. We painted and read together; or I listened, as if in a dream, to the wild improvisations of his speaking guitar. And thus, as a closer and still closer intimacy admitted me more unreservedly into the recesses of his spirit, the more bitterly did I perceive the futility of all attempt at cheering a mind from which darkness, as if an inherent positive quality, poured forth upon all objects of the moral and physical universe, in one unceasing radiation of gloom.

I shall ever bear about me a memory of the many solemn hours I thus spent alone with the master of the House of Usher. Yet I should fail in any attempt to convey an idea of the exact character of the studies, or of the occupations, in which he involved me, or led me the way. An excited and highly distempered ideality threw a sulphureous lustre over all. His long improvised dirges will ring forever in my ears. Among other things, I hold painfully in mind a certain singular perversion and amplification of the wild air of the last waltz of Von Weber. From the paintings over which his elaborate fancy brooded, and which grew, touch by touch, into vaguenesses at which I shuddered the more thrillingly, because I shuddered knowing not why;—from these paintings (vivid as their images now are before me) I would in vain endeavour to educe more than a small portion which should lie within the compass of merely written words. By the utter simplicity, by the nakedness of his designs, he arrested and overawed attention. If ever mortal painted an idea, that mortal was Roderick Usher. For me at least—in the circumstances then surrounding me—there arose out of the pure abstractions which the hypochondriac contrived to throw upon his canvas, an intensity of intolerable awe, no shadow of which felt I ever yet in the contemplation of the certainly glowing yet too concrete reveries of Fuseli.

One of the phantasmagoric conceptions of my friend, partaking not so rigidly of the spirit of abstraction, may be shadowed forth, although feebly, in words. A small picture presented the interior of an immensely long and rectangular vault or tunnel, with low walls, smooth, white, and without interruption or device. Certain accessory points of the design served well to convey the idea that this excavation lay at an exceeding depth below the surface of the earth. No outlet was observed in any portion of its vast extent, and no torch, or other artificial source of light was discernible; yet a flood of intense rays rolled throughout, and bathed the whole in a ghastly and inappropriate splendour.

I have just spoken of that morbid condition of the auditory nerve which rendered all music intolerable to the sufferer, with the exception of certain effects of stringed instruments. It was, perhaps, the narrow limits to which he thus confined himself upon the guitar, which gave birth, in great measure, to the fantastic character of his performances. But the fervid *facility* of his *impromptus* could not be so accounted for. They must have been, and were, in the notes, as well as in the words of his wild fantasias (for he not unfrequently accompanied himself with rhymed verbal improvisations), the result of that intense mental collectedness and concentration to which I have previously alluded as observable only in particular moments of the highest artificial excitement. The words of one of these rhapsodies I have easily remembered. I was, perhaps, the more forcibly impressed with it, as he gave it, because, in the under or mystic current of its meaning, I fancied that I perceived, and for the first time, a full consciousness on the part of Usher, of the tottering of his lofty reason upon her throne. The verses, which were entitled, "The Haunted Palace," ran very nearly, if not accurately, thus:

I

In the greenest of our valleys,
    By good angels tenanted,
Once a fair and stately palace—
    Radiant palace—reared its head.
In the monarch Thought's dominion—
    It stood there!
Never seraph spread a pinion
    Over fabric half so fair.

II

Banners yellow, glorious, golden,
    On its roof did float and flow;
(This—all this—was in the olden
    Time long ago)
And every gentle air that dallied,
    In that sweet day,
Along the ramparts plumed and pallid,
    A winged odour went away.

III

Wanderers in that happy valley
    Through two luminous windows saw
Spirits moving musically
    To a lute's well-tunèd law,
Round about a throne, where sitting
    (Porphyrogene!)
In state his glory well befitting,
    The ruler of the realm was seen.

IV

And all with pearl and ruby glowing
    Was the fair palace door,
Through which came flowing, flowing, flowing
    And sparkling evermore,
A troop of Echoes whose sweet duty
    Was but to sing,
In voices of surpassing beauty,
    The wit and wisdom of their king.

V

But evil things, in robes of sorrow,
    Assailed the monarch's high estate;
(Ah, let us mourn, for never morrow
    Shall dawn upon him, desolate!)
And, round about his home, the glory
    That blushed and bloomed
Is but a dim-remembered story
    Of the old time entombed.

VI

And travellers now within that valley,
    Through the red-litten windows, see
Vast forms that move fantastically
    To a discordant melody;
While, like a rapid ghastly river,
    Through the pale door,
A hideous throng rush out forever,
    And laugh—but smile no more.

I well remember that suggestions arising from this ballad, led us into a train of thought wherein there became manifest an opinion of Usher's which I mention not so much on account of its novelty, (for other men* have thought thus,) as on account of the pertinacity with which he maintained it. This opinion, in its general form, was that of the sentience of all vegetable things. But, in his disordered fancy, the idea had assumed a more daring character, and trespassed, under certain conditions, upon the kingdom of inorganization. I lack words to express the full extent, or the earnest *abandon* of his persuasion. The belief, however, was connected (as I have previously hinted) with the gray stones of the home of his forefathers. The conditions of the sentience had been here, he imagined, fulfilled in the method of collocation of these stones—in the order of their arrangement, as well as in that of the many *fungi* which overspread them, and of the decayed trees which stood around—above all, in the long undisturbed endurance of this arrangement, and in its reduplication in the still waters of the tarn. Its evidence—the evidence of the sentience—was to be seen, he said, (and I here started as he spoke,) in the gradual yet certain condensation of an atmosphere of their own about the waters and the walls. The result was discoverable, he added, in that silent, yet importunate and terrible influence which for centuries had moulded the destinies of his family, and which made *him* what I now saw him—what he was. Such opinions need no comment, and I will make none.

Our books—the books which, for years, had formed no small portion of the mental existence of the invalid—were, as might be supposed, in strict keeping with this character of phantasm. We pored together over such works as the Ververt et Chartreuse of Gresset; the Belphegor of Machiavelli; the Heaven and Hell of Swedenborg; the Subterranean Voyage of Nicholas Klimm by Holberg; the Chiromancy of Robert Flud, of Jean D'Indaginé, and of De la Chambre; the Journey into the Blue Distance of Tieck; and the City of the Sun of Campanella. One favourite volume was a small octavo edition of the *Directorium Inquisitorum,* by the Dominican Eymeric de Gironne; and there were passages in Pomponius Mela, about the old African

Edgar Allan Poe

---

* Watson, Dr. Percival, Spallanzani, and especially the Bishop of Landaff.— See "Chemical Essays," vol. v.

Satyrs and Ægipans, over which Usher would sit dreaming for hours. His chief delight, however, was found in the perusal of an exceedingly rare and curious book in quarto Gothic—the manual of a forgotten church—the *Vigiliæ Mortuorum secundum Chorum Ecclesiæ Maguntinæ.*

I could not help thinking of the wild ritual of this work, and of its probable influence upon the hypochondriac, when, one evening, having informed me abruptly that the lady Madeline was no more, he stated his intention of preserving her corpse for a fortnight, (previously to its final interment,) in one of the numerous vaults within the main walls of the building. The worldly reason, however, assigned for this singular proceeding, was one which I did not feel at liberty to dispute. The brother had been led to his resolution (so he told me) by consideration of the unusual character of the malady of the deceased, of certain obtrusive and eager inquiries on the part of her medical men, and of the remote and exposed situation of the burial-ground of the family. I will not deny that when I called to mind the sinister countenance of the person whom I met upon the staircase, on the day of my arrival at the house, I had no desire to oppose what I regarded as at best but a harmless, and by no means an unnatural, precaution.

At the request of Usher, I personally aided him in the arrangements for the temporary entombment. The body having been encoffined, we two alone bore it to its rest. The vault in which we placed it (and which had been so long unopened that our torches, half smothered in its oppressive atmosphere, gave us little opportunity for investigation) was small, damp, and entirely without means of admission for light; lying, at great depth, immediately beneath that portion of the building in which was my own sleeping apartment. It had been used, apparently, in remote feudal times, for the worst purposes of a donjon-keep, and, in later days, as a place of deposit for powder, or some other highly combustible substance, as a portion of its floor, and the whole interior of a long archway through which we reached it, were carefully sheathed with copper. The door, of massive iron, had been, also, similarly protected. Its immense weight caused an unusually sharp grating sound, as it moved upon its hinges.

Having deposited our mournful burden upon tressels within this region of horror, we partially turned aside the yet unscrewed lid of the coffin, and looked upon the face of the tenant. A striking similitude between the brother and sister now first arrested my attention; and Usher, divining, perhaps, my thoughts, murmured out some few words from which I learned that the deceased and himself had been twins, and that sympathies of a scarcely intelligible nature had always existed between them. Our glances, however, rested not long upon the dead—for we could not regard her unawed. The disease which had thus entombed the lady in the maturity of youth, had left, as usual in all maladies of a strictly cataleptical character, the mockery of a faint blush upon the bosom and the face, and that suspiciously lingering smile upon the lip which is so terrible in death. We replaced and screwed down the lid, and, having secured the door of iron, made our way, with toil, into the scarcely less gloomy apartments of the upper portion of the house.

And now, some days of bitter grief having elapsed, an observable change came over the features of the mental disorder of my friend. His ordinary manner had vanished. His ordinary occupations were neglected or forgotten. He roamed from chamber to chamber with hurried, unequal, and objectless step. The pallor of his countenance had assumed, if possible, a more ghastly hue—but the luminousness of his eye had utterly gone out. The once occasional huskiness of his tone was heard no more; and a tremulous quaver, as if of extreme terror, habitually characterized his utterance. There were times, indeed, when I thought his unceasingly agitated mind was labouring with some oppressive secret, to divulge which he struggled for the necessary courage. At times, again, I was obliged to resolve all into the mere inexplicable vagaries of madness, for I beheld him gazing upon vacancy for long hours, in an attitude of the profoundest attention, as if listening to some imaginary sound. It was no wonder that his condition terrified—that it infected me. I felt creeping upon me, by slow yet certain degrees, the wild influences of his own fantastic yet impressive superstitions.

It was, especially, upon retiring to bed late in the night of the seventh or eighth day after the placing of the lady Madeline within the donjon, that I experienced the full power of such feelings. Sleep came not near my couch—while the hours waned and waned away. I struggled to reason off the nervousness which had dominion over me. I endeavoured to believe that much, if not all of what I felt, was due to the bewildering influence of the gloomy furniture of the room—of the dark and tattered draperies, which, tortured into motion by the breath of a rising tempest, swayed fitfully to and fro upon the walls, and rustled uneasily about the decorations of the bed. But my efforts were fruitless. An irrepressible tremour gradually pervaded my frame; and, at length, there sat upon my very heart an incubus of utterly causeless alarm. Shaking this off with a gasp and a struggle, I uplifted myself upon the pillows, and, peering earnestly within the intense darkness of the chamber, hearkened—I know not why, except that an instinctive spirit prompted me—to certain low and indefinite sounds which came through the pauses of the storm, at long intervals, I knew not whence. Overpowered by an intense sentiment of horror, unaccountable yet unendurable, I threw on my clothes with haste (for I felt that I should sleep no more during the night), and endeavoured to arouse myself from the pitiable condition to which I had fallen, by pacing rapidly to and fro through the apartment.

I had taken but few turns in this manner, when a light step on an adjoining staircase arrested my attention. I presently recognised it as that of Usher. In an instant afterward he rapped, with a gentle touch, at my door, and entered, bearing a lamp. His countenance was, as usual, cadaverously wan—but, moreover, there was a species of mad hilarity in his eyes—an evidently restrained *hysteria* in his whole demeanour. His air appalled me—but anything was preferable to the solitude which I had so long endured, and I even welcomed his presence as a relief.

"And you have not seen it?" he said abruptly, after having stared about him for some moments in silence—"you have not then seen it?—but, stay! you shall." Thus speaking, and having carefully shaded his lamp, he hurried to one of the casements, and threw it freely open to the storm.

The impetuous fury of the entering gust nearly lifted us

from our feet. It was, indeed, a tempestuous yet sternly beautiful night, and one wildly singular in its terror and its beauty. A whirlwind had apparently collected its force in our vicinity; for there were frequent and violent alterations in the direction of the wind; and the exceeding density of the clouds (which hung so low as to press upon the turrets of the house) did not prevent our perceiving the life-like velocity with which they flew careering from all points against each other, without passing away into the distance. I say that even their exceeding density did not prevent our perceiving this—yet we had no glimpse of the moon or stars—nor was there any flashing forth of the lightning. But the under surfaces of the huge masses of agitated vapour, as well as all terrestrial objects immediately around us, were glowing in the unnatural light of a faintly luminous and distinctly visible gaseous exhalation which hung about and enshrouded the mansion.

"You must not—you shall not behold this!" said I, shudderingly, to Usher, as I led him, with a gentle violence, from the window to a seat. "These appearances, which bewilder you, are merely electrical phenomena not uncommon—or it may be that they have their ghastly origin in the rank miasma of the tarn. Let us close this casement;—the air is chilling and dangerous to your frame. Here is one of your favourite romances. I will read, and you shall listen;—and so we will pass away this terrible night together."

The antique volume which I had taken up was the "Mad Trist" of Sir Launcelot Canning; but I had called it a favourite of Usher's more in sad jest than in earnest; for, in truth, there is little in its uncouth and unimaginative prolixity which could have had interest for the lofty and spiritual ideality of my friend. It was, however, the only book immediately at hand; and I indulged a vague hope that the excitement which now agitated the hypochondriac, might find relief (for the history of mental disorder is full of similar anomalies) even in the extremeness of the folly which I should read. Could I have judged, indeed, by the wild overstrained air of vivacity with which he hearkened, or apparently hearkened, to the words of the tale, I might well have congratulated myself upon the success of my design.

I had arrived at that well-known portion of the story where Ethelred, the hero of the Trist, having sought in vain for peaceable admission into the dwelling of the hermit, proceeds to make good an entrance by force. Here, it will be remembered, the words of the narrative run thus:

"And Ethelred, who was by nature of a doughty heart, and who was now mighty withal, on account of the powerfulness of the wine which he had drunken, waited no longer to hold parley with the hermit, who, in sooth, was of an obstinate and maliceful turn, but, feeling the rain upon his shoulders, and fearing the rising of the tempest, uplifted his mace outright, and, with blows, made quickly room in the plankings of the door for his gauntleted hand; and now pulling therewith sturdily, he so cracked, and ripped, and tore all asunder, that the noise of the dry and hollow-sounding wood alarumed and reverberated throughout the forest."

At the termination of this sentence I started, and for a moment, paused; for it appeared to me (although I at once concluded that my excited fancy had deceived me)—it appeared to me that, from some very remote portion of the mansion, there came, indistinctly, to my ears, what might have been, in its exact similarity of character, the echo (but a stifled and dull one certainly) of the very cracking and ripping sound which Sir Launcelot had so particularly described. It was, beyond doubt, the coincidence alone which had arrested my attention; for, amid the rattling of the sashes of the casements, and the ordinary commingled noises of the still increasing storm, the sound, in itself, had nothing, surely, which should have interested or disturbed me. I continued the story:

"But the good champion Ethelred, now entering within the door, was sore enraged and amazed to perceive no signal of the maliceful hermit; but, in the stead thereof, a dragon of a scaly and prodigious demeanour, and of a fiery tongue, which sate in guard before a palace of gold, with a floor of silver; and upon the wall there hung a shield of shining brass with this legend enwritten—

Who entereth herein, a conqueror hath bin;
Who slayeth the dragon, the shield he shall win;

And Ethelred uplifted his mace, and struck upon the head of the dragon, which fell before him, and gave up his pesty breath, with a shriek so horrid and harsh, and withal so piercing, that Ethelred had fain to close his ears with his hands against the dreadful noise of it, the like whereof was never before heard."

Here again I paused abruptly, and now with a feeling of wild amazement—for there could be no doubt whatever that, in this instance, I did actually hear (although from what direction it proceeded I found it impossible to say) a low and apparently distant, but harsh, protracted, and most unusual screaming or grating sound—the exact counterpart of what my fancy had already conjured up for the dragon's unnatural shriek as described by the romancer.

Oppressed, as I certainly was, upon the occurrence of the second and most extraordinary coincidence, by a thousand conflicting sensations, in which wonder and extreme terror were predominant, I still retained sufficient presence of mind to avoid exciting, by any observation, the sensitive nervousness of my companion. I was by no means certain that he had noticed the sounds in question; although, assuredly, a strange alteration had, during the last few minutes, taken place in his demeanour. From a position fronting my own, he had gradually brought round his chair, so as to sit with his face to the door of the chamber; and thus I could but partially perceive his features, although I saw that his lips trembled as if he were murmuring inaudibly. His head had dropped upon his breast—yet I knew that he was not asleep, from the wide and rigid opening of the eye as I caught a glance of it in profile. The motion of his body, too, was at variance with this idea—for he rocked from side to side with a gentle yet constant and uniform sway. Having rapidly taken notice of all this, I resumed the narrative of Sir Launcelot, which thus proceeded:

"And now, the champion, having escaped from the terrible fury of the dragon, bethinking himself of the brazen shield, and of the breaking up of the enchantment which was upon it, removed the carcass from out of the way before him, and approached valorously over the silver pavement of the castle to where the shield was upon the wall; which in sooth tarried not for his full coming, but fell down at his feet upon the silver floor, with a mighty great and terrible ringing sound."

No sooner had these syllables passed my lips, than—as if a shield of brass had indeed, at the moment, fallen heavily upon a floor of silver—I became aware of a distinct, hollow, metallic, and clangorous, yet apparently muffled reverberation. Completely unnerved, I leaped to my feet; but the measured rocking movement of Usher was undisturbed. I rushed to the chair in which he sat. His eyes were bent fixedly before him, and throughout his whole countenance there reigned a stony rigidity. But, as I placed my hand upon his shoulder, there came a strong shudder over his whole person; a sickly smile quivered about his lips; and I saw that he spoke in a low, hurried, and gibbering murmur, as if unconscious of my presence. Bending closely over him, I at length drank in the hideous import of his words.

"Not hear it?—yes, I hear it, and *have* heard it. Long—long—long—many minutes, many hours, many days, have I heard it—yet I dared not—oh, pity me, miserable wretch that I am!—I dared not—I *dared* not speak! *We have put her living in the tomb!* Said I not that my senses were acute? I *now* tell you that I heard her first feeble movements in the hollow coffin. I heard them—many, many days ago—yet I dared not—*I dared not speak!* And now—to-night—Ethelred—ha! ha!—the breaking of the hermit's door, and the death-cry of the dragon, and the clangour of the shield!—say, rather, the rending of her coffin, and the grating of the iron hinges of her prison, and her struggles within the coppered archway of the vault! Oh whither shall I fly? Will she not be here anon? Is she not hurrying to upbraid me for my haste? Have I not heard her footstep on the stair? Do I not distinguish that heavy and horrible beating of her heart? MADMAN!" here he sprang furiously to his feet, and shrieked out his syllables, as if in the effort he were giving up his soul—"MADMAN! I TELL YOU THAT SHE NOW STANDS WITHOUT THE DOOR!"

As if in the superhuman energy of his utterance there had been found the potency of a spell—the huge antique panels to which the speaker pointed, threw slowly back, upon the instant, their ponderous and ebony jaws. It was the work of the rushing gust—but then without those doors there did stand the lofty and enshrouded figure of the lady Madeline of Usher. There was blood upon her white robes, and the evidence of some bitter struggle upon every portion of her emaciated frame. For a moment she remained trembling and reeling to and fro upon the threshold, then, with a low moaning cry, fell heavily inward upon the person of her brother, and in her violent and now final death-agonies, bore him to the floor a corpse, and a victim to the terrors he had anticipated.

From that chamber, and from that mansion, I fled aghast. The storm was still abroad in all its wrath as I found myself crossing the old causeway. Suddenly there shot along the path a wild light, and I turned to see whence a gleam so unusual could have issued; for the vast house and its shadows were alone behind me. The radiance was that of the full, setting, and blood-red moon which now shone vividly through that once barely-discernible fissure of which I have before spoken as extending from the roof of the building, in a zigzag direction, to the base. While I gazed, this fissure rapidly widened—there came a fierce breath of the whirlwind—the entire orb of the satellite burst at once upon my sight—my brain reeled as I saw the mighty walls rushing asunder—there was a long tumultuous shouting sound like the voice of a thousand waters—and the deep and dank tarn at my feet closed sullenly and silently over the fragments of the "House of Usher."

FITZ-JAMES O'BRIEN

Fitz-James O'Brien was born in County Cork, Ireland, in 1828. He had already published many stories and poems in British and Irish periodicals before emigrating to the United States in 1852. Settling in New York City, he wrote prolifically in a number of genres, including poems, plays, stories, and sketches. At the outbreak of the Civil War, O'Brien enlisted in the Seventh New York Regiment and was decorated for bravery. He died of an infection in 1862.

O'Brien's short fiction is pervaded by a fascination with the supernatural and the bizarre. Aside from "What Was It?," O'Brien wrote such celebrated tales as "The Diamond Lens" (1858), in which a scientist discovers an entire world of living creatures in a drop of water and falls in love with a microscopic female figure he sees there; "The Lost Room" (1858), about spirits of the past invading a room and making it disappear; and "The Wondersmith" (1859), a story about animated dolls probably influenced by E. T. A. Hoffmann. O'Brien's work was posthumously collected by William Winter in *The Poems and Stories of Fitz-James O'Brien* (1881) and, later, by his descendant, the critic and editor Edward J. O'Brien, in *Collected Stories of Fitz-James O'Brien* (1925). Jessica Amanda Salmonson has prepared a definitive two-volume edition, *The Supernatural Tales of Fitz-James O'Brien* (1988). Some of O'Brien's newspaper work has been collected in *Selected Literary Journalism, 1852–1860,* edited by Wayne R. Kine (2003).

"What Was It?" (first published in *Harper's* in March 1859) remains O'Brien's best-known story and is a prototypical account of an invisible monster; it very likely influenced several later stories on the same subject, including Guy de Maupassant's "The Horla" (1886), Ambrose Bierce's "The Damned Thing" (1893), Algernon Blackwood's "The Wendigo" (1907), and H. P. Lovecraft's "The Dunwich Horror" (1928).

WHAT WAS IT?

It is, I confess, with considerable diffidence that I approach the strange narrative which I am about to relate. The events which I purpose detailing are of so extraordinary a character that I am quite prepared to meet with an unusual amount of incredulity and scorn. I accept all such beforehand. I have, I trust, the literary courage to face unbelief. I have, after mature consideration, resolved to narrate, in as simple and straightforward a manner as I can compass, some facts that passed under my observation, in the month of July last, and which, in the annals of the mysteries of physical science, are wholly unparalleled.

I live at No. — Twenty-sixth Street, in New York. The house is in some respects a curious one. It has enjoyed for the last two years the reputation of being haunted. It is a large and stately residence, surrounded by what was once a garden, but which is now only a green enclosure used for bleaching clothes. The dry basin of what has been a fountain, and a few fruit-trees ragged and unpruned, indicate that this spot in past days was a pleasant, shady retreat, filled with fruits and flowers and the sweet murmur of waters.

The house is very spacious. A hall of noble size leads to a large spiral staircase winding through its centre, while the various apartments are of imposing dimensions. It was built some fifteen or twenty years since by Mr. A——, the well-known New York merchant, who five years ago threw the commercial world into convulsions by a stupendous bank fraud. Mr. A——, as every one knows, escaped to Europe, and died not long after, of a broken heart. Almost immediately after the news of his decease reached this country and was verified, the report spread in Twenty-sixth Street that No. — was haunted. Legal measures had dispossessed the widow of its former owner, and it was inhabited merely by a care-taker and his wife, placed there by the house-agent in whose hands it had passed for purposes of renting or sale. These people declared that they were troubled with unnatural noises. Doors were opened without any visible agency. The remnants of furniture scattered through the various rooms were, during the night, piled one upon the other by unknown hands. Invisible feet passed up and down the stairs in broad daylight, accompanied by the rustle of unseen silk dresses, and the gliding of viewless hands along the massive balusters. The care-taker and his wife declared they would live there no longer. The house-agent laughed, dismissed them, and put others in their place. The noises and supernatural manifestations continued. The neighborhood caught up the story, and the house remained untenanted for three years. Several persons negotiated for it; but, somehow, always before the bargain was closed they heard the unpleasant rumors and declined to treat any further.

It was in this state of things that my landlady, who at that time kept a boarding-house in Bleecker Street, and who wished to move further up town, conceived the bold idea of renting No. — Twenty-sixth Street. Happening to have in her house rather a plucky and philosophical set of boarders, she laid her scheme before us, stating candidly everything she had heard respecting the ghostly qualities of the establishment to which she wished to remove us. With the exception of two timid persons,—a sea-captain and a returned Californian, who immediately gave notice that they would leave,—all of Mrs. Moffat's guests declared that they would accompany her in her chivalric incursion into the abode of spirits.

Our removal was effected in the month of May, and we were charmed with our new residence. The portion of Twenty-sixth Street where our house is situated, between Seventh and Eighth Avenues, is one of the pleasantest localities in New York. The gardens back of the houses, running down nearly to the Hudson, form, in the summer time, a perfect avenue of verdure. The air is pure and invigorating, sweeping, as it does, straight across the river from the Weehawken heights, and even the ragged garden which surrounded the house, although displaying on washing days rather too much clothesline, still gave us a piece of greensward to look at, and a cool retreat in the summer evenings, where we smoked our cigars in the dusk, and watched the fireflies flashing their dark-lanterns in the long grass.

Of course we had no sooner established ourselves at No. — than we began to expect the ghosts. We absolutely awaited their advent with eagerness. Our dinner conversation was supernatural. One of the boarders, who had purchased Mrs. Crowe's "Night Side of Nature" for his own private delectation, was regarded as a public enemy by the entire household for not having bought twenty copies. The man led a life of supreme wretchedness while he was reading this volume. A system of espionage was established, of which he was the victim. If he incautiously laid the book down for an instant and left the room, it was immediately seized and read aloud in secret places to a select few. I found myself a person of immense importance, it having leaked out that I was tolerably well versed in the history of supernaturalism, and had once written a story the foundation of which was a ghost. If a table or a wainscot panel happened to warp when we were assembled in the large drawing-room, there was an instant silence, and every one was prepared for an immediate clanking of chains and a spectral form.

After a month of psychological excitement, it was with the utmost dissatisfaction that we were forced to acknowledge that nothing in the remotest degree approaching the supernatural had manifested itself. Once the black butler asseverated that his candle had been blown out by some invisible agency while he was undressing himself for the night; but as I had more than once discovered this colored gentleman in a condition when one candle must have appeared to him like two, I thought it possible that, by going a step further in his potations, he might have reversed this phenomenon, and seen no candle at all where he ought to have beheld one.

Things were in this state when an incident took place so awful and inexplicable in its character that my reason fairly reels at the bare memory of the occurrence. It was the tenth of July. After dinner was over I repaired, with my friend Dr. Hammond, to the garden to smoke my evening pipe. Independent of certain mental sympathies which existed between the Doctor and myself, we were linked together by a vice. We both smoked opium. We knew each other's secret, and respected it. We enjoyed together that wonderful expansion of thought, that marvellous intensifying of the perceptive faculties, that boundless feeling of existence when we seem to have points of contact with the whole universe,—in short, that unimaginable spiritual bliss, which I would not surrender for a throne, and which I hope you, reader, will never—never taste.

Those hours of opium happiness which the Doctor and I spent together in secret were regulated with a scientific accuracy. We did not blindly smoke the drug of paradise, and leave our dreams to chance. While smoking, we carefully steered our conversation through the brightest and calmest channels of thought. We talked of the East, and endeavored to recall the magical panorama of its glowing scenery. We criticised the most sensuous poets,—those who painted life ruddy with health, brimming with passion, happy in the possession of youth and strength. If we talked of Shakespeare's "Tempest," we lingered over Ariel, and avoided Caliban. Like the Guebers, we turned our faces to the east, and saw only the sunny side of the world.

This skilful coloring of our train of thought produced in our subsequent visions a corresponding tone. The splendor of Arabian fairy-land dyed our dreams. We paced that narrow strip of grass with the tread and port of kings. The song of the *rana arborea,* while he clung to the bark of the ragged plum-tree, sounded like the strains of divine musicians. Houses, walls, and streets melted like rain-clouds, and vistas of unimaginable glory stretched away before us. It was a rapturous companionship. We enjoyed the vast delight more perfectly because, even in our most ecstatic moments, we were conscious of each other's presence. Our pleasures, while individual, were still twin, vibrating and moving in musical accord.

On the evening in question, the tenth of July, the Doctor and myself drifted into an unusually metaphysical mood. We lit our large meerschaums, filled with fine Turkish tobacco, in the core of which burned a little black nut of opium, that, like the nut in the fairy tale, held within its narrow limits wonders beyond the reach of kings; we paced to and fro, conversing. A strange perversity dominated the currents of our thought. They would *not* flow through the sun-lit channels into which we strove to divert them. For some unaccountable reason, they constantly diverged into dark and lonesome beds, where a continual gloom brooded. It was in vain that, after our old fashion, we flung ourselves on the shores of the East, and talked of its gay bazaars, of the splendors of the time of Haroun, of harems and golden palaces. Black afreets continually arose from the depths of our talk, and expanded, like the one the fisherman released from the copper vessel, until they blotted everything bright from our vision. Insensibly, we yielded to the occult force that swayed us, and indulged in gloomy speculation. We had talked some time upon the proneness of the human mind to mysticism, and the almost universal love of the terrible, when Hammond suddenly said to me, "What do you consider to be the greatest element of terror?"

The question puzzled me. That many things were terrible, I knew. Stumbling over a corpse in the dark; beholding, as I once did, a woman floating down a deep and rapid river, with wildly lifted arms, and awful, upturned face, uttering, as she drifted, shrieks that rent one's heart, while we, the spectators, stood frozen at a window which overhung the river at a height of sixty feet, unable to make the slightest effort to save her, but dumbly watching her last supreme agony and her disappearance. A shattered wreck, with no life visible, encountered floating listlessly on the ocean, is a terrible object, for it suggests a huge terror, the proportions of which are veiled. But it now struck me, for the first time, that there must be one great and ruling embodiment of fear,—a King of Terrors, to which all others must succumb. What might it be? To what train of circumstances would it owe its existence?

"I confess, Hammond," I replied to my friend, "I never

considered the subject before. That there must be one Something more terrible than any other thing, I feel. I cannot attempt, however, even the most vague definition."

"I am somewhat like you, Harry," he answered. "I feel my capacity to experience a terror greater than anything yet conceived by the human mind;—something combining in fearful and unnatural amalgamation hitherto supposed incompatible elements. The calling of the voices in Brockden Brown's novel of 'Wieland' is awful; so is the picture of the Dweller of the Threshold, in Bulwer's 'Zanoni'; but," he added, shaking his head gloomily, "there is something more terrible still than these."

"Look here, Hammond," I rejoined, "let us drop this kind of talk, for heaven's sake! We shall suffer for it, depend on it."

"I don't know what's the matter with me to-night," he replied, "but my brain is running upon all sorts of weird and awful thoughts. I feel as if I could write a story like Hoffmann, to-night, if I were only master of a literary style."

"Well, if we are going to be Hoffmannesque in our talk, I'm off to bed. Opium and nightmares should never be brought together. How sultry it is! Good-night, Hammond."

"Good-night, Harry. Pleasant dreams to you."

"To you, gloomy wretch, afreets, ghouls, and enchanters."

We parted, and each sought his respective chamber. I undressed quickly and got into bed, taking with me, according to my usual custom, a book, over which I generally read myself to sleep. I opened the volume as soon as I had laid my head upon the pillow, and instantly flung it to the other side of the room. It was Goudon's "History of Monsters,"—a curious French work, which I had lately imported from Paris, but which, in the state of mind I had then reached, was anything but an agreeable companion. I resolved to go to sleep at once; so, turning down my gas until nothing but a little blue point of light glimmered on the top of the tube, I composed myself to rest.

The room was in total darkness. The atom of gas that still remained alight did not illuminate a distance of three inches round the burner. I desperately drew my arms across my eyes, as if to shut out the darkness, and tried to think of nothing. It was in vain. The confounded themes touched on by Hammond in the garden kept obtruding themselves on my brain. I battled against them. I erected ramparts of would-be blankness of intellect to keep them out. They still crowded upon me. While I was lying still as a corpse, hoping that by a perfect physical inaction I should hasten mental repose, an awful incident occurred. A Something dropped, as it seemed, from the ceiling, plum upon my chest, and the next instant I felt two bony hands encircling my throat, endeavoring to choke me.

I am no coward, and am possessed of considerable physical strength. The suddenness of the attack, instead of stunning me, strung every nerve to its highest tension. My body acted from instinct, before my brain had time to realize the terrors of my position. In an instant I wound two muscular arms around the creature, and squeezed it, with all the strength of despair, against my chest. In a few seconds the bony hands that had fastened on my throat loosened their hold, and I was free to breathe once more. Then commenced a struggle of awful intensity. Immersed in the most profound darkness, totally ignorant of the nature of the Thing by which I was so suddenly attacked, finding my grasp slipping every moment, by reason, it seemed to me, of the entire nakedness of my assailant, bitten with sharp teeth in the shoulder, neck, and chest, having every moment to protect my throat against a pair of sinewy, agile hands, which my utmost efforts could not confine,—these were a combination of circumstances to combat which required all the strength, skill and courage that I possessed.

At last, after a silent, deadly, exhausting struggle, I got my assailant under by a series of incredible efforts of strength. Once pinned, with my knee on what I made out to be its chest, I knew that I was victor. I rested for a moment to breathe. I heard the creature beneath me panting in the darkness, and felt the violent throbbing of a heart. It was apparently as exhausted as I was; that was one comfort. At this moment I remembered that I usually placed under my pillow, before going to bed, a large yellow silk pocket-handkerchief. I felt for it instantly; it was there. In a few seconds more I had, after a fashion, pinioned the creature's arms.

I now felt tolerably secure. There was nothing more to be

done but to turn on the gas, and, having first seen what my midnight assailant was like, arouse the household. I will confess to being actuated by a certain pride in not giving the alarm before; I wished to make the capture alone and unaided.

Never losing my hold for an instant, I slipped from the bed to the floor, dragging my captive with me. I had but a few steps to make to reach the gas-burner; these I made with the greatest caution, holding the creature in a grip like a vise. At last I got within arm's-length of the tiny speck of blue light which told me where the gas-burner lay. Quick as lightning I released my grasp with one hand and let on the full flood of light. Then I turned to look at my captive.

I cannot even attempt to give any definition of my sensations the instant after I turned on the gas. I suppose I must have shrieked with terror, for in less than a minute afterward my room was crowded with the inmates of the house. I shudder now as I think of that awful moment. *I saw nothing!* Yes; I had one arm firmly clasped round a breathing, panting, corporeal shape, my other hand gripped with all its strength a throat as warm, and apparently fleshy, as my own; and yet, with this living substance in my grasp, with its body pressed against my own, and all in the bright glare of a large jet of gas, I absolutely beheld nothing! Not even in an outline—a vapor!

I do not, even at this hour, realize the situation in which I found myself. Imagination in vain tries to compass the awful paradox.

It breathed. I felt its warm breath upon my cheek. It struggled fiercely. It had hands. They clutched me. Its skin was smooth, like my own. There it lay, pressed close up against me, solid as stone,—and yet utterly invisible!

I wonder that I did not faint or go mad on the instant. Some wonderful instinct must have sustained me; for, absolutely, in place of loosening my hold on the terrible Enigma, I seemed to gain an additional strength in my moment of horror, and tightened my grasp with such wonderful force that I felt the creature shivering with agony.

Just then Hammond entered the room at the head of the

household. As soon as he beheld my face—which, I suppose, must have been an awful sight to look at—he hastened forward, crying, "Great heaven, Harry! what has happened?"

"Hammond! Hammond!" I cried, "come here. O, this is awful! I have been attacked in bed by something or other, which I have hold of; but I can't see it—I can't see it!"

Hammond, doubtless struck by the unfeigned horror expressed in my countenance, made one or two steps forward with an anxious yet puzzled expression. A very audible titter burst from the remainder of my visitors. This suppressed laughter made me furious. To laugh at a human being in my position! It was the worst species of cruelty. *Now,* I can understand why the appearance of a man struggling violently, as it would seem, with an airy nothing, and calling for assistance against a vision, should have appeared ludicrous. *Then,* so great was my rage against the mocking crowd that had I the power I would have stricken them dead where they stood.

"Hammond! Hammond!" I cried again, despairingly, "for God's sake come to me. I can hold the—the thing but a short while longer. It is overpowering me. Help me! Help me!"

"Harry," whispered Hammond, approaching me, "you have been smoking too much opium."

"I swear to you, Hammond, that this is no vision," I answered, in the same low tone. "Don't you see how it shakes my whole frame with its struggles? If you don't believe me, convince yourself. Feel it,—touch it."

Hammond advanced and laid his hand in the spot I indicated. A wild cry of horror burst from him. He had felt it!

In a moment he had discovered somewhere in my room a long piece of cord, and was the next instant winding it and knotting it about the body of the unseen being that I clasped in my arms.

"Harry," he said, in a hoarse, agitated voice, for, though he preserved his presence of mind, he was deeply moved, "Harry, it's all safe now. You may let go, old fellow, if you're tired. The Thing can't move."

I was utterly exhausted, and I gladly loosed my hold.

Hammond stood holding the ends of the cord that bound the Invisible, twisted round his hand, while before him, self-supporting as it were, he beheld a rope laced and interlaced, and stretching tightly around a vacant space. I never saw a man look so thoroughly stricken with awe. Nevertheless his face expressed all the courage and determination which I knew him to possess. His lips, although white, were set firmly, and one could perceive at a glance that, although stricken with fear, he was not daunted.

The confusion that ensued among the guests of the house who were witnesses of this extraordinary scene between Hammond and myself,—who beheld the pantomime of binding this struggling Something,—who beheld me almost sinking from physical exhaustion when my task of jailer was over,—the confusion and terror that took possession of the bystanders, when they saw all this, was beyond description. The weaker ones fled from the apartment. The few who remained clustered near the door and could not be induced to approach Hammond and his Charge. Still incredulity broke out through their terror. They had not the courage to satisfy themselves, and yet they doubted. It was in vain that I begged of some of the men to come near and convince themselves by touch of the existence in that room of a living being which was invisible. They were incredulous, but did not dare to undeceive themselves. How could a solid, living, breathing body be invisible, they asked. My reply was this. I gave a sign to Hammond, and both of us—conquering our fearful repugnance to touch the invisible creature—lifted it from the ground, manacled as it was, and took it to my bed. Its weight was about that of a boy of fourteen.

"Now, my friends," I said, as Hammond and myself held the creature suspended over the bed, "I can give you self-evident proof that here is a solid, ponderable body, which, nevertheless, you cannot see. Be good enough to watch the surface of the bed attentively."

I was astonished at my own courage in treating this strange event so calmly; but I had recovered from my first terror, and felt a sort of scientific pride in the affair, which dominated every other feeling.

The eyes of the bystanders were immediately fixed on my bed. At a given signal Hammond and I let the creature fall. There was the dull sound of a heavy body alighting on a soft mass. The timbers of the bed creaked. A deep impression marked itself distinctly on the pillow, and on the bed itself. The crowd who witnessed this gave a low cry, and rushed from the room. Hammond and I were left alone with our Mystery.

We remained silent for some time, listening to the low, irregular breathing of the creature on the bed, and watching the rustle of the bed-clothes as it impotently struggled to free itself from confinement. Then Hammond spoke.

"Harry, this is awful."

"Ay, awful."

"But not unaccountable."

"Not unaccountable! What do you mean? Such a thing has never occurred since the birth of the world. I know not what to think, Hammond. God grant that I am not mad, and that this is not an insane fantasy!"

"Let us reason a little, Harry. Here is a solid body which we touch, but which we cannot see. The fact is so unusual that it strikes us with terror. Is there no parallel, though, for such a phenomenon? Take a piece of pure glass. It is tangible and transparent. A certain chemical coarseness is all that prevents its being so entirely transparent as to be totally invisible. It is not *theoretically impossible*, mind you, to make a glass which shall not reflect a single ray of light,—a glass so pure and homogeneous in its atoms that the rays from the sun will pass through it as they do through the air, refracted but not reflected. We do not see the air, and yet we feel it."

"That's all very well, Hammond, but these are inanimate substances. Glass does not breathe, air does not breathe. This *thing* has a heart that palpitates,—a will that moves it,—lungs that play, and inspire and respire."

"You forget the phenomena of which we have so often heard of late," answered the Doctor, gravely. "At the meetings called 'spirit circles,' invisible hands have been thrust into the hands of those persons round the table,—warm, fleshy hands that seemed to pulsate with mortal life."

"What? Do you think, then, that this thing is—"

"I don't know what it is," was the solemn reply; "but please the gods I will, with your assistance, thoroughly investigate it."

We watched together, smoking many pipes, all night long, by the bedside of the unearthly being that tossed and panted until it was apparently wearied out. Then we learned by the low, regular breathing that it slept.

The next morning the house was all astir. The boarders congregated on the landing outside my room, and Hammond and myself were lions. We had to answer a thousand questions as to the state of our extraordinary prisoner, for as yet not one person in the house except ourselves could be induced to set foot in the apartment.

The creature was awake. This was evidenced by the convulsive manner in which the bed-clothes were moved in its efforts to escape. There was something truly terrible in beholding, as it were, those secondhand indications of the terrible writhings and agonized struggles for liberty which themselves were invisible.

Hammond and myself had racked our brains during the long night to discover some means by which we might realize the shape and general appearance of the Enigma. As well as we could make out by passing our hands over the creature's form, its outlines and lineaments were human. There was a mouth; a round, smooth head without hair; a nose, which, however, was little elevated above the cheeks; and its hands and feet felt like those of a boy. At first we thought of placing the being on a smooth surface and tracing its outline with chalk, as shoemakers trace the outline of the foot. This plan was given up as being of no value. Such an outline would give not the slightest idea of its conformation.

A happy thought struck me. We could take a cast of it in plaster of Paris. This would give us the solid figure, and satisfy all our wishes. But how to do it? The movements of the creature would disturb the setting of the plastic covering, and distort the mould. Another thought. Why not give it chloroform? It had respiratory organs,—that was evident by its breathing. Once reduced to a state of insensibility, we could do with it what we would. Doctor X—— was sent for; and after the worthy physician had recovered from the first shock of amazement, he proceeded to administer the chloroform. In three minutes afterward we were enabled to remove the fetters from the creature's body, and a modeller was busily engaged in covering the invisible form with the moist clay. In five minutes more we had a mould, and before evening a rough fac-simile of the Mystery. It was shaped like a man,—distorted, uncouth, and horrible, but still a man. It was small, not over four feet and some inches in height, and its limbs revealed a muscular development that was unparalleled. Its face surpassed in hideousness anything I had ever seen. Gustave Doré, or Callot, or Tony Johannot, never conceived anything so horrible. There is a face in one of the latter's illustrations to *Un Voyage où il vous plaira,* which somewhat approaches the countenance of this creature, but does not equal it. It was the physiognomy of what I should fancy a ghoul might be. It looked as if it was capable of feeding on human flesh.

Having satisfied our curiosity, and bound every one in the house to secrecy, it became a question what was to be done with our Enigma? It was impossible that we should keep such a horror in our house; it was equally impossible that such an awful being should be let loose upon the world. I confess that I would have gladly voted for the creature's destruction. But who would shoulder the responsibility? Who would undertake the execution of this horrible semblance of a human being? Day after day this question was deliberated gravely. The boarders all left the house. Mrs. Moffat was in despair, and threatened Hammond and myself with all sorts of legal penalties if we did not remove the Horror. Our answer was, "We will go if you like, but we decline taking this creature with us. Remove it yourself if you please. It appeared in your house. On you the responsibility rests." To this there was, of course, no answer. Mrs. Moffat could not obtain for love or money a person who would even approach the Mystery.

The most singular part of the affair was that we were entirely ignorant of what the creature habitually fed on. Everything in the way of nutriment that we could think of was placed before it, but was never touched. It was awful to stand by, day after day, and see the clothes toss, and hear the hard breathing, and know that it was starving.

Ten, twelve days, a fortnight passed, and it still lived. The pulsations of the heart, however, were daily growing fainter, and had now nearly ceased. It was evident that the creature was dying for want of sustenance. While this terrible life-struggle was going on, I felt miserable. I could not sleep. Horrible as the creature was, it was pitiful to think of the pangs it was suffering.

At last it died. Hammond and I found it cold and stiff one morning in the bed. The heart had ceased to beat, the lungs to inspire. We hastened to bury it in the garden. It was a strange funeral, the dropping of that viewless corpse into the damp hole. The cast of its form I gave to Doctor X——, who keeps it in his museum in Tenth Street.

As I am on the eve of a long journey from which I may not return, I have drawn up this narrative of an event the most singular that has ever come to my knowledge.

AMBROSE BIERCE

Ambrose Gwinnett Bierce was born in Meigs County, Ohio, in 1842. His family later moved to Indiana. At the outbreak of the Civil War in 1861, Bierce immediately volunteered; he served for nearly the entire conflict, suffering a serious head wound in 1864. After the war, Bierce went to San Francisco, where he eventually became a journalist, serving as a columnist for the *San Francisco News Letter* (1867–72). After a stay in England (1872–75), where he wrote prolifically for British magazines, he returned to San Francisco, writing for the *Argonaut* (1877–79), the *Wasp* (1881–86), and, most famously, for the young William Randolph Hearst's *San Francisco Examiner* (1887–1906). Bierce became one of the most feared journalists of his day, his biting, satirical columns skewering many contemporary notable figures.

Bierce's writing of short stories was sporadic, but his tales of the Civil War were gathered in *Tales of Soldiers and Civilians* (1891; revised as *In the Midst of Life,* 1898), while his supernatural tales were collected in *Can Such Things Be?* (1893). Such tales as "Chickamauga" (1889) and "An Occurrence at Owl Creek Bridge" (1890) are classics of Civil War literature, while "The Middle Toe of the Right Foot" (1890) and "The Moonlit Road" (1907) give Bierce an unassailable rank in supernatural fiction. Bierce attained greater celebrity for his *Cynic's Word Book* (1906), revised as *The Devil's Dictionary* (1911). He edited his own *Collected Works* (1909–12) in twelve volumes. Bierce vanished in Mexico in early 1914; he is believed to have died in one of the battles of the Mexican Civil War.

"The Death of Halpin Frayser" (first published in the *Wave*, December 19, 1891), is Bierce's most celebrated horror tale. Although narrated in a highly fragmented manner, it can be pieced together to reveal a hideous series of events: Halpin Frayser, moving to California, had married his mother, Catherine, living under the name Larue. Frayser later kills her, but, overwrought by his actions, loses his memory of these events. Catherine's reanimated corpse then exacts revenge upon him by killing him over her own grave in a California cemetery.

THE DEATH OF HALPIN FRAYSER

I

For by death is wrought greater change than hath been shown. Whereas in general the spirit that removed cometh back upon occasion, and is sometimes seen of those in flesh (appearing in the form of the body it bore) yet it hath happened that the veritable body without the spirit hath walked. And it is attested of those encountering who have lived to speak thereon that a lich so raised up hath no natural affection, nor remembrance thereof, but only hate. Also, it is known that some spirits which in life were benign become by death evil altogether.

—Hali.

One dark night in midsummer a man waking from a dreamless sleep in a forest lifted his head from the earth, and staring a few moments into the blackness, said: "Catherine Larue." He said nothing more; no reason was known to him why he should have said so much.

The man was Halpin Frayser. He lived in St. Helena, but where he lives now is uncertain, for he is dead. One who practices sleeping in the woods with nothing under him but the dry leaves and the damp earth, and nothing over him but the branches from which the leaves have fallen and the sky from which the earth has fallen, cannot hope for great longevity, and Frayser had already attained the age of thirty-two. There are persons in this world, millions of persons, and far and away the best persons, who regard that as a very advanced age. They are the children. To those who view the voyage of life from the port of departure the bark that has accomplished any considerable distance appears already in close approach to the farther shore. However, it is not certain that Halpin Frayser came to his death by exposure.

He had been all day in the hills west of the Napa Valley, looking for doves and such small game as was in season. Late in the afternoon it had come on to be cloudy, and he had lost his bearings; and although he had only to go always downhill— everywhere the way to safety when one is lost—the absence of trails had so impeded him that he was overtaken by night while still in the forest. Unable in the darkness to penetrate the thickets of manzanita and other undergrowth, utterly bewildered and overcome with fatigue, he had lain down near the root of a large madroño and fallen into a dreamless sleep. It was hours later, in the very middle of the night, that one of God's mysterious messengers, gliding ahead of the incalculable host of his companions sweeping westward with the dawn line, pronounced the awakening word in the ear of the sleeper, who sat upright and spoke, he knew not why, a name, he knew not whose.

Halpin Frayser was not much of a philosopher, nor a scientist. The circumstance that, waking from a deep sleep at night in the midst of a forest, he had spoken aloud a name that he had not in memory and hardly had in mind did not arouse an enlightened curiosity to investigate the phenomenon. He thought it odd, and with a little perfunctory shiver, as if in deference to a seasonal presumption that the night was chill, he lay down again and went to sleep. But his sleep was no longer dreamless.

He thought he was walking along a dusty road that showed white in the gathering darkness of a summer night. Whence and whither it led, and why he traveled it, he did not know, though all seemed simple and natural, as is the way in dreams; for in the Land Beyond the Bed surprises cease from troubling and the judgment is at rest. Soon he came to a parting of the ways; leading from the highway was a road less traveled, having the appearance, indeed, of having been long abandoned, because, he thought, it led to something evil; yet he turned into it without hesitation, impelled by some imperious necessity.

As he pressed forward he became conscious that his way was haunted by invisible existences whom he could not definitely figure to his mind. From among the trees on either side he caught broken and incoherent whispers in a strange tongue which yet he partly understood. They seemed to him fragmentary utterances of a monstrous conspiracy against his body and soul.

It was now long after nightfall, yet the interminable forest through which he journeyed was lit with a wan glimmer having no point of diffusion, for in its mysterious lumination nothing cast a shadow. A shallow pool in the guttered depression of an old wheel rut, as from a recent rain, met his eye with a crimson gleam. He stooped and plunged his hand into it. It stained his fingers; it was blood! Blood, he then observed, was about him everywhere. The weeds growing rankly by the roadside showed it in blots and splashes on their big, broad leaves. Patches of dry dust between the wheelways were pitted and spattered as with a red rain. Defiling the trunks of the trees were broad maculations of crimson, and blood dripped like dew from their foliage.

All this he observed with a terror which seemed not incompatible with the fulfillment of a natural expectation. It seemed to him that it was all in expiation of some crime which, though conscious of his guilt, he could not rightly remember. To the menaces and mysteries of his surroundings the consciousness was an added horror. Vainly he sought by tracing life backward in memory, to reproduce the moment of his sin; scenes and incidents came crowding tumultuously into his mind, one picture effacing another, or commingling with it in confusion and obscurity, but nowhere could he catch a glimpse of what he sought. The failure augmented his terror; he felt as one who has murdered in the dark, not knowing whom or why. So frightful was the situation—the mysterious light burned with so silent and awful a menace; the noxious plants, the trees that by common consent are invested with a melancholy or baleful character, so openly in his sight conspired against his peace; from overhead and all about came so audible and startling whispers and the sighs of creatures so obviously not of earth—that he could endure it no longer, and with a great effort to break some malign spell that bound his faculties to silence and inaction, he shouted with the full strength of his lungs! His voice broken, it seemed, into an infinite multitude of unfamiliar sounds, went babbling and stammering away into the distant reaches of the forest, died into silence, and all was as before. But he had made a beginning at resistance and was encouraged. He said:

"I will not submit unheard. There may be powers that are not malignant traveling this accursed road. I shall leave them a record and an appeal. I shall relate my wrongs, the persecutions that I endure—I, a helpless mortal, a penitent, an unoffending poet!" Halpin Frayser was a poet only as he was a penitent: in his dream.

Taking from his clothing a small red-leather pocketbook, one-half of which was leaved for memoranda, he discovered that he was without a pencil. He broke a twig from a bush, dipped it into a pool of blood and wrote rapidly. He had hardly touched the paper with the point of his twig when a low, wild peal of laughter broke out at a measureless distance away, and growing ever louder, seemed approaching ever nearer; a soulless, heartless, and unjoyous laugh, like that of the loon, solitary by the lakeside at midnight; a laugh which culminated in an unearthly shout close at hand, then died away by slow gradations, as if the accursed being that uttered it had withdrawn over the verge of the world whence it had come. But the man felt that this was not so—that it was near by and had not moved.

A strange sensation began slowly to take possession of his body and his mind. He could not have said which, if any, of his senses was affected; he felt it rather as a consciousness—a mysterious mental assurance of some overpowering presence—some supernatural malevolence different in kind from the invisible existences that swarmed about him, and superior to them in power. He knew that it had uttered that hideous laugh. And now it seemed to be approaching him; from what direction he did not know—dared not conjecture. All his former fears were forgotten or merged in the gigantic terror that now held him in thrall. Apart from that, he had but one thought: to complete his written appeal to the benign powers who, traversing the haunted wood, might some time rescue him if he should be denied the blessing of annihilation. He wrote with terrible rapidity, the twig in his fingers rilling blood without renewal; but in the middle of a sentence his hands denied their service to his will, his arms fell to his sides, the book to the earth; and powerless to move or cry out, he found himself staring into the sharply drawn face and blank, dead eyes of his own mother, standing white and silent in the garments of the grave!

II

In his youth Halpin Frayser had lived with his parents in Nashville, Tennessee. The Fraysers were well-to-do, having a good position in such society as had survived the wreck wrought by civil war. Their children had the social and educational opportunities of their time and place, and had responded to good associations and instruction with agreeable manners and cultivated minds. Halpin being the youngest and not over robust was perhaps a trifle "spoiled." He had the double disadvantage of a mother's assiduity and a father's neglect. Frayser *père* was what no Southern man of means is not—a politician. His country, or rather his section and State, made demands upon his time and attention so exacting that to those of his family he was compelled to turn an ear partly deafened by the thunder of the political captains and the shouting, his own included.

Young Halpin was of a dreamy, indolent and rather romantic turn, somewhat more addicted to literature than law, the profession to which he was bred. Among those of his relations who professed the modern faith of heredity it was well understood that in him the character of the late Myron Bayne, a maternal great-grandfather, had revisited the glimpses of the moon—by which orb Bayne had in his lifetime been sufficiently affected to be a poet of no small Colonial distinction. If not specially observed, it was observable that while a Frayser who was not the proud possessor of a sumptuous copy of the ancestral "poetical works" (printed at the family expense, and long ago withdrawn from an inhospitable market) was a rare Frayser indeed, there was an illogical indisposition to honor the great deceased in the person of his spiritual successor. Halpin was pretty generally deprecated as an intellectual black sheep who was likely at any moment to disgrace the flock by bleating in meter. The Tennessee Fraysers were a practical folk—not practical in the popular sense of devotion to sordid pursuits, but having a robust contempt for any qualities unfitting a man for the wholesome vocation of politics.

In justice to young Halpin it should be said that while in him were pretty faithfully reproduced most of the mental and moral characteristics ascribed by history and family tradition to the famous Colonial bard, his succession to the gift and faculty divine was purely inferential. Not only had he never been known to court the muse, but in truth he could not have written correctly a line of verse to save himself from the Killer of the Wise. Still, there was no knowing when the dormant faculty might wake and smite the lyre.

In the meantime the young man was rather a loose fish, anyhow. Between him and his mother was the most perfect sympathy, for secretly the lady was herself a devout disciple of the late and great Myron Bayne, though with the tact so generally and justly admired in her sex (despite the hardy calumniators who insist that it is essentially the same thing as cunning) she had always taken care to conceal her weakness from all eyes but those of him who shared it. Their common guilt in respect of that was an added tie between them. If in Halpin's youth his mother had "spoiled" him, he had assuredly done his part toward being spoiled. As he grew to such manhood as is attainable by a Southerner who does not care which way elections go the attachment between him and his beautiful mother—whom from early childhood he had called Katy—became yearly stronger and more tender. In these two romantic natures was manifest in a signal way that neglected phenomenon, the dominance of the sexual element in all the relations of life, strengthening, softening, and beautifying even those of consanguinity. The two were nearly inseparable, and by strangers observing their manner were not infrequently mistaken for lovers.

Entering his mother's boudoir one day Halpin Frayser kissed her upon the forehead, toyed for a moment with a lock of her dark hair which had escaped from its confining pins, and said, with an obvious effort at calmness:

"Would you greatly mind, Katy, if I were called away to California for a few weeks?"

It was hardly needful for Katy to answer with her lips a question to which her telltale cheeks had made instant reply. Evidently she would greatly mind; and the tears, too, sprang into her large brown eyes as corroborative testimony.

"Ah, my son," she said, looking up into his face with infinite tenderness, "I should have known that this was coming. Did I not lie awake a half of the night weeping because, during the other half, Grandfather Bayne had come to me in a dream, and standing by his portrait—young, too, and handsome as that—pointed to yours on the same wall? And when I looked it seemed that I could not see the features; you had been painted with a face cloth, such as we put upon the dead. Your father has laughed at me, but you and I, dear, know that such things are not for nothing. And I saw below the edge of the cloth the marks of hands on your throat—forgive me, but we have not been used to keep such things from each other. Perhaps you have another interpretation. Perhaps it does not mean that you will go to California. Or maybe you will take me with you?"

It must be confessed that this ingenious interpretation of the dream in the light of newly discovered evidence did not wholly commend itself to the son's more logical mind; he had, for the moment at least, a conviction that it foreshadowed a more simple and immediate, if less tragic, disaster than a visit to the Pacific Coast. It was Halpin Frayser's impression that he was to be garroted on his native heath.

"Are there not medicinal springs in California?" Mrs. Frayser resumed before he had time to give her the true reading of the dream—"places where one recovers from rheumatism and neuralgia? Look—my fingers feel so stiff; and I am almost sure they have been giving me great pain while I slept."

She held out her hands for his inspection. What diagnosis of her case the young man may have thought it best to conceal with a smile the historian is unable to state, but for himself he feels bound to say that fingers looking less stiff, and showing fewer evidences of even insensible pain, have seldom been submitted for medical inspection by even the fairest patient desiring a prescription of unfamiliar scenes.

The outcome of it was that of these two odd persons having equally odd notions of duty, the one went to California, as the interest of his client required, and the other remained at home in compliance with a wish that her husband was scarcely conscious of entertaining.

While in San Francisco Halpin Frayser was walking one dark night along the water front of the city, when, with a suddenness that surprised and disconcerted him, he became a sailor. He was in fact "shanghaied" aboard a gallant, gallant ship, and sailed for a far countree. Nor did his misfortunes end with the voyage; for the ship was cast ashore on an island of the South Pacific, and it was six years afterward when the survivors were taken off by a venturesome trading schooner and brought back to San Francisco.

Though poor in purse, Frayser was no less proud in spirit than he had been in the years that seemed ages and ages ago. He would accept no assistance from strangers, and it was while living with a fellow survivor near the town of St. Helena, awaiting news and remittances from home, that he had gone gunning and dreaming.

III

The apparition confronting the dreamer in the haunted wood—the thing so like, yet so unlike his mother—was horrible! It stirred no love nor longing in his heart; it came unattended with pleasant memories of a golden past—inspired no sentiment of any kind; all the finer emotions were swallowed up in fear. He tried to turn and run from before it, but his legs were as lead; he was unable to lift his feet from the ground. His arms hung helpless at his sides; of his eyes only he retained control, and these he dared not remove from the lusterless orbs of the apparition, which he knew was not a soul without a body, but that most dreadful of all existences infesting that haunted wood—a body without a soul! In its blank stare was neither love, nor pity, nor intelligence—nothing to which to address an appeal for mercy. "An appeal will not lie," he thought, with an absurd reversion to professional slang, making the situation more horrible, as the fire of a cigar might light up a tomb.

For a time, which seemed so long that the world grew gray with age and sin, and the haunted forest, having fulfilled its purpose in this monstrous culmination of its terrors, vanished out of his consciousness with all its sights and sounds, the apparition stood within a pace, regarding him with the mindless malevolence of a wild brute; then thrust its hands forward and sprang upon him with appalling ferocity! The act released his physical energies without unfettering his will; his mind was still spellbound, but his powerful body and agile limbs, endowed with a blind, insensate life of their own, resisted stoutly and well. For an instant he seemed to see this unnatural contest between a dead intelligence and a breathing mechanism only as a spectator—such fancies are in dreams; then he regained his identity almost as if by a leap forward into his body, and the straining automation had a directing will as alert and fierce as that of its hideous antagonist.

But what mortal can cope with a creature of his dream? The imagination creating the enemy is already vanquished; the combat's result is the combat's cause. Despite his struggles—despite his strength and activity, which seemed wasted in a void, he felt the cold fingers close upon his throat. Borne backward to the earth, he saw above him the dead and drawn face within a hand's breadth of his own, and then all was black. A sound as of the beating of distant drums—a murmur of swarming voices, a sharp, far cry signing all to silence, and Halpin Frayser dreamed that he was dead.

IV

A warm, clear night had been followed by a morning of drenching fog. At about the middle of the afternoon of the preceding day a little whiff of light vapor—a mere thickening of the atmosphere, the ghost of a cloud—had been observed clinging to the western side of Mount St. Helena, away up along the barren altitudes near the summit. It was so thin, so diaphanous, so like a fancy made visible, that one would have said: "Look quickly! in a moment it will be gone."

In a moment it was visibly larger and denser. While with one edge it clung to the mountain, with the other it reached farther and farther out into the air above the lower slopes. At the same time it extended itself to north and south, joining small patches of mist that appeared to come out of the mountainside on exactly the same level, with an intelligent design to be absorbed. And so it grew and grew until the summit was shut out of view from the valley, and over the valley itself was an ever-extending canopy, opaque and gray. At Calistoga, which lies near the head of the valley and the foot of the mountain, there were a starless night and a sunless morning. The fog, sinking into the valley, had reached southward, swallowing up ranch after ranch, until it had blotted out the town of St. Helena, nine miles away. The dust in the road was laid; trees were adrip with moisture; birds sat silent in their coverts; the morning light was wan and ghastly, with neither color nor fire.

Two men left the town of St. Helena at the first glimmer of dawn, and walked along the road northward up the valley toward Calistoga. They carried guns on their shoulders, yet no one having knowledge of such matters could have mistaken them for hunters of bird or beast. They were a deputy sheriff from Napa and a detective from San Francisco—Holker and Jaralson, respectively. Their business was man-hunting.

"How far is it?" inquired Holker, as they strode along, their feet stirring white the dust beneath the damp surface of the road.

"The White Church? Only a half mile farther," the other

answered. "By the way," he added, "it is neither white nor a church; it is an abandoned schoolhouse, gray with age and neglect. Religious services were once held in it—when it was white, and there is a graveyard that would delight a poet. Can you guess why I sent for you, and told you to come heeled?"

"Oh, I never have bothered you about things of that kind. I've always found you communicative when the time came. But if I may hazard a guess, you want me to help you arrest one of the corpses in the graveyard."

"You remember Branscom?" said Jaralson, treating his companion's wit with the inattention that it deserved.

"The chap who cut his wife's throat? I ought; I wasted a week's work on him and had my expenses for my trouble. There is a reward of five hundred dollars, but none of us ever got a sight of him. You don't mean to say——"

"Yes, I do. He has been under the noses of you fellows all the time. He comes by night to the old graveyard at the White Church."

"The devil! That's where they buried his wife."

"Well, you fellows might have had sense enough to suspect that he would return to her grave some time."

"The very last place that anyone would have expected him to return to."

"But you had exhausted all the other places. Learning your failure at them, I 'laid for him' there."

"And you found him?"

"Damn it! he found *me*. The rascal got the drop on me— regularly held me up and made me travel. It's God's mercy that he didn't go through me. Oh, he's a good one, and I fancy the half of that reward is enough for me if you're needy."

Holker laughed good humoredly, and explained that his creditors were never more importunate.

"I wanted merely to show you the ground, and arrange a plan with you," the detective explained. "I thought it as well for us to be heeled, even in daylight."

"The man must be insane," said the deputy sheriff. "The reward is for his capture and conviction. If he's mad he won't be convicted."

Mr. Holker was so profoundly affected by that possible failure of justice that he involuntarily stopped in the middle of the road, then resumed his walk with abated zeal.

"Well, he looks it," assented Jaralson. "I'm bound to admit that a more unshaven, unshorn, unkempt, and uneverything wretch I never saw outside the ancient and honorable order of tramps. But I've gone in for him, and can't make up my mind to let go. There's glory in it for us, anyhow. Not another soul knows that he is this side of the Mountains of the Moon."

"All right," Holker said; "we will go and view the ground," and he added, in the words of a once favorite inscription for tombstones: "'where you must shortly lie'—I mean, if old Branscom ever gets tired of you and your impertinent intrusion. By the way, I heard the other day that 'Branscom' was not his real name."

"What is?"

"I can't recall it. I had lost all interest in the wretch, and it did not fix itself in my memory—something like Pardee. The woman whose throat he had the bad taste to cut was a widow when he met her. She had come to California to look up some relatives—there are persons who will do that sometimes. But you know all that."

"Naturally."

"But not knowing the right name, by what happy inspiration did you find the right grave? The man who told me what the name was said it had been cut on the headboard."

"I don't know the right grave." Jaralson was apparently a trifle reluctant to admit his ignorance of so important a point of his plan. "I have been watching about the place generally. A part of our work this morning will be to identify that grave. Here is the White Church."

For a long distance the road had been bordered by fields on both sides, but now on the left there was a forest of oaks, madroños, and gigantic spruces whose lower parts only could be seen, dim and ghostly in the fog. The undergrowth was, in places, thick, but nowhere impenetrable. For some moments Holker saw nothing of the building, but as they turned into the woods it revealed itself in faint gray outline through the fog, looking huge and far away. A few steps more, and it was within an arm's length, distinct, dark with moisture, and insignificant in size. It had the usual country-schoolhouse form—belonged to the packing-box order of architecture; had an underpinning of stones, a moss-grown roof, and blank window spaces, whence both glass and sash had long departed. It was ruined, but not a ruin—a typical Californian substitute for what are known to guide-bookers abroad as "monuments of the past." With scarcely a glance at this uninteresting structure Jaralson moved on into the dripping undergrowth beyond.

"I will show you where he held me up," he said. "This is the graveyard."

Here and there among the bushes were small inclosures containing graves, sometimes no more than one. They were recognized as graves by the discolored stones or rotting boards at head and foot, leaning at all angles, some prostrate; by the ruined picket fences surrounding them; or, infrequently, by the mound itself showing its gravel through the fallen leaves. In many instances nothing marked the spot where lay the vestiges of some poor mortal—who, leaving "a large circle of sorrowing friends," had been left by them in turn—except a depression in the earth, more lasting than that in the spirits of the mourners. The paths, if any paths had been, were long obliterated; trees of a considerable size had been permitted to grow up from the graves and thrust aside with root or branch the inclosing fences. Over all was that air of abandonment and decay which seems nowhere so fit and significant as in a village of the forgotten dead.

As the two men, Jaralson leading, pushed their way through the growth of young trees, that enterprising man suddenly stopped and brought up his shotgun to the height of his breast, uttered a low note of warning, and stood motionless, his eyes fixed upon something ahead. As well as he could, obstructed by brush, his companion, though seeing nothing, imitated the posture and so stood, prepared for what might ensue. A moment later Jaralson moved cautiously forward, the other following.

Under the branches of an enormous spruce lay the dead body of a man. Standing silent above it they noted such particulars as first strike the attention—the face, the attitude, the clothing; whatever most promptly and plainly answers the unspoken question of a sympathetic curiosity.

The body lay upon its back, the legs wide apart. One arm was thrust upward, the other outward; but the latter was bent acutely, and the hand was near the throat. Both hands were tightly clenched. The whole attitude was that of desperate but ineffectual resistance to—what?

Near by lay a shotgun and a game bag through the meshes of which was seen the plumage of shot birds. All about were evidences of a furious struggle; small sprouts of poison-oak were bent and denuded of leaf and bark; dead and rotting leaves had been pushed into heaps and ridges on both sides of the legs by the action of other feet than theirs; alongside the hips were unmistakable impressions of human knees.

The nature of the struggle was made clear by a glance at the dead man's throat and face. While breast and hands were white, those were purple—almost black. The shoulders lay upon a low mound, and the head was turned back at an angle otherwise impossible, the expanded eyes staring blankly backward in a direction opposite to that of the feet. From the froth filling the open mouth the tongue protruded, black and swollen. The throat showed horrible contusions; not mere fingermarks, but bruises and lacerations wrought by two strong hands that must have buried themselves in the yielding flesh, maintaining their terrible grasp until long after death. Breast, throat, face, were wet; the clothing was saturated; drops of water, condensed from the fog, studded the hair and mustache.

All this the two men observed without speaking—almost at a glance. Then Holker said:

"Poor devil! he had a rough deal."

Jaralson was making a vigilant circumspection of the forest, his shotgun held in both hands and at full cock, his finger upon the trigger.

"The work of a maniac," he said, without withdrawing his eyes from the inclosing wood. "It was done by Branscom—Pardee."

Something half hidden by the disturbed leaves on the earth caught Holker's attention. It was a red-leather pocketbook. He picked it up and opened it. It contained leaves of white paper for memoranda, and upon the first leaf was the name "Halpin Frayser." Written in red on several succeeding leaves—scrawled as if in haste and barely legible—were the following lines, which Holker read aloud, while his companion continued scanning the dim gray confines of their narrow world and hearing matter of apprehension in the drip of water from every burdened branch:

"Enthralled by some mysterious spell, I stood
  In the lit gloom of an enchanted wood.
    The cypress there and myrtle twined their boughs,
    Significant, in baleful brotherhood.

"The brooding willow whispered to the yew;
  Beneath, the deadly nightshade and the rue,
    With immortelles self-woven into strange
    Funereal shapes, and horrid nettles grew.

"No song of bird nor any drone of bees,
  Nor light leaf lifted by the wholesome breeze:
    The air was stagnant all, and Silence was
    A living thing that breathed among the trees.

"Conspiring spirits whispered in the gloom,
  Half-heard, the stilly secrets of the tomb.
    With blood the trees were all adrip; the leaves
    Shone in the witch-light with a ruddy bloom.

"I cried aloud!—the spell, unbroken still,
  Rested upon my spirit and my will.
    Unsouled, unhearted, hopeless and forlorn,
    I strove with monstrous presages of ill!

"At last the viewless——"

Holker ceased reading; there was no more to read. The manuscript broke off in the middle of a line.

"That sounds like Bayne," said Jaralson, who was something of a scholar in his way. He had abated his vigilance and stood looking down at the body.

"Who's Bayne?" Holker asked rather incuriously.

"Myron Bayne, a chap who flourished in the early years of the nation—more than a century ago. Wrote mighty dismal stuff; I have his collected works. That poem is not among them, but it must have been omitted by mistake."

"It is cold," said Holker; "let us leave here; we must have up the coroner from Napa."

Jaralson said nothing, but made a movement in compliance. Passing the end of the slight elevation of earth upon which the dead man's head and shoulders lay, his foot struck some hard substance under the rotting forest leaves, and he took the trouble to kick it into view. It was a fallen headboard, and painted on it were the hardly decipherable words, "Catharine Larue."

"Larue, Larue!" exclaimed Holker, with sudden animation. "Why, that is the real name of Branscom—not Pardee. And—bless my soul! how it all comes to me—the murdered woman's name had been Frayser!"

"There is some rascally mystery here," said Detective Jaralson. "I hate anything of that kind."

There came to them out of the fog—seemingly from a great distance—the sound of a laugh, a low, deliberate, soulless laugh, which had no more of joy than that of a hyena night-prowling in the desert; a laugh that rose by slow gradation, louder and louder, clearer, more distinct and terrible, until it seemed barely outside the narrow circle of their vision; a laugh so unnatural, so unhuman, so devilish, that it filled those hardy man-hunters with a sense of dread unspeakable! They did not move their weapons nor think of them; the menace of that horrible sound was not of the kind to be met with arms. As it had grown out of silence, so now it died away; from a culminating shout which had seemed almost in their ears, it drew itself away into the distance, until its failing notes, joyless and mechanical to the last, sank to silence at a measureless remove.

ROBERT W. CHAMBERS

Robert William Chambers was born in 1865 in Brooklyn, New York. An early interest in painting led him to study art in Paris; he skillfully made use of the atmosphere of Bohemian decadence he found there in his first novel, *In the Quarter* (1894). His next volume, *The King in Yellow* (1895), largely consisting of tales of the supernatural, has become a classic in the field. Chambers went on to write other volumes of horror and fantasy, including *The Maker of Moons* (1896), *The Mystery of Choice* (1897), and *In Search of the Unknown* (1904). But he gradually turned his attention to sentimental romances and popular historical tales, achieving bestseller status with an array of books including *Cardigan* (1901), *The Younger Set* (1907), *Some Ladies in Haste* (1908), *The Common Law* (1911), and *The Restless Sex* (1918). These books, while making him one of the wealthiest authors of his period, also spelled his aesthetic damnation. He returned to the supernatural only occasionally in his later years, with such works as *The Tree of Heaven* (1906), *The Tracer of Lost Persons* (1907), *Police!!!* (1915), and the mediocre "Yellow Peril" novel, *The Slayer of Souls* (1920). From the proceeds of his writing he purchased a lavish estate in Mamaroneck, New York, where he died in 1933. Chambers's complete supernatural tales are now collected in *The Yellow Sign and Other Stories* (2000).

"The Yellow Sign" is perhaps the most horrific story in

The King in Yellow. This nightmarish tale of the reanimated dead plaguing art students in New York makes tangential use of a leitmotif that runs through many of the stories: a play entitled *The King in Yellow,* the reading of which induces despair or madness. Other stories in the volume include "The Repairer of Reputations," a bizarre story of New York City in the future; "The Demoiselle d'Ys," a delicate tale of the medieval past impinging upon the present; and "The Mask," a story exquisitely fusing beauty and horror in its account of a chemical that freezes living entities in a state of suspended animation.

THE YELLOW SIGN

"Let the red dawn surmise
What we shall do,
When this blue starlight dies
And all is through."

There are so many things which are impossible to explain!
Why should certain chords in music make me think of
the brown and golden tints of autumn foliage? Why should the
Mass of Sainte Cécile send my thoughts wandering among caverns whose walls blaze with ragged masses of virgin silver? What
was it in the roar and turmoil of Broadway at six o'clock that
flashed before my eyes the picture of a still Breton forest where
sunlight filtered through spring foliage and Sylvia bent, half curiously, half tenderly, over a small green lizard, murmuring:
"To think that this also is a little ward of God!"

When I first saw the watchman his back was toward me. I
looked at him indifferently until he went into the church. I paid
no more attention to him than I had to any other man who
lounged through Washington Square that morning, and when
I shut my window and turned back into my studio I had forgotten him. Late in the afternoon, the day being warm, I raised
the window again and leaned out to get a sniff of air. A man was
standing in the courtyard of the church, and I noticed him
again with as little interest as I had that morning. I looked across
the square to where the fountain was playing and then, with my
mind filled with vague impressions of trees, asphalt drives, and
the moving groups of nursemaids and holiday-makers, I started
to walk back to my easel. As I turned, my listless glance included
the man below in the churchyard. His face was toward me now,

and with a perfectly involuntary movement I bent to see it. At the same moment he raised his head and looked at me. Instantly I thought of a coffin-worm. Whatever it was about the man that repelled me I did not know, but the impression of a plump white grave-worm was so intense and nauseating that I must have shown it in my expression, for he turned his puffy face away with a movement which made me think of a disturbed grub in a chestnut.

I went back to my easel and motioned the model to resume her pose. After working awhile I was satisfied that I was spoiling what I had done as rapidly as possible, and I took up a palette knife and scraped the color out again. The flesh tones were sallow and unhealthy, and I did not understand how I could have painted such sickly color into a study which before that had glowed with healthy tones.

I looked at Tessie. She had not changed, and the clear flush of health dyed her neck and cheeks as I frowned.

"Is it something I've done?" she said.

"No,—I've made a mess of this arm, and for the life of me I can't see how I came to paint such mud as that into the canvas," I replied.

"Don't I pose well?" she insisted.

"Of course, perfectly."

"Then it's not my fault?"

"No. It's my own."

"I'm very sorry," she said.

I told her she could rest while I applied rag and turpentine to the plague spot on my canvas, and she went off to smoke a cigarette and look over the illustrations in the *Courier Français*.

I did not know whether it was something in the turpentine or a defect in the canvas, but the more I scrubbed the more that gangrene seemed to spread. I worked like a beaver to get it out, and yet the disease appeared to creep from limb to limb of the study before me. Alarmed I strove to arrest it, but now the color on the breast changed and the whole figure seemed to absorb the infection as a sponge soaks up water. Vigorously I plied palette knife, turpentine, and scraper, thinking all the time what a séance I should hold with Duval who had sold me the canvas;

but soon I noticed that it was not the canvas which was defective nor yet the colors of Edward. "It must be the turpentine," I thought angrily, "or else my eyes have become so blurred and confused by the afternoon light that I can't see straight." I called Tessie, the model. She came and leaned over my chair blowing rings of smoke into the air.

"What *have* you been doing to it?" she exclaimed.

"Nothing," I growled, "it must be this turpentine!"

"What a horrible color it is now," she continued. "Do you think my flesh resembles green cheese?"

"No, I don't," I said angrily, "did you ever know me to paint like that before?"

"No, indeed!"

"Well, then!"

"It must be the turpentine, or something," she admitted.

She slipped on a Japanese robe and walked to the window. I scraped and rubbed until I was tired and finally picked up my brushes and hurled them through the canvas with a forcible expression, the tone alone of which reached Tessie's ears.

Nevertheless she promptly began: "That's it! Swear and act silly and ruin your brushes! You have been three weeks on that study, and now look! What's the good of ripping the canvas? What creatures artists are!"

I felt about as much ashamed as I usually did after such an outbreak, and I turned the ruined canvas to the wall. Tessie helped me clean my brushes, and then danced away to dress. From the screen she regaled me with bits of advice concerning whole or partial loss of temper, until, thinking, perhaps, I had been tormented sufficiently, she came out to implore me to button her waist where she could not reach it on the shoulder.

"Everything went wrong from the time you came back from the window and talked about that horrid-looking man you saw in the churchyard," she announced.

"Yes, he probably bewitched the picture," I said, yawning. I looked at my watch.

"It's after six, I know," said Tessie, adjusting her hat before the mirror.

"Yes," I replied, "I didn't mean to keep you so long." I leaned out of the window but recoiled with disgust, for the young man with the pasty face stood below in the churchyard. Tessie saw my gesture of disapproval and leaned from the window.

"Is that the man you don't like?" she whispered.

I nodded.

"I can't see his face, but he does look fat and soft. Someway or other," she continued, turning to look at me, "he reminds me of a dream,—an awful dream I once had. Or," she mused, looking down at her shapely shoes, "was it a dream after all?"

"How should I know?" I smiled.

Tessie smiled in reply.

"You were in it," she said, "so perhaps you might know something about it."

"Tessie! Tessie!" I protested, "don't you dare flatter by saying that you dream about me!"

"But I did," she insisted; "shall I tell you about it?"

"Go ahead," I replied, lighting a cigarette.

Tessie leaned back on the open window-sill and began very seriously.

"One night last winter I was lying in bed thinking about nothing at all in particular. I had been posing for you and I was tired out, yet it seemed impossible for me to sleep. I heard the bells in the city ring ten, eleven, and midnight. I must have fallen asleep about midnight because I don't remember hearing the bells after that. It seemed to me that I had scarcely closed my eyes when I dreamed that something impelled me to go to the window. I rose, and raising the sash leaned out. Twenty-fifth Street was deserted as far as I could see. I began to be afraid; everything outside seemed so—so black and uncomfortable. Then the sound of wheels in the distance came to my ears, and it seemed to me as though that was what I must wait for. Very slowly the wheels approached, and, finally, I could make out a vehicle moving along the street. It came nearer and nearer, and when it passed beneath my window I saw it was a hearse. Then, as I trembled with fear, the driver turned and looked straight at me. When I awoke I was standing by the open window shivering with cold, but the black-plumed hearse and the driver were gone. I dreamed this dream again in March last, and again awoke beside the open window. Last night the dream came again. You remember how it was raining; when I awoke, standing at the open window, my night-dress was soaked."

"But where did I come into the dream?" I asked.

"You—you were in the coffin; but you were not dead."

"In the coffin?"

"Yes."

"How did you know? Could you see me?"

"No; I only knew you were there."

"Had you been eating Welsh rarebits, or lobster salad?" I began laughing, but the girl interrupted me with a frightened cry.

"Hello! What's up?" I said, as she shrank into the embrasure by the window.

"The—the man below in the churchyard;—he drove the hearse."

"Nonsense," I said, but Tessie's eyes were wide with terror. I went to the window and looked out. The man was gone. "Come, Tessie," I urged, "don't be foolish. You have posed too long; you are nervous."

"Do you think I could forget that face?" she murmured. "Three times I saw the hearse pass below my window, and every time the driver turned and looked up at me. Oh, his face was so white and—and soft? It looked dead—it looked as if it had been dead a long time."

I induced the girl to sit down and swallow a glass of Marsala. Then I sat down beside her, and tried to give her some advice.

"Look here, Tessie," I said, "you go to the country for a week or two, and you'll have no more dreams about hearses. You pose all day, and when night comes your nerves are upset. You can't keep this up. Then again, instead of going to bed when your day's work is done, you run off to picnics at Sulzer's Park, or go to the Eldorado or Coney Island, and when you come down here next morning you are fagged out. There was no real hearse. That was a soft-shell crab dream."

She smiled faintly.

"What about the man in the churchyard?"

"Oh, he's only an ordinary unhealthy, everyday creature."

"As true as my name is Tessie Reardon, I swear to you, Mr. Scott, that the face of the man below in the churchyard is the face of the man who drove the hearse!"

"What of it?" I said. "It's an honest trade."

"Then you think I *did* see the hearse?"

"Oh," I said, diplomatically, "if you really did, it might not be unlikely that the man below drove it. There is nothing in that."

Tessie rose, unrolled her scented handkerchief, and taking a bit of gum from a knot in the hem, placed it in her mouth. Then drawing on her gloves she offered me her hand, with a frank, "Good-night, Mr. Scott," and walked out.

II

The next morning, Thomas, the bellboy, brought me the *Herald* and a bit of news. The church next door had been sold. I thanked Heaven for it, not that it being a Catholic I had any repugnance for the congregation next door, but because my nerves were shattered by a blatant exhorter, whose every word echoed through the aisle of the church as if it had been my own rooms, and who insisted on his r's with a nasal persistence which revolted my every instinct. Then, too, there was a fiend in human shape, an organist, who reeled off some of the grand old hymns with an interpretation of his own, and I longed for the blood of a creature who could play the doxology with an amendment of minor chords which one hears only in a quartet of very young undergraduates. I believe the minister was a good man, but when he bellowed: "And the Lorrrd said unto Moses, the Lorrrd is a man of war; the Lorrrd is his name. My wrath shall wax hot and I will kill you with the sworrrd!" I wondered how many centuries of purgatory it would take to atone for such a sin.

"Who bought the property?" I asked Thomas.

"Nobody that I knows, sir. They do say the gent wot owns this 'ere 'Amilton flats was lookin' at it. 'E might be a bildin' more studios."

I walked to the window. The young man with the unhealthy face stood by the churchyard gate, and at the mere sight of him the same overwhelming repugnance took possession of me.

"By the way, Thomas," I said, "who is that fellow down there?"

Thomas sniffed. "That there worm, sir? 'E's night-watchman of the church, sir. 'E maikes me tired a-sittin' out all night on them steps and lookin' at you insultin' like. I'd a punched 'is 'ed, sir—beg pardon, sir——"

"Go on, Thomas."

"One night a comin' 'ome with 'Arry, the other English boy, I sees 'im sittin' there on them steps. We 'ad Molly and Jen with us, sir, the two girls on the tray service, an' 'e looks so insultin' at us that I up and sez: 'Wat you looking hat, you fat slug?'—beg pardon, sir, but that's 'ow I sez, sir. Then 'e don't say nothin' and I sez: 'Come out and I'll punch that puddin' 'ed.' Then I hopens the gate an' goes in, but 'e don't say nothin', only looks insultin' like. Then I 'its 'im one, but, ugh! 'is 'ed was that cold and mushy it ud sicken you to touch 'im."

"What did he do then?" I asked, curiously.

"'Im? Nawthin'."

"And you, Thomas?"

The young fellow flushed with embarrassment and smiled uneasily.

"Mr. Scott, sir, I ain't no coward an' I can't make it out at all why I run. I was in the 5th Lawncers, sir, bugler at Tel-el-Kebir, an' was shot by the wells."

"You don't mean to say you ran away?"

"Yes, sir; I run."

"Why?"

"That's just what I want to know, sir. I grabbed Molly an' run, an' the rest was as frightened as I."

"But what were they frightened at?"

Thomas refused to answer for a while, but now my curiosity was aroused about the repulsive young man below and I pressed him. Three years' sojourn in America had not only modified Thomas' cockney dialect but had given him the American's fear of ridicule.

"You won't believe me, Mr. Scott, sir?"

"Yes, I will."

"You will lawf at me, sir?"

"Nonsense!"

He hesitated. "Well, sir, it's Gawd's truth that when I 'it 'im 'e grabbed me wrists, sir, and when I twisted 'is soft, mushy fist one of 'is fingers come off in me 'and."

The utter loathing and horror of Thomas' face must have been reflected in my own for he added:

"It's orful, an' now when I see 'im I just go away. 'E maikes me hill."

When Thomas had gone I went to the window. The man stood beside the church-railing with both hands on the gate, but I hastily retreated to my easel again, sickened and horrified, for I saw that the middle finger of his right hand was missing.

At nine o'clock Tessie appeared and vanished behind the screen with a merry "good-morning, Mr. Scott." When she had reappeared and taken her pose upon the model stand I started a new canvas much to her delight. She remained silent as long as I was on the drawing, but as soon as the scrape of the charcoal ceased and I took up my fixative she began to chatter.

"Oh, I had such a lovely time last night. We went to Tony Pastor's."

"Who are 'we'?" I demanded.

"Oh, Maggie, you know, Mr. Whyte's model, and Pinkie McCormick—we call her Pinkie because she's got that beautiful red hair you artists like so much—and Lizzie Burke."

I sent a shower of spray from the fixative over the canvas, and said: "Well, go on."

"We saw Kelly and Baby Barnes the skirt-dancer and—all the rest. I made a mash."

"Then you have gone back on me, Tessie?"

She laughed and shook her head.

"He's Lizzie Burke's brother, Ed. He's a perfect gen'l'man."

I felt constrained to give her some parental advice concerning mashing, which she took with a bright smile.

"Oh, I can take care of a strange mash," she said, examining her chewing gum, "but Ed is different. Lizzie is my best friend."

Then she related how Ed had come back from the stocking mill in Lowell, Massachusetts, to find her and Lizzie grown up, and what an accomplished young man he was, and how he thought nothing of squandering half a dollar for ice-cream and oysters to celebrate his entry as clerk into the woollen department of Macy's. Before she finished I began to paint, and she resumed the pose, smiling and chattering like a sparrow. By noon I had the study fairly well rubbed in and Tessie came to look at it.

"That's better," she said.

I thought so too, and ate my lunch with a satisfied feeling that all was going well. Tessie spread her lunch on a drawing table opposite me and we drank our claret from the same bottle and lighted our cigarettes from the same match. I was very much attached to Tessie. I had watched her shoot up into a slender but exquisitely formed woman from a frail, awkward child. She had posed for me during the last three years, and among all my models she was my favorite. It would have troubled me very much indeed had she become "tough" or "fly," as the phrase goes, but I never noticed any deterioration of her manner, and felt at heart that she was all right. She and I never discussed morals at all, and I had no intention of doing so, partly because I had none myself, and partly because I knew she would do what she liked in spite of me. Still I did hope she would steer clear of complications, because I wished her well, and then also I had a selfish desire to retain the best model I had. I knew that mashing, as she termed it, had no significance with girls like Tessie, and that such things in America did not resemble in the least the same things in Paris. Yet, having lived with my eyes open, I also knew that somebody would take Tessie away some day, in one manner or another, and though I professed to myself that marriage was nonsense, I sincerely hoped that, in this case, there would be a priest at the end of the vista. I am a Catholic. When I listen to high mass, when I sign myself, I feel that everything, including myself, is more cheerful, and when I confess, it does me good. A man who lives as much alone as I do, must confess to somebody. Then, again, Sylvia was Catholic, and it was reason enough for me. But I was speaking of Tessie, which is very different. Tessie also was Catholic and much more devout than I, so, taking it all in all, I had little fear for my pretty model until she should fall in love. But *then* I knew that fate alone would decide her future for her, and I prayed inwardly that fate would keep her away from men like me and throw into her path nothing but Ed Burkes and Jimmy McCormicks, bless her sweet face!

Tessie sat blowing rings of smoke up to the ceiling and tinkling the ice in her tumbler.

"Do you know that I also had a dream last night?" I observed.

"Not about that man," she laughed.

"Exactly. A dream similar to yours, only much worse."

It was foolish and thoughtless of me to say this, but you know how little tact the average painter has.

"I must have fallen asleep about 10 o'clock," I continued, "and after awhile I dreamt that I awoke. So plainly did I hear the midnight bells, the wind in the tree-branches, and the whistle of steamers from the bay, that even now I can scarcely believe I was not awake. I seemed to be lying in a box which had a glass cover. Dimly I saw the street lamps as I passed, for I must tell you, Tessie, the box in which I reclined appeared to lie in a cushioned wagon which jolted me over a stony pavement. After a while I became impatient and tried to move but the box was too narrow. My hands were crossed on my breast so I could not raise them to help myself. I listened and then tried to call. My voice was gone. I could hear the trample of the horses attached to the wagon and even the breathing of the driver. Then another sound broke upon my ears like the raising of a window sash. I managed to turn my head a little, and found I could look, not only through the glass cover of my box, but also through the glass panes in the side of the covered vehicle. I saw houses, empty and silent, with neither light nor life about any of them excepting one. In that house a window was open on the first floor and a figure all in white stood looking down into the street. It was you."

Tessie had turned her face away from me and leaned on the table with her elbow.

"I could see your face," I resumed, "and it seemed to me to

be very sorrowful. Then we passed on and turned into a narrow black lane. Presently the horses stopped. I waited and waited, closing my eyes with fear and impatience, but all was silent as the grave. After what seemed to me hours, I began to feel uncomfortable. A sense that somebody was close to me made me unclose my eyes. Then I saw the white face of the hearse-driver looking at me through the coffin-lid——"

A sob from Tessie interrupted me. She was trembling like a leaf. I saw I had made an ass of myself and attempted to repair the damage.

"Why, Tess," I said, "I only told you this to show you what influence your story might have on another person's dreams. You don't suppose I really lay in a coffin, do you? What are you trembling for? Don't you see that your dream and my unreasonable dislike for that inoffensive watchman of the church simply set my brain working as soon as I fell asleep?"

She laid her head between her arms and sobbed as if her heart would break. What a precious triple donkey I had made of myself! But I was about to break my record. I went over and put my arm about her.

"Tessie dear, forgive me," I said; "I had no business to frighten you with such nonsense. You are too sensible a girl, too good a Catholic to believe in dreams."

Her hand tightened on mine and her head fell back upon my shoulder, but she still trembled and I petted her and comforted her.

"Come, Tess, open your eyes and smile."

Her eyes opened with a slow languid movement and met mine, but their expression was so queer that I hastened to reassure her again.

"It's all humbug, Tessie, you surely are not afraid that any harm will come to you because of that."

"No," she said, but her scarlet lips quivered.

"Then what's the matter? Are you afraid?"

"Yes. Not for myself."

"For me, then?" I demanded gayly.

"For you," she murmured in a voice almost inaudible, "I—I care for you."

At first I started to laugh, but when I understood her, a shock passed through me and I sat like one turned to stone. This was the crowning bit of idiocy I had committed. During the moment which elapsed between her reply and my answer I thought of a thousand responses to that innocent confession. I could pass it by with a laugh, I could misunderstand her and re-assure her as to my health, I could simply point out that it was impossible she could love me. But my reply was quicker than my thoughts, and I might think and think now when it was too late, for I had kissed her on the mouth.

That evening I took my usual walk in Washington Park, pondering over the occurrences of the day. I was thoroughly committed. There was no back out now, and I stared the future straight in the face. I was not good, not even scrupulous, but I had no idea of deceiving either myself or Tessie. The one passion of my life lay buried in the sunlit forests of Brittany. Was it buried forever? Hope cried "No!" For three years I had been listening to the voice of Hope, and for three years I had waited for a footstep on my threshold. Had Sylvia forgotten? "No!" cried Hope.

I said that I was not good. That is true, but still I was not exactly a comic opera villain. I had led an easy-going reckless life, taking what invited me of pleasure, deploring and sometimes bitterly regretting consequences. In one thing alone, except my painting, was I serious, and that was something which lay hidden if not lost in the Breton forests.

It was too late now for me to regret what had occurred during the day. Whatever it had been, pity, a sudden tenderness for sorrow, or the more brutal instinct of gratified vanity, it was all the same now, and unless I wished to bruise an innocent heart my path lay marked before me. The fire and strength, the depth of passion of a love which I had never even suspected, with all my imagined experience in the world, left me no alternative but to respond or send her away. Whether because I am so cowardly about giving pain to others, or whether it was that I have little of the gloomy Puritan in me, I do not know, but I shrank from disclaiming responsibility for that thoughtless kiss, and in fact had no time to do so before the gates of her heart opened and the flood poured forth. Others who habitually do their duty and find a sullen satisfaction in making themselves and everybody else unhappy, might have withstood it. I did not. I dared not. After the storm had abated I did tell her that she might better have loved Ed Burke and worn a plain gold ring, but she would not hear of it, and I thought perhaps that as long as she had decided to love somebody she could not marry, it had better be me. I at least could treat her with an intelligent affection, and whenever she became tired of her infatuation she could go none the worse for it. For I was decided on that point although I knew how hard it would be. I remembered the usual termination of Platonic liaisons and thought how disgusted I had been whenever I heard of one. I knew I was undertaking a great deal for so unscrupulous a man as I was, and I dreaded the future, but never for one moment did I doubt that she was safe with me. Had it been anybody but Tessie I should not have bothered my head about scruples. For it did not occur to me to sacrifice Tessie as I would have sacrificed a woman of the world. I looked the future squarely in the face and saw the several probable endings to the affair. She would either tire of the whole thing, or become so unhappy that I should have either to marry her or go away. If I married her we would be unhappy. I with a wife unsuited to me, and she with a husband unsuitable for any woman. For my past life could scarcely entitle me to marry. If I went away she might either fall ill, recover, and marry some Eddie Burke, or she might recklessly or deliberately go and do something foolish. On the other hand if she tired of me, then her whole life would be before her with beautiful vistas of Eddie Burkes and marriage rings and twins and Harlem flats and Heaven knows what. As I strolled along through the trees by the Washington Arch, I decided that she should find a substantial friend in me anyway and the future could take care of itself. Then I went into the house and put on my evening dress for the little faintly perfumed note on my dresser said, "Have a cab at the stage door at eleven," and the note was signed "Edith Carmichel, Metropolitan Theatre."

I took supper that night, or rather we took supper, Miss Carmichel and I, at Solari's and the dawn was just beginning to gild the cross on the Memorial Church as I entered Washington Square after leaving Edith at the Brunswick. There was not a soul in the park as I passed among the trees and took the walk which leads from the Garibaldi statue to the Hamilton Apartment House, but as I passed the churchyard I saw a figure sitting on the stone steps. In spite of myself a chill crept over me at the sight of the white puffy face, and I hastened to pass. Then he said something which might have been addressed to me or might merely have been a mutter to himself, but a sudden furious anger flamed up within me that such a creature should address me. For an instant I felt like wheeling about and smashing my stick over his head, but I walked on, and entering the Hamilton went to my apartment. For some time I tossed about the bed trying to get the sound of his voice out of my ears, but could not. It filled my head, that muttering sound, like thick oily smoke from a fat-rendering vat or an odor of noisome decay. And as I lay and tossed about, the voice in my ears seemed more distinct, and I began to understand the words he had muttered. They came to me slowly as if I had forgotten them, and at last I could make some sense out of the sounds. It was this:

"Have you found the Yellow Sign?"
"Have you found the Yellow Sign?"
"Have you found the Yellow Sign?"

I was furious. What did he mean by that? Then with a curse upon him and his I rolled over and went to sleep, but when I awoke later I looked pale and haggard, for I had dreamed the dream of the night before and it troubled me more than I cared to think.

I dressed and went down into my studio. Tessie sat by the window, but as I came in she rose and put both arms around my neck for an innocent kiss. She looked so sweet and dainty that I kissed her again and then sat down before the easel.

"Hello! Where's the study I began yesterday?" I asked.

Tessie looked conscious, but did not answer. I began to hunt among the pile of canvases, saying, "Hurry up, Tess, and get ready; we must take advantage of the morning light."

Robert W. Chambers

When at last I gave up the search among the other canvases and turned to look around the room for the missing study I noticed Tessie standing by the screen with her clothes still on.

"What's the matter," I asked, "don't you feel well?"

"Yes."

"Then hurry."

"Do you want me to pose as—as I have always posed?"

Then I understood. Here was a new complication. I had lost, of course, the best nude model I had ever seen. I looked at Tessie. Her face was scarlet. Alas! Alas! We had eaten of the tree of knowledge, and Eden and native innocence were dreams of the past—I mean for her.

I suppose she noticed the disappointment on my face, for she said: "I will pose if you wish. The study is behind the screen here where I put it."

"No," I said, "we will begin something new;" and I went into my wardrobe and picked out a Moorish costume which fairly blazed with tinsel. It was a genuine costume, and Tessie retired to the screen with it enchanted. When she came forth again I was astonished. Her long black hair was bound above her forehead with a circlet of turquoises, and the ends curled about her glittering girdle. Her feet were encased in the embroidered pointed slippers and the skirt of her costume, curiously wrought with arabesques in silver, fell to her ankles. The deep metallic blue vest embroidered with silver and the short Mauresque jacket spangled and sewn with turquoises became her wonderfully. She came up to me and held up her face smiling. I slipped my hand into my pocket and drawing out a gold chain with a cross attached, dropped it over her head.

"It's yours, Tessie."

"Mine?" she faltered.

"Yours. Now go and pose." Then with a radiant smile she ran behind the screen and presently re-appeared with a little box on which was written my name.

"I had intended to give it to you when I went home to-night," she said, "but I can't wait now."

I opened the box. On the pink cotton inside lay a clasp of

black onyx, on which was inlaid a curious symbol or letter in gold. It was neither Arabic nor Chinese, nor as I found afterwards did it belong to any human script.

"It's all I had to give you for a keepsake," she said, timidly.

I was annoyed, but I told her how much I should prize it, and promised to wear it always. She fastened it on my coat beneath the lapel.

"How foolish, Tess, to go and buy me such a beautiful thing as this," I said.

"I did not buy it," she laughed.

"Where did you get it?"

Then she told me how she had found it one day while coming from the Aquarium in the Battery, how she had advertised it and watched the papers, but at last gave up all hopes of finding the owner.

"That was last winter," she said, "the very day I had the first horrid dream about the hearse."

I remembered my dream of the previous night but said nothing, and presently my charcoal was flying over a new canvas, and Tessie stood motionless on the model stand.

III

The day following was a disastrous one for me. While moving a framed canvas from one easel to another my foot slipped on the polished floor and I fell heavily on both wrists. They were so badly sprained that it was useless to attempt to hold a brush, and I was obliged to wander about the studio, glaring at unfinished drawings and sketches until despair seized me and I sat down to smoke and twiddle my thumbs with rage. The rain blew against the windows and rattled on the roof of the church, driving me into a nervous fit with its interminable patter. Tessie sat sewing by the window, and every now and then raised her head and looked at me with such innocent compassion that I began to feel ashamed of my irritation and looked about for something to occupy me. I had read all the papers and all the books in the library, but for the sake of something to do I went to the bookcases and shoved them open with my elbow. I knew every volume by its color and examined them all, passing slowly around the library and whistling to keep up my spirits. I was turning to go into the dining-room when my eye fell upon a book bound in serpent skin, standing in a corner of the top shelf of the last bookcase. I did not remember it and from the floor could not decipher the pale lettering on the back, so I went to the smoking-room and called Tessie. She came in from the studio and climbed up to reach the book.

"What is it?" I asked.

"'The King in Yellow.'"

I was dumfounded. Who had placed it there? How came it in my rooms? I had long ago decided that I should never open that book, and nothing on earth could have persuaded me to buy it. Fearful lest curiosity might tempt me to open it, I had never even looked at it in book-stores. If I ever had had any curiosity to read it, the awful tragedy of young Castaigne, whom I knew, prevented me from exploring its wicked pages. I had always refused to listen to any description of it, and indeed, nobody ever ventured to discuss the second part aloud, so I had absolutely no knowledge of what those leaves might reveal. I stared at the poisonous mottled binding as I would at a snake.

"Don't touch it, Tessie," I said; "come down."

Of course my admonition was enough to arouse her curiosity, and before I could prevent it she took the book and, laughing, danced off into the studio with it. I called to her but she slipped away with a tormenting smile at my helpless hands, and I followed her with some impatience.

"Tessie!" I cried, entering the library, "listen, I am serious. Put that book away. I do not wish you to open it!" The library was empty. I went into both drawing-rooms, then into the bed-rooms, laundry, kitchen and finally returned to the library and began a systematic search. She had hidden herself so well that it was half an hour later when I discovered her crouching white and silent by the latticed window in the store-room above. At the first glance I saw she had been punished for her foolishness. "The King in Yellow" lay at her feet, but the book was open at the second part. I looked at Tessie and saw it was too late. She had opened "The King in Yellow." Then I took her by the hand and led her into the studio. She seemed dazed, and when I told her to lie down on the sofa she obeyed me without a word. After a while she closed her eyes and her breathing became regular and deep, but I could not determine whether or not she slept. For a long while I sat silently beside her, but she neither stirred nor spoke, and at last I rose and entering the unused store-room took the book in my least injured hand. It seemed heavy as lead, but I carried it into the studio again, and sitting down on the rug beside the sofa, opened it and read it through from beginning to end.

When, faint with the excess of my emotions, I dropped the volume and leaned wearily back against the sofa, Tessie opened her eyes and looked at me.

We had been speaking for some time in a dull monotonous strain before I realized that we were discussing "The King in Yellow." Oh the sin of writing such words,—words which are clear as crystal, limpid and musical as bubbling springs, words which sparkle and glow like the poisoned diamonds of the Medicis! Oh the wickedness, the hopeless damnation of a soul who could fascinate and paralyze human creatures with such words,—words understood by the ignorant and wise alike, words which are more precious than jewels, more soothing than music, more awful than death!

We talked on, unmindful of the gathering shadows, and she was begging me to throw away the clasp of black onyx quaintly inlaid with what we now knew to be the Yellow Sign. I never shall know why I refused, though even at this hour, here in my bedroom as I write this confession, I should be glad to know *what* it was that prevented me from tearing the Yellow Sign from my breast and casting it into the fire. I am sure I wished to do so, and yet Tessie pleaded with me in vain. Night fell and the hours dragged on, but still we murmured to each other of the King and the Pallid Mask, and midnight sounded from the misty spires in the fog-wrapped city. We spoke of Hastur and of Cassilda, while outside the fog rolled against the blank window-panes as the cloud waves roll and break on the shores of Hali.

The house was very silent now and not a sound came up from the misty streets. Tessie lay among the cushions, her face a gray blot in the gloom, but her hands were clasped in mine and I knew that she knew and read my thoughts as I read hers, for we had understood the mystery of the Hyades and the Phantom of Truth was laid. Then as we answered each other, swiftly, silently, thought on thought, the shadows stirred in the gloom about us, and far in the distant streets we heard a sound. Nearer and nearer it came, the dull crunching of wheels, nearer and yet nearer, and now, outside before the door it ceased, and I dragged myself to the window and saw a black-plumed hearse. The gate below opened and shut, and I crept shaking to my door and bolted it, but I knew no bolts, no locks, could keep that creature out who was coming for the Yellow Sign. And now I heard him moving very softly along the hall. Now he was at the door, and the bolts rotted at his touch. Now he had entered. With eyes starting from my head I peered into the darkness, but when he came into the room I did not see him. It was only when I felt him envelop me in his cold soft grasp that I cried out and struggled with deadly fury, but my hands were useless and he tore the onyx clasp from my coat and struck me full in the face. Then, as I fell, I heard Tessie's soft cry and her spirit fled: and even while falling I longed to follow her, for I knew that the King in Yellow had opened his tattered mantle and there was only God to cry to now.

I could tell more, but I cannot see what help it will be to the world. As for me I am past human help or hope. As I lie here, writing, careless even whether or not I die before I finish, I can see the doctor gathering up his powders and phials with a vague gesture to the good priest beside me, which I understand.

They will be very curious to know the tragedy—they of the outside world who write books and print millions of newspapers, but I shall write no more, and the father confessor will seal my last words with the seal of sanctity when his holy office is done. They of the outside world may send their creatures into wrecked homes and death-smitten firesides, and their newspapers will batten on blood and tears, but with me their spies must halt before the confessional. They know that Tessie is dead and that I am dying. They know how the people in the house, aroused by an infernal scream, rushed into my room and found one living and two dead, but they do not know what I shall tell them now; they do not know that the doctor said as he pointed to a horrible decomposed heap on the floor—the livid corpse of the watchman from the church: "I have no theory, no explanation. That man must have been dead for months!"

I think I am dying. I wish the priest would——

HENRY JAMES

Henry James was born in 1843 in New York, the son of the philosopher Henry James, Sr., and the brother of the philosopher and psychologist William James. James and his brother received most of their education in a succession of schools in Europe, thereby gaining the cosmopolitanism that would color his outlook throughout his life. In 1862 he entered Harvard Law School but left after a year. In 1864 his first story was published; his first novel, *Watch and Ward,* appeared in 1871. In 1875 James permanently left the United States, settling in England in 1876. It was there that his most celebrated novels were written: *The American* (1877), *Daisy Miller* (1879), *Portrait of a Lady* (1881), *The Bostonians* (1886), *What Maisie Knew* (1897), *The Awkward Age* (1899), *The Wings of the Dove* (1902), *The Ambassadors* (1903), and *The Golden Bowl* (1903). Many of these novels examine, with an unparalleled subtlety of psychological analysis, the effect of sophisticated European culture upon Americans. James was naturalized as a British citizen in 1915. He died in London in 1916, shortly after receiving the Order of Merit.

For James, the supernatural was a lifelong concern, chiefly as a means of probing psychological states. Leon Edel's edition of *The Ghostly Tales of Henry James* (1949) includes eighteen short stories and novelettes written between 1868 and 1908, the most celebrated of which, *The*

Turn of the Screw (first published in *The Two Magics,* 1898), has spawned a veritable library of critical analysis, largely centering on whether the supernatural—in the form of the ghosts of the valet Peter Quint and the governess Miss Jessel, who appear to haunt two young children—actually comes into play. Other tales, such as "The Romance of Certain Old Clothes" (1868), a tale of jealousy between sisters, "Sir Edmund Orme" (1891), about a daytime ghost, and "The Jolly Corner" (1908), a story that dances between the supernatural and the psychological, are also well known. "The Real Right Thing" (first published in *Collier's Weekly,* December 16, 1899) is another ambiguous tale, in which we can never be certain whether the ghost of a dead author has genuinely manifested itself.

THE REAL RIGHT THING

I

When, after the death of Ashton Doyne—but three months after—George Withermore was approached, as the phrase is, on the subject of a "volume," the communication came straight from his publishers, who had been, and indeed much more, Doyne's own; but he was not surprised to learn, on the occurrence of the interview they next suggested, that a certain pressure as to the early issue of a Life had been applied them by their late client's widow. Doyne's relations with his wife had been to Withermore's knowledge a special chapter—which would present itself, by the way, as a delicate one for the biographer; but a sense of what she had lost, and even of what she had lacked, had betrayed itself, on the poor woman's part, from the first days of her bereavement, sufficiently to prepare an observer at all initiated for some attitude of reparation, some espousal even exaggerated of the interests of a distinguished name. George Withermore was, as he felt, initiated; yet what he had not expected was to hear that she had mentioned him as the person in whose hands she would most promptly place the materials for a book.

These materials—diaries, letters, memoranda, notes, documents of many sorts—were her property and wholly in her control, no conditions at all attaching to any portion of her heritage; so that she was free at present to do as she liked—free in particular to do nothing. What Doyne would have arranged had he had time to arrange could be but supposition and guess. Death had taken him too soon and too suddenly, and there was all the pity that the only wishes he was known to have expressed were wishes leaving it positively out. He had broken short off—that was the way of it; and the end was ragged and needed trimming. Withermore was conscious, abundantly, of how close he had stood to him, but also was not less aware of his comparative obscurity. He was young, a journalist, a critic, a hand-to-mouth character, with little, as yet, of any striking sort, to show. His writings were few and small, his relations scant and vague. Doyne, on the other hand, had lived long enough—above all had had talent enough—to become great, and among his many friends gilded also with greatness were several to whom his wife would have affected those who knew her as much more likely to appeal.

The preference she had at all events uttered—and uttered in a roundabout considerate way that left him a measure of freedom—made our young man feel that he must at least see her and that there would be in any case a good deal to talk about. He immediately wrote to her, she as promptly named an hour, and they had it out. But he came away with his particular idea immensely strengthened. She was a strange woman, and he had never thought her an agreeable, yet there was something that touched him now in her bustling blundering zeal. She wanted the book to make up, and the individual whom, of her husband's set, she probably believed she might most manipulate was in every way to help it to do so. She hadn't taken Doyne seriously enough in life, but the biography should be a full reply to every imputation on herself. She had scantly known how such books were constructed, but she had been looking and had learned something. It alarmed Withermore a little from the first to see that she'd wish to go in for quantity. She talked of "volumes," but he had his notion of that.

"My thought went straight to *you*, as his own would have done," she had said almost as soon as she rose before him there in her large array of mourning—with her big black eyes, her big black wig, her big black fan and gloves, her general gaunt ugly tragic, but striking and, as might have been thought from a certain point of view, "elegant" presence. "You're the one he liked most; oh *much!*"—and it had quite sufficed to turn Withermore's head. It little mattered that he could afterwards wonder if she had known Doyne enough, when it came to that, to be sure. He would have said for himself indeed that her testimony on such a point could scarcely count. Still, there was no smoke without fire; she knew at least what she meant, and he wasn't a person she could have an interest in flattering. They went up together without delay to the great man's vacant study at the back of the house and looking over the large green garden—a beautiful and inspiring scene to poor Withermore's view—common to the expensive row.

"You can perfectly work here, you know," said Mrs. Doyne: "you shall have the place quite to yourself—I'll give it all up to you; so that in the evenings in particular, don't you see? It will be perfection for quiet and privacy."

Perfection indeed, the young man felt as he looked about—having explained that, as his actual occupation was an evening paper and his earlier hours, for a long time yet, regularly taken up, he should have to come always at night. The place was full of their lost friend; everything in it had belonged to him; everything they touched had been part of his life. It was all at once too much for Withermore—too great an honour and even too great a care; memories still recent came back to him, so that, while his heart beat faster and his eyes filled with tears, the pressure of his loyalty seemed almost more than he could carry. At the sight of his tears Mrs. Doyne's own rose to her lids, and the two for a minute only looked at each other. He half-expected her to break out "Oh help me to feel as I know you know I want to feel!" And after a little one of them said, with the other's deep assent—it didn't matter which: "It's here that we're *with* him." But it was definitely the young man who put it, before they left the room, that it was there he was with themselves.

The young man began to come as soon as he could arrange it, and then it was, on the spot, in the charmed stillness, between the lamp and the fire and with the curtains drawn, that a certain intenser consciousness set in for him. He escaped from the black London November; he passed through the large hushed house and up the red-carpeted staircase where he only found in his path the whisk of a soundless trained maid or the reach, out of an open room, of Mrs. Doyne's queenly weeds and approving tragic face; and then, by a mere touch of the well-made door that gave so sharp and pleasant a click, shut himself in for three or four warm hours with the spirit—as he had always distinctly declared it—of his master. He was not a little frightened when, even the first night, it came over him that he had really been most affected, in the whole matter, by the prospect, the privilege and the luxury, of this sensation. He hadn't, he could now reflect, definitely considered the question of the book—as to which there was here even already much to consider: he had simply let his affection and admiration—to say nothing of his gratified pride—meet to the full the temptation Mrs. Doyne had offered them.

How did he know without more thought, he might begin to ask himself, that the book was on the whole to be desired? What warrant had he ever received from Ashton Doyne himself for so direct and, as it were, so familiar an approach? Great was the art of biography, but there were lives and lives, there were subjects and subjects. He confusedly recalled, so far as that went, old words dropped by Doyne over contemporary compilations, suggestions of how he himself discriminated as to other heroes and other panoramas. He even remembered how his friend would at moments have shown himself as holding that the "literary" career might—save in the case of a Johnson and a Scott, with a Boswell and a Lockhart to help—best content itself to be represented. The artist was what he *did*—he was nothing else. Yet how on the other hand wasn't *he*, George Withermore, poor devil, to have jumped at the chance of spending his winter in an intimacy so rich? It had been simply dazzling—that was the fact. It hadn't been the "terms," from the publishers—though these were, as they said at the office, all right; it had been Doyne himself, his company and contact and presence, it had been just what it was turning out, the possibility of an intercourse closer than that of life. Strange that death, of the two things, should have the fewer mysteries and secrets! The first night our young man was alone in the room it struck him his master and he were really for the first time together.

II

Mrs. Doyne had for the most part let him expressively alone, but she had on two or three occasions looked in to see if his needs had been met, and he had had the opportunity of thanking her on the spot for the judgement and zeal with which she had smoothed his way. She had to some extent herself been looking things over and had been able already to muster several groups of letters; all the keys of drawers and cabinets she had moreover from the first placed in his hands, with helpful information as to the apparent whereabouts of different matters. She had put him, to be brief, in the fullest possible possession, and whether or no her husband had trusted her she at least, it was clear, trusted her husband's friend. There grew upon Withermore nevertheless the impression that in spite of all these offices she wasn't yet at peace and that a certain unassuageable anxiety continued even to keep step with her confidence. Though so full of consideration she was at the same time perceptibly *there:* he felt her, through a supersubtle sixth sense that the whole connexion had already brought into play, hover, in the still hours, at the top of landings and on the other side of doors; he gathered from the soundless brush of her skirts the hint of her watchings and waitings. One evening when, at his friend's table, he had lost himself in the depths of correspondence, he was made to start and turn by the suggestion that some one was behind him. Mrs. Doyne had come in without his hearing the door, and she gave a strained smile, as he sprang to his feet. "I hope," she said, "I haven't frightened you."

"Just a little—I was so absorbed. It was as if, for the instant," the young man explained, "it had been himself."

The oddity of her face increased in her wonder. "Ashton?"

"He does seem so near," said Withermore.

"To you too?"

This naturally struck him. "He does then to you?"

She waited, not moving from the spot where she had first stood, but looking round the room as if to penetrate its duskier angles. She had a way of raising to the level of her nose the big black fan which she apparently never laid aside and with which she thus covered the lower half of her face, her rather hard eyes, above it, becoming the more ambiguous. "Sometimes."

"Here," Withermore went on, "it's as if he might at any moment come in. That's why I jumped just now. The time's so short since he really used to—it only *was* yesterday. I sit in his chair, I turn his books, I use his pens, I stir his fire—all exactly as if, learning he would presently be back from a walk, I had come up here contentedly to wait. It's delightful—but it's strange."

Mrs. Doyne, her fan still up, listened with interest. "Does it worry you?"

"No—I like it."

Again she faltered. "Do you ever feel as if he were—a—quite—a—personally in the room?"

"Well, as I said just now," her companion laughed, "on hearing you behind me I seemed to take it so. What do we want, after all," he asked, "but that he shall be with us?"

"Yes, as you said he'd be—that first time." She gazed in full assent. "He *is* with us."

She was rather portentous, but Withermore took it smiling. "Then we must keep him. We must do only what he'd like."

"Oh only that of course—only. But if he *is* here——?" And her sombre eyes seemed to throw it out in vague distress over her fan.

"It proves he's pleased and wants only to help? Yes, surely; it must prove that."

She gave a light gasp and looked again round the room. "Well," she said as she took leave of him, "remember that I too want only to help." On which, when she had gone, he felt sufficiently that she had come in simply to see he was all right.

He was all right more and more, it struck him after this, for as he began to get into his work he moved, as it appeared to him, but the closer to the idea of Doyne's personal presence. When once this fancy had begun to hang about him he welcomed it, persuaded it, encouraged it, quite cherished it, looking forward all day to feeling it renew itself in the evening, and waiting for the growth of dusk very much as one of a pair of lovers might wait for the hour of their appointment. The smallest accidents humoured and confirmed it, and by the end of three or four weeks he had come fully to regard it as the consecration of his enterprise. Didn't it just settle the question of what Doyne would have thought of what they were doing? What they were doing was what he wanted done, and they could go on from step to step without scruple or doubt. Withermore rejoiced indeed at moments to feel this certitude: there were times of dipping deep into some of Doyne's secrets when it was particularly pleasant to be able to hold that Doyne desired him, as it were, to know them. He was learning many things he hadn't suspected—drawing many curtains, forcing many doors, reading many riddles, going, in general, as they said, behind almost everything. It was at an occasional sharp turn of some of the duskier of these wanderings "behind" that he really, of a sudden, most felt himself, in the intimate sensible way, face to face with his friend; so that he could scarce have told, for the instant, if their meeting occurred in the narrow passage and tight squeeze of the past or at the hour and in the place that actually held him. Was it a matter of '67?—or but of the other side of the table?

Happily, at any rate, even in the vulgarest light publicity could ever shed, there would be the great fact of the way Doyne was "coming out." He was coming out too beautifully—better yet than such a partisan as Withermore could have supposed. All the while as well, nevertheless, how would this partisan have represented to any one else the special state of his own consciousness? It wasn't a thing to talk about—it was only a thing to feel. There were moments for instance when, while he bent over his papers, the light breath of his dead host was as distinctly in his hair as his own elbows were on the table before him. There were moments when, had he been able to look up, the other side of the table would have shown him this companion as vividly as the shaded lamplight showed him his page. That he couldn't at such a juncture look up was his own affair, for the situation was ruled—that was but natural—by deep delicacies and fine timidities, the dread of too sudden or too rude an advance. What was intensely in the air was that if Doyne *was* there it wasn't nearly so much for himself as for the young priest of his altar. He hovered and lingered, he came and went, he might almost have been, among the books and the papers, a hushed discreet librarian, doing the particular things, rendering the quiet aid, liked by men of letters.

Withermore himself meanwhile came and went, changed his place, wandered on quests either definite or vague; and more than once when, taking a book down from a shelf and finding in it marks of Doyne's pencil, he got drawn on and lost he had heard documents on the table behind him gently shifted and stirred, had literally, on his return, found some letter mislaid pushed again into view, some thicket cleared by the opening of an old journal at the very date he wanted. How should he have gone so, on occasion, to the special box or drawer, out of fifty receptacles, that would help him, had not his mystic assistant happened, in fine prevision, to tilt its lid or pull it half-open, just in the way that would catch his eye?—in spite, after all, of the fact of lapses and intervals in which, *could* one have really looked, one would have seen somebody standing before the fire a trifle detached and over-erect—somebody fixing one the least bit harder than in life.

III

That this auspicious relation had in fact existed, had continued, for two or three weeks, was sufficiently shown by the dawn of the distress with which our young man found himself aware of having, for some reason, from the close of a certain day, begun to miss it. The sign of that was an abrupt surprised sense—on the occasion of his mislaying a marvellous unpublished page which, hunt where he would, remained stupidly irrecoverably lost—that his protected state was, with all said, exposed to some confusion and even to some depression. If, for the joy of the business, Doyne and he had, from the start, been together, the situation had within a few days of his first suspicion of it suffered the odd change of their ceasing to be so. That was what was the matter, he mused, from the moment an impression of mere mass and quantity struck him as taking, in his happy outlook at his material, the place of the pleasant assumption of a clear course and a quick pace. For five nights he struggled; then, never at his table, wandering about the room, taking up his references only to lay them down, looking out of the window, poking the fire, thinking strange thoughts and listening for signs and sounds not as he suspected or imagined, but as he vainly desired and invoked them, he yielded to the view that he was for the time at least forsaken.

The extraordinary thing thus became that it made him not only sad but in a high degree uneasy not to feel Doyne's presence. It was somehow stranger he shouldn't be there than it had ever been he *was*—so strange indeed at last that Withermore's nerves found themselves quite illogically touched. They had taken kindly enough to what was of an order impossible to explain, perversely reserving their sharpest state for the return to the normal, the supersession of the false. They were remarkably beyond control when finally, one night after his resisting them an hour or two, he simply edged out of the room. It had now but for the first time become impossible to him to stay. Without design, but panting a little and positively as a man scared, he passed along his usual corridor and reached the top of the staircase. From this point he saw Mrs. Doyne look up at him from the bottom quite as if she had known he would come; and the most singular thing of all was that, though he had been conscious of no motion to resort to her, had only been prompted to relieve himself by escape, the sight of her position made him recognise it as just, quickly feel it as a part of some monstrous oppression that was closing over them both. It was wonderful how, in the mere modern London hall, between the Tottenham Court Road rugs and the electric light, it came up to him from the tall black lady, and went again from him down to her, that he knew what she meant by looking as if he would know. He descended straight, she turned into her own little lower room, and there, the next thing, with the door shut, they were, still in silence and with queer faces, confronted over confessions that had taken sudden life from these two or three movements. Withermore gasped as it came to him why he had lost his friend. "He has been with *you?*"

With this it was all out—out so far that neither had to explain and that, when "What do you suppose is the matter?" quickly passed between them, one appeared to have said it as much as the other. Withermore looked about at the small bright room in which, night after night, she had been living her life as he had been living his own upstairs. It was pretty, cosy, rosy; but she had by turns felt in it what he had felt and heard in it what he had heard. Her effect there—fantastic black, plumed and extravagant, upon deep pink—was that of some "decadent" coloured print, some poster of the newest school. "You understood he had left me?" he asked.

She markedly wished to make it clear. "This evening—yes. I've made things out."

"You knew—before—that he was with me?"

She hesitated again. "I felt he wasn't with *me*. But on the stairs—"

"Yes?"

"Well—he passed; more than once. He was in the house. And at your door—"

"Well?" he went on as she once more faltered.

"If I stopped I could sometimes tell. And from your face," she added, "to-night, at any rate, I knew your state."

"And that was why you came out?"

"I thought you'd come to me."

He put out to her, on this, his hand, and they thus for a minute of silence held each other clasped. There was no peculiar presence for either now—nothing more peculiar than that of each for the other. But the place had suddenly become as if consecrated, and Withermore played over it again his anxiety. "What *is* then the matter?"

"I only want to do the real right thing," she returned after her pause.

"And aren't we doing it?"

"I wonder. Aren't *you*?"

He wondered too. "To the best of my belief. But we must think."

"We must think," she echoed. And they did think—thought with intensity the rest of that evening together, and thought independently (Withermore at least could answer for himself) during many days that followed. He intermitted a little his visits and his work, trying, all critically, to catch himself in the act of some mistake that might have accounted for their disturbance. Had he taken, on some important point—or looked as if he might take—some wrong line or wrong view? had he somewhere benightedly falsified or inadequately insisted? He went back at last with the idea of having guessed two or three questions he might have been on the way to muddle; after which he had abovestairs, another period of agitation, presently followed by another interview below with Mrs. Doyne, who was still troubled and flushed.

"He's there?"

"He's there."

"I knew it!" she returned in an odd gloom of triumph. Then as to make it clear: "He hasn't been again with *me*."

"Nor with me again to help," said Withermore.

She considered. "Not to help?"

"I can't make it out—I'm at sea. Do what I will I feel I'm wrong."

She covered him a moment with her pompous pain. "How do you feel it?"

"Why by things that happen. The strangest things. I can't describe them—and you wouldn't believe them."

"Oh yes I should!" Mrs. Doyne cried.

"Well, he intervenes." Withermore tried to explain. "However I turn I find him."

She earnestly followed. "'Find' him?"

"I meet him. He seems to rise there before me."

Staring, she waited a little. "Do you mean you see him?"

"I feel as if at any moment I may. I'm baffled. I'm checked." Then he added: "I'm afraid."

"Of *him*?" asked Mrs. Doyne.

He thought. "Well—of what I'm doing."

"Then what, that's so awful, *are* you doing?"

"What you proposed to me. Going into his life."

She showed, in her present gravity, a new alarm. "And don't you *like* that?"

"Doesn't *he?* That's the question. We lay him bare. We serve him up. What is it called? We give him to the world."

Poor Mrs. Doyne, as if on a menace to her hard atonement, glared at this for an instant in deeper gloom. "And why shouldn't we?"

"Because we don't know. There are natures, there are lives, that shrink. He mayn't wish it," said Withermore. "We never asked him."

"How *could* we?"

He was silent a little. "Well, we ask him now. That's after all what our start has so far represented. We've put it to him."

"Then—if he has been with us—we've had his answer."

Withermore spoke now as if he knew what to believe. "He hasn't been 'with' us—he has been against us."

"Then why did you think—"

"What I *did* think at first—that what he wishes to make us feel is his sympathy? Because I was in my original simplicity mistaken. I was—I don't know what to call it—so excited and charmed that I didn't understand. But I understand at last. He only wanted to communicate. He strains forward out of his darkness, he reaches toward us out of his mystery, he makes us dim signs out of his horror."

"'Horror'?" Mrs. Doyne gasped with her fan up to her mouth.

"At what we're doing." He could by this time piece it all together. "I see now that at first—"

"Well, what?"

"One had simply to feel he was there and therefore not indifferent. And the beauty of that misled me. But he's there as a protest."

"Against *my* Life?" Mrs. Doyne wailed.

"Against *any* Life. He's there to *save* his Life. He's there to be let alone."

"So you give up?" she almost shrieked.

He could only meet her. "He's there as a warning."

For a moment, on this, they looked at each other deep. "You *are* afraid!" she at last brought out.

It affected him, but he insisted. "He's there as a curse!"

With that they parted, but only for two or three days; her last word to him continuing to sound so in his ears that, between his need really to satisfy her and another need presently to be noted, he felt he mightn't yet take up his stake. He finally went back at his usual hour and found her in her usual place. "Yes, I *am* afraid," he announced as if he had turned that well over and knew now all it meant. "But I gather you're not."

She faltered, reserving her word. "What is it you fear?"

"Well, that if I go on I *shall* see him."

"And then—?"

"Oh then," said George Withermore, "I *should* give up!"

She weighed it with her proud but earnest air. "I think, you know, we must have a clear sign."

"You wish me to try again?"

She debated. "You see what it means—for me—to give up."

"Ah but *you* needn't," Withermore said.

She seemed to wonder, but in a moment went on. "It would mean that he won't take from me—" But she dropped for despair.

"Well, what?"

"Anything," said poor Mrs. Doyne.

He faced her a moment more. "I've thought myself of the clear sign. I'll try again."

As he was leaving her however she remembered. "I'm only afraid that to-night there's nothing ready—no lamp and no fire."

"Never mind," he said from the foot of the stairs; "I'll find things."

To which she answered that the door of the room would probably at any rate be open; and retired again as to wait for him. She hadn't long to wait; though, with her own door wide and her attention fixed, she may not have taken the time quite as it appeared to her visitor. She heard him, after an interval, on the stair, and he presently stood at her entrance, where, if he hadn't been precipitate, but rather, for step and sound, backward and vague, he showed at least as livid and blank.

"I give up."

"Then you've seen him?"

"On the threshold—guarding it."

"Guarding it?" She glowed over her fan. "Distinct?"

"Immense. But dim. Dark. Dreadful," said poor George Withermore.

She continued to wonder. "You didn't go in?"

The young man turned away. "He forbids!"

"You say *I* needn't," she went on after a moment. "Well then need I?"

"See him?" George Withermore asked.

She waited an instant. "Give up."

"You must decide." For himself he could at last but sink to the sofa with his bent face in his hands. He wasn't quite to know afterwards how long he had sat so; it was enough that what he did next know was that he was alone among her favourite objects. Just as he gained his feet however, with this sense and that of the door standing open to the hall, he found himself afresh confronted, in the light, the warmth, the rosy space, with her big black perfumed presence. He saw at a glance, as she offered him a huger bleaker stare over the mask of her fan, that she had been above; and so it was that they for the last time faced together their strange question. "You've seen him?" Withermore asked.

He was to infer later on from the extraordinary way she closed her eyes and, as if to steady herself, held them tight and long, in silence, that beside the unutterable vision of Ashton Doyne's wife his own might rank as an escape. He knew before she spoke that all was over. "I give up."

H. P. LOVECRAFT

Howard Phillips Lovecraft was born in 1890 in Providence, Rhode Island, where he remained for most of his life. Plagued by illness, Lovecraft led a sheltered life in youth; his upbringing was conducted by his overly protective mother, his aunts, and—following the death of his father from syphilis in 1898—by his maternal grandfather, Whipple Van Buren Phillips, a successful businessman. Lovecraft's formal education was spotty, and poor health compelled his departure from high school in 1908 without a diploma. After a period of reclusiveness, he joined the amateur journalism movement, prolifically writing essays, poems, and a few stories during the period 1914–1924. The founding of the pulp magazine *Weird Tales* allowed him to sell his early horror tales with regularity, and he became a fixture in the magazine. After a failed marriage and a move to Brooklyn (1924–26), Lovecraft returned to Providence and began his most vigorous period of fiction writing, with such works as "The Colour out of Space" (1927), "The Dunwich Horror" (1928), "The Whisperer in Darkness" (1930), *At the Mountains of Madness* (1931), and "The Shadow Out of Time" (1934–35). In these works, Lovecraft fashioned a pseudomythology that August Derleth later coined the "Cthulhu Mythos," which postulates the existence of immense, godlike forces who have come to earth from the depths of space; this mythology embodies

Lovecraft's strongly atheistic stance, in which humanity is a helpless pawn amid the infinite depths of the universe. The Cthulhu Mythos has been widely imitated by other writers, although many (including Derleth) misunderstood its philosophical substance. Lovecraft died in Providence in 1937. Derleth and Donald Wandrei founded the publishing firm of Arkham House to issue Lovecraft's works in book form, and he has since become recognized as the leading American writer of supernatural fiction in the twentieth century.

"The Call of Cthulhu," written in 1926 and published in *Weird Tales* (February 1928), is the first major tale of the Cthulhu Mythos and features Lovecraft's use of the documentary style and his dense, richly evocative prose style.

THE CALL OF CTHULHU

(Found Among the Papers of
the Late Francis Wayland Thurston, of Boston)

"Of such great powers or beings there may be conceivably a
survival . . . a survival of a hugely remote period when . . .
consciousness was manifested, perhaps, in shapes and forms
long since withdrawn before the tide of advancing
humanity . . . forms of which poetry and legend alone have
caught a flying memory and called them gods, monsters,
mythical beings of all sorts and kinds. . . ."

—*Algernon Blackwood*

I
THE HORROR IN CLAY

he most merciful thing in the world, I think, is the inabil-
ity of the human mind to correlate all its contents. We live
on a placid island of ignorance in the midst of black seas of infinity, and it was not meant that we should voyage far. The sciences, each straining in its own direction, have hitherto harmed
us little; but some day the piecing together of dissociated knowledge will open up such terrifying vistas of reality, and of our
frightful position therein, that we shall either go mad from the
revelation or flee from the deadly light into the peace and safety
of a new dark age.

Theosophists have guessed at the awesome grandeur of the
cosmic cycle wherein our world and human race form transient
incidents. They have hinted at strange survivals in terms which

would freeze the blood if not masked by a bland optimism. But it is not from them that there came the single glimpse of forbidden aeons which chills me when I think of it and maddens me when I dream of it. That glimpse, like all dread glimpses of truth, flashed out from an accidental piecing together of separated things—in this case an old newspaper item and the notes of a dead professor. I hope that no one else will accomplish this piecing out; certainly, if I live, I shall never knowingly supply a link in so hideous a chain. I think that the professor, too, intended to keep silent regarding the part he knew, and that he would have destroyed his notes had not sudden death seized him.

My knowledge of the thing began in the winter of 1926–27 with the death of my grand-uncle George Gammell Angell, Professor Emeritus of Semitic Languages in Brown University, Providence, Rhode Island. Professor Angell was widely known as an authority on ancient inscriptions, and had frequently been resorted to by the heads of prominent museums; so that his passing at the age of ninety-two may be recalled by many. Locally, interest was intensified by the obscurity of the cause of death. The professor had been stricken whilst returning from the Newport boat; falling suddenly, as witnesses said, after having been jostled by a nautical-looking negro who had come from one of the queer dark courts on the precipitous hillside which formed a short cut from the waterfront to the deceased's home in Williams Street. Physicians were unable to find any visible disorder, but concluded after perplexed debate that some obscure lesion of the heart, induced by the brisk ascent of so steep a hill by so elderly a man, was responsible for the end. At the time I saw no reason to dissent from this dictum, but latterly I am inclined to wonder—and more than wonder.

As my grand-uncle's heir and executor, for he died a childless widower, I was expected to go over his papers with some thoroughness; and for that purpose moved his entire set of files and boxes to my quarters in Boston. Much of the material which I correlated will be later published by the American Archaeological Society, but there was one box which I found exceedingly puzzling, and which I felt much averse from shewing to other eyes. It had been locked, and I did not find the key till it occurred to me to examine the personal ring which the professor carried always in his pocket. Then indeed I succeeded in opening it, but when I did so seemed only to be confronted by a greater and more closely locked barrier. For what could be the meaning of the queer clay bas-relief and the disjointed jottings, ramblings, and cuttings which I found? Had my uncle, in his latter years, become credulous of the most superficial impostures? I resolved to search out the eccentric sculptor responsible for this apparent disturbance of an old man's peace of mind.

The bas-relief was a rough rectangle less than an inch thick and about five by six inches in area; obviously of modern origin. Its designs, however, were far from modern in atmosphere and suggestion; for although the vagaries of cubism and futurism are many and wild, they do not often reproduce that cryptic regularity which lurks in prehistoric writing. And writing of some kind the bulk of these designs seemed certainly to be; though my memory, despite much familiarity with the papers and collections of my uncle, failed in any way to identify this particular species, or even to hint at its remotest affiliations.

Above these apparent hieroglyphics was a figure of evidently pictorial intent, though its impressionistic execution forbade a very clear idea of its nature. It seemed to be a sort of monster, or symbol representing a monster, of a form which only a diseased fancy could conceive. If I say that my somewhat extravagant imagination yielded simultaneous pictures of an octopus, a dragon, and a human caricature, I shall not be unfaithful to the spirit of the thing. A pulpy, tentacled head surmounted a grotesque and scaly body with rudimentary wings; but it was the *general outline* of the whole which made it most shockingly frightful. Behind the figure was a vague suggestion of a Cyclopean architectural background.

The writing accompanying this oddity was, aside from a stack of press cuttings, in Professor Angell's most recent hand; and made no pretence to literary style. What seemed to be the main document was headed "CTHULHU CULT" in characters painstakingly printed to avoid the erroneous reading of a word so unheard-of. This manuscript was divided into two sections, the first of which was headed "1925—Dream and Dream Work of H. A. Wilcox, 7 Thomas St., Providence, R.I.", and the second, "Narrative of Inspector John R. Legrasse, 121 Bienville St., New Orleans, La., at 1908 A. A. S. Mtg.—Notes on Same, & Prof. Webb's Acct." The other manuscript papers were all brief notes, some of them accounts of the queer dreams of different persons, some of them citations from theosophical books and magazines (notably W. Scott-Elliot's *Atlantis and the Lost Lemuria*), and the rest comments on long-surviving secret societies and hidden cults, with references to passages in such mythological and anthropological source-books as Frazer's *Golden Bough* and Miss Murray's *Witch-Cult in Western Europe*. The cuttings largely alluded to outré mental illnesses and outbreaks of group folly or mania in the spring of 1925.

The first half of the principal manuscript told a very peculiar tale. It appears that on March 1st, 1925, a thin, dark young man of neurotic and excited aspect had called upon Professor Angell bearing the singular clay bas-relief, which was then exceedingly damp and fresh. His card bore the name of Henry Anthony Wilcox, and my uncle had recognised him as the youngest son of an excellent family slightly known to him, who had latterly been studying sculpture at the Rhode Island School of Design and living alone at the Fleur-de-Lys Building near that institution. Wilcox was a precocious youth of known genius but great eccentricity, and had from childhood excited attention through the strange stories and odd dreams he was in the habit of relating. He called himself "psychically hypersensitive", but the staid folk of the ancient commercial city dismissed him as merely "queer". Never mingling much with his kind, he had dropped gradually from social visibility, and was now known only to a small group of aesthetes from other towns. Even the Providence Art Club, anxious to preserve its conservatism, had found him quite hopeless.

On the occasion of the visit, ran the professor's manuscript, the sculptor abruptly asked for the benefit of his host's archaeological knowledge in identifying the hieroglyphics on the bas-relief. He spoke in a dreamy, stilted manner which suggested pose and alienated sympathy; and my uncle shewed some sharpness in replying, for the conspicuous freshness of the tablet implied kinship with anything but archaeology. Young Wilcox's rejoinder, which impressed my uncle enough to make him recall and record it verbatim, was of a fantastically poetic cast which must have typified his whole conversation, and which I have since found highly characteristic of him. He said, "It is new, indeed, for I made it last night in a dream of strange cities; and dreams are older than brooding Tyre, or the contemplative Sphinx, or garden-girdled Babylon."

It was then that he began that rambling tale which suddenly played upon a sleeping memory and won the fevered interest of my uncle. There had been a slight earthquake tremor the night before, the most considerable felt in New England for some years; and Wilcox's imagination had been keenly affected. Upon retiring, he had had an unprecedented dream of great Cyclopean cities of titan blocks and sky-flung monoliths, all dripping with green ooze and sinister with latent horror. Hieroglyphics had covered the walls and pillars, and from some undetermined point below had come a voice that was not a voice; a chaotic sensation which only fancy could transmute into sound, but which he attempted to render by the almost unpronounceable jumble of letters, *"Cthulhu fhtagn."*

This verbal jumble was the key to the recollection which excited and disturbed Professor Angell. He questioned the sculptor with scientific minuteness; and studied with almost frantic intensity the bas-relief on which the youth had found himself working, chilled and clad only in his night-clothes, when waking had stolen bewilderingly over him. My uncle blamed his old age, Wilcox afterward said, for his slowness in recognising both hieroglyphics and pictorial design. Many of his questions seemed highly out-of-place to his visitor, especially those which tried to connect the latter with strange cults or societies; and Wilcox could not understand the repeated promises of silence which he was offered in exchange for an admission of membership in some widespread mystical or paganly religious body. When Professor Angell became convinced that the sculptor was indeed ignorant of any cult or system of cryptic lore, he besieged his visitor with demands for future reports of dreams. This bore regular fruit, for after the first interview the manuscript records daily calls of the young man, during which he related startling fragments of nocturnal imagery whose burden was always some terrible Cyclopean vista of dark and dripping stone, with a subterrene voice or intelligence shouting monotonously in enigmatical sense-impacts uninscribable save as gibberish. The two sounds most frequently repeated are those rendered by the letters *"Cthulhu"* and *"R'lyeh."*

On March 23d, the manuscript continued, Wilcox failed to appear; and inquiries at his quarters revealed that he had been stricken with an obscure sort of fever and taken to the home of his family in Waterman Street. He had cried out in the night, arousing several other artists in the building, and had manifested since then only alternations of unconsciousness and delirium. My uncle at once telephoned the family, and from that time forward kept close watch of the case; calling often at the Thayer Street office of Dr. Tobey, whom he learned to be in charge. The youth's febrile mind, apparently, was dwelling on strange things; and the doctor shuddered now and then as he spoke of them. They included not only a repetition of what he had formerly dreamed, but touched wildly on a gigantic thing "miles high" which walked or lumbered about. He at no time fully described this object, but occasional frantic words, as repeated by Dr. Tobey, convinced the professor that it must be identical with the nameless monstrosity he had sought to depict in his dream-sculpture. Reference to this object, the doctor added, was invariably a prelude to the young man's subsidence into lethargy. His temperature, oddly enough, was not greatly above normal; but his whole condition was otherwise such as to suggest true fever rather than mental disorder.

On April 2nd at about 3 p.m. every trace of Wilcox's malady suddenly ceased. He sat upright in bed, astonished to find himself at home and completely ignorant of what had happened in dream or reality since the night of March 22nd. Pronounced well by his physician, he returned to his quarters in three days; but to Professor Angell he was of no further assistance. All traces of strange dreaming had vanished with his recovery, and my uncle kept no record of his night-thoughts after a week of pointless and irrelevant accounts of thoroughly usual visions.

Here the first part of the manuscript ended, but references to certain of the scattered notes gave me much material for thought—so much, in fact, that only the ingrained scepticism then forming my philosophy can account for my continued distrust of the artist. The notes in question were those descriptive of the dreams of various persons covering the same period as that in which young Wilcox had had his strange visitations. My uncle, it seems, had quickly instituted a prodigiously far-flung body of inquiries amongst nearly all the friends whom he could question without impertinence, asking for nightly reports of their dreams, and the dates of any notable visions for some time past. The reception of his request seems to have been varied; but he must, at the very least, have received more responses than any ordinary man could have handled without a secretary. This original correspondence was not preserved, but his notes formed a thorough and really significant digest. Average people in society and business—New England's traditional "salt of the earth"—gave an almost completely negative result, though scattered cases of uneasy but formless nocturnal impressions appear here and there, always between March 23d and April 2nd—the period of young Wilcox's delirium. Scientific men were little more affected, though four cases of vague description suggest fugitive glimpses of strange landscapes, and in one case there is mentioned a dread of something abnormal.

It was from the artists and poets that the pertinent answers came, and I know that panic would have broken loose had they been able to compare notes. As it was, lacking their original letters, I half suspected the compiler of having asked leading questions, or of having edited the correspondence in corroboration of what he had latently resolved to see. That is why I continued to feel that Wilcox, somehow cognisant of the old data which my uncle had possessed, had been imposing on the veteran scientist. These responses from aesthetes told a disturbing tale. From February 28th to April 2nd a large proportion of them had dreamed very bizarre things, the intensity of the dreams being immeasurably the stronger during the period of the sculptor's delirium. Over a fourth of those who reported anything, reported scenes and half-sounds not unlike those which

Wilcox had described; and some of the dreamers confessed acute fear of the gigantic nameless thing visible toward the last. One case, which the note describes with emphasis, was very sad. The subject, a widely known architect with leanings toward theosophy and occultism, went violently insane on the date of young Wilcox's seizure, and expired several months later after incessant screamings to be saved from some escaped denizen of hell. Had my uncle referred to these cases by name instead of merely by number, I should have attempted some corroboration and personal investigation; but as it was, I succeeded in tracing down only a few. All of these, however, bore out the notes in full. I have often wondered if all the objects of the professor's questioning felt as puzzled as did this fraction. It is well that no explanation shall ever reach them.

The press cuttings, as I have intimated, touched on cases of panic, mania, and eccentricity during the given period. Professor Angell must have employed a cutting bureau, for the number of extracts was tremendous and the sources scattered throughout the globe. Here was a nocturnal suicide in London, where a lone sleeper had leaped from a window after a shocking cry. Here likewise a rambling letter to the editor of a paper in South America, where a fanatic deduces a dire future from visions he has seen. A despatch from California describes a theosophist colony as donning white robes en masse for some "glorious fulfilment" which never arrives, whilst items from India speak guardedly of serious native unrest toward the end of March. Voodoo orgies multiply in Hayti, and African outposts report ominous mutterings. American officers in the Philippines find certain tribes bothersome about this time, and New York policemen are mobbed by hysterical Levantines on the night of March 22–23. The west of Ireland, too, is full of wild rumour and legendry, and a fantastic painter named Ardois-Bonnot hangs a blasphemous "Dream Landscape" in the Paris spring salon of 1926. And so numerous are the recorded troubles in insane asylums, that only a miracle can have stopped the medical fraternity from noting strange parallelisms and drawing mystified conclusions. A weird bunch of cuttings, all told; and I can at this date scarcely envisage the callous rationalism with which I set them aside. But I was then convinced that young Wilcox had known of the older matters mentioned by the professor.

II
THE TALE OF INSPECTOR LEGRASSE

The older matters which had made the sculptor's dream and bas-relief so significant to my uncle formed the subject of the second half of his long manuscript. Once before, it appears, Professor Angell had seen the hellish outlines of the nameless monstrosity, puzzled over the unknown hieroglyphics, and heard the ominous syllables which can be rendered only as *"Cthulhu"*; and all this in so stirring and horrible a connexion that it is small wonder he pursued young Wilcox with queries and demands for data.

This earlier experience had come in 1908, seventeen years before, when the American Archaeological Society held its annual meeting in St. Louis. Professor Angell, as befitted one of his authority and attainments, had had a prominent part in all the deliberations; and was one of the first to be approached by the several outsiders who took advantage of the convocation to offer questions for correct answering and problems for expert solution.

The chief of these outsiders, and in a short time the focus of interest for the entire meeting, was a commonplace-looking middle-aged man who had travelled all the way from New Orleans for certain special information unobtainable from any local source. His name was John Raymond Legrasse, and he was by profession an Inspector of Police. With him he bore the subject of his visit, a grotesque, repulsive, and apparently very ancient stone statuette whose origin he was at a loss to determine. It must not be fancied that Inspector Legrasse had the least interest in archaeology. On the contrary, his wish for enlightenment was prompted by purely professional considerations. The statuette, idol, fetish, or whatever it was, had been captured some months before in the wooded swamps south of New Orleans during a raid on a supposed voodoo meeting; and so singular and hideous were the rites connected with it, that the police could not but realise that they had stumbled on a dark cult totally unknown to them, and infinitely more diabolic than even the blackest of the African voodoo circles. Of its origin, apart from the erratic and unbelievable tales extorted from the captured members, absolutely nothing was to be discovered; hence the anxiety of the police for any antiquarian lore which might help them to place the frightful symbol, and through it track down the cult to its fountain-head.

Inspector Legrasse was scarcely prepared for the sensation which his offering created. One sight of the thing had been enough to throw the assembled men of science into a state of tense excitement, and they lost no time in crowding around him to gaze at the diminutive figure whose utter strangeness and air of genuinely abysmal antiquity hinted so potently at un-opened and archaic vistas. No recognised school of sculpture had animated this terrible object, yet centuries and even thou-sands of years seemed recorded in its dim and greenish surface of unplaceable stone.

The figure, which was finally passed slowly from man to man for close and careful study, was between seven and eight inches in height, and of exquisitely artistic workmanship. It rep-resented a monster of vaguely anthropoid outline, but with an octopus-like head whose face was a mass of feelers, a scaly, rubbery-looking body, prodigious claws on hind and fore feet, and long, narrow wings behind. This thing, which seemed in-stinct with a fearsome and unnatural malignancy, was of a somewhat bloated corpulence, and squatted evilly on a rectan-gular block or pedestal covered with undecipherable charac-ters. The tips of the wings touched the back edge of the block, the seat occupied the centre, whilst the long, curved claws of the doubled-up, crouching hind legs gripped the front edge and extended a quarter of the way down toward the bottom of the pedestal. The cephalopod head was bent forward, so that the ends of the facial feelers brushed the backs of huge fore paws which clasped the croucher's elevated knees. The aspect of the whole was abnormally life-like, and the more subtly fear-ful because its source was so totally unknown. Its vast, awesome, and incalculable age was unmistakable; yet not one link did it shew with any known type of art belonging to civilisation's youth—or indeed to any other time. Totally separate and apart, its very material was a mystery; for the soapy, greenish-black stone with its golden or iridescent flecks and striations resembled nothing familiar to geology or mineralogy. The characters along the base were equally baffling; and no member present, despite a representation of half the world's expert learning in this field, could form the least notion of even their remotest linguistic kinship. They, like the subject and material, belonged to something horribly remote and distinct from mankind as we know it; something frightfully suggestive of old and unhallowed cycles of life in which our world and our conceptions have no part.

And yet, as the members severally shook their heads and confessed defeat at the Inspector's problem, there was one man in that gathering who suspected a touch of bizarre familiarity in the monstrous shape and writing, and who presently told with some diffidence of the odd trifle he knew. This person was the late William Channing Webb, Professor of Anthropology in Princeton University, and an explorer of no slight note. Professor Webb had been engaged, forty-eight years before, in a tour of Greenland and Iceland in search of some Runic inscriptions which he failed to unearth; and whilst high up on the West Greenland coast had encountered a singular tribe or cult of degenerate Esquimaux whose religion, a curious form of devil-worship, chilled him with its deliberate bloodthirstiness and repulsiveness. It was a faith of which other Esquimaux knew little, and which they mentioned only with shudders, saying that it had come down from horribly ancient aeons before ever the world was made. Besides nameless rites and human sacrifices there were certain queer hereditary rituals addressed to a supreme elder devil or *tornasuk;* and of this Professor Webb had taken a careful phonetic copy from an aged *angekok* or wizard-priest, expressing the sounds in Roman letters as best he knew how. But just now of prime significance was the fetish which this cult had cherished, and around which they danced when the aurora leaped high over the ice cliffs. It was, the professor stated, a very crude bas-relief of stone, comprising a hideous picture and some cryptic writing. And so far as he could tell, it was a rough parallel in all essential features of the bestial thing now lying before the meeting.

This data, received with suspense and astonishment by the assembled members, proved doubly exciting to Inspector Legrasse; and he began at once to ply his informant with questions. Having noted and copied an oral ritual among the swamp cult-worshippers his men had arrested, he besought the professor to remember as best he might the syllables taken down amongst the diabolist Esquimaux. There then followed an exhaustive comparison of details, and a moment of really awed silence when both detective and scientist agreed on the virtual identity of the phrase common to two hellish rituals so many worlds of distance apart. What, in substance, both the Esquimau wizards and the Louisiana swamp-priests had chanted to their kindred idols was something very like this—the word-divisions being guessed at from traditional breaks in the phrase as chanted aloud:

"Ph'nglui mglw'nafh Cthulhu R'lyeh wgah'nagl fhtagn."

Legrasse had one point in advance of Professor Webb, for several among his mongrel prisoners had repeated to him what older celebrants had told them the words meant. This text, as given, ran something like this:

"In his house at R'lyeh dead Cthulhu waits dreaming."

And now, in response to a general and urgent demand, Inspector Legrasse related as fully as possible his experience with the swamp worshippers; telling a story to which I could see my uncle attached profound significance. It savoured of the wildest dreams of myth-maker and theosophist, and disclosed an astonishing degree of cosmic imagination among such half-castes and pariahs as might be least expected to possess it.

On November 1st, 1907, there had come to the New Orleans police a frantic summons from the swamp and lagoon country to the south. The squatters there, mostly primitive but good-natured descendants of Lafitte's men, were in the grip of stark terror from an unknown thing which had stolen upon them in the night. It was voodoo, apparently, but voodoo of a more terrible sort than they had ever known; and some of their women and children had disappeared since the malevolent tom-tom had begun its incessant beating far within the black haunted woods where no dweller ventured. There were insane shouts and harrowing screams, soul-chilling chants and dancing devil-flames; and, the frightened messenger added, the people could stand it no more.

So a body of twenty police, filling two carriages and an automobile, had set out in the late afternoon with the shivering squatter as a guide. At the end of the passable road they alighted, and for miles splashed on in silence through the terrible cypress woods where day never came. Ugly roots and malignant hanging nooses of Spanish moss beset them, and now and then a pile of dark stones or fragment of a rotting wall intensified by its hint of morbid habitation a depression which every malformed tree and every fungous islet combined to create. At length the squatter settlement, a miserable huddle of huts, hove in sight; and hysterical dwellers ran out to cluster around the group of bobbing lanterns. The muffled beat of tom-toms was now faintly audible far, far ahead; and a curdling shriek came at infrequent intervals when the wind shifted. A reddish glare, too, seemed to filter through the pale undergrowth beyond endless avenues of forest night. Reluctant even to be left alone again, each one of the cowed squatters refused point-blank to advance another inch toward the scene of unholy worship, so Inspector Legrasse and his nineteen colleagues plunged on unguided into black arcades of horror that none of them had ever trod before.

The region now entered by the police was one of traditionally evil repute, substantially unknown and untraversed by white men. There were legends of a hidden lake unglimpsed by mortal sight, in which dwelt a huge, formless white polypous thing with luminous eyes; and squatters whispered that batwinged devils flew up out of caverns in inner earth to worship it at midnight. They said it had been there before D'Iberville, before La Salle, before the Indians, and before even the wholesome beasts and birds of the woods. It was nightmare itself, and to see it was to die. But it made men dream, and so they knew enough to keep away. The present voodoo orgy was, indeed, on the merest fringe of this abhorred area, but that location was bad enough; hence perhaps the very place of the worship had terrified the squatters more than the shocking sounds and incidents.

Only poetry or madness could do justice to the noises heard by Legrasse's men as they ploughed on through the black morass toward the red glare and the muffled tom-toms. There are vocal qualities peculiar to men, and vocal qualities peculiar to beasts; and it is terrible to hear the one when the source should yield the other. Animal fury and orgiastic licence here whipped themselves to daemoniac heights by howls and squawking ecstasies that tore and reverberated through those nighted woods like pestilential tempests from the gulfs of hell. Now and then the less organised ululation would cease, and from what seemed a well-drilled chorus of hoarse voices would rise in sing-song chant that hideous phrase or ritual:

"Ph'nglui mglw'nafh Cthulhu R'lyeh wgah'nagl fhtagn."

Then the men, having reached a spot where the trees were thinner, came suddenly in sight of the spectacle itself. Four of them reeled, one fainted, and two were shaken into a frantic cry which the mad cacophony of the orgy fortunately deadened. Legrasse dashed swamp water on the face of the fainting man, and all stood trembling and nearly hypnotised with horror.

In a natural glade of the swamp stood a grassy island of perhaps an acre's extent, clear of trees and tolerably dry. On this now leaped and twisted a more indescribable horde of human abnormality than any but a Sime or an Angarola could paint. Void of clothing, this hybrid spawn were braying, bellowing, and writhing about a monstrous ring-shaped bonfire; in the centre of which, revealed by occasional rifts in the curtain of flame, stood a great granite monolith some eight feet in height; on top of which, incongruous in its diminutiveness, rested the noxious carven statuette. From a wide circle of ten scaffolds set up at regular intervals with the flame-girt monolith as a centre hung, head downward, the oddly marred bodies of the helpless squatters who had disappeared. It was inside this circle that the ring of worshippers jumped and roared, the general direction of the mass motion being from left to right in endless Bacchanal between the ring of bodies and the ring of fire.

It may have been only imagination and it may have been only echoes which induced one of the men, an excitable Spaniard, to fancy he heard antiphonal responses to the ritual from some far and unillumined spot deeper within the wood of ancient legendry and horror. This man, Joseph D. Galvez, I later met and questioned; and he proved distractingly imaginative. He indeed went so far as to hint of the faint beating of great wings, and of a glimpse of shining eyes and a mountainous white bulk beyond the remotest trees—but I suppose he had been hearing too much native superstition.

Actually, the horrified pause of the men was of comparatively brief duration. Duty came first; and although there must have been nearly a hundred mongrel celebrants in the throng, the police relied on their firearms and plunged determinedly into the nauseous rout. For five minutes the resultant din and chaos were beyond description. Wild blows were struck, shots were fired, and escapes were made; but in the end Legrasse was able to count some forty-seven sullen prisoners, whom he forced to dress in haste and fall into line between two rows of policemen. Five of the worshippers lay dead, and two severely wounded ones were carried away on improvised stretchers by their fellow-prisoners. The image on the monolith, of course, was carefully removed and carried back by Legrasse.

Examined at headquarters after a trip of intense strain and weariness, the prisoners all proved to be men of a very low, mixed-blooded, and mentally aberrant type. Most were seamen, and a sprinkling of negroes and mulattoes, largely West Indians or Brava Portuguese from the Cape Verde Islands, gave a colouring of voodooism to the heterogeneous cult. But before many questions were asked, it became manifest that something far deeper and older than negro fetishism was involved. Degraded and ignorant as they were, the creatures held with surprising consistency to the central idea of their loathsome faith.

They worshipped, so they said, the Great Old Ones who lived ages before there were any men, and who came to the young world out of the sky. Those Old Ones were gone now, inside the earth and under the sea; but their dead bodies had told their secrets in dreams to the first men, who formed a cult which had never died. This was that cult, and the prisoners said it had always existed and always would exist, hidden in distant wastes and dark places all over the world until the time when the great priest Cthulhu, from his dark house in the mighty city of R'lyeh under the waters, should rise and bring the earth again beneath his sway. Some day he would call, when the stars were ready, and the secret cult would always be waiting to liberate him.

Meanwhile no more must be told. There was a secret which even torture could not extract. Mankind was not absolutely alone among the conscious things of earth, for shapes came out of the dark to visit the faithful few. But these were not the Great Old Ones. No man had ever seen the Old Ones. The carven idol was great Cthulhu, but none might say whether or not the others were precisely like him. No one could read the old writing now, but things were told by word of mouth. The chanted ritual was not the secret—that was never spoken aloud, only whispered. The chant meant only this: "In his house at R'lyeh dead Cthulhu waits dreaming."

Only two of the prisoners were found sane enough to be hanged, and the rest were committed to various institutions. All denied a part in the ritual murders, and averred that the killing had been done by Black Winged Ones which had come to them from their immemorial meeting-place in the haunted wood. But of those mysterious allies no coherent account could ever be gained. What the police did extract, came mainly from an immensely aged mestizo named Castro, who claimed to have sailed to strange ports and talked with undying leaders of the cult in the mountains of China.

Old Castro remembered bits of hideous legend that paled the speculations of theosophists and made man and the world seem recent and transient indeed. There had been aeons when other Things ruled on the earth, and They had had great cities. Remains of Them, he said the deathless Chinamen had told him, were still to be found as Cyclopean stones on islands in the Pacific. They all died vast epochs of time before men came, but there were arts which could revive Them when the stars had come round again to the right positions in the cycle of eternity. They had, indeed, come themselves from the stars, and brought Their images with Them.

These Great Old Ones, Castro continued, were not composed altogether of flesh and blood. They had shape—for did not this star-fashioned image prove it?—but that shape was not made of matter. When the stars were right, They could plunge from world to world through the sky; but when the stars were wrong, They could not live. But although They no longer lived, They would never really die. They all lay in stone houses in Their great city of R'lyeh, preserved by the spells of mighty Cthulhu for a glorious resurrection when the stars and the earth might once more be ready for Them. But at that time some force from outside must serve to liberate Their bodies. The spells that preserved Them intact likewise prevented Them from making an initial move, and They could only lie awake in the dark and think whilst uncounted millions of years rolled by. They knew all that was occurring in the universe, for Their mode of speech was transmitted thought. Even now They talked in Their tombs. When, after infinities of chaos, the first men came, the Great Old Ones spoke to the sensitive among them by moulding their dreams; for only thus could Their language reach the fleshly minds of mammals.

Then, whispered Castro, those first men formed the cult around small idols which the Great Ones shewed them; idols brought in dim aeras from dark stars. That cult would never die till the stars came right again, and the secret priests would take great Cthulhu from His tomb to revive His subjects and resume His rule of earth. That time would be easy to know, for then mankind would have become as the Great Old Ones; free and wild and beyond good and evil, with laws and morals thrown aside and all men shouting and killing and revelling in joy. Then the liberated Old Ones would teach them new ways to shout and kill and revel and enjoy themselves, and all the earth would flame with a holocaust of ecstasy and freedom. Meanwhile the cult, by appropriate rites, must keep alive the memory of those ancient ways and shadow forth the prophecy of their return.

In the elder time chosen men had talked with the entombed Old Ones in dreams, but then something had happened. The great stone city R'lyeh, with its monoliths and sepulchres, had sunk beneath the waves; and the deep waters, full of the one primal mystery through which not even thought can pass, had cut off the spectral intercourse. But memory never died, and high-priests said that the city would rise again when the stars were right. Then came out of the earth the black spirits of earth, mouldy and shadowy, and full of dim rumours picked up in caverns beneath forgotten sea-bottoms. But of them old Castro dared not speak much. He cut himself off hurriedly, and no amount of persuasion or subtlety could elicit more in this direction. The *size* of the Old Ones, too, he curiously declined to mention. Of the cult, he said that he thought the centre lay amid the pathless deserts of Arabia, where Irem, the City of Pillars, dreams hidden and untouched. It was not allied to the European witch-cult, and was virtually unknown beyond its members. No book had ever really hinted of it, though the deathless Chinamen said that there were double meanings in the *Necronomicon* of the mad Arab Abdul Alhazred which the initiated might read as they chose, especially the much-discussed couplet:

> "That is not dead which can eternal lie,
> And with strange aeons even death may die."

Legrasse, deeply impressed and not a little bewildered, had inquired in vain concerning the historic affiliations of the cult. Castro, apparently, had told the truth when he said that it was wholly secret. The authorities at Tulane University could shed no light upon either cult or image, and now the detective had come to the highest authorities in the country and met with no more than the Greenland tale of Professor Webb.

The feverish interest aroused at the meeting by Legrasse's tale, corroborated as it was by the statuette, is echoed in the subsequent correspondence of those who attended; although scant mention occurs in the formal publications of the society. Caution is the first care of those accustomed to face occasional charlatanry and imposture. Legrasse for some time lent the image to Professor Webb, but at the latter's death it was returned to him and remains in his possession, where I viewed it not long ago. It is truly a terrible thing, and unmistakably akin to the dream-sculpture of young Wilcox.

That my uncle was excited by the tale of the sculptor I did not wonder, for what thoughts must arise upon hearing, after a knowledge of what Legrasse had learned of the cult, of a sensitive young man who had *dreamed* not only the figure and exact hieroglyphics of the swamp-found image and the Greenland devil tablet, but had come *in his dreams* upon at least three of the precise words of the formula uttered alike by Esquimau diabolists and mongrel Louisianans? Professor Angell's instant start on an investigation of the utmost thoroughness was eminently natural; though privately I suspected young Wilcox of having heard of the cult in some indirect way, and of having invented a series of dreams to heighten and continue the mystery at my uncle's expense. The dream-narratives and cuttings collected by the professor were, of course, strong corroboration; but the rationalism of my mind and the extravagance of the whole subject led me to adopt what I thought the most sensible conclusions. So, after thoroughly studying the manuscript again and correlating the theosophical and anthropological notes with the cult narrative of Legrasse, I made a trip to Providence to see the sculptor and give him the rebuke I thought proper for so boldly imposing upon a learned and aged man.

Wilcox still lived alone in the Fleur-de-Lys Building in Thomas Street, a hideous Victorian imitation of seventeenth-century Breton architecture which flaunts its stuccoed front amidst the lovely colonial houses on the ancient hill, and under the very shadow of the finest Georgian steeple in America. I found him at work in his rooms, and at once conceded from the specimens scattered about that his genius is indeed profound and authentic. He will, I believe, some time be heard from as one of the great decadents; for he has crystallised in clay and will one day mirror in marble those nightmares and phantasies which Arthur Machen evokes in prose, and Clark Ashton Smith makes visible in verse and in painting.

Dark, frail, and somewhat unkempt in aspect, he turned languidly at my knock and asked me my business without rising. When I told him who I was, he displayed some interest; for my uncle had excited his curiosity in probing his strange dreams, yet had never explained the reason for the study. I did not enlarge his knowledge in this regard, but sought with some subtlety to draw him out. In a short time I became convinced of his absolute sincerity, for he spoke of the dreams in a manner none could mistake. They and their subconscious residuum had influenced his art profoundly, and he shewed me a morbid statue whose contours almost made me shake with the potency of its black suggestion. He could not recall having seen the original of this thing except in his own dream bas-relief, but the outlines had formed themselves insensibly under his hands. It was, no doubt, the giant shape he had raved of in delirium. That he really knew nothing of the hidden cult, save from what my uncle's relentless catechism had let fall, he soon made clear; and again I strove to think of some way in which he could possibly have received the weird impressions.

He talked of his dreams in a strangely poetic fashion; making me see with terrible vividness the damp Cyclopean city of slimy green stone—whose *geometry*, he oddly said, was *all wrong*—and hear with frightened expectancy the ceaseless, half-mental calling from underground: *"Cthulhu fhtagn," "Cthulhu fhtagn."* These words had formed part of that dread ritual which told of dead Cthulhu's dream-vigil in his stone vault at R'lyeh, and I felt deeply moved despite my rational beliefs. Wilcox, I was sure, had heard of the cult in some casual way, and had soon forgotten it amidst the mass of his equally weird reading and imagining. Later, by virtue of its sheer impressiveness, it had found subconscious expression in dreams, in the bas-relief, and in the terrible statue I now beheld; so that his imposture upon my uncle had been a very innocent one. The youth was of a type, at once slightly affected and slightly ill-mannered, which I could never like; but I was willing enough now to admit both his genius and his honesty. I took leave of him amicably, and wish him all the success his talent promises.

The matter of the cult still remained to fascinate me, and

at times I had visions of personal fame from researches into its origin and connexions. I visited New Orleans, talked with Legrasse and others of that old-time raiding-party, saw the frightful image, and even questioned such of the mongrel prisoners as still survived. Old Castro, unfortunately, had been dead for some years. What I now heard so graphically at first-hand, though it was really no more than a detailed confirmation of what my uncle had written, excited me afresh; for I felt sure that I was on the track of a very real, very secret, and very ancient religion whose discovery would make me an anthropologist of note. My attitude was still one of absolute materialism, *as I wish it still were,* and I discounted with almost inexplicable perversity the coincidence of the dream notes and odd cuttings collected by Professor Angell.

One thing I began to suspect, and which I now fear I *know,* is that my uncle's death was far from natural. He fell on a narrow hill street leading up from an ancient waterfront swarming with foreign mongrels, after a careless push from a negro sailor. I did not forget the mixed blood and marine pursuits of the cult-members in Louisiana, and would not be surprised to learn of secret methods and poison needles as ruthless and as anciently known as the cryptic rites and beliefs. Legrasse and his men, it is true, have been let alone; but in Norway a certain seaman who saw things is dead. Might not the deeper inquiries of my uncle after encountering the sculptor's data have come to sinister ears? I think Professor Angell died because he knew too much, or because he was likely to learn too much. Whether I shall go as he did remains to be seen, for I have learned much now.

III
THE MADNESS FROM THE SEA

If heaven ever wishes to grant me a boon, it will be a total effacing of the results of a mere chance which fixed my eye on a certain stray piece of shelf-paper. It was nothing on which I would naturally have stumbled in the course of my daily round, for it was an old number of an Australian journal, the *Sydney Bulletin* for April 18, 1925. It had escaped even the cutting bureau which had at the time of its issuance been avidly collecting material for my uncle's research.

I had largely given over my inquiries into what Professor Angell called the "Cthulhu Cult," and was visiting a learned friend in Paterson, New Jersey; the curator of a local museum and a mineralogist of note. Examining one day the reserve specimens roughly set on the storage shelves in a rear room of the museum, my eye was caught by an odd picture in one of the old papers spread beneath the stones. It was the *Sydney Bulletin* I have mentioned, for my friend has wide affiliations in all conceivable foreign parts; and the picture was a half-tone cut of a hideous stone image almost identical with that which Legrasse had found in the swamp.

Eagerly clearing the sheet of its precious contents, I scanned the item in detail; and was disappointed to find it of only moderate length. What it suggested, however, was of portentous significance to my flagging quest; and I carefully tore it out for immediate action. It read as follows:

MYSTERY DERELICT FOUND AT SEA
Vigilant Arrives With Helpless Armed New Zealand Yacht in Tow.
One Survivor and Dead Man Found Aboard. Tale of
Desperate Battle and Deaths at Sea.
Rescued Seaman Refuses
Particulars of Strange Experience.
Odd Idol Found in His Possession. Inquiry
to Follow.

The Morrison Co.'s freighter *Vigilant*, bound from Valparaiso, arrived this morning at its wharf in Darling Harbour, having in tow the battled and disabled but heavily armed steam yacht *Alert* of Dunedin, N. Z., which was sighted April 12th in S. Latitude 34° 21', W. Longitude 152° 17' with one living and one dead man aboard.

The *Vigilant* left Valparaiso March 25th, and on April 2nd was driven considerably south of her course by exceptionally heavy storms and monster waves. On April 12th the derelict was sighted; and though apparently deserted, was found upon boarding to contain one survivor in a half-delirious condition and one man who had evidently been dead for more than a week. The living man was clutching a horrible stone idol of unknown origin, about a foot in height, regarding whose nature authorities at Sydney University, the Royal Society, and the Museum in College Street all profess complete bafflement, and which the survivor says he found in the cabin of the yacht, in a small carved shrine of common pattern.

This man, after recovering his senses, told an exceedingly strange story of piracy and slaughter. He is Gustaf Johansen, a Norwegian of some intelligence, and had been second mate of the two-masted schooner *Emma* of Auckland, which sailed for Callao February 20th with a complement of eleven men. The *Emma*, he says, was delayed and thrown widely south of her course by the great storm of March 1st, and on March 22nd, in S. Latitude 49° 51', W. Longitude 128° 34', encountered the *Alert*, manned by a queer and evil-looking crew of Kanakas and half-castes. Being ordered peremptorily to turn back, Capt. Collins refused; whereupon the strange crew began to fire savagely and without warning upon the schooner with a peculiarly heavy battery of brass cannon forming part of the yacht's equipment. The *Emma*'s men shewed fight, says the survivor, and though the schooner began to sink from shots beneath the waterline they managed to heave alongside their enemy and board her, grappling with the savage crew on the yacht's deck, and being forced to kill them all, the number being slightly superior, because of their particularly abhorrent and desperate though rather clumsy mode of fighting.

Three of the *Emma*'s men, including Capt. Collins and First Mate Green, were killed; and the remaining eight under Second Mate Johansen proceeded to navigate the captured yacht, going ahead in their original direction to see if any reason for their ordering back had existed. The next day, it appears, they raised and landed on a small island, although none is known to exist in that part of the ocean; and six of the men somehow died ashore, though Johansen is queerly reticent about this part of his story, and speaks only of their falling into a rock chasm. Later, it seems, he and one companion boarded the yacht and tried to manage her, but were beaten about by the storm of April 2nd. From that time till his rescue on the 12th the man remembers little, and he does not even recall when William Briden, his companion, died. Briden's death reveals no apparent cause, and was probably due to excitement or exposure. Cable advices from Dunedin report that the *Alert* was well known there as an island trader, and bore an evil reputation along the waterfront. It was owned by a curious group of half-castes whose frequent meetings and night trips to the woods attracted no little curiosity; and it had set sail in great haste just after the storm and earth tremors of March 1st. Our Auckland correspondent gives the *Emma* and her crew an excellent reputation, and Johansen is described as a sober and worthy man. The admiralty will institute an inquiry on the whole matter beginning tomorrow, at which every effort will be made to induce Johansen to speak more freely than he has done hitherto.

This was all, together with the picture of the hellish image; but what a train of ideas it started in my mind! Here were new treasuries of data on the Cthulhu Cult, and evidence that it had strange interests at sea as well as on land. What motive prompted the hybrid crew to order back the *Emma* as they sailed about with their hideous idol? What was the unknown island on which six of the *Emma*'s crew had died, and about which the mate Johansen was so secretive? What had the vice-admiralty's investigation brought out, and what was known of the noxious cult in Dunedin? And most marvellous of all, what deep and more than natural linkage of dates was this which gave a malign and now undeniable significance to the various turns of events so carefully noted by my uncle?

March 1st—our February 28th according to the International Date Line—the earthquake and storm had come. From Dunedin the *Alert* and her noisome crew had darted eagerly forth as if imperiously summoned, and on the other side of the earth poets and artists had begun to dream of a strange, dank Cyclopean city whilst a young sculptor had moulded in his sleep the form of the dreaded Cthulhu. March 23d the crew of the *Emma* landed on an unknown island and left six men dead; and on that date the dreams of sensitive men assumed a heightened vividness and darkened with dread of a giant monster's malign pursuit, whilst an architect had gone mad and a sculptor had lapsed suddenly into delirium! And what of this storm of April 2nd—the date on which all dreams of the dank city ceased, and Wilcox emerged unharmed from the bondage of strange fever? What of all this—and of those hints of old Castro about the sunken, star-born Old Ones and their coming reign; their faithful cult *and their mastery of dreams?* Was I tottering on the brink of cosmic horrors beyond man's power to bear? If so, they must be horrors of the mind alone, for in some way the second of April had put a stop to whatever monstrous menace had begun its siege of mankind's soul.

That evening, after a day of hurried cabling and arranging, I bade my host adieu and took a train for San Francisco. In less than a month I was in Dunedin; where, however, I found that little was known of the strange cult-members who had lingered in the old sea-taverns. Waterfront scum was far too common for special mention; though there was vague talk about one inland trip these mongrels had made, during which faint drumming and red flame were noted on the distant hills. In Auckland I learned that Johansen had returned *with yellow hair turned white* after a perfunctory and inconclusive questioning at Sydney, and had thereafter sold his cottage in West Street and sailed with his wife to his old home in Oslo. Of his stirring experience he would tell his friends no more than he had told the admiralty officials, and all they could do was to give me his Oslo address.

After that I went to Sydney and talked profitlessly with seamen and members of the vice-admiralty court. I saw the *Alert,* now sold and in commercial use, at Circular Quay in Sydney Cove, but gained nothing from its non-committal bulk. The crouching image with its cuttlefish head, dragon body, scaly wings, and hieroglyphed pedestal, was preserved in the Museum at Hyde Park; and I studied it long and well, finding it a thing of balefully exquisite workmanship, and with the same utter mystery, terrible antiquity, and unearthly strangeness of material which I had noted in Legrasse's smaller specimen. Geologists, the curator told me, had found it a monstrous puzzle; for they vowed that the world held no rock like it. Then I thought with a shudder of what old Castro had told Legrasse about the primal Great Ones: "They had come from the stars, and had brought Their images with Them."

Shaken with such a mental revolution as I had never before known, I now resolved to visit Mate Johansen in Oslo. Sailing for London, I reëmbarked at once for the Norwegian capital; and one autumn day landed at the trim wharves in the shadow of the Egeberg. Johansen's address, I discovered, lay in the Old Town of King Harold Haardrada, which kept alive the name of Oslo during all the centuries that the greater city masqueraded as "Christiana." I made the brief trip by taxicab, and knocked with palpitant heart at the door of a neat and ancient building with plastered front. A sad-faced woman in black answered my summons, and I was stung with disappointment when she told me in halting English that Gustaf Johansen was no more.

He had not long survived his return, said his wife, for the doings at sea in 1925 had broken him. He had told her no more than he had told the public, but had left a long manuscript—of "technical matters" as he said—written in English, evidently in order to safeguard her from the peril of casual perusal. During a walk through a narrow lane near the Gothenburg dock, a bundle of papers falling from an attic window had knocked him down. Two Lascar sailors at once helped him to his feet, but before the ambulance could reach him he was dead. Physicians found no adequate cause for the end, and laid it to heart trouble and a weakened constitution.

I now felt gnawing at my vitals that dark terror which will never leave me till I, too, am at rest; "accidentally" or otherwise. Persuading the widow that my connexion with her husband's "technical matters" was sufficient to entitle me to his manuscript, I bore the document away and began to read it on the London boat. It was a simple, rambling thing—a naive sailor's effort at a post-facto diary—and strove to recall day by day that last awful voyage. I cannot attempt to transcribe it verbatim in all its cloudiness and redundance, but I will tell its gist enough to shew why the sound of the water against the vessel's sides became so unendurable to me that I stopped my ears with cotton.

Johansen, thank God, did not know quite all, even though he saw the city and the Thing, but I shall never sleep calmly again when I think of the horrors that lurk ceaselessly behind life in time and in space, and of those unhallowed blasphemies from elder stars which dream beneath the sea, known and favoured by a nightmare cult ready and eager to loose them on the world whenever another earthquake shall heave their monstrous stone city again to the sun and air.

Johansen's voyage had begun just as he told it to the vice-admiralty. The *Emma,* in ballast, had cleared Auckland on February 20th, and had felt the full force of that earthquake-born tempest which must have heaved up from the sea-bottom the horrors that filled men's dreams. Once more under control, the ship was making good progress when held up by the *Alert* on March 22nd, and I could feel the mate's regret as he wrote of her bombardment and sinking. Of the swarthy cult-fiends on the *Alert* he speaks with significant horror. There was some peculiarly abominable quality about them which made their destruction seem almost a duty, and Johansen shews ingenuous wonder at the charge of ruthlessness brought against his party during the proceedings of the court of inquiry. Then, driven ahead by curiosity in their captured yacht under Johansen's command, the men sight a great stone pillar sticking out of the sea, and in S. Latitude 47° 9', W. Longitude 126° 43' come upon a coast-line of mingled mud, ooze, and weedy Cyclopean masonry which can be nothing less than the tangible substance of earth's supreme terror—the nightmare corpse-city of R'lyeh, that was built in measureless aeons behind history by the vast, loathsome shapes that seeped down from the dark stars. There lay great Cthulhu and his hordes, hidden in green slimy vaults and sending out at last, after cycles incalculable, the thoughts that spread fear to the dreams of the sensitive and called imperiously to the faithful to come on a pilgrimage of liberation and restoration. All this Johansen did not suspect, but God knows he soon saw enough!

I suppose that only a single mountain-top, the hideous monolith-crowned citadel whereon great Cthulhu was buried, actually emerged from the waters. When I think of the *extent* of all that may be brooding down there I almost wish to kill myself forthwith. Johansen and his men were awed by the cosmic majesty of this dripping Babylon of elder daemons, and must have guessed without guidance that it was nothing of this or of any sane planet. Awe at the unbelievable size of the greenish stone blocks, at the dizzying height of the great carven monolith, and at the stupefying identity of the colossal statues and bas-reliefs with the queer image found in the shrine on the *Alert,* is poignantly visible in every line of the mate's frightened description.

Without knowing what futurism is like, Johansen achieved something very close to it when he spoke of the city; for instead of describing any definite structure or building, he dwells only on broad impressions of vast angles and stone surfaces—surfaces too great to belong to any thing right or proper for this earth, and impious with horrible images and hieroglyphs. I mention his talk about *angles* because it suggests something Wilcox had told me of his awful dreams. He had said that the *geometry* of the dream-place he saw was abnormal, non-Euclidean, and loathsomely redolent of spheres and dimensions apart from ours. Now an unlettered seaman felt the same thing whilst gazing at the terrible reality.

Johansen and his men landed at a sloping mud-bank on this monstrous Acropolis, and clambered slipperily up over titan oozy blocks which could have been no mortal staircase. The very sun of heaven seemed distorted when viewed through the polarising miasma welling out from this sea-soaked perversion, and twisted menace and suspense lurked leeringly in those crazily elusive angles of carven rock where a second glance shewed concavity after the first shewed convexity.

Something very like fright had come over all the explorers before anything more definite than rock and ooze and weed was seen. Each would have fled had he not feared the scorn of the others, and it was only half-heartedly that they searched—vainly, as it proved—for some portable souvenir to bear away.

It was Rodriguez the Portuguese who climbed up the foot of the monolith and shouted of what he had found. The rest followed him, and looked curiously at the immense carved door with the now familiar squid-dragon bas-relief. It was, Johansen said, like a great barn-door; and they all felt that it was a door because of the ornate lintel, threshold, and jambs around it, though they could not decide whether it lay flat like a trap-door or slantwise like an outside cellar-door. As Wilcox would have said, the geometry of the place was all wrong. One could not be sure that the sea and the ground were horizontal, hence the relative position of everything else seemed phantasmally variable.

Briden pushed at the stone in several places without result. Then Donovan felt over it delicately around the edge, pressing each point separately as he went. He climbed interminably along the grotesque stone moulding—that is, one would call it climbing if the thing was not after all horizontal—and the men wondered how any door in the universe could be so vast. Then, very softly and slowly, the acre-great panel began to give inward at the top; and they saw that it was balanced. Donovan slid or somehow propelled himself down or along the jamb and rejoined his fellows, and everyone watched the queer recession of the monstrously carven portal. In this phantasy of prismatic distortion it moved anomalously in a diagonal way, so that all the rules of matter and perspective seemed upset.

The aperture was black with a darkness almost material. That tenebrousness was indeed a *positive quality;* for it obscured such parts of the inner walls as ought to have been revealed, and actually burst forth like smoke from its aeon-long imprisonment, visibly darkening the sun as it slunk away into the shrunken and gibbous sky on flapping membraneous wings. The odour arising from the newly opened depths was intolerable, and at length the quick-eared Hawkins thought he heard a nasty, slopping sound down there. Everyone listened, and everyone was listening still when It lumbered slobberingly into sight and gropingly squeezed Its gelatinous green immensity through the black doorway into the tainted outside air of that poison city of madness.

Poor Johansen's handwriting almost gave out when he wrote of this. Of the six men who never reached the ship, he thinks two perished of pure fright in that accursed instant. The Thing cannot be described—there is no language for such abysms of shrieking and immemorial lunacy, such eldritch contradictions of all matter, force, and cosmic order. A mountain walked or stumbled. God! What wonder that across the earth a great architect went mad, and poor Wilcox raved with fever in that telepathic instant? The Thing of the idols, the green, sticky spawn of the stars, had awaked to claim his own. The stars were right again, and what an age-old cult had failed to do by design, a band of innocent sailors had done by accident. After vigintillions of years great Cthulhu was loose again, and ravening for delight.

Three men were swept up by the flabby claws before anybody turned. God rest them, if there be any rest in the universe. They were Donovan, Guerrera, and Ångstrom. Parker slipped as the other three were plunging frenziedly over endless vistas of green-crusted rock to the boat, and Johansen swears he was swallowed up by an angle of masonry which shouldn't have been there; an angle which was acute, but behaved as if it were obtuse. So only Briden and Johansen reached the boat, and pulled desperately for the *Alert* as the mountainous monstrosity flopped down the slimy stones and hesitated floundering at the edge of the water.

Steam had not been suffered to go down entirely, despite the departure of all hands for the shore; and it was the work of only a few moments of feverish rushing up and down between wheel and engines to get the *Alert* under way. Slowly, amidst the distorted horrors of that indescribable scene, she began to churn the lethal waters; whilst on the masonry of that charnel shore that was not of earth the titan Thing from the stars slavered and gibbered like Polypheme cursing the fleeing ship of Odysseus. Then, bolder than the storied Cyclops, great Cthulhu slid greasily into the water and began to pursue with vast wave-raising strokes of cosmic potency. Briden looked back and went mad, laughing shrilly as he kept on laughing at intervals till death found him one night in the cabin whilst Johansen was wandering deliriously.

But Johansen had not given out yet. Knowing that the Thing could surely overtake the *Alert* until steam was fully up, he resolved on a desperate chance; and, setting the engine for full speed, ran lightning-like on deck and reversed the wheel. There was a mighty eddying and foaming in the noisome brine, and as the steam mounted higher and higher the brave Norwegian drove his vessel head on against the pursuing jelly which rose above the unclean froth like the stern of a daemon galleon. The awful squid-head with writhing feelers came nearly up to the bowsprit of the sturdy yacht, but Johansen drove on relentlessly. There was a bursting as of an exploding bladder, a slushy nastiness as of a cloven sunfish, a stench as of a thousand opened graves, and a sound that the chronicler would not put on paper. For an instant the ship was befouled by an acrid and blinding green cloud, and then there was only a venomous seething astern; where—God in heaven!—the scattered plasticity of that nameless sky-spawn was nebulously *recombining* in its hateful original form, whilst its distance widened every second as the *Alert* gained impetus from its mounting steam.

That was all. After that Johansen only brooded over the idol in the cabin and attended to a few matters of food for himself and the laughing maniac by his side. He did not try to navigate after the first bold flight, for the reaction had taken something out of his soul. Then came the storm of April 2nd, and a gathering of the clouds about his consciousness. There is a sense of spectral whirling through liquid gulfs of infinity, of dizzying rides through reeling universes on a comet's tail, and of hysterical plunges from the pit to the moon and from the moon back again to the pit, all livened by a cachinnating chorus of the distorted, hilarious elder gods and the green, bat-winged mocking imps of Tartarus.

Out of that dream came rescue—the *Vigilant,* the vice-admiralty court, the streets of Dunedin, and the long voyage back home to the old house by the Egeberg. He could not tell—they would think him mad. He would write of what he knew before death came, but his wife must not guess. Death would be a boon if only it could blot out the memories.

That was the document I read, and now I have placed it in the tin box beside the bas-relief and the papers of Professor Angell. With it shall go this record of mine—this test of my own sanity, wherein is pieced together that which I hope may never be pieced together again. I have looked upon all that the universe has to hold of horror, and even the skies of spring and the flowers of summer must ever afterward be poison to me. But I do not think my life will be long. As my uncle went, as poor Johansen went, so I shall go. I know too much, and the cult still lives.

Cthulhu still lives, too, I suppose, again in that chasm of stone which has shielded him since the sun was young. His accursed city is sunken once more, for the *Vigilant* sailed over the spot after the April storm; but his ministers on earth still bellow and prance and slay around idol-capped monoliths in lonely places. He must have been trapped by the sinking whilst within his black abyss, or else the world would by now be screaming with fright and frenzy. Who knows the end? What has risen may sink, and what has sunk may rise. Loathsomeness waits and dreams in the deep, and decay spreads over the tottering cities of men. A time will come—but I must not and cannot think! Let me pray that, if I do not survive this manuscript, my executors may put caution before audacity and see that it meets no other eye.

CLARK ASHTON SMITH

Clark Ashton Smith was born in Long Valley, California, in 1893, and spent most of his life in Auburn, in the foothills of the Sierras. Largely self-educated, Smith developed an impressive vocabulary by reading a dictionary and encyclopedia from cover to cover. His earliest literary work was poetry, and in 1912 he attained celebrity as a child prodigy by publishing *The Star-Treader and Other Poems,* a volume of "cosmic" verse largely inspired by his mentor, the well-known California poet George Sterling. Other volumes of poetry followed: *Odes and Sonnets* (1918), *Ebony and Crystal* (1922), *Sandalwood* (1925). But Smith's stately, formal poetry was increasingly out of fashion with the Modernist poets of the day, and Smith became discouraged at his lack of recognition as a poet.

Smith came into contact with H. P. Lovecraft in 1922, and their substantial correspondence may have helped turn Smith's attention to fiction writing. In 1929 he began the voluminous production of short stories of horror, fantasy, and science fiction, chiefly for the pulp magazines, and in large part to support his ailing parents. Many of these stories constituted components of loose story cycles based in such fantastic realms as Hyperborea (an ancient continent in the far north), Zothique (the earth's last continent), Averoigne (a province in medieval France), and the like. By 1937 Smith's fiction writing largely ended, and he resumed the writing of poetry, also taking up the carving of fantastic sculptures. His tales were gathered in numerous volumes published by Arkham House: *Out of Space and Time* (1942), *Lost Worlds* (1944), *Genius Loci* (1948), *The Abominations of Yondo* (1960), and several others. Smith died in Pacific Grove, California, in 1961. His *Selected Poems* appeared in 1971.

"The Vaults of Yoh-Vombis" (*Weird Tales*, May 1932), one of several tales set on the planet Mars, demonstrates Smith's blending of supernatural horror and science fiction and his dense, idiosyncratic prose style.

THE VAULTS OF YOH-VOMBIS

PREFACE

As an interne in the terrestrial hospital at Ignarh, I had charge of the singular case of Rodney Severn, the one surviving member of the Octave Expedition to Yoh-Vombis, and took down the following story from his dictation. Severn had been brought to the hospital by the Martian guides of the Expedition. He was suffering from a horribly lacerated and inflamed condition of the scalp and brow, and was wildly delirious part of the time and had to be held down in his bed during recurrent seizures of a mania whose violence was doubly inexplicable in view of his extreme debility.

The lacerations, as will be learned from the story, were mainly self-inflicted. They were mingled with numerous small round wounds, easily distinguished from the knife-slashes, and arranged in regular circles, through which an unknown poison had been injected into Severn's scalp. The causation of these wounds was difficult to explain; unless one were to believe that Severn's story was true, and was no mere figment of his illness. Speaking for myself, in the light of what afterwards occurred, I feel that I have no other recourse than to believe it. There are strange things on the red planet; and I can only second the wish that was expressed by the doomed archaeologist in regard to future explorations.

The night after he finished telling me his story, while another doctor than myself was supposedly on duty, Severn managed to escape from the hospital, doubtless in one of the strange seizures at which I have hinted: a most astonishing thing, for he had seemed weaker than ever after the long strain of his terrible narrative, and his demise had been hourly expected. More astonishing still, his bare footsteps were found in the desert, going toward Yoh-Vombis, till they vanished in the path of a light sand-storm; but no trace of Severn himself has yet been discovered.

THE NARRATIVE OF RODNEY SEVERN

If the doctors are correct in their prognostication, I have only a few Martian hours of life remaining to me. In those hours I shall endeavor to relate, as a warning to others who might follow in our footsteps, the singular and frightful happenings that terminated our researches among the ruins of Yoh-Vombis. Somehow, even in my extremity, I shall contrive to tell the story; since there is no one else to do it. But the telling will be toilsome and broken; and after I am done, the madness will recur, and several men will restrain me, lest I should leave the hospital and return across many desert leagues to those abominable vaults beneath the compulsion of the malignant and malevolent virus which is permeating my brain. Perhaps death will release me from that abhorrent control, which would urge me down to bottomless underworld warrens of terror for which the saner planets of the solar system can have no analogue. I say *perhaps* . . . for, remembering what I have seen, I am not sure that even death will end my bondage. . . .

There were eight of us, professional archaeologists with more or less terrene and interplanetary experience, who set forth with native guides from Ignarh, the commercial metropolis of Mars, to inspect that ancient, aeon-deserted city. Allan Octave, our official leader, held his primacy by virtue of knowing more about Martian archaeology than any other Terrestrial on the planet; and others of the party, such as William Harper and Jonas Halgren, had been associated with him in many of his previous researches. I, Rodney Severn, was more of a newcomer, having spent but a few months on Mars; and the greater part of my own ultra-terrene delvings had been confined to Venus.

I had often heard of Yoh-Vombis, in a vague and legendary sort of manner, and never at first hand. Even the ubiquitous Octave had never seen it. Builded by an extinct people whose history has been lost in the latter, decadent eras of the planet, it remains a dim and fascinating riddle whose solution has never been approached . . . and which, I trust, may endure forevermore unsolved by man. Certainly I hope that no one will ever follow in our steps. . . .

Contrary to the impression we had received from Martian stories, we found that the semi-fabulous ruins lay at no great distance from Ignarh with its terrestrial colony and consulates. The nude, spongy-chested natives had spoken deterringly of vast deserts filled with ever-swirling sand-storms, through which we must pass to reach Yoh-Vombis; and in spite of our munificent offers of payment, it had been difficult to secure guides for the journey. We had provisioned ourselves amply and had prepared for all emergencies that might eventuate during a long trip. Therefore, we were pleased as well as surprised when we came to the ruins after seven hours of plodding across the flat, treeless, orange-yellow desolation to the south-west of Ignarh. On account of the lesser gravity, the journey was far less tiring than one who is unfamiliar with Martian conditions might expect. But because of the thin, Himalaya-like air, and the possible strain on our hearts, we had been careful not to hasten.

Our coming to Yoh-Vombis was sudden and spectacular. Climbing the low slope of a league-long elevation of bare and deeply eroded stone, we saw before us the shattered walls of our destination, whose highest tower was notching the small, remote sun that glared in stifled crimson through the floating haze of fine sand. For a little, we thought that the domeless, three-angled towers and broken-down monoliths were those of some unlegended city, other than the one we sought. But the disposition of the ruins, which lay in a sort of arc for almost the entire extent of the low and gneissic elevation, together with the type of architecture, soon convinced us that we had found our goal. No other ancient city on Mars had been laid out in that manner; and the strange, many-terraced buttresses of the thick walls, like the stairways of forgotten Anakim, were peculiar to the prehistoric race that had built Yoh-Vombis. Moreover, Yoh-Vombis was the one remaining example of this architecture, aside from a few fragments in the neighborhood of Ignarh, which we had previously examined.

I have seen the hoary, sky-confronting walls of Macchu Pichu amid the desolate Andes, and the teocallis that are buried in the Mexican jungles. And I have seen the frozen, giant-builded battlements of Uogam on the glacial tundras of the nightward hemisphere of Venus. But these were as things of yesteryear, bearing at least the memory or the intimation of life, compared with the awesome and lethiferous antiquity, the cycle-enduring doom of a petrified sterility, that seemed to invest Yoh-Vombis. The whole region was far from the life-giving canals beyond whose environs even the more noxious flora and fauna are seldom found; and we had seen no living thing since our departure from Ignarh. But here, in this place of eternal bareness and solitude, it seemed that life could never have been. The stark, eroded stones were things that might have been reared by the toil of the dead, to house the monstrous ghouls and demons of primal desolation.

I think we all received the same impression as we stood staring in silence while the pale, sanies-like sunset fell on the dark and megalithic ruins. I remember gasping a little, in an air that seemed to have been touched by the irrespirable chill of death; and I heard the same sharp, laborious intake of breath from others of our party.

"That place is deader than an Egyptian morgue," observed Harper.

"Certainly it is far more ancient," Octave assented. "According to the most reliable legends, the Yorhis, who built Yoh-Vombis, were wiped out by the present ruling race at least forty thousand years ago."

"There's a story, isn't there," said Harper, "that the last remnant of the Yorhis was destroyed by some unknown agency—something too horrible and outré to be mentioned even in a myth?"

"Of course, I've heard that legend," agreed Octave. "Maybe we'll find evidence among the ruins, to prove or disprove it. The Yorhis may have been cleaned out by some terrible epidemic, such as the Yashta pestilence, which was a kind of green mould that ate all the bones of the body, starting with the teeth and nails. But we needn't be afraid of getting it, if there are any mummies in Yoh-Vombis—the bacteria will all be dead as their victims, after so many cycles of planetary desiccation. Anyway, there ought to be a lot for us to learn. The Aihais have always been more or less shy of the place. Few have ever visited it: and none, as far as I can find, have made a thorough examination of the ruins."

The sun had gone down with uncanny swiftness, as if it had disappeared through some sort of prestidigitation rather than the normal process of setting. We felt the instant chill of the blue-green twilight: and the ether above us was like a huge, transparent dome of sunless ice, shot with a million bleak sparklings that were the stars. We donned the coats and helmets of Martian fur, which must always be worn at night; and going on to westward of the walls, we established our camp in their lee, so that we might be sheltered a little from the *jaar*, that cruel desert wind that always blows from the east before dawn. Then, lighting the alcohol lamps that had been brought along for cooking purposes, we huddled around them while the evening meal was prepared and eaten.

Afterwards, for comfort rather than because of weariness, we retired early to our sleeping-bags; and the two Aihais, our guides, wrapped themselves in the cerement-like folds of grey *bassa*-cloth which are all the protection their leathery skins appear to require even in sub-zero temperatures.

Even in my thick, double-lined bag, I still felt the rigor of the night air; and I am sure it was this, rather than anything else, which kept me awake for a long while and rendered my eventual slumber somewhat restless and broken. Of course, the strangeness of our situation, and the weird proximity of those aeonian walls and towers may in some measure have contributed to my unrest. But at any rate, I was not troubled by even the least presentiment of alarm or danger; and I should have laughed at the idea that anything of peril could lurk on Yoh-Vombis, amid whose undreamable and stupefying antiquities the very phantoms of its dead must long since have faded into nothingness.

I remember little, however, except the feeling of interminable duration that often marks a shallow and interrupted sleep. I recall the marrow-piercing wind that moaned above us toward midnight, and the sand that stung my face like a fine hail as it passed, blowing from desert to immemorial desert; and I recall the still, inflexible stars that grew dim for awhile with that fleeing ancient dust. Then the wind went by; and I drowsed again, with starts of semi-wakefulness. At last, in one of these, I knew vaguely that the small twin moons, Phobos and Deimos, had risen and were making huge and spectral shadows with the ruins and were casting an ashen glimmer on the shrouded forms of my companions.

I must have been half-asleep; for the memory of that which I saw is doubtful as any dream. I watched beneath drooping lids the tiny moons that had topped the domeless triangular towers; and I saw the far-flung shadows that almost touched the bodies of my fellow-archaeologists.

The whole scene was locked in a petrific stillness; and none of the sleepers stirred. Then, as my lids were about to close, I received an impression of movement in the frozen gloom; and it seemed to me that a portion of the foremost shadow had detached itself and was crawling toward Octave, who lay nearer to the ruins than we others.

Even through my heavy lethargy, I was disturbed by a warning of something unnatural and perhaps ominous. I started to sit up; and even as I moved, the shadowy object, whatever it was, drew back and became merged once more in the greater shadow. Its vanishment startled me into full wakefulness; and yet I could not be sure that I had actually seen the thing. In that brief, final glimpse, it had seemed like a roughly circular piece of cloth or leather, dark and crumpled, and twelve or fourteen inches in diameter, that ran along the ground with the doubling movement of an inch-worm, causing it to fold and unfold in a startling manner as it went.

I did not go to sleep again for nearly an hour; and if it had not been for the extreme cold, I should doubtless have gotten up to investigate and make sure whether I had really beheld an object of such bizarre nature or had merely dreamt it. I lay staring at the deep ebon shadow in which it had disappeared, while a series of fanciful wonderings followed each other in antic procession through my mind. Even then, though somewhat perturbed, I was not aware of any actual fear or intuition of possible menace. And more and more I began to convince myself that the thing was too unlikely and fantastical to have been anything but the figment of a dream. And at last I nodded off into light slumber.

The chill, demoniac sighing of the *jaar* across the jagged walls awoke me, and I saw that the faint moonlight had received the hueless accession of early dawn. We all arose, and prepared our breakfast with fingers that grew numb in spite of the spirit-lamps. Then, shivering, we ate, while the sun leapt over the horizon like a juggler's ball. Enormous, gaunt, without gradations of shadow or luminosity, the ruins beetled before us in the thin light, like the mausolea of primordial giants, that abide from darkness-eaten aeons to confront the last dawn of an expiring orb.

My queer visual experience during the night had taken on more than ever a fantasmagoric unreality; and I gave it no more than a passing thought and did not speak of it to the others. But, even as the faint, distorted shadows of slumber often tinge one's waking hours, it may have contributed to the nameless mood in which I found myself: a mood in which I felt the unhuman alienage of our surroundings and the black, fathomless antiquity of the ruins like an almost unbearable oppression. The feeling seemed to be made of a million spectral adumbrations that oozed unseen but palpable from the great, unearthly architecture; that weighed upon me like tomb-born incubi, but were void of form and meaning such as could be comprehended by human thought. I appeared to move, not in the open air, but in the smothering gloom of sealed sepulchral vaults; to choke with a death-fraught atmosphere, with the miasmata of aeon-old corruption.

My companions were all eager to explore the ruins; and of course it was impossible for me to even mention the apparently absurd and baseless shadows of my mood. Human beings on other worlds than their own are often subject to nervous and psychic symptoms of this sort, engendered by the unfamiliar forces, the novel radiations of their environment. But, as we approached the buildings in our preliminary tour of examination, I lagged behind the others, seized by a paralyzing panic that left me unable to move or breathe for a few moments. A dark, freezing clamminess seemed to pervade my brain and muscles and suspend their inmost working. Then it lifted; and I was free to go on and follow the others.

Strangely, as it seemed, the two Martians refused to accompany us. Stolid and taciturn, they gave no explicit reason; but evidently nothing would induce them to enter Yoh-Vombis. Whether or not they were afraid of the ruins, we were unable to determine: their enigmatic faces, with the small oblique eyes and huge, flaring nostrils, betrayed neither fear nor any other emotion intelligible to man. In reply to our questions, they merely said that no Aihai had set foot among the ruins for ages. Apparently there was some mysterious tabu in connection with the place.

For equipment in that preliminary tour, we took along only a crowbar and two picks. Our other tools, and some cartridges of high explosives, we left at our camp, to be used later if necessary, after we had surveyed the ground. One or two of us owned automatics: but these also were left behind; for it seemed absurd to imagine that any form of life would be encountered among the ruins.

Octave was visibly excited as we began our inspection, and maintained a running-fire of exclamatory comment. The rest of us were subdued and silent; and I think that my own feeling, in a measure, was shared by many of the others. It was impossible to shake off the somber awe and wonder that fell upon us from those megalithic stones.

I have no time to describe the ruins minutely, but must hasten on with my story. There is much that I could not describe

Clark Ashton Smith

anyway; for the main area of the city was destined to remain unexplored.

We went on for some distance among the triangular, terraced buildings, following the zig-zag streets that conformed to this peculiar architecture. Most of the towers were more or less dilapidated; and everywhere we saw the deep erosion wrought by cycles of blowing wind and sand, which, in many cases, had worn into roundness the sharp angles of the mighty walls. We entered some of the towers through high, narrow doorways, but found utter emptiness within. Whatever they had contained in the way of furnishings must long ago have crumbled into dust; and the dust had been blown away by the searching desert gales. On some of the outer walls, there was evidence of carving or lettering; but all of it was so worn down and obliterated by time that we could trace only a few fragmentary outlines, of which we could make nothing.

At length we came to a wide thoroughfare, which ended in the wall of a vast terrace, several hundred yards long by perhaps forty in height, on which the central buildings were grouped like a sort of citadel or acropolis. A flight of broken steps, designed for longer limbs than those of men or even the gangling modern Martians, afforded access to the terrace, which had seemingly been hewn from the plateau itself.

Pausing, we decided to defer our investigation of the higher buildings, which, being more exposed than the others, were doubly ruinous and dilapidated, and in all likelihood would offer little for our trouble. Octave had begun to voice his disappointment over our failure to find anything in the nature of artifacts or carvings that would throw light on the history of Yoh-Vombis.

Then, a little to the right of the stairway, we perceived an entrance in the main wall, half-choked with ancient debris. Behind the heap of detritus, we found the beginning of a downward flight of steps. Darkness poured from the opening like a visible flood, noisome and musty with primordial stagnancies of decay; and we could see nothing below the first steps, which gave the appearance of being suspended over a black gulf.

Octave and myself and several others had brought along electric torches, in case we should need them in our explorations. It had occurred to us that there might be subterranean vaults or catacombs in Yoh-Vombis, even as in the latter-day cities of Mars, which are often more extensive underground than above; and such vaults would be the likeliest place in which to look for vestiges of the Yorhi civilization.

Throwing his torch-beam into the abyss, Octave began to descend the stairs. His eager voice called us to follow.

Again, for an instant, the unknown, irrational panic froze my faculties, and I hesitated while the others pressed forward behind me. Then, as before, the terror passed; and I wondered at myself for being overcome by anything so absurd and unfounded. I followed Octave down the steps, and the others came trooping after me.

At the bottom of the high, awkward steps, we found ourselves in a long and roomy vault, like a subterranean hallway. Its floor was deep with siftings of immemorial dust; and in places there were heaps of a coarse grey powder, such as might be left by the decomposition of certain fungi that grow in the Martian catacombs, under the canals. Such fungi, at one time, might conceivably have existed in Yoh-Vombis; but, owing to the prolonged and excessive dehydration, they must have died out long ago. Nothing, surely, not even a fungus, could have lived in those arid vaults for many aeons past.

The air was singularly heavy, as if the lees of an ancient atmosphere, less tenuous than that of Mars today, had settled down and remained in that stagnant darkness. It was harder to breathe than the outer air; it was filled with unknown effluvia; and the light dust arose before us at every step, diffusing a faintness of bygone corruption, like the dust of powdered mummies.

At the end of the vault, before a strait and lofty doorway our torches revealed an immense shallow urn or pan, supported on short cube-shaped legs, and wrought from a dull blackish-green material which suggested some bizarre alloy of metal and porcelain. The thing was about four feet across, with a thick rim adorned by writhing indecipherable figures, deeply etched as if by acid. In the bottom of the bowl we perceived a deposit of dark and cinder-like fragments, which gave off a slight but disagreeable pungence, like the phantom of some more powerful odor. Octave, bending over the rim, began to cough and sneeze as he inhaled it.

"That stuff, whatever it was, must have been a pretty strong fumigant," he observed. "The people of Yoh-Vombis may have used it to disinfect the vaults."

The doorway beyond the shallow urn admitted us to a larger chamber, whose floor was comparatively free of dust. We found that the dark stone beneath our feet was marked off in multiform geometric patterns, traced with ochreous ore, amid which, as in Egyptian cartouches, hieroglyphics and highly formalized drawings were enclosed. We could make little from most of them; but the figures in many were doubtless designed to represent the Yorhis themselves. Like the Aihais, they were tall and angular, with great bellows-like chests; and they were depicted as possessing a supplementary third arm, which issued from the bosom; a characteristic which, in vestigial form, sometimes occurs among the Aihais. The ears and nostrils, as far as we could judge, were not so huge and flaring as those of the modern Martians. All of these Yorhis were represented as being nude; but in one of the cartouches, done in a far hastier style than the others, we perceived two figures whose high, conical craniums were wrapped in what seemed to be a sort of turban, which they were about to remove or adjust. The artist seemed to have laid a peculiar emphasis on the odd gesture with which the sinuous, four-jointed fingers were plucking at these head-dresses; and the whole posture was unexplainably contorted.

From the second vault, passages ramified in all directions, leading to a veritable warren of catacombs. Here, enormous pot-bellied urns of the same material as the fumigating-pan, but taller than a man's head and fitted with angular-handled stoppers, were ranged in solemn rows along the walls, leaving scant room for two of us to walk abreast. When we succeeded in removing one of the huge stoppers, we saw that the jar was filled to the rim with ashes and charred fragments of bone.

Doubtless (as is still the Martian custom) the Yorhis had stored the cremated remains of whole families in single urns.

Even Octave became silent as we went on; and a sort of meditative awe seemed to replace his former excitement. We others, I think, were utterly weighed down to a man by the solid gloom of a concept-defying antiquity, into which it seemed that we were going further and further at every step.

The shadows fluttered before us like the monstrous and misshapen wings of phantom bats. There was nothing anywhere but the atom-like dust of ages, and the jars that held the ashes of a long-extinct people. But, clinging to the high roof in one of the further vaults, I saw a dark and corrugated patch of circular form, like a withered fungus. It was impossible to reach the thing; and we went on after peering at it with many futile conjectures. Oddly enough, I failed to remember at that moment the crumpled, shadowy object I had seen or dreamt the night before.

I have no idea how far we had gone, when we came to the last vault; but it seemed that we had been wandering for ages in that forgotten underworld. The air was growing fouler and more irrespirable, with a thick, sodden quality, as if from a sediment of material rottenness; and we had about decided to turn back. Then, without warning, at the end of a long, urn-lined catacomb, we found ourselves confronted by a blank wall.

Here, we came upon one of the strangest and most mystifying of our discoveries—a mummified and incredibly desiccated figure, standing erect against the wall. It was more than seven feet in height, of a brown, bituminous color, and was wholly nude except for a sort of black cowl that covered the upper head and drooped down at the sides in wrinkled folds. From the three arms, and general contour, it was plainly one of the ancient Yorhis—perhaps the sole member of this race whose body had remained intact.

We all felt an inexpressible thrill at the sheer age of this shrivelled thing, which, in the dry air of the vault, had endured through all the historic and geologic vicissitudes of the planet, to provide a visible link with lost cycles.

Then, as we peered closer with our torches, we saw *why* the mummy had maintained an upright position. At ankles, knees, waist, shoulders and neck it was shackled to the wall by heavy metal bands, so deeply eaten and embrowned with a sort of rust that we had failed to distinguish them at first sight in the shadow. The strange cowl on the head, when closelier studied, continued to baffle us. It was covered with a fine, mould-like pile, unclean and dusty as ancient cobwebs. Something about it, I know not what, was abhorrent and revolting.

"By Jove! this is a real find!" ejaculated Octave, as he thrust his torch into the mummified face, where shadows moved like living things in the pit-deep hollows of the eyes and the huge triple nostrils and wide ears that flared upward beneath the cowl.

Still lifting the torch, he put out his free hand and touched the body very lightly. Tentative as the touch had been, the lower part of the barrel-like torso, the legs, the hands and forearms all seemed to dissolve into powder, leaving the head and upper body and arms still hanging in their metal fetters. The progress of decay had been queerly unequal, for the remnant portions gave no sign of disintegration.

Octave cried out in dismay, and then began to cough and sneeze, as the cloud of brown powder, floating with airy lightness, enveloped him. We others all stepped back to avoid the powder. Then, above the spreading cloud, I saw an unbelievable thing. The black cowl on the mummy's head began to curl and twitch upward at the corners, it writhed with a verminous motion, it fell from the withered cranium, seeming to fold and unfold convulsively in mid-air as it fell. Then it dropped on the bare head of Octave who, in his disconcertment at the crumbling of the mummy, had remained standing close to the wall. At that instant, in a start of profound terror, I remembered the thing that had inched itself from the shadows of Yoh-Vombis in the light of the twin moons, and had drawn back like a figment of slumber at my first waking movement.

Cleaving closely as a tightened cloth, the thing enfolded Octave's hair and brow and eyes, and he shrieked wildly, with incoherent pleas for help, and tore with frantic fingers at the cowl, but failed to loosen it. Then his cries began to mount in a mad crescendo of agony, as if beneath some instrument of infernal torture; and he danced and capered blindly about the vault, eluding us with strange celerity as we all sprang forward in an effort to reach him and release him from his weird incumbrance. The whole happening was mysterious as a nightmare; but the thing that had fallen on his head was plainly some unclassified form of Martian life, which, contrary to all the known laws of science, had survived in those primordial catacombs. We must rescue him from its clutches if we could.

We tried to close in on the frenzied figure of our chief—which, in the far from roomy space between the last urns and the wall, should have been an easy matter. But, darting away, in a manner doubly incomprehensible because of his blindfolded condition, he circled about us and ran past, to disappear among the urns toward the outer labyrinth of intersecting catacombs.

"My God! What has happened to him?" cried Harper. "The man acts as if he were possessed."

There was obviously no time for a discussion of the enigma, and we all followed Octave as speedily as our astonishment would permit. We had lost sight of him in the darkness, and when we came to the first division of the vaults, we were doubtful as to which passage he had taken, till we heard a shrill scream, several times repeated, in a catacomb on the extreme left. There was a weird, unearthly quality in those screams, which may have been due to the long-stagnant air or the peculiar acoustics of the ramifying cavens. But somehow I could not imagine them as issuing from human lips—at least not from those of a living man. They seemed to contain a soulless, mechanical agony, as if they had been wrung from a devil-driven corpse.

Thrusting our torches before us into the lurching, fleeing shadows, we raced along between rows of mighty urns. The screaming had died away in sepulchral silence; but far off we heard the light and muffled thud of running feet. We followed in headlong pursuit; but, gasping painfully in the vitiated, miasmal air, we were soon compelled to slacken our pace without coming in sight of Octave. Very faintly, and further away than ever, like the tomb-swallowed steps of a phantom, we heard his vanishing footfalls. Then they ceased; and we heard nothing, except our own convulsive breathing, and the blood that throbbed in our temple-veins like steadily beaten drums of alarm.

We went on, dividing our party into three contingents when we came to a triple branching of the caverns. Harper and Halgren and myself took the middle passage; and after we had gone on for an endless interval without finding any trace of Octave, and had threaded our way through recesses piled to the roof with colossal urns that must have held the ashes of a hundred generations, we came out in the huge chamber with the geometric floor designs. Here, very shortly, we were joined by the others, who had likewise failed to locate our missing leader.

It would be useless to detail our renewed and hour-long search of the myriad vaults, many of which we had not hitherto explored. All were empty, as far as any sign of life was concerned. I remember passing once more through the vault in which I had seen the dark, rounded patch on the ceiling, and noting with a shudder that the patch was gone. It was a miracle that we did not lose ourselves in that underworld maze; but at last we came back to the final catacomb in which we had found the shackled mummy.

We heard a measured and recurrent clangor as we neared the place—a most alarming and mystifying sound under the circumstances. It was like the hammering of ghouls on some forgotten mausoleum. When we drew nearer, the beams of our torches revealed a sight that was no less unexplainable than unexpected. A human figure, with its back toward us and the head concealed by a swollen black object that had the size and form of a sofa cushion, was standing near the remains of the mummy and was striking at the wall with a pointed metal bar. How long Octave had been there, and where he had found the bar, we could not know. But the blank wall had crumbled away beneath his furious blows, leaving on the floor a pile of cement-like fragments; and a small, narrow door, of the same ambiguous material as the cinerary urns and the fumigating-pan, had been laid bare.

Amazed, uncertain, inexpressibly bewildered, we were all

incapable of action or volition at that moment. The whole business was too fantastic and too horrifying, and it was plain that Octave had been overcome by some sort of madness. I, for one, felt the violent upsurge of sudden nausea when I had identified the loathsomely bloated thing that clung to Octave's head and drooped in obscene tumescence on his neck. I did not dare to surmise the causation of its bloating.

Before any of us could recover our faculties, Octave flung aside the metal bar and began to fumble for something in the wall. It must have been a hidden spring; though how he could have known its location or existence is beyond all legitimate conjecture. With a dull, hideous grating, the uncovered door swung inward, thick and ponderous as a mausolean slab, leaving an aperture from which the nether midnight seemed to well like a flood of aeon-buried foulness. Somehow, at that instant, our electric torches appeared to flicker and grow dim; and we all breathed a suffocating fetor, like a draft from inner worlds of immemorial putrescence.

Octave had turned toward us now, and he stood in an idle posture before the open door, like one who has finished some ordained task. I was the first of our party to throw off the paralyzing spell; and pulling out a clasp-knife—the only semblance of a weapon which I carried—I ran over to him. He moved back, but not quickly enough to evade me, when I stabbed with the four-inch blade at the black, turgescent mass that enveloped his whole upper head and hung down upon his eyes.

What the thing was, I should prefer not to imagine—if it were possible to imagine. It was formless as a great slug, with neither head nor tail nor apparent organs—an unclean, puffy, leathery thing, covered with that fine, mould-like fur of which I have spoken. The knife tore into it as if through rotten parchment, making a long gash, and the horror appeared to collapse like a broken bladder. Out of it there gushed a sickening torrent of human blood, mingled with dark, filiated masses that may have been half-dissolved hair, and floating gelatinous lumps like molten bone, and shreds of a curdy white substance. At the same time, Octave began to stagger, and went down at full length on the floor. Disturbed by his fall, the mummy-dust arose about him in a curling cloud, beneath which he lay mortally still.

Conquering my revulsion, and choking with the dust, I bent over him and tore the flaccid, oozing horror from his head. It came with unexpected ease, as if I had removed a limp rag: but I wish to God that I had let it remain. Beneath, there was no longer a human cranium, for all had been eaten away, even to the eyebrows, and the half-devoured brain was laid bare as I lifted the cowl-like object. I dropped the unnamable thing from fingers that had grown suddenly nerveless, and it turned over as it fell, revealing on the nether side many rows of pinkish suckers, arranged in circles about a pallid disk that was covered with nerve-like filaments, suggesting a sort of plexus.

My companions had pressed forward behind me; but, for an appreciable interval, no one spoke.

"How long do you suppose he has been dead?" It was Halgren who whispered the awful question, which we had all been asking ourselves. Apparently no one felt able or willing to answer it; and we could only stare in horrible, timeless fascination at Octave.

At length I made an effort to avert my gaze; and turning at random, I saw the remnants of the shackled mummy, and noted for the first time, with mechanical, unreal horror, the half-eaten condition of the withered head. From this, my gaze was diverted to the newly opened door at one side, without perceiving for a moment what had drawn my attention. Then, startled, I beheld beneath my torch, far down beyond the door, as if in some nether pit, a seething, multitudinous, worm-like movement of crawling shadows. They seemed to boil up in the darkness; and then, over the broad threshold of the vault, there poured the verminous vanguard of a countless army: things that were kindred to the monstrous, diabolic leech I had torn from Octave's eaten head. Some were thin and flat, like writhing, doubling disks of cloth or leather, and others were more or less poddy, and crawled with glutted slowness. What they had found to feed on in the sealed, eternal midnight I do not know; and I pray that I never shall know.

I sprang back and away from them, electrified with terror,

sick with loathing, and the black army inched itself unendingly with nightmare swiftness from the unsealed abyss, like the nauseous vomit of horror-sated hells. As it poured toward us, burying Octave's body from sight in a writhing wave, I saw a stir of life from the seemingly dead thing I had cast aside, and saw the loathly struggle which it made to right itself and join the others.

But neither I nor my companions could endure to look longer. We turned and ran between the mighty rows of urns, with the slithering mass of demon leeches close upon us, and scattered in blind panic when we came to the first division of the vaults. Heedless of each other or of anything but the urgency of flight, we plunged into the ramifying passages at random. Behind me, I heard someone stumble and go down, with a curse that mounted to an insane shrieking; but I knew that if I halted and went back, it would be only to invite the same baleful doom that had overtaken the hindmost of our party.

Still clutching the electric torch and my open clasp-knife, I ran along a minor passage which, I seemed to remember, would conduct with more or less directness upon the large outer vault with the painted floor. Here I found myself alone. The others had kept to the main catacombs; and I heard far off a muffled babel of mad cries, as if several of them had been seized by their pursuers.

It seemed that I must have been mistaken about the direction of the passage; for it turned and twisted in an unfamiliar manner, with many intersections, and I soon found that I was lost in the black labyrinth, where the dust had lain unstirred by living feet for inestimable generations. The cinerary warren had grown still once more; and I heard my own frenzied panting, loud and stertorous as that of a Titan in the dead silence.

Suddenly, as I went on, my torch disclosed a human figure coming toward me in the gloom. Before I could master my startlement, the figure had passed me with long, machine-like strides, as if returning to the inner vaults. I think it was Harper, since the height and build were about right for him; but I am not altogether sure, for the eyes and upper head were muffled by a dark, inflated cowl, and the pale lips locked as if in a silence of tetanic torture—or death. Whoever he was, he had dropped his torch; and he was running blindfold, in utter darkness, beneath the impulsion of that unearthly vampirism, to seek the very fountain-head of the unloosed horror. I knew that he was beyond human help; and I did not even dream of trying to stop him.

Trembling violently, I resumed my flight, and was passed by two more of our party, stalking by with mechanical swiftness and sureness, and cowled with those Satanic leeches. The others must have returned by way of the main passages; for I did not meet them; and was never to see them again.

The remainder of my flight is a blur of pandemonian terror. Once more, after thinking that I was near the outer cavern, I found myself astray, and fled through a ranged eternity of monstrous urns, in vaults that must have extended for an unknown distance beyond our explorations. It seemed that I had gone on for years; and my lungs were choking with the aeon-dead air, and my legs were ready to crumble beneath me, when I saw far off a tiny point of blessed daylight. I ran toward it, with all the terrors of the alien darkness crowding behind me, and accursed shadows flittering before, and saw that the vault ended in a low, ruinous entrance, littered by rubble on which there fell an arc of thin sunshine.

It was another entrance than the one by which we had penetrated this lethal underworld. I was within a dozen feet of the opening when, without sound or other intimation, something dropped upon my head from the roof above, blinding me instantly and closing upon me like a tautened net. My brow and scalp, at the same time, were shot through with a million needle-like pangs—a manifold, ever-growing agony that seemed to pierce the very bone and converge from all sides upon my inmost brain.

The terror and suffering of that moment were worse than aught which the hells of earthly madness or delirium could ever contain. I felt the foul, vampiric clutch of an atrocious death—and of more than death.

I believe that I dropped the torch: but the fingers of my right hand had still retained the open knife. Instinctively—since I was hardly capable of conscious volition—I raised the knife and slashed blindly, again and again, many times, at the thing that had fastened its deadly folds upon me. The blade must have gone through and through the clinging monstrosity, to gash my own flesh in a score of places; but I did not feel the pain of those wounds in the million-throbbing torment that possessed me.

At last I saw light, and saw that a black strip, loosened from above my eyes and dripping with my own blood, was hanging down my cheek. It writhed a little, even as it hung, and I ripped it away, and ripped the other remnants of the thing, tatter by oozing, bloody tatter, from off my brow and head. Then I staggered toward the entrance; and the wan light turned to a far, receding, dancing flame before me as I lurched and fell outside the cavern—a flame that fled like the last star of creation above the yawning, sliding chaos and oblivion into which I descended . . .

I am told that my unconsciousness was of brief duration. I came to myself, with the cryptic faces of the two Martian guides bending over me. My head was full of lancinating pains, and half-remembered terrors closed upon my mind like the shadows of mustering harpies. I rolled over, and looked back toward the cavern-mouth, from which the Martians, after finding me, had seemingly dragged me for some little distance. The mouth was under the terraced angle of an outer building, and within sight of our camp.

I stared at the black opening with hideous fascination, and descried a shadowy stirring in the gloom—the writhing, verminous movement of things that pressed forward from the darkness but did not emerge into the light. Doubtless they could not endure the sun, those creatures of ultramundane night and cycle-sealed corruption.

It was then that the ultimate horror, the beginning madness, came upon me. Amid my crawling revulsion, my nausea-prompted desire to flee from that seething cavern-mouth, there rose an abhorrently conflicting impulse to return; to thread my backward way through all the catacombs, as the others had done; to go down where never men save they, the inconceivably doomed and accursed, had ever gone; to seek beneath that damnable compulsion a nether world that human thought can never picture. There was a black light, a soundless calling, in the vaults of my brain: the implanted summons of the Thing, like a permeating and sorcerous poison. It lured me to the subterranean door that was walled up by the dying people of Yoh-Vombis, to immure those hellish and immortal leeches, those dark parasites that engraft their own abominable life on the half-eaten brains of the dead. It called me to the depths beyond, where dwell the noisome, necromantic Ones, of whom the leeches, with all their powers of vampirism and diabolism, are but the merest minions . . .

It was only the two Aihais who prevented me from going back. I struggled, I fought them insanely as they strove to retard me with their spongy arms; but I must have been pretty thoroughly exhausted from all the superhuman adventures of the day; and I went down once more, after a little, into fathomless nothingness, from which I floated out at long intervals, to realize that I was being carried across the desert toward Ignarh.

Well, that is all my story. I have tried to tell it fully and coherently, at a cost that would be unimaginable to the sane . . . to tell it before the madness falls upon me again, as it will very soon—as it is doing now . . . Yes, I have told my story . . . and you have written it all out, haven't you? Now I must go back to Yoh-Vombis— back across the desert and down through all the catacombs to the vaster vaults beneath. Something is in my brain, that commands me and will direct me . . . I tell you, I must go . . .

ROBERT E. HOWARD

Robert Ervin Howard was born in 1906 in Peaster, Texas, and spent most of his life in the nearby town of Cross Plains. He was the son of one of the pioneer physicians of Texas and early developed a devotion to his native land and, by extension, to frontier and barbarian peoples throughout history. Largely self-educated, Howard graduated from Brownwood High School and spent only a year studying bookkeeping at Howard Payne College Academy. In 1924 he sold his first story to *Weird Tales,* and for the next dozen years he wrote prolifically for the horror and adventure pulp magazines.

Much of Howard's work falls into cycles focused around a dynamic hero, usually of barbarian cast, including Bran Mak Morn (a British chieftain in Roman times), Solomon Kane (an English Puritan of the seventeenth century), King Kull (a warrior-king in the imaginary prehistoric realm of Valusia), and, most famously, Conan the Cimmerian, introduced to readers in "The Phoenix on the Sword" (*Weird Tales,* December 1932); these latter two cycles virtually established the subgenre of sword-and-sorcery as a powerful subset of the fantasy tale. In 1930 Howard came into contact with H. P. Lovecraft, and in their voluminous correspondence over the next six years Howard articulated his yearning for the freedom, courage, and adventurousness that he saw in barbarism as opposed to the softness and decadence of civilization. Howard also wrote poignantly of his native Texas in such stories as "The Horror from the Mound" (*Weird Tales,* May 1932) and "Black Canaan" (*Weird Tales,* June 1936). Despondent over the imminent death of his mother, Howard committed suicide in 1936.

Howard's Conan has become emblematic of his work; it has been widely imitated by other writers and also adapted into films, comic books, and other media. His brief involvement with Novalyne Price has been depicted in the film *The Whole Wide World* (1996).

"Old Garfield's Heart" (*Weird Tales,* December 1933) is typical of Howard's weird work in its deft use of the supernatural and in its topographical realism.

OLD GARFIELD'S HEART

I was sitting on the porch when my grandfather hobbled out and sank down on his favorite chair with the cushioned seat, and began to stuff tobacco in his old corncob-pipe.

"I thought you'd be goin' to the dance," he said.

"I'm waiting for Doc Blaine," I answered. "I'm going over to old man Garfield's with him."

My grandfather sucked at his pipe awhile before he spoke again.

"Old Jim purty bad off?"

"Doc says he hasn't a chance."

"Who's takin' care of him?"

"Joe Braxton—against Garfield's wishes. But somebody had to stay with him."

My grandfather sucked his pipe noisily, and watched the heat lightning playing away off up in the hills; then he said: "You think old Jim's the biggest liar in this county, don't you?"

"He tells some pretty tall tales," I admitted. "Some of the things he claimed he took part in, must have happened before he was born."

"I came from Tennessee to Texas in 1870," my grandfather said abruptly. "I saw this town of Lost Knob grow up from nothin'. There wasn't even a log-hut store here when I came. But old Jim Garfield was here, livin' in the same place he lives now, only then it was a log cabin. He don't look a day older now than he did the first time I saw him."

"You never mentioned that before," I said in some surprise.

"I knew you'd put it down to an old man's maunderin's," he answered. "Old Jim was the first white man to settle in this country. He built his cabin a good fifty miles west of the frontier. God knows how he done it, for these hills swarmed with Comanches then.

"I remember the first time I ever saw him. Even then everybody called him 'old Jim.'

"I remember him tellin' me the same tales he's told you— how he was at the battle of San Jacinto when he was a youngster, and how he'd rode with Ewen Cameron and Jack Hayes. Only I believe him, and you don't."

"That was so long ago—" I protested.

"The last Indian raid through this country was in 1874," said my grandfather, engrossed in his own reminiscences. "I was in on that fight, and so was old Jim. I saw him knock old Yellow Tail off his mustang at seven hundred yards with a buffalo rifle.

"But before that I was with him in a fight up near the head of Locust Creek. A band of Comanches came down Mesquital, lootin' and burnin', rode through the hills and started back up Locust Creek, and a scout of us were hot on their heels. We ran onto them just at sundown in a mesquite flat. We killed seven of them, and the rest skinned out through the brush on foot. But three of our boys were killed, and Jim Garfield got a thrust in the breast with a lance.

"It was an awful wound. He lay like a dead man, and it seemed sure nobody could live after a wound like that. But an old Indian came out of the brush, and when we aimed our guns at him, he made the peace sign and spoke to us in Spanish. I don't know why the boys didn't shoot him in his tracks, because our blood was heated with the fightin' and killin', but somethin' about him made us hold our fire. He said he wasn't a Comanche, but was an old friend of Garfield's, and wanted to help him. He asked us to carry Jim into a clump of mesquite, and leave him alone with him, and to this day I don't know why we did, but we did. It was an awful time—the wounded moanin' and callin' for water, the starin' corpses strewn about the camp, night comin' on, and no way of knowin' that the Indians wouldn't return when dark fell.

"We made camp right there, because the horses were fagged out, and we watched all night, but the Comanches didn't come back. I don't know what went on out in the mesquite where Jim Garfield's body lay, because I never saw that strange Indian again; but durin' the night I kept hearin' a weird moanin' that wasn't made by the dyin' men, and an owl hooted from midnight till dawn.

"And at sunrise Jim Garfield came walkin' out of the mesquite, pale and haggard, but alive, and already the wound in his breast had closed and begun to heal. And since then he's never mentioned that wound, nor that fight, nor the strange Indian who came and went so mysteriously. And he hasn't aged a bit; he looks now just like he did then—a man of about fifty."

In the silence that followed, a car began to purr down the road, and twin shafts of light cut through the dusk.

"That's Doc Blaine," I said. "When I come back I'll tell you how Garfield is."

Doc Blaine was prompt with his predictions as we drove the three miles of post-oak covered hills that lay between Lost Knob and the Garfield farm.

"I'll be surprized to find him alive," he said, "smashed up like he is. A man his age ought to have more sense than to try to break a young horse."

"He doesn't look so old," I remarked.

"I'll be fifty, my next birthday," answered Doc Blaine. "I've known him all my life, and he must have been at least fifty the first time I ever saw him. His looks are deceiving."

Old Garfield's dwelling-place was reminiscent of the past. The boards of the low squat house had never known paint. Orchard fence and corrals were built of rails.

Old Jim lay on his rude bed, tended crudely but efficiently by the man Doc Blaine had hired over the old man's protests. As I looked at him, I was impressed anew by his evident vitality. His frame was stooped but unwithered, his limbs rounded out with springy muscles. In his corded neck and in his face, drawn though it was with suffering, was apparent an innate virility. His eyes, though partly glazed with pain, burned with the same unquenchable element.

"He's been ravin'," said Joe Braxton stolidly.

"First white man in this country," muttered old Jim, becoming intelligible. "Hills no white man ever set foot in before. Gettin' too old. Have to settle down. Can't move on like I used to. Settle down here. Good country before it filled up with cow-men and squatters. Wish Ewen Cameron could see this country. The Mexicans shot him. Damn 'em!"

Doc Blaine shook his head. "He's all smashed up inside. He won't live till daylight."

Garfield unexpectedly lifted his head and looked at us with clear eyes.

"Wrong, Doc," he wheezed, his breath whistling with pain. "I'll live. What's broken bones and twisted guts? Nothin'! It's the heart that counts. Long as the heart keeps pumpin', a man can't die. My heart's sound. Listen to it! Feel of it!"

He groped painfully for Doc Blaine's wrist, dragged his hand to his bosom and held it there, staring up into the doctor's face with avid intensity.

"Regular dynamo, ain't it?" he gasped. "Stronger'n a gasoline engine!"

Blaine beckoned me. "Lay your hand here," he said, placing my hand on the old man's bare breast. "He does have a remarkable heart action."

I noted, in the light of the coal-oil lamp, a great livid scar in the gaunt arching breast—such a scar as might be made by a flint-headed spear. I laid my hand directly on this scar, and an exclamation escaped my lips.

Under my hand old Jim Garfield's heart pulsed, but its throb was like no other heart action I have ever observed. Its power was astounding; his ribs vibrated to its steady throb. It felt more like the vibrating of a dynamo than the action of a human organ. I could feel its amazing vitality radiating from his breast, stealing up into my hand and up my arm, until my own heart seemed to speed up in response.

"I can't die," old Jim gasped. "Not so long as my heart's in my breast. Only a bullet through the brain can kill me. And even then I wouldn't be rightly dead, as long as my heart beats in my breast. Yet it ain't rightly mine, either. It belongs to Ghost Man, the Lipan chief. It was the heart of a god the Lipans worshipped before the Comanches drove 'em out of their native hills.

"I knew Ghost Man down on the Rio Grande, when I was with Ewen Cameron. I saved his life from the Mexicans once. He tied the string of ghost wampum between him and me—the wampum no man but me and him can see or feel. He came when he knowed I needed him, in that fight up on the headwaters of Locust Creek, when I got this scar.

"I was dead as a man can be. My heart was sliced in two, like the heart of a butchered beef steer.

"All night Ghost Man did magic, callin' my ghost back from spirit-land. I remember that flight, a little. It was dark, and gray-like, and I drifted through gray mists and heard the dead wailin' past me in the mist. But Ghost Man brought me back.

"He took out what was left of my mortal heart, and put the heart of the god in my bosom. But it's his, and when I'm through with it, he'll come for it. It's kept me alive and strong for the lifetime of a man. Age can't touch me. What do I care if these fools around here call me an old liar? What I know, I know. But hark'ee!"

His fingers became claws, clamping fiercely on Doc Blaine's wrist. His old eyes, old yet strangely young, burned fierce as those of an eagle under his bushy brows.

"If by some mischance I *should* die, now or later, promise me this! Cut into my bosom and take out the heart Ghost Man lent me so long ago! It's his. And as long as it beats in my body, my spirit'll be tied to that body, though my head be crushed like an egg underfoot! A livin' thing in a rottin' body! Promise!"

"All right, I promise," replied Doc Blaine, to humor him, and old Jim Garfield sank back with a whistling sigh of relief.

He did not die that night, nor the next, nor the next. I well remember the next day, because it was that day that I had the fight with Jack Kirby.

People will take a good deal from a bully, rather than to spill blood. Because nobody had gone to the trouble of killing him, Kirby thought the whole countryside was afraid of him.

He had bought a steer from my father, and when my father went to collect for it, Kirby told him that he had paid the money to me—which was a lie. I went looking for Kirby, and came upon him in a bootleg joint, boasting of his toughness, and telling the crowd that he was going to beat me up and make me say that he had paid me the money, and that I had stuck it into my own pocket. When I heard him say that, I saw red, and ran in on him with a stockman's knife, and cut him across the face, and in the neck, side, breast and belly, and the only thing that saved his life was the fact that the crowd pulled me off.

There was a preliminary hearing, and I was indicted on a charge of assault, and my trial was set for the following term of court. Kirby was as tough-fibered as a post-oak country bully ought to be, and he recovered, swearing vengeance, for he was vain of his looks, though God knows why, and I had permanently impaired them.

And while Jack Kirby was recovering, old man Garfield recovered too, to the amazement of everybody, especially Doc Blaine.

I well remember the night Doc Blaine took me again out to old Jim Garfield's farm. I was in Shifty Corlan's joint, trying to drink enough of the slop he called beer to get a kick out of it, when Doc Blaine came in and persuaded me to go with him.

As we drove along the winding old road in Doc's car, I asked: "Why are you insistent that I go with you this particular night? This isn't a professional call, is it?"

"No," he said. "You couldn't kill old Jim with a post-oak maul. He's completely recovered from injuries that ought to have killed an ox. To tell the truth, Jack Kirby is in Lost Knob, swearing he'll shoot you on sight."

"Well, for God's sake!" I exclaimed angrily. "Now everybody'll think I left town because I was afraid of him. Turn around and take me back, damn it!"

"Be reasonable," said Doc. "Everybody knows you're not afraid of Kirby. Nobody's afraid of him now. His bluff's broken, and that's why he's so wild against you. But you can't afford to have any more trouble with him now, and your trial only a short time off."

I laughed and said: "Well, if he's looking for me hard enough, he can find me as easily at old Garfield's as in town, because Shifty Corlan heard you say where we were going. And Shifty's hated me ever since I skinned him in that horse-swap last fall. He'll tell Kirby where I went."

"I never thought of that," said Doc Blaine, worried.

"Hell, forget it," I advised. "Kirby hasn't got guts enough to do anything but blow."

But I was mistaken. Puncture a bully's vanity and you touch his one vital spot.

Old Jim had not gone to bed when we got there. He was sitting in the room opening on to his sagging porch, the room which was at once living-room and bedroom, smoking his old cob pipe and trying to read a newspaper by the light of his coal-oil lamp. All the windows and doors were wide open for the coolness, and the insects which swarmed in and fluttered around the lamp didn't seem to bother him.

We sat down and discussed the weather—which isn't so inane as one might suppose, in a country where men's livelihood depends on sun and rain, and is at the mercy of wind and drouth. The talk drifted into other kindred channels, and after some time, Doc Blaine bluntly spoke of something that hung in his mind.

"Jim," he said, "that night I thought you were dying, you babbled a lot of stuff about your heart, and an Indian who lent you his. How much of that was delirium?"

"None, Doc," said Garfield, pulling at his pipe. "It was gospel truth. Ghost Man, the Lipan priest of the Gods of Night, replaced my dead, torn heart with one from somethin' he worshipped. I ain't sure myself just what that somethin' is—somethin' from away back and a long way off, he said. But bein' a god, it can do without its heart for awhile. But when I die—if I ever get my head smashed so my consciousness is destroyed—the heart must be given back to Ghost Man."

"You mean you were in earnest about cutting out your heart?" demanded Doc Blaine.

"It has to be," answered old Garfield. "A livin' thing in a dead thing is opposed to nat'er. That's what Ghost Man said."

"Who the devil *was* Ghost Man?"

"I told you. A witch-doctor of the Lipans, who dwelt in this country before the Comanches came down from the Staked Plains and drove 'em south across the Rio Grande. I was a friend to 'em. I reckon Ghost Man is the only one left alive."

"Alive? Now?"

"I dunno," confessed old Jim. "I dunno whether he's alive or dead. I dunno whether he was alive when he came to me after the fight on Locust Creek, or even if he was alive when I knowed him in the southern country. Alive as we understand life, I mean."

"What balderdash is this?" demanded Doc Blaine uneasily, and I felt a slight stirring in my hair. Outside was stillness, and the stars, and the black shadows of the post-oak woods. The lamp cast old Garfield's shadow grotesquely on the wall, so that it did not at all resemble that of a human, and his words were strange as words heard in a nightmare.

"I knowed you wouldn't understand," said old Jim. "I don't understand myself, and I ain't got the words to explain them things I feel and know without understandin'. The Lipans were kin to the Apaches, and the Apaches learnt curious things from the Pueblos. Ghost Man *was*—that's all I can say—alive or dead, I don't know, but he *was*. What's more, he *is*."

"Is it you or me that's crazy?" asked Doc Blaine.

"Well," said old Jim, "I'll tell you this much—Ghost Man knew Coronado."

"Crazy as a loon!" murmured Doc Blaine. Then he lifted his head. "What's that?"

"Horse turning in from the road," I said. "Sounds like it stopped."

I stepped to the door, like a fool, and stood etched in the light behind me. I got a glimpse of a shadowy bulk I knew to be a man on a horse; then Doc Blaine yelled: "Look out!" and threw himself against me, knocking us both sprawling. At the same instant I heard the smashing report of a rifle, and old Garfield grunted and fell heavily.

"Jack Kirby!" screamed Doc Blaine. "He's killed Jim!"

I scrambled up, hearing the clatter of retreating hoofs, snatched old Jim's shotgun from the wall, rushed recklessly out on to the sagging porch and let go both barrels at the fleeing shape, dim in the starlight. The charge was too light to kill at that range, but the bird-shot stung the horse and maddened him. He swerved, crashed headlong through a rail fence and charged across the orchard, and a peach tree limb knocked his rider out of the saddle. He never moved after he hit the ground. I ran out there and looked down at him. It was Jack Kirby, right enough, and his neck was broken like a rotten branch.

I let him lie, and ran back to the house. Doc Blaine had stretched old Garfield out on a bench he'd dragged in from the porch, and Doc's face was whiter than I'd ever seen it. Old Jim was a ghastly sight; he had been shot with an old-fashioned .45-70, and at that range the heavy ball had literally torn off the top of his head. His features were masked with blood and brains. He had been directly behind me, poor old devil, and he had stopped the slug meant for me.

Doc Blaine was trembling, though he was anything but a stranger to such sights.

"Would you pronounce him dead?" he asked.

"That's for you to say," I answered. "But even a fool could tell that he's dead."

"He *is* dead," said Doc Blaine in a strained unnatural voice. "Rigor mortis is already setting in. But feel his heart!"

I did, and cried out. The flesh was already cold and clammy; but beneath it that mysterious heart still hammered steadily away, like a dynamo in a deserted house. No blood coursed through those veins; yet the heart pounded, pounded, pounded, like the pulse of Eternity.

"A living thing in a dead thing," whispered Doc Blaine, cold sweat on his face. "This is opposed to nature. I am going to keep the promise I made him. I'll assume full responsibility. This is too monstrous to ignore."

Our implements were a butcher-knife and a hack-saw. Outside only the still stars looked down on the black post-oak shadows and the dead man that lay in the orchard. Inside, the old lamp flickered, making strange shadows move and shiver and cringe in the corners, and glistened on the blood on the floor, and the red-dabbled figure on the bench. The only sound inside was the crunch of the saw-edge in bone; outside an owl began to hoot weirdly.

Doc Blaine thrust a red-stained hand into the aperture he had made, and drew out a red, pulsing object that caught the lamplight. With a choked cry he recoiled, and the thing slipped from his fingers and fell on the table. And I too cried out involuntarily. For it did not fall with a soft meaty thud, as a piece of flesh should fall. It *thumped* hard on the table.

Impelled by an irresistible urge, I bent and gingerly picked up old Garfield's heart. The feel of it was brittle, unyielding, like steel or stone, but smoother than either. In size and shape it was the duplicate of a human heart, but it was slick and smooth, and its crimson surface reflected the lamplight like a jewel more lambent than any ruby; and in my hand it still throbbed mightily, sending vibratory radiations of energy up my arm until my own heart seemed swelling and bursting in response. It was cosmic *power*, beyond my comprehension, concentrated into the likeness of a human heart.

The thought came to me that here was a dynamo of life, the nearest approach to immortality that is possible for the destructible human body, the materialization of a cosmic secret more wonderful than the fabulous fountain sought for by Ponce de Leon. My soul was drawn into that unterrestrial gleam, and I suddenly wished passionately that it hammered and thundered in my own bosom in place of my paltry heart of tissue and muscle.

Doc Blaine ejaculated incoherently. I wheeled.

The noise of his coming had been no greater than the whispering of a night wind through the corn. There in the doorway he stood, tall, dark, inscrutable—an Indian warrior, in the paint, war bonnet, breech-clout and moccasins of an elder age. His dark eyes burned like fires gleaming deep under fathomless black lakes. Silently he extended his hand, and I dropped Jim Garfield's heart into it. Then without a word he turned and stalked into the night. But when Doc Blaine and I rushed out into the yard an instant later, there was no sign of any human being. He had vanished like a phantom of the night, and only something that looked like an owl was flying, dwindling from sight, into the rising moon.

ROBERT BLOCH

Robert Albert Bloch was born in Chicago in 1917. An early love of pulp fiction led him to write to H. P. Lovecraft in 1933, and for the next four years, until Lovecraft's death, Bloch engaged in a virtual tutelage in the art of writing. By 1935 Bloch had begun appearing in *Weird Tales* with somewhat flamboyant tales of supernatural horror; but in a few years he began exercising more restraint, developing the tight-lipped, hard-boiled manner representative of his later work. His first short story collection, *The Opener of the Way*, appeared in 1945 from Arkham House; two years later, *The Scarf,* a chilling novel fusing psychological and supernatural horror, was published. Bloch subsequently alternated between such works of suspense as the novels *Psycho* (1959), *The Dead Beat* (1960), and *Night-World* (1972) and supernatural tales such as the classic "Yours Truly, Jack the Ripper" (*Weird Tales,* July 1943) and "The Skull of the Marquis de Sade" (*Weird Tales,* September 1945; filmed as *The Skull,* 1965). Alfred Hitchcock's film adaptation of *Psycho* (1960) brought Bloch great celebrity but also a certain pressure to duplicate its success, and his two sequels (*Psycho II,* 1982; *Psycho House,* 1990) do not represent him to best advantage. Late in life he wrote a charming autobiography, *Once Around the Bloch* (1993). Robert Bloch died in Beverly Hills, California, in 1994.

Bloch's most representative work in supernatural horror is found in his bountiful array of short stories, collected in such volumes as *Pleasant Dreams—Nightmares* (1958), *Tales in a Jugular Vein* (1965), *Chamber of Horrors* (1966), *Such Stuff as Screams Are Made Of* (1979), and many others. The best of them are found in the three-volume *Selected Stories* (1988).

"Black Bargain" (*Weird Tales*, May 1942; collected in *Flowers from the Moon and Other Lunacies*, 1998) is representative of Bloch's work in its air of mundane realism, which allows the subtle incursion of the supernatural to enter in a spectacular denouement. It makes use of a fictitious volume, *De Vermis Mysteriis* (*The Mysteries of the Worm*), devised in Bloch's early Lovecraftian tales.

BLACK BARGAIN

It was getting late when I switched off the neon and got busy behind the fountain with my silver polish. The fruit syrup came off easily, but the chocolate stuck and the hot fudge was greasy. I wish to God they wouldn't order hot fudge.

I began to get irritated as I scrubbed away. Five hours on my feet, every night, and what did I have to show for it? Varicose veins. Varicose veins, and the memory of a thousand foolish faces. The veins were easier to bear than the memories. They were so depressing, those customers of mine. I knew them all by heart.

In early evening all I got was "cokes." I could spot the "cokes" a mile away. Giggling high-school girls, with long shocks of uncombed brown hair, with their shapeless tan fingertip coats and the repulsively thick legs bulging over boots. They were all "cokes." For forty-five minutes they'd monopolize a booth, messing up the tile table top with cigarette ashes, crushed napkins daubed in lipstick and little puddles of spilled water. Whenever a high-school girl came in, I automatically reached for the cola pump.

A little later in the evening I got the "gimmie two packs" crowd. Sports shirts hanging limply over hairy arms meant the filtertips. Blue work shirts with rolled sleeves disclosing tattooing meant the unfiltered cigarettes.

Once in awhile I got a fat boy. He was always a "cigar." If he wore glasses he was a two-for-thirty-fiver. If not, I merely had to indicate the box on the counter. Ten cents straight, Mild Havana—all long filler.

Oh, it was monotonous. The "notions" family, who invariably departed with aspirin, Ex-Lax, candy bars, and a pint of ice cream. The "public library" crowd—tall, skinny youths bending the pages of magazines on the rack and never buying. The "soda waters" with their trousers wrinkled by the sofa of a one room apartment, the "curlers," always looking furtively toward the baby buggy outside. And around ten, the "pineapple sundaes"—fat women Bingo players. Followed by the "chocolate sodas" when the show let out. More booth parties, giggling girls and red-necked young men in sloppy mod outfits.

In and out, all day long. The rushing "telephones," the doddering old "five-cent stamps," the bachelor "toothpastes" and "razor blades."

I could spot them all at a glance. Night after night they dragged up to the counter. I don't know why they even bothered to tell me what they wanted. One look was all I needed to anticipate their slightest wishes. I could have given them what they needed without their asking.

Or, rather, I suppose I couldn't. Because what most of them really needed was a good long drink of arsenic as far as I was concerned.

Arsenic! Good Lord, how long had it been since I'd been called upon to fill out a *prescription!* None of these stupid idiots wanted *drugs* from a drugstore. Why had I bothered to study pharmacy? All I really needed was a two week course in pouring chocolate syrup over melting ice cream, and a month's study of how to set up cardboard figures in the window so as to emphasize their enormous busts.

Well—

He came in then. I heard the slow footsteps without bothering to look up. For amusement I tried to guess before I glanced. A "gimme two packs?" A "toothpaste?" Well the hell with him. I was closing up.

The male footsteps had shuffled up to the counter before I raised my head. They halted, timidly. I still refused to give any recognition of his presence. Then came a hesitant cough. That did it.

I found myself staring at a middle-aged, thin little fellow with sandy hair and rimless glasses perched on a snub nose. The crease of his froggish mouth underlined the despair of his face.

He wore a frayed $36.50 suit, a wrinkled white shirt, and a string tie—but humility was his real garment. It covered him completely, that aura of hopeless resignation.

"I beg your pardon, please, but have you any tincture of aconite?"

Well, miracles *do* happen. I was going to get a chance to sell drugs after all. Or was I? When despair walks in and asks for aconite, it means suicide.

I shrugged. "Aconite?" I echoed. "I don't know."

He smiled, a little. Or rather, that crease wrinkled back in a poor imitation of amusement. But on his face a smile had no more mirth in it than the grin you see on a skull.

"I know what you're thinking," he mumbled. "But you're wrong. I'm—I'm a chemist. I'm doing some experiments, and I must have four ounces of aconite at once. And some belladonna. Yes, and—wait a minute."

Then he dragged the book out of his pocket.

I craned my neck, and it was worth it.

The book had rusty metal covers, and was obviously very old. When the thick yellow pages fluttered open under his trembling thumb I saw flecks of dust rise from the binding. The heavy black-lettered type was German, but I couldn't read anything at that distance.

"Let me see now," he murmured. "Aconite—belladonna— yes, and I have this—the cat, of course—nightshade—um hum—oh, yes, I'll need some phosphorus of course—have you any blue chalk?—Good—and I guess that's all."

I was beginning to catch on. But what the devil did it matter to me? A weirdo more or less was nothing new in my life. All I wanted to do was get out of here and soak my feet.

I went back and got the stuff for him, quickly. I peered

through the slot above the prescription counter, but he wasn't doing anything—just paging through that black, iron-bound book and moving his lips.

Wrapping the parcel, I came out. "Anything else, sir?"

"Oh—yes. Could I have about a dozen candles? The large size?"

I opened a drawer and scrabbled for them under the dust.

"I'll have to melt them down and reblend them with the fat," he said.

"What?"

"Nothing. I was just figuring."

Sure. That's the kind of figuring you do best when you're counting the pads in your cell. But it wasn't my business, was it?

So I handed over the package, like a fool.

"Thank you. You've been very kind. I must ask you to be kinder—to charge this."

Oh, great!

"You see, I'm temporarily out of funds. But I can assure you, in a very short time, in fact within three days, I shall pay you in full. Yes."

A very convincing plea. I wouldn't give him a cup of coffee on it—and that's what moochers usually ask for, instead of aconite and candles. But if his words didn't move me, his eyes did. They were so lonely behind his spectacles, so pitifully alone, those two little puddles of hope in the desert of despair that was his face.

All right. Let him have his dreams. Let him take his old iron-bound dream book home with him and make like crazy. Let him light his tapers and draw his phosphorescent circle and recite his spells or whatever the hell he wanted to do.

No, I wouldn't give him coffee, but I'd give him a dream.

"That's okay, buddy," I said. "We're all down on our luck some time, I guess."

That was wrong. I shouldn't have patronized. He stiffened at once and his mouth curled into a sneer—of superiority, if you please!

"I'm not asking charity," he said. "You'll get paid, never

fear, my good man. In three days, mark my words. Now good evening. I have work to do."

Out he marched, leaving "my good man" with his mouth open. Eventually I closed my mouth, but I couldn't clamp a lid on my curiosity.

That night, walking home, I looked down the dark street with new interest. The black houses bulked like a barrier behind which lurked fantastic mysteries. Row upon row, not houses any more, but dark dungeons of dreams. In what house did my stranger hide? In what room was he intoning to what strange gods?

Once again I sensed the presence of wonder in the world of lurking strangeness behind the scenes of drugstore and highrise civilization. Black books still were read, and wild-eyed strangers walked and muttered, candles burned into the night, and a missing alley cat might mean a chosen sacrifice.

But my feet hurt, so I went home.

Same old malted milks, cherry cokes, Vaseline, Listerine, hairnets, bathing caps, cigarettes, and what have you?

Me, I had a headache. It was four days later, almost the same time of night, when I found myself scrubbing off the soda-taps again.

Sure enough, he walked in.

I kept telling myself all evening that I didn't expect him—but I *did* expect him, really. I had that crawling feeling when the door clicked. I waited for the shuffle of the Tom McCann shoes.

Instead there was a brisk tapping of Oxfords. English Oxfords. The $40 kind.

I looked up in a hurry this time.

It *was* my stranger.

At least he was there, someplace beneath the flashy blue weave of his suit, the immaculate shirt and foulard tie. He had had a shave, a haircut, a manicure, and evidently a winning ticket in the Irish Sweepstakes.

"Hello there." Nothing wrong with that voice—I've heard it in the big hotel lobbies for years, brimming over with pep and confidence and authority.

"Well, well, well," was all I could say.

He chuckled. His mouth wasn't a crease any more. It was a trumpet of command. Out of that mouth could come orders, and directions. This wasn't a mouth shaped for hesitant excuses any longer. It was a mouth for requesting expensive dinners, choice vintage wines, heavy cigars; a mouth that barked at taxi drivers and doormen.

"Surprised to see me, eh? Well, I told you it would take three days. Want to pay you your money, thank you for your kindness."

That was nice. Not the thanks, the money. I like money. The thought of getting some I didn't expect made me genial.

"So your prayers were answered, eh?" I said.

He frowned.

"Prayers—what prayers?"

"Why I thought that—"

"I don't understand," he snapped, understanding perfectly well. "Did you perhaps harbor some misapprehension concerning my purchases of the other evening? A few necessary chemicals, that's all—to complete the experiment I spoke of. And the candles, I must confess were to light my room. They shut off my electricity the day before."

Well, it *could* be.

"Might as well tell you the experiment was a howling success. Yes, sir. Went right down to Newsohm with the results and they put me on as assistant research director. Quite a break."

Newsohm was the biggest chemical supply house in our section of the country. And he went right down in his rags and was "put on" as assistant research director. Well, live and learn.

"So here's the money. $5.39, wasn't it? Can you change a fifty?"

I couldn't.

"That's all right, keep it."

I refused, I don't know why. Made me feel crawling again, somehow.

"Well, then, tell you what let's do. You are closing up, aren't you? Why not step down the street to the tavern for a little drink? I'll get change there. Come on, I feel like celebrating."

So it was that five minutes later I walked down the street with Mr. Fritz Gulther.

We took a table in the tavern and ordered quietly. Neither he nor I was at ease. Somehow there was an unspoken secret between us. It seemed almost as though I harbored criminal knowledge against him—I, of all men, alone knowing that behind this immaculately clad figure of success, there lurked a shabby spectre just three days in the past. A spectre that owed me $5.39.

We drank quickly, both of us. The spectre got a little fainter. We had another. I insisted on paying for the third round.

"It's a celebration," I argued.

He laughed. "Certainly is. And let me tell you, this is only the beginning! From now on I'm going to climb so fast it'll make your head swim. I'll be running that place within six months. Going to get a lot of new orders in from the government, and expand."

"Wait a minute," I cautioned, reserve gone. "You're way ahead of yourself. If I were in your shoes I'd still be flipping with what happened to me in the past three days."

Fritz Gulther smiled. "Oh, that? I expected *that*. Didn't I tell you so in the store? I've been working for over a year and I knew just what to expect. It was no surprise, I assure you. I had it all planned. I was willing to starve to carry out my necessary studies, and I did starve. Might as well admit it."

"Sure." I was on my third drink now, over the barriers. "When you came into the store I said to myself, 'Here's a guy who's been through hell!'"

"Truer words were never spoken," said Gulther. "I've been through hell all right, quite literally. But it's all over now, and I didn't get burned."

"Say, confidentially—what kind of magic did you use?"

"Magic? Magic? I don't know anything about magic."

"Oh, yes you do, Gulther," I said. "What about that little black book with the iron covers you were mumbling around with in the store?"

"German inorganic chemistry text," he snapped. "Pretty old. Here, drink up and have another."

I had another. Gulther began to babble, a bit. About his new clothes and his new apartment and the new car he was going to buy next week. About how he was going to have everything he wanted now, by God, he'd show the fools that laughed at him all these years, he'd pay back the nagging landladies and the cursing grocers, and the sneering rats who told him he was soft in the head for studying the way he did.

Then he got into the kindly stage.

"How'd you like a job at Newsohm?" he asked me. "You're a good pharmacist. You know your chemistry. You're a nice enough fellow, too—but you've got a terrible imagination. How about it? Be my secretary. Sure, that's it. Be my secretary. I'll put you on tomorrow."

"I'll drink on that," I declared. The prospect intoxicated me. The thought of escape from the damned store, escape from the "coke"-faces, the "ciggies"-voices, very definitely intoxicated me. So did the next drink.

I began to see something.

We were sitting against the wall and the tavern lights were low. Couples around us were babbling in monotone that was akin to silence. We sat in shadow against the wall. Now I looked at my shadow—an ungainly, flickering caricature of myself, hunched over the table. What a contrast it presented before *his* suddenly erect bulk!

His shadow, now—

His shadow, now—

I saw it. He was sitting up straight across the table from me. But his shadow on the wall was *standing!*

"No more Scotch for me," I said, as the waiter came up.

But I continued to stare at his shadow. He was sitting and the shadow was standing. It was a larger shadow than mine, and a blacker shadow. For fun I moved my hands up and down, making heads and faces in silhouette. He wasn't watching me, he was gesturing to the waiter.

His shadow didn't gesture. I just stood there, I watched and stared and tried to look away. His hands moved but the black outline stood poised and silent, hands dangling at the sides.

And yet I saw the familiar shape of his head and nose; unmistakably his.

"Say, Gulther," I said. "Your shadow—there on the wall—"

I slurred my words. My eyes were blurred.

But I felt his attitude pierce my consciousness below the alcohol.

Fritz Gulther rose to his feet and then shoved a dead white face against mine. He didn't look at his shadow. He looked at me, through me, at some horror behind my face, my thoughts, my brain. He looked *at* me, and *into* some private hell of his own.

"Shadow," he said. "There's nothing wrong with my shadow. You're mistaken. Remember that, you're mistaken. And if you ever mention it again, I'll bash your skull in."

Then Fritz Gulther got up and walked away. I watched him march across the room, moving swiftly but a little unsteadily. Behind him, moving very slowly and not a bit unsteadily, a tall black shadow followed him from the room.

If you can build a better mousetrap than your neighbor, you're liable to put your foot in it.

That's certainly what I had done with Gulther. Here I was ready to accept his offer of a good job as his secretary, and I had to go and pull a drunken boner!

I was still cursing myself for a fool two days later. Shadows that don't follow body movements, indeed! Who was that shadow I saw you with last night? That was no shadow, that was the Scotch I was drinking. Oh, fine!

So I stood in the drugstore and sprinkled my sundaes with curses as well as chopped nuts.

I nearly knocked the pecans off the counter that second night, when Fritz Gulther walked in again.

He hurried up to the counter and flashed me a tired smile.

"Got a minute to spare?"

"Sure—wait till I serve these people in the booth."

I dumped the sundaes and raced back. Gulther perched himself on a stool and took off his hat. He was sweating profusely.

"Say—I want to apologize for the way I blew my stack the other night."

"Why, that's all right, Mr. Gulther."

"I got a little too excited, that's all. Liquor and success went to my head. No hard feelings, I want you to understand that. It's just that I was nervous. Your ribbing me about my shadow, that stuff sounded too much like the way I was always kidded for sticking to my studies in my room. Landlady used to accuse me of all sorts of things. Claimed I dissected her cat, that I was burning incense, messing the floor up with chalk. Some damn fool college punks downstairs began to yap around that I was some kind of nut dabbling in witchcraft."

I wasn't asking for his autobiography, remember. All this sounded a little hysterical. But then, Gulther looked the part. His sweating, the way his mouth wobbled and twitched as he got this out.

"But say, reason I stopped in was to see if you could fix me up a sedative. No, no bromo or aspirin. I've been taking plenty of that stuff ever since the other evening. My nerves are all shot. That job of mine down at Newsohm takes it all out of me."

"Wait a minute, I'll get something."

I made for the back room. As I compounded I sneaked a look at Gulther through the slot.

All right, I'll be honest. It wasn't Gulther I wanted to look at. It was his shadow.

When a customer sits at the counter stools, the storelights hit him so that his shadow is just a little black pool beneath his feet.

Gulther's shadow was a complete silhouette of his body, in outline. A black, deep shadow.

I blinked, but that didn't help.

Stranger still, the shadow seemed to be cast *parallel* with his body, instead of at an angle from it. It grew out from his chest instead of his legs. I don't know refraction, the laws of light, all that technical stuff. All I know is that Fritz Gulther had a big black shadow sitting beside him on the floor, and that the sight of it sent cold shivers along my spine.

I wasn't drunk. Neither was he. Neither was the shadow. All three of us existed.

Now Gulther was putting his hat back on.

But not the shadow. It just sat there. Crouched.

It was all wrong.

The shadow was no denser at one spot than at another. It was evenly dark, and—I noted this particularly—the outlines did not blur or fade. They were solid.

I stared and stared. I saw a lot now I'd never noticed. The shadow wore no clothes. Of course! Why should it put on a hat? It was naked, that shadow. But it belonged to Gulther—it wore spectacles. It was his shadow, all right. Which suited me fine, because *I* didn't want it.

Now Gulther was looking down over his shoulder. *He* was looking at his shadow now. Even from a distance I fancied I saw new beads of sweat string a rosary of fear across his forehead.

He knew, all right!

I came out, finally.

"Here it is," I said. I kept my eyes from his face.

"Good. Hope it works. Must get some sleep. And say—that job offer still goes. How about coming down tomorrow morning?"

I nodded, forcing a smile.

Gulther paid me, rose.

"See you then."

"Certainly." And why not? After all, what if you do work for a boss with an unnatural shadow? Most bosses have other faults, worse ones and more concrete. That shadow—whatever it was and whatever was wrong with it—wouldn't bite me. Though Gulther acted as though it might bite *him*.

As he turned away I looked at his departing back, and at the long, swooping black outline which followed it. The shadow rose and stalked after him. Stalked. Yes, it followed quite purposefully. To my now bewildered eyes it seemed larger than it had in the tavern. Larger, and a bolder black.

Then the night swallowed Gulther and his nonexistent companion.

I went back to the rear of the store and swallowed the other half of the sedative I'd made up for that purpose. After seeing that shadow, I needed it as much as he did.

The girl in the ornate outer office smiled prettily. "Go right in," she warbled. "He's expecting you."

So it was true, then. Gulther was assistant research director, and I was to be his secretary.

I floated in. In the morning sunshine I forgot all about shadows.

The inner office was elaborately furnished—a huge place with elegant walnut paneling associated with business authority. There was a kidney desk set before closed venetian blinds, and a variety of comfortable leather armchairs. Fluorescent lighting gleamed pleasantly.

But there was no Gulther. Probably on the other side of the little door at the back, talking to his Chief.

I sat down, with the tight feeling of anticipation hugged somewhere within my stomach. I glanced around, taking in the room again. My gaze swept the glass-topped desk. It was bare. Except in the corner, where a small box of cigars rested.

No, wait a minute. That wasn't a cigar-box. It was metal. I'd seen it somewhere before.

Of course! It was Gulther's iron-bound book.

"German inorganic chemistry." Who was I to doubt his word? So naturally, I just had to sneak a look before he came in.

I opened the yellowed pages.

De Vermis Mysteriis.

"Mysteries of the Worm."

This was no inorganic chemistry text. It was something entirely different. Something that told you how you could compound aconite and belladonna and draw circles of phosphorescent fire on the floor when the stars were right. Something that spoke of melting tallow candles and blending them with corpsefat, whispered of the uses to which animal sacrifice might be put.

It spoke of meetings that could be arranged with various parties most people don't either care to meet or even believe in.

The thick black letters crawled across the pages, and the detestable odor arising from the musty thing formed a background for the nastiness of the text. I won't say whether or not I believed what I was reading, but I will admit that there was an air, a suggestion about those cold, deliberate directions for traffic with alien evil, which made me shiver with repulsion. Such thoughts have no place in sanity, even as fantasy. And if *this* is what Gulther had done with the materials he'd bought himself for $5.39 . . .

"Years of study," eh? "Experiments." What was Gulther trying to call up, what did he call up, and what bargain did he make?

The man who could answer these questions sidled out from behind the door. Gone was the Fritz Gulther of the come-on-strong personality. It was my original moocher who creased his mouth at me in abject fear. He looked like a man—I had to say it—who was afraid of his own shadow.

The shadow trailed him through the doorway. To my eyes it had grown overnight. Its arms were slightly raised, though Gulther had both hands pressed against his sides. I saw it cross the wall as he walked toward me—and it moved more swiftly than he did.

Make no mistake. I saw the shadow. Since then I've talked to wise boys who assure me that under even fluorescence no shadow is cast. They're wise boys all right, but I saw that shadow.

Gulther saw that book in my hands.

"All right," he said, simply. "You know. And maybe it's just as well."

"Know?"

"Yes. Know that I made a bargain with—someone. I thought I was being smart. He promised me success, and wealth, anything I wanted, on only one condition. Those damned conditions; you always read about them and you always forget, because they sound so foolish! He told me that I'd have only one rival, and that this rival would be a part of myself. It would grow with my success."

I sat mute. Gulther was wound up for a long time.

"Silly, wasn't it? Of course I accepted. And then I found out what my rival was—what it would be. This shadow of mine. It's independent of me, you know that, and it keeps growing! Oh, not in size, but in *depth*, in intensity. It's becoming—maybe I *am* crazy but you see it, too—more solid. Thicker. As though it had palpable substance."

Crease-mouth wobbled violently, but the words choked on.

"The further I go the more it grows. Last night I took your sedative and it didn't work. Didn't work at all. I sat up in the darkness and watched my shadow."

"In darkness?"

"Yes. It doesn't need light. It really *exists*, now. Permanently. In the dark it's just a blacker blur. But you can see it. It doesn't sleep, or rest. It just waits."

"And you're afraid of it? Why?"

"I don't know. It doesn't threaten me, or make gestures, or even take any notice of me. Shadows taking notice—sounds crazy, doesn't it? But you see it as I do. You can see it waiting. And that's why I'm afraid. What's it waiting for?"

The shadow crept closer over his shoulder. Eavesdropping.

"I don't need you for a secretary. I need a nurse."

"What you need is a good rest."

"Rest? How can I rest? I just came out of Newsohm's office. He doesn't notice anything—yet. Too stupid, I suppose. The girls in the office look at me when I pass, and I wonder if they see something peculiar. But Newsohm doesn't. He just made me head of research. Completely in charge."

"In five days? Marvelous!"

"Isn't it? Except for our bargain—whenever I succeed, my rival gains power with me. That will make the shadow stronger. How, I don't know. I'm waiting. And I can't find rest."

"I'll find it for you. Just lie down and wait—I'll be back."

I left him hastily—left him sitting at his desk, all alone. Not quite alone. The shadow was there, too.

Before I went I had the funniest temptation. I wanted to run my hand along the wall, through that shadow. And yet I didn't. It was too black, too solid. What if my hand should actually encounter *something*?

So I just left.

I was back in half an hour. I grabbed Gulther's arm, bared it, plunged the needle home.

"Morphine," I whispered. "You'll sleep now."

He did, resting on the leather sofa. I sat at his side, watching the shadow that didn't sleep.

It stood there towering above him unnaturally. I tried to ignore it, but it was a third party in the room. Once, when I turned my back, it moved. I began to pace up and down. I opened my mouth, trying to hold back a scream.

The phone buzzed. I answered mechanically, my eyes never leaving the black outline on the wall that swayed over Gulther's recumbent form.

"Yes? No—he's not in right now. This is Mr. Gulther's secretary speaking. Your message? Yes, I'll tell him. I certainly will. Thank you."

It had been a woman's voice—a deep, rich voice. Her message was to tell Mr. Gulther she'd changed her mind. She'd be happy to meet him that evening at dinner.

Another conquest for Fritz Gulther!

Conquest—two conquests in a row. That meant conquests for the shadow, too. But *how?*

I turned to the shadow on the wall, and got a shock. It was lighter! Grayer, thinner, wavering a little!

What was wrong?

I glanced down at Gulther's sleeping face. Then I got another shock. Gulther's face was dark. Not tanned, but dark. Blackish. Sooty. *Shadowy.*

Then I did scream, a little.

Gulther awoke.

I just pointed to his face and indicated the wall mirror. He almost fainted. "It's combining with me," he whispered.

His skin was slate-colored. I turned my back because I couldn't look at him.

"We must do something," he mumbled. "Fast."

"Perhaps if you were to use—that book again, you could make another bargain."

It was a fantastic idea, but it popped out. I faced Gulther again and saw him smile.

"That's it! If you could get the materials now—you know what I need—go to the drugstore—but hurry up because—"

I shook my head. Gulther was nebulous, shimmery. I saw him through a mist.

Then I heard him yell.

"You damned fool! Look at *me*. That's my shadow you're staring at!"

I ran out of the room, and in less than ten minutes I was trying to fill a vial with belladonna with fingers that trembled like lumps of jelly.

I must have looked like a fool, carrying that armful of packages through the outer office. Candles, chalk, phosphorus, aconite, belladonna, and—blame it on my hysteria—the dead body of an alleycat I decoyed behind the store.

Certainly I felt like a fool when Fritz Gulther met me at the door of his sanctum.

"Come on in," he snapped.

Yes, snapped.

It took only a glance to convince me that Gulther had his cool again. Whatever the black change that frightened us so had been, he'd shook it off while I was gone.

Once again the trumpet voice held authority. Once again the sneering smile replaced the apologetic crease in the mouth.

Gulther's skin was white, normal. His movements were brisk and no longer frightened. He didn't need any wild spells—or had he ever, really?

Suddenly I felt as though I'd been a victim of my own imagination. After all, men don't make bargains with demons, they don't change places with their shadows.

The moment Gulther closed the door his words corroborated my mood.

"Well, I've snapped out of it. Foolish nonsense, wasn't it?" He smiled easily. "Guess we won't need that junk after all. Right when you left I began to feel better. Here, sit down and take it easy."

I sat. Gulther rested on the desk nonchalantly swinging his legs.

"All that nervousness, that strain, has disappeared. But before I forget it, I'd like to apologize for telling you that crazy story about sorcery and my obsession. Matter of fact, I'd feel better about the whole thing in the future if you just forgot all this ever happened."

I nodded.

Gulther smiled again.

"That's right. Now we're ready to get down to business. I tell you, it's a real relief to realize the progress we're going to make. I'm head research director already, and if I play my cards right I think I'll be running this place in another three months. Some of the things Newsohm told me today tipped me off. So just play ball with me and we'll go a long way. A long way. And I can promise you one thing—I'll never have any of these crazy spells again."

There was nothing wrong with what Gulther said here. Nothing wrong with any of it. There was nothing wrong with the way Gulther lolled and smiled at me, either.

Then why did I suddenly get that old crawling sensation along my spine?

For a moment I couldn't place it—and then I realized.

Fritz Gulther sat on his desk, before the wall, *but now he cast no shadow.*

Where had it gone?

There was only one place for it to go. And if it had gone there, then—*where was Fritz Gulther?*

He read it in my eyes.

I read it in his swift gesture.

Gulther's hand dipped into his pocket and reemerged. As it rose, I rose, and sprang across the room.

I gripped the revolver, pressed it back and away, and stared into his convulsed countenance, into his eyes. Behind the glasses, behind the human pupils, there was only a blackness. The cold, grinning blackness of a shadow.

Then he snarled, arms clawing up as he tried to wrest the weapon free, aim it. His body was cold, curiously weightless, but filled with a slithering strength. I felt myself go limp under those icy, scrabbling talons, but as I gazed into those two dark pools of hate that were his eyes, fear and desperation lent me aid.

A single gesture, and I turned the muzzle in. The gun exploded, and Gulther slumped to the floor.

They crowded in then; they stood and stared down, too. We all stood and stared down at the body lying on the floor.

Body? There was Fritz Gulther's shoes, his shirt, his tie, his expensive blue suit. The toes of his shoes pointed up, the shirt and tie and suit were creased and filled out to support a body beneath.

But there was no body on the floor. There was only a shadow—a deep, black shadow, encased in Fritz Gulther's clothes.

Nobody said a word for a long minute. Then one of the girls whispered, "Look—it's just a shadow."

I bent down quickly and shook the clothes. As I did so, the shadow seemed to move beneath my fingers, to move and to melt.

In an instant it slithered free from the garments. There was a flash—or a final retinal impression of blackness, and the shadow was gone. The clothing sagged down into an empty huddled heap on the floor.

I rose and faced them. I couldn't say it loud, but I could say it gratefully, very gratefully.

"No," I said. "You're mistaken. There's no shadow there. There's nothing at all—absolutely nothing at all."

AUGUST DERLETH

August William Derleth was born in 1909 in Sauk City, Wisconsin, where he spent most of his life. He sold his first story to *Weird Tales* at the age of seventeen, in 1926, and contributed prolifically to that pulp magazine for much of its run. Also in 1926, he came into contact with H. P. Lovecraft, whose influence upon his work would be decisive. Corresponding prolifically with Lovecraft, he became acquainted with many of Lovecraft's colleagues, including Donald Wandrei, Clark Ashton Smith, and Robert E. Howard. After Lovecraft's death in 1937, Derleth and Wandrei established the publishing firm of Arkham House to issue Lovecraft's tales in hardcover; Arkham House would become the most prestigious small-press publisher of supernatural fiction in the United States.

Derleth established a mainstream reputation with such works as *Place of Hawks* (1935) and *Evening in Spring* (1941), which richly evoked the history, topography, and personalities of his native Wisconsin. Sinclair Lewis wrote a laudatory article on him in *Esquire* in 1945. But Derleth failed to become a mainstream author recognized outside his home state, largely because his prodigious literary work in many different fields tended to dissipate his energies. Aside from his publishing activities, he edited several important anthologies of horror and science fiction, notably *The Night Side* (1944) and *Dark of the Moon: Poems of*

Fantasy and the Macabre (1947). He wrote many tales of the Cthulhu Mythos under Lovecraft's inspiration, although he failed to understand the philosophical direction of Lovecraft's invention and has been much criticized for leading it in a direction Lovecraft would probably not have approved. Derleth died in Sauk City in 1971.

"The Lonesome Place," first published in *Famous Fantastic Mysteries* (February 1948) and collected in *Lonesome Places* (1962), is perhaps Derleth's finest supernatural tale. Like much of his supernatural work, it relies on relatively conventional supernatural manifestations, but its execution is remarkably skillful.

THE LONESOME PLACE

You who sit in your houses of nights, you who sit in the theatres, you who are gay at dances and parties—all you who are enclosed by four walls—you have no conception of what goes on outside in the dark. In the lonesome places. And there are so many of them, all over—in the country, in the small towns, in the cities. If you were out in the evenings, in the night, you would know about them, you would pass them and wonder, perhaps, and if you were a small boy you might be frightened . . . frightened the way Johnny Newell and I were frightened, the way thousands of small boys from one end of the country to the other are being frightened when they have to go out alone at night, past lonesome places, dark and lightless, sombre and haunted. . . .

I want you to understand that if it had not been for the lonesome place at the grain elevator, the place with the big old trees and the sheds up close to the sidewalk, and the piles of lumber—if it had not been for that place Johnny Newell and I would never have been guilty of murder. I say it even if there is nothing the law can do about it. They cannot touch us, but it is true, and I know, and Johnny knows, but we never talk about it, we never say anything; it is just something we keep here, behind our eyes, deep in our thoughts where it is a fact which is lost among thousands of others, but no less there, something we know beyond cavil.

It goes back a long way. But as time goes, perhaps it is not long. We were young, we were little boys in a small town. Johnny lived three houses away and across the street from me, and both of us lived in the block west of the grain elevator. We were never afraid to go past the lonesome place together. But we were not often together. Sometimes one of us had to go that way alone, sometimes the other. I went that way most of the time—there was no other, except to go far around, because that was the straight way down town, and I had to walk there, when my father was too tired to go.

In the evenings it would happen like this. My mother would discover that she had no sugar or salt or bologna, and she would say, "Steve, you go down town and get it. Your father's too tired."

I would say, "I don't wanna."

She would say, "You go."

I would say, "I can go in the morning before school."

She would say, "You go now. I don't want to hear another word out of you. Here's the money."

And I would have to go.

Going down was never quite so bad, because most of the time there was still some afterglow in the west, and a kind of pale light lay there, a luminousness, like part of the day lingering there, and all around town you could hear the kids hollering in the last hour they had to play, and you felt somehow not alone, you could go down into that dark place under the trees and you would never think of being lonesome. But when you came back—that was different. When you came back the afterglow was gone; if the stars were out, you could never see them for the trees; and though the streetlights were on—the old fashioned lights arched over the cross-roads—not a ray of them penetrated the lonesome place near the elevator. There it was, half a block long, black as black could be, dark as the deepest night, with the shadows of the trees making it a solid place of darkness, with the faint glow of light where a streetlight pooled at the end of the street, far away it seemed, and that other glow behind, where the other corner light lay.

And when you came that way you walked slower and slower. Behind you lay the brightly-lit stores; all along the way there had been houses, with lights in the windows and music playing and voices of people sitting to talk on their porches—but up there, ahead of you, there was the lonesome place, with no house nearby, and up beyond it the tall, dark grain elevator, gaunt and forbidding, the lonesome place of trees and sheds and lumber, in which anything might be lurking, anything at all, the lonesome place where you were sure that something haunted the darkness waiting for the moment and the hour and the night when you came through to burst forth from its secret place and leap upon you, tearing you and rending you and doing unmentionable things before it had done with you.

That was the lonesome place. By day it was oak and maple trees over a hundred years old, low enough so that you could almost touch the big spreading limbs; it was sheds and lumber piles which were seldom disturbed; it was a sidewalk and long grass, never mowed or kept down until late fall, when somebody burned it off; it was a shady place in the hot summer days where some cool air always lingered. You were never afraid of it by day, but by night it was a different place; for then it was lonesome, away from sight or sound, a place of darkness and strangeness, a place of terror for little boys haunted by a thousand fears.

And every night, coming home from town, it happened like this. I would walk slower and slower, the closer I got to the lonesome place. I would think of every way around it. I would keep hoping somebody would come along, so that I could walk with him, Mr. Newell, maybe, or old Mrs. Potter, who lived farther up the street, or Reverend Bislor, who lived at the end of the block beyond the grain elevator. But nobody ever came. At this hour it was too soon after supper for them to go out, or, already out, too soon for them to return. So I walked slower and slower, until I got to the edge of the lonesome place—and then I ran as fast as I could, sometimes with my eyes closed.

Oh, I knew what was there, all right. I knew there was something in that dark, lonesome place. Perhaps it was the bogey-man. Sometimes my grandmother spoke of him, of how he waited in dark places for bad boys and girls. Perhaps it was an ogre. I knew about ogres in the books of fairy tales. Perhaps it was something else, something worse. I ran. I ran hard. Every blade of grass, every leaf, every twig that touched me was *its* hand reaching for me. The sound of my footsteps slapping the sidewalk were *its* steps pursuing. The hard breathing which was my own became *its* breathing in its frenetic struggle to reach me, to rend and tear me, to imbue my soul with terror.

I would burst out of that place like a flurry of wind, fly past the gaunt elevator, and not pause until I was safe in the yellow glow of the familiar streetlight. And then, in a few steps, I was home.

And mother would say, "For the Lord's sake, have you been running on a hot night like this?"

I would say, "I hurried."

"You didn't have to hurry that much. I don't need it till breakfast time."

And I would say, "I could-a got it in the morning. I could-a run down before breakfast. Next time, that's what I'm gonna do."

Nobody would pay any attention.

Some nights Johnny had to go down town, too. Things then weren't the way they are today, when every woman makes a ritual of afternoon shopping and seldom forgets anything; in those days, they didn't go down town so often, and when they did, they had such lists they usually forgot something. And after Johnny and I had been through the lonesome place on the same night, we compared notes next day.

"Did you see anything?" he would ask.

"No, but I heard it," I would say.

"I felt it," he would whisper tensely. "It's got big, flat clawed feet. You know what's the ugliest feet around?"

"Sure, one of those stinking yellow softshell turtles."

"It's got feet like that. Oh, ugly, and soft, and sharp claws! I saw one out of the corner of my eye," he would say.

"Did you see its face?" I would ask.

"It ain't got no face. Cross my heart an' hope to die, there ain't no face. That's worse'n if there was one."

Oh, it was a horrible beast—not an animal, not a man— that lurked in the lonesome place and came forth predatorily at night, waiting there for us to pass. It grew like this, out of our mutual experiences. We discovered that it had scales, and a great long tail, like a dragon. It breathed from somewhere, hot as fire, but it had no face and no mouth in it, just a horrible opening in its throat. It was as big as an elephant, but it did not look like anything so friendly. It belonged there in the lonesome place; it would never go away; that was its home, and it had to wait for its food to come to it—the unwary boys and girls who had to pass through the lonesome place at night.

How I tried to keep from going near the lonesome place after dark!

"Why can't Mady go?" I would ask.

"Mady's too little," mother would answer.

"I'm not so big."

"Oh, shush! You're a big boy now. You're going to be seven years old. Just think of it."

"I don't think seven is old," I would say. I didn't, either. Seven wasn't nearly old enough to stand up against what was in the lonesome place.

"Your Sears-Roebuck pants are long ones," she would say.

"I don't care about any old Sears-Roebuck pants. I don't wanna go."

"I want you to go. You never get up early enough in the morning."

"But I will. I promise I will. I promise, Ma!" I would cry out.

"Tomorrow morning it will be a different story. No, you go."

That was the way it went every time. I had to go. And Mady was the only one who guessed. "Fraidycat," she would whisper. Even she never really knew. She never had to go through the lonesome place after dark. They kept her at home. She never knew how something could lie up in those old trees, lie right along those old limbs across the sidewalk and drop down without a sound, clawing and tearing, something without a face, with ugly clawed feet like a softshell turtle's, with scales and a tail like a dragon, something as big as a house, all black, like the darkness in that place.

But Johnny and I knew.

"It almost got me last night," he would say, his voice low, looking anxiously out of the woodshed where we sat as if *it* might hear us.

"Gee, I'm glad it didn't," I would say. "What was it like?"

"Big and black. Awful black. I looked around when I was running, and all of a sudden there wasn't any light way back at the other end. Then I knew it was coming. I ran like everything to get out of there. It was almost on me when I got away. Look there!"

And he would show me a rip in his shirt where a claw had come down.

"And you?" he would ask excitedly, big-eyed. "What about you?"

"It was back behind the lumber piles when I came through," I said. "I could just feel it waiting. I was running, but it got right up—you look, there's a pile of lumber tipped over there."

And we would walk down into the lonesome place in mid-day and look. Sure enough, there would be a pile of lumber tipped over, and we would look to where something had been lying down, the grass all pressed down. Sometimes we would find a handkerchief and wonder whether *it* had caught somebody; then we would go home and wait to hear if anyone was missing, speculating apprehensively all the way home whether *it* had got Mady or Christine or Helen, or any one of the girls in our class or Sunday School, or whether maybe *it* had got Miss Doyle, the young primary grades teacher who had to walk that way sometimes after supper. But no one was ever reported missing, and the mystery grew. Maybe *it* had got some stranger who happened to be passing by and didn't know about the Thing that lived there in the lonesome place. We were sure *it* had got somebody. It scared us, bad, and after something like this I hated all the more to go down town after supper, even for candy or ice-cream.

"Some night I won't come back, you'll see," I would say.

"Oh, don't be silly," my mother would say.

"You'll see. You'll see. It'll get me next, you'll see."

"What'll get you?" she would ask offhandedly.

"Whatever it is out there in the dark," I would say.

"There's nothing out there but the dark," she would say.

"What about the bogey-man?" I would protest.

"They caught him," she would say. "A long time ago. He's locked up for good."

But Johnny and I knew better. His parents didn't know, either. The minute he started to complain, his dad reached for a hickory switch they kept behind the door. He had to go out fast and never mind what was in the lonesome place.

What do grown-up people know about the things boys are afraid of? Oh, hickory switches and such like, they know that. But what about what goes on in their minds when they have to come home alone at night through the lonesome places? What do they know about lonesome places where no light from the street-corner ever comes? What do they know about a place and time when a boy is very small and very alone, and the night is as big as the town, and the darkness is the whole world? When grown-ups are big, old people who cannot understand anything, no matter how plain? A boy looks up and out, but he can't look very far when the trees bend down over and press close, when the sheds rear up along one side and the trees on the other, when the darkness lies like a cloud along the sidewalk and the arc-lights are far, far away. No wonder then that Things grow in the darkness of lonesome places that way *it* grew in that dark place near the grain elevator. No wonder a boy runs like the wind until his heartbeats sound like a drum and push up to suffocate him.

"You're white as a sheet," mother would say sometimes. "You've been running again."

"Yes," I would say. "I've been running." But I never said why; I knew they wouldn't believe me; I knew nothing I could say would convince them about the Thing that lived back there, down the block, down past the grain elevator in that dark, lonesome place.

"You don't have to run," my father would say. "Take it easy."

"I ran," I would say. But I wanted the worst way to say I had to run and to tell them why I had to; but I knew they wouldn't believe me any more than Johnny's parents believed him when he told them, as he did once.

He got a licking with a strap and had to go to bed.

I never got licked. I never told them.

But now it must be told, now it must be set down.

For a long time we forgot about the lonesome place. We grew older and we grew bigger. We went on through school into high school, and somehow we forgot about the Thing in the lonesome place. That place never changed. The trees grew older. Sometimes the lumber piles were bigger or smaller. Once the sheds were painted—red, like blood. Seeing them that way the first time, I remembered. Then I forgot again. We took to playing baseball and basketball and football. We began to swim in the river and to date the girls. We never talked about the Thing in the lonesome place any more, and when we went through there at night it was like something forgotten that lurked back in a corner of the mind. We thought of something we ought to remember, but never could quite remember; that was the way it seemed—like a memory locked away, far away in childhood. We never ran through that place, and sometimes it was even a good place to walk through with a girl, because she always snuggled up close and said how spooky it was there under the overhanging trees. But even then we never lingered there, not exactly lingered; we didn't run through there, but we walked without faltering or loitering, no matter how pretty a girl she was.

The years went past, and we never thought about the lonesome place again.

We never thought how there would be other little boys going through it at night, running with fast-beating hearts, breathless with terror, anxious for the safety of the arc-light beyond the margin of the shadow which confined the dweller in that place, the light-fearing creature that haunted the dark, like so many terrors dwelling in similar lonesome places in the cities and small towns and countrysides all over the world, waiting to frighten little boys and girls, waiting to invade them with horror and unshakable fear—waiting for something more. . . .

Three nights ago little Bobby Jeffers was killed in the lonesome place. He was all mauled and torn and partly crushed, as if something big had fallen on him. Johnny, who was on the Village Board, went to look at the place, and after he had been there, he telephoned me to go, too, before other people walked there.

I went down and saw the marks, too. It was just as the coroner said, only not an "animal of some kind," as he put it. Something with a dragging tail, with scales, with great clawed feet—and I knew it had no face.

I knew, too, that Johnny and I were guilty. We had murdered Bobby Jeffers because the thing that killed him was the thing Johnny and I had created out of our childhood fears and left in that lonesome place to wait for some scared little boy at some minute in some hour during some dark night, a little boy who, like fat Bobby Jeffers, couldn't run as fast as Johnny and I could run.

And the worst is not that there is nothing to do, but that the lonesome place is being changed. The village is cutting down some of the trees now, removing the sheds, and putting up a streetlight in the middle of that place; it will not be dark and lonesome any longer, and the Thing that lives there will have to go somewhere else, where people are unsuspecting, to some other lonesome place in some other small town or city or countryside, where it will wait as it did here, for some frightened little boy or girl to come along, waiting in the dark and the lonesomeness . . .

FRITZ LEIBER

Fritz Reuter Leiber, Jr., was born in Chicago in 1910. He was the son of a noted actor, Fritz Leiber, Sr., and he himself appeared sporadically in plays and films. Shortly after his marriage in 1936 to Jonquil Stephens, Leiber came in touch with H. P. Lovecraft, with whom he had a brief but influential correspondence. Leiber began publishing tales of fantasy, science fiction, and horror in the late 1930s. Many of them focus around a pair of characters named Fafhrd and the Gray Mouser, loosely based upon himself and his friend Harry O. Fischer; these jaunty, self-deprecating tales established the subgenre of sword-and-sorcery as a viable literary form. Leiber's first book, the short story collection *Night's Black Agents* (1947), was the first in a long succession of publications that would establish Leiber as one of the premier authors of science fiction and fantasy since Lovecraft. Among his achievements are the novel *Conjure Wife* (1943), a deft updating of the witchcraft legend; *The Sinful Ones* (1953), a novel of existential terror; and the futuristic novel *The Big Time* (1958). Leiber definitively modernized the supernatural tale by setting it in the present-day amid the common landmarks of urban civilization, as in such tales as "The Automatic Pistol" (1940) and "Smoke Ghost" (1941); this tendency reached its pinnacle in the late novel *Our Lady of Darkness* (1977), set in the San Francisco that was Leiber's home for decades prior to his death in 1992. Leiber was the recipient of every major award in the fields of fantasy, horror, and science fiction.

"The Girl with the Hungry Eyes" (first published in *The Girl with the Hungry Eyes,* edited by Donald A. Wollheim, 1949) is representative of Leiber's updating of supernatural tropes: in this account of a woman who exercises a fatal sexual lure upon men by the ubiquitous presence of her image on billboards and other advertising, Leiber has transformed the traditional vampire of legend into a kind of "psychic vampirism" that does not require the sucking of blood to engender its effects. Written in a clipped, Hemingwayesque prose, the story is a masterful exposition of the temptations of the "eternal feminine."

THE GIRL WITH THE HUNGRY EYES

All right, I'll tell you why the Girl gives me the creeps. Why I can't stand to go downtown and see the mob slavering up at her on the tower, with that pop bottle or pack of cigarettes or whatever it is beside her. Why I hate to look at magazines any more because I know she'll turn up somewhere in a brassiere or a bubble bath. Why I don't like to think of millions of Americans drinking in that poisonous half smile. It's quite a story—more story than you're expecting.

No, I haven't suddenly developed any long-haired indignation at the evils of advertising and the national glamour-girl complex. That'd be a laugh for a man in my racket, wouldn't it?

Though I think you'll agree there's something a little perverted about trying to capitalize on sex that way. But it's okay with me. And I know we've had the Face and the Body and the Look and what not else, so why shouldn't someone come along who sums it all up so completely, that we have to call her the Girl and blazon her on all the billboards from Times Square to Telegraph Hill?

But the Girl isn't like any of the others. She's unnatural. She's morbid. She's unholy.

Oh it's 1948, is it, and the sort of thing I'm hinting at went out with witchcraft? But you see I'm not altogether sure myself what I'm hinting at, beyond a certain point. There are vampires and vampires, and not all of them suck blood.

And there were the murders, if they were murders.

Besides, let me ask you this. Why, when America is obsessed with the Girl, don't we find out more about her? Why doesn't she rate a *Time* cover with a droll biography inside? Why hasn't there been a feature in *Life* or the *Post*? A Profile in the *New Yorker*? Why hasn't *Charm* or *Mademoiselle* done her career saga? Not ready for it? Nuts!

Why haven't the movies snapped her up? Why hasn't she been on *Information, Please*? Why don't we see her kissing candidates at political rallies? Why isn't she chosen queen of some sort of junk or other at a convention?

Why don't we read about her tastes and hobbies, her views of the Russian situation? Why haven't the columnists interviewed her in a kimono on the top floor of the tallest hotel in Manhattan and told us who her boy-friends are?

Finally—and this is the real killer—why hasn't she ever been drawn or painted?

Oh, no she hasn't. If you knew anything about commercial art you'd know that. Every blessed one of those pictures was worked up from a photograph. Expertly? Of course. They've got the top artists on it. But that's how it's done.

And now I'll tell you the *why* of all that. It's because from the top to the bottom of the whole world of advertising, news, and business, there isn't a solitary soul who knows where the Girl came from, where she lives, what she does, who she is, even what her name is.

You heard me. What's more, not a single solitary soul ever *sees* her—except one poor damned photographer, who's making more money off her than he ever hoped to in his life and who's scared and miserable as hell every minute of the day.

No, I haven't the faintest idea who he is or where he has his studio. But I know there has to be such a man and I'm morally certain he feels just like I *said*.

Yes, I might be able to find her, if I tried. I'm not sure though—by now she probably has other safeguards. Besides, I don't want to.

Oh, I'm off my rocker, am I? That sort of thing can't happen in this Year of our Atom 1948? People can't keep out of sight that way, not even Garbo?

Well I happen to know they can, because last year I was that poor damned photographer I was telling you about. Yes, last year, in 1947, when the Girl made her first poisonous splash right here in this big little city of ours.

Yes, I knew you weren't here last year and you don't know about it. Even the Girl had to start small. But if you hunted through the files of the local newspapers, you'd find some ads, and I might be able to locate you some of the old displays—I think Lovelybelt is still using one of them. I used to have a mountain of photos myself, until I burned them.

Yes, I made my cut off her. Nothing like what that other photographer must be making, but enough so it still bought this whisky. She was funny about money. I'll tell you about that.

But first picture me in 1947. I had a fourth floor studio in that rathole the Hauser Building, catty-corner from Ardleigh Park.

I'd been working at the Marsh-Mason studios until I'd gotten my bellyful of it and decided to start in for myself. The Hauser Building was crummy—I'll never forget how the stairs creaked—but it was cheap and there was a skylight.

Business was lousy. I kept making the rounds of all the advertisers and agencies, and some of them didn't object to me too much personally, but my stuff never clicked. I was pretty near broke. I was behind on my rent. Hell, I didn't even have enough money to have a girl.

It was one of those dark grey afternoons. The building was awfully quiet—even with the shortage they can't half rent the Hauser. I'd just finished developing some pix I was doing on speculation for Lovelybelt Girdles and Buford's Pool and Playground—the last a faked-up beach scene. My model had left. A Miss Leon. She was a civics teacher at one of the high schools and modelled for me on the side, just lately on speculation too. After one look at the prints, I decided that Miss Leon probably wasn't just what Lovelybelt was looking for—or my photography either. I was about to call it a day.

And then the street door slammed four storeys down and there were steps on the stairs and she came in.

She was wearing a cheap, shiny black dress. Black pumps.

No stockings. And except that she had a grey cloth coat over one of them, those skinny arms of hers were bare. Her arms are pretty skinny, you know, or can you see things like that any more?

And then the thin neck, the slightly gaunt, almost prim face, the tumbling mass of dark hair, and looking out from under it the hungriest eyes in the world.

That's the real reason she's plastered all over the country today, you know—those eyes. Nothing vulgar, but just the same they're looking at you with a hunger that's all sex and something more than sex. That's what everybody's been looking for since the Year One—something a little more than sex.

Well, boys, there I was, alone with the Girl, in an office that was getting shadowy, in a nearly empty building. A situation that a million male Americans have undoubtedly pictured to themselves with various lush details. How was I feeling? Scared.

I know sex can be frightening. That cold, heart-thumping when you're alone with a girl and feel you're going to touch her. But if it was sex this time, it was overlaid with something else.

At least I wasn't thinking about sex.

I remember that I took a backward step and that my hand jerked so that the photos I was looking at sailed to the floor.

There was the faintest dizzy feeling like something was being drawn out of me. Just a little bit.

That was all. Then she opened her mouth and everything was back to normal for a while.

"I see you're a photographer, mister," she said. "Could you use a model?"

Her voice wasn't very cultivated.

"I doubt it," I told her, picking up the pix. You see, I wasn't impressed. The commercial possibilities of her eyes hadn't registered on me yet, by a long shot. "What have you done?"

Well she gave me a vague sort of story and I began to check her knowledge of model agencies and studios and rates and what not and pretty soon I said to her,

"Look here, you never modelled for a photographer in your life. You just walked in here cold."

Well, she admitted that was more or less so.

All along through our talk I got the idea she was feeling her way, like someone in a strange place. Not that she was uncertain of herself, or of me, but just of the general situation.

"And you think anyone can model?" I asked her pityingly.

"Sure," she said.

"Look," I said, "a photographer can waste a dozen negatives trying to get one half-way human photo of an average woman. How many do you think he'd have to waste before he got a real catchy, glamorous pix of her?"

"I think I could do it," she said.

Well, I should have kicked her out right then. Maybe I admired the cool way she stuck to her dumb little guns. Maybe I was touched by her underfed look. More likely I was feeling mean on account of the way my pix had been snubbed by everybody and I wanted to take it out on her by showing her up.

"Okay, I'm going to put you on the spot," I told her. "I'm going to try a couple of shots of you. Understand, it's strictly on spec. If somebody should ever want to use a photo of you, which is about one chance in two million, I'll pay you regular rates for your time. Not otherwise."

She gave me a smile. The first. "That's swell by me," she said.

Well, I took three or four shots, closeups of her face since I didn't fancy her cheap dress, and at least she stood up to my sarcasm. Then I remembered I still had the Lovelybelt stuff and I guess the meanness was still working in me because I handed her a girdle and told her to go back of the screen and get into it and she did, without getting flustered as I'd expected, and since we'd gone that far I figured we might as well shoot the beach scene to round it out, and that was that.

All this time I wasn't feeling anything particular in one way or the other except every once in a while I'd get one of those faint dizzy flashes and wonder if there was something wrong with my stomach or if I could have been a bit careless with my chemicals. Still, you know, I think the uneasiness was in me all the while.

I tossed her a card and pencil. "Write your name and address and phone," I told her and made for the darkroom.

A little later she walked out. I didn't call any good-byes. I was irked because she hadn't fussed around or seemed anxious about her poses, or even thanked me, except for that one smile.

I finished developing the negatives, made some prints, glanced at them, decided they weren't a great deal worse than Miss Leon. On an impulse I slipped them in with the pix I was going to take on the rounds next morning.

By now I'd worked long enough so I was a bit fagged and nervous, but I didn't dare waste enough money on liquor to help that. I wasn't very hungry. I think I went to a cheap movie.

I didn't think of the Girl at all, except maybe to wonder faintly why in my present womanless state I hadn't made a pass at her. She had seemed to belong to a, well, distinctly more approachable social strata than Miss Leon. But then of course there were all sorts of arguable reasons for my not doing that.

Next morning I made the rounds. My first step was Munsch's Brewery. They were looking for a "Munsch Girl." Papa Munsch had a sort of affection for me, though he razzed my photography. He had a good natural judgement about that, too. Fifty years ago he might have been one of the shoestring boys who made Hollywood.

Right now he was out in the plant pursuing his favourite occupation. He put down the beaded can, smacked his lips, gabbled something technical to someone about hops, wiped his fat hands on the big apron he was wearing, and grabbed my thin stack of pix.

He was about half-way through, making noises with his tongue and teeth, when he came to her. I kicked myself for even having stuck her in.

"That's her," he said. "The photography's not so hot, but that's the girl."

It was all decided. I wondered now why Papa Munsch sensed what the girl had right away, while I didn't. I think it was because I saw her first in the flesh, if that's the right word.

At the time I just felt faint.

"Who is she?" he asked.

"One of my new models," I tried to make it casual.

"Bring her out tomorrow morning," he told me. "And your stuff. We'll photograph her here. I want to show you."

"Here, don't look so sick," he added. "Have some beer."

Well I went away telling myself it was just a fluke, so that she'd probably blow it tomorrow with her inexperience and so on.

Just the same, when I reverently laid my next stack of pix on Mr. Fitch, of Lovelybelt's, rose-coloured blotter, I had hers on top.

Mr. Fitch went through the motions of being an art critic. He leaned over backward, squinted his eyes, waved his long fingers, and said, "Hmm. What do you think, Miss Willow? Here, in this light. Of course the photograph doesn't show the bias cut. And perhaps we should use the Lovelybelt Imp instead of the Angel. Still, the girl . . . Come over here, Binns." More finger-waving. "I want a married man's reaction."

He couldn't hide the fact that he was hooked.

Exactly the same thing happened at Buford's Pool and Playground, except that Da Costa didn't need a married man's say-so.

"Hot stuff," he said, sucking his lips. "Oh boy, you photographers!"

I hot-footed it back to the office and grabbed up the card I'd given her to put down her name and address.

It was blank.

I don't mind telling you that the next five days were about the worst I ever went through, in an ordinary way. When next morning rolled around and I still hadn't got hold of her, I had to start stalling.

"She's sick," I told Papa Munsch over the phone.

"She's at a hospital?" he asked me.

"Nothing that serious," I told him.

"Get her out here then. What's a little headache?"

"Sorry, I can't."

Papa Munsch got suspicious. "You really got this girl?"

"Of course I have."

"Well, I don't know, I'd think it was some New York model, except I recognized your lousy photography."

I laughed.

"Well look, you get her here tomorrow morning, you hear?"

"I'll try."

"Try nothing. You get her out here."

He didn't know half of what I tried. I went around to all the model and employment agencies. I did some slick detective work at the photographic and art studios. I used up some of my last dimes putting advertisements in all three papers. I looked at high school yearbooks and at employee photos in local house organs. I went to restaurants and drugstores, looking at waitresses, and to dime stores and department stores, looking at clerks. I watched the crowds coming out of movie theatres. I roamed the streets.

Evenings I spent quite a bit of time along Pick-up Row. Somehow that seemed the right place.

The fifth afternoon I knew I was licked. Papa Munsch's deadline—he'd given me several, but this was it—was due to run out at six o'clock. Mr. Fitch had already cancelled.

I was at the studio window, looking out at Ardleigh Park. She walked in.

I'd gone over this moment so often in my mind that I had no trouble putting on my act. Even the faint dizzy feeling didn't throw me off.

"Hello," I said, hardly looking at her.

"Hello," she said.

"Not discouraged yet?"

"No." It didn't sound uneasy or defiant. It was just a statement.

I snapped a look at my watch, got up and said curtly, "Look here, I'm going to give you a chance. There's a client of mine looking for a girl your general type. If you do a real good job you may break into the modelling business.

"We can see him this afternoon if we hurry," I said. I picked up my stuff. "Come on. And next time if you expect favours, don't forget to leave your phone number."

"Uh, uh," she said, not moving.

"What do you mean?" I said.

"I'm not going out to see any client of yours."

"The hell you aren't," I said. "You little nut, I'm giving you a break."

She shook her head slowly. "You're not fooling me, baby, you're not fooling me at all. They *want* me." And she gave me the second smile.

At the time I thought she must have seen my newspaper ad. Now I'm not so sure.

"And now I'll tell you how we're going to work," she went on. "You aren't going to have my name or address or phone number. Nobody is. And we're going to do all the pictures right here. Just you and me."

You can imagine the roar I raised at that. I was everything—angry, sarcastic, patiently explanatory, off my nut, threatening, pleading.

I would have slapped her face off, except it was photographic capital.

In the end all I could do was phone Papa Munsch and tell him her conditions. I know I didn't have a chance, but I had to take it.

He gave me a really angry bawling out, said "no" several times and hung up.

It didn't faze her. "We'll start shooting at ten o'clock tomorrow," she said.

It was just like her, using that corny line from the movie magazines.

About midnight Papa Munsch called me up.

"I don't know what insane asylum you're renting this girl from," he said, "but I'll take her. Come around tomorrow morning and I'll try to get it through your head just how I want the pictures. And I'm glad I got you out of bed!"

After that it was a breeze. Even Mr. Fitch reconsidered and after taking two days to tell me it was quite impossible he accepted the conditions too.

Of course you're all under the spell of the Girl, so you can't understand how much self-sacrifice it represented on Mr. Fitch's part when he agreed to forgo supervising the photography of my model in the Lovelybelt Imp or Vixen or whatever it was we finally used.

Next morning she turned up on time according to her schedule, and we went to work. I'll say one thing for her, she never got tired and she never kicked at the way I fussed over shots. I got along okay except I still had that feeling of something being shoved away gently. Maybe you've felt it just a little, looking at her picture.

When we finished I found out there were still more rules. It was about the middle of the afternoon. I started down with her to get a sandwich and coffee.

"Uh uh," she said, "I'm going down alone. And look, baby, if you ever try to follow me, if you ever so much as stick your head out that window when I go, you can hire yourself another model."

You can imagine how all this crazy stuff strained my temper—and my imagination. I remember opening the window after she was gone—I waited a few minutes first—and standing there getting some fresh air and trying to figure out what could be back of it, whether she was hiding from the police, or was somebody's ruined daughter, or maybe had got the idea it was smart to be temperamental, or more likely Papa Munsch was right and she was partly nuts.

But I had my pix to finish up.

Looking back it's amazing to think how fast her magic began to take hold of the city after that. Remembering what came after, I'm frightened of what's happening to the whole country—and maybe the world. Yesterday I read something in *Time* about the Girl's picture turning up on billboards in Egypt.

The rest of my story will help show you why I'm frightened in that big general way. But I have a theory, too, that helps explain, though it's one of those things that's beyond that "certain point." It's about the Girl. I'll give it to you in a few words.

You know how modern advertising gets everybody's mind set in the same direction, wanting the same things, imagining the same things. And you know the psychologists aren't so sceptical of telepathy as they used to be.

Add up the two ideas. Suppose the identical desires of millions of people focused on one telepathic person. Say a girl. Shaped her in their image.

Imagine her knowing the hiddenmost hungers of millions of men. Imagine her seeing deeper into those hungers than the people that had them, seeing the hatred and the wish for death behind the lust. Imagine her shaping herself in that complete image, keeping herself as aloof as marble. Yet imagine the hunger she might feel in answer to their hunger.

But that's getting a long way from the facts of my story. And some of those facts are darn solid. Like money. We made money.

That was the funny thing I was going to tell you. I was afraid the Girl was going to hold me up. She really had me over a barrel, you know.

But she didn't ask for anything but the regular rates. Later on I insisted on pushing more money at her, a whole lot. But she always took it with that same contemptuous look, as if she were going to toss it down the first drain when she got outside. Maybe she did.

At any rate, I had money. For the first time in months I had money enough to get drunk, buy new clothes, take taxicabs. I could make a play for any girl I wanted to. I only had to pick.

And so of course I had to go and pick—

But first let me tell you about Papa Munsch.

Papa Munsch wasn't the first of the boys to try to meet my model but I think he was the first to really go soft on her. I could watch the change in his eyes as he looked at her pictures. They began to get sentimental, reverent. Mama Munsch had been dead for two years.

He was smart about the way he planned it. He got me to drop some information which told him when she came to work, and then one morning he came pounding up the stairs a few minutes before.

"I've got to see her, Dave," he told me.

I argued with him, I kidded him, I explained he didn't know just how serious she was about her crazy ideas. I pointed out he was cutting both our throats. I even amazed myself by bawling him out.

He didn't take any of it in his usual way. He just kept repeating, "But, Dave, I've got to see her."

The street door slammed.

"That's her," I said, lowering my voice. "You've got to get out."

He wouldn't, so I shoved him in the darkroom. "And keep quiet," I whispered. "I'll tell her I can't work today."

I knew he'd try to look at her and probably come busting in, but there wasn't anything else I could do.

The footsteps came to the fourth floor. But she never showed at the door. I got uneasy.

"Get that bum out of there!" she yelled suddenly from beyond the door. Not very loud, but in her commonest voice.

"I'm going up to the next landing," she said. "And if that fat-bellied bum doesn't march straight down to the street, he'll never get another pix of me except spitting in his lousy beer."

Papa Munsch came out of the darkroom. He was white. He didn't look at me as he went out. He never looked at her pictures in front of me again.

That was Papa Munsch. Now it's me I'm telling about. I talked around the subject with her, I hinted, eventually I made my pass.

She lifted my hand off her as if it were a damp rag.

"Nix, baby," she said. "This is working time."

"But afterwards . . ." I pressed.

"The rules still hold." And I got what I think was the fifth smile.

It's hard to believe, but she never budged an inch from that crazy line. I mustn't make a pass at her in the office, because our work was very important and she loved it and there mustn't be any distractions. And I couldn't see her anywhere else, because if I tried to, I'd never snap another picture of her—and all this with more money coming in all the time and me never so stupid as to think my photography had anything to do with it.

Of course I wouldn't have been human if I hadn't made more passes. But they always got the wet-rag treatment and there weren't any more smiles.

I changed. I went sort of crazy and light-headed—only sometimes I felt my head was going to burst. And I started to talk to her all the time. About myself.

It was like being in a constant delirium that never interfered with business. I didn't pay any attention to the dizzy feeling. It seemed natural.

I'd walk around and for a moment the reflector would look like a sheet of white-hot steel, or the shadows would seem like armies of moths, or the camera would be a big black coal car. But the next instant they'd come all right again.

I think sometimes I was scared to death of her. She'd seem the strangest, horriblest person in the world. But other times . . .

And I talked. It didn't matter what I was doing—lighting her, posing her, fussing with props, snapping my pix—or where she was—on the platform, behind the screen, relaxing with a magazine—I kept up a steady gab.

I told her everything I knew about myself. I told her about my first girl. I told her about my brother Bob's bicycle. I told her about running away on a freight, and the licking Pa gave me when I came home. I told her about shipping to South America and the blue sky at night. I told her about Betty. I told her about my mother dying of cancer. I told her about being beaten up in a fight in an alley back of a bar. I told her about Mildred. I told her about the first picture I ever sold. I told her how Chicago looked from a sailboat. I told her about the longest drunk I was ever on. I told her about Marsh-Mason. I told her about Gwen. I told her about how I met Papa Munsch. I told her about hunting her. I told her about how I felt now.

She never paid the slightest attention to what I said. I couldn't even tell if she heard me.

It was when we were getting our first nibble from national advertisers that I decided to follow her when she went home.

Wait, I can place it better than that. Something you'll remember from the out-of-town papers—those maybe murders I mentioned. I think there were six.

I say "maybe," because the police could never be sure they weren't heart attacks. But there's bound to be suspicion when heart attacks happen to people whose hearts have been okay, and always at night when they're alone and away from home and there's a question of what they were doing.

The six deaths created one of those "mystery poisoner"

scares. And afterwards there was a feeling that they hadn't really stopped, but were being continued in a less suspicious way.

That's one of the things that scares me now.

But at that time my only feeling was relief that I'd decided to follow her.

I made her work until dark one afternoon. I didn't need any excuses, we were snowed under with orders. I waited until the street door slammed, then I ran down. I was wearing rubber-soled shoes. I'd slipped on a dark coat she'd never seen me in, and a dark hat.

I stood in the doorway until I spotted her. She was walking by Ardleigh Park toward the heart of town. It was one of those warm fall nights. I followed her on the other side of the street. My idea for tonight was just to find out where she lived. That would give me a hold on her.

She stopped in front of a display window of Everly's department store, standing back from the glow. She stood there looking in.

I remembered we'd done a big photograph of her for Everly's, to make a flat model for a lingerie display. That was what she was looking at.

At the time it seemed all right to me that she should adore herself, if that was what she was doing.

When people passed she'd turn away a little or drift back farther into the shadows.

Then a man came by alone. I couldn't see his face very well, but he looked middle-aged. He stopped and stood looking in the window.

She came out of the shadows and stepped up beside him.

How would you boys feel if you were looking at a poster of the Girl and suddenly she was there beside you, her arm linked with yours?

This fellow's reaction showed plain as day. A crazy dream had come to life for him.

They talked for a moment. Then he waved a taxi to the kerb. They got in and drove off.

I got drunk that night. It was almost as if she'd known I was following her and had picked that way to hurt me. Maybe she had. Maybe this was the finish.

But the next morning she turned up at the usual time and I was back in the delirium, only now with some new angles added.

That night when I followed her she picked a spot under a street lamp, opposite one of the Munsch Girl billboards.

Now it frightens me to think of her lurking that way.

After about twenty minutes a convertible slowed down going past her, backed up, swung in to the kerb.

I was closer this time. I got a good look at the fellow's face. He was a little younger, about my age.

Next morning the same face looked up at me from the front page of the paper. The convertible had been found parked on a side street. He had been in it. As in the other maybe-murders, the cause of death was uncertain.

All kinds of thoughts were spinning in my head that day, but there were only two things I knew for sure. That I'd got the first real offer from a national advertiser, and that I was going to take the Girl's arm and walk down the stairs with her when we quit work.

She didn't seem surprised. "You know what you're doing?" she said.

"I know."

She smiled. "I was wondering when you'd get around to it."

I began to feel good. I was kissing everything good-bye, but I had my arm around hers.

It was another of those warm fall evenings. We cut across into Ardleigh Park. It was dark there, but all around the sky was a sallow pink from the advertising signs.

We walked for a long time in the park. She didn't say anything and she didn't look at me, but I could see her lips twitching and after a while her hand tightened on my arm.

We stopped. We'd been walking across the grass. She dropped down and pulled me after her. She put her hands on my shoulders. I was looking down at her face. It was the faintest sallow pink from the glow in the sky. The hungry eyes were dark smudges.

I was fumbling with her blouse. She took my hand away, not like she had in the studio. "I don't want that," she said.

First I'll tell you what I did afterwards. Then I'll tell you why I did it. Then I'll tell you what she said.

What I did was run away. I don't remember all of that because I was dizzy, and the pink sky was swinging against the dark trees. But after a while I staggered into the lights of the street. The next day I closed up the studio. The telephone was ringing when I locked the door and there were unopened letters on the floor. I never saw the Girl again in the flesh, if that's the right word.

I did it because I didn't want to die. I didn't want the life drawn out of me. There are vampires and vampires, and the ones that suck blood aren't the worst. If it hadn't been for the warning of those dizzy flashes, and Papa Munsch and the face in the morning paper, I'd have gone the way the others did. But I realized what I was up against while there was still time to tear myself away. I realized that wherever she came from, whatever shaped her, she's the quintessence of the horror behind the bright billboard. She's the smile that tricks you into throwing away your money and your life. She's the eyes that lead you on and on, and then show you death. She's the creature you give everything for and never really get. She's the being that takes everything you've got and gives nothing in return. When you yearn towards her face on the billboards, remember that. She's the lure. She's the bait. She's the Girl.

And this is what she said, "I want you. I want your high spots. I want everything that's made you happy and everything that's hurt you bad. I want your first girl. I want that shiny bicycle. I want that licking. I want that pinhole camera. I want Betty's legs. I want the blue sky filled with stars. I want your mother's death. I want your blood on the cobblestones. I want Mildred's mouth. I want the first picture you sold. I want the lights of Chicago. I want the gin. I want Gwen's hands. I want your wanting me. I want your life. Feed me, baby, feed me."

RAY BRADBURY

Ray Douglas Bradbury was born in Waukegan, Illinois, in 1920. Graduating from Los Angeles High School in 1938, Bradbury was inspired by his readings of H. P. Lovecraft and Clark Ashton Smith in the pulp magazines to begin writing tales of fantasy and horror, and he began publishing in *Weird Tales* and other venues in the early 1940s. His first volume, the story collection *Dark Carnival* (1947), was published by Arkham House. Bradbury went on to become one of the most distinguished and prolific writers in the field. He laid the foundations for literary science fiction with such pioneering works as *The Martian Chronicles* (1950), *The Illustrated Man* (1951), and the dystopian novel *Fahrenheit 451* (1953), while in the realm of fantasy and horror he produced such delicate and winsome works as *Dandelion Wine* (1957), a tale of wonders and terrors in a small town in Illinois; *Something Wicked This Way Comes* (1962), about a sinister traveling carnival show; the children's novel *The Halloween Tree* (1972); and *Death Is a Lonely Business* (1985), a roman à clef about Bradbury's writing for the pulps. Along with Fritz Leiber and Richard Matheson, Bradbury transformed the field of supernatural horror by relocating it in the modern age and among the mundane settings of small-town or suburban life. His hundreds of short stories have appeared in many volumes, including *The October Country* (1955), *The Machineries of Joy* (1964), *I Sing the Body Electric!*

(1969), and *The Toynbee Convector* (1988). The best of them are gathered in *The Stories of Ray Bradbury* (1980). Bradbury also worked extensively in film and television. He died in 2012.

"The Fog Horn" (first published in the *Saturday Evening Post* for June 23, 1951) is one of Bradbury's most effective short stories and a poignant tale of horrors from the sea. It was credited as the basis for the film *The Beast from 20,000 Fathoms* (1953), although Bradbury himself remarked on the similarity of the screenplay to his story when he read it while visiting his friend Ray Harryhausen; the next day Bradbury received a telegram offering to buy the film rights to his story.

THE FOG HORN

ut there in the cold water, far from land, we waited every night for the coming of the fog, and it came, and we oiled the brass machinery and lit the fog light up in the stone tower. Feeling like two birds in the gray sky, McDunn and I sent the light touching out, red, then white, then red again, to eye the lonely ships. And if they did not see our light, then there was always our Voice, the great deep cry of our Fog Horn shuddering through the rags of mist to startle the gulls away like decks of scattered cards and make the waves turn high and foam.

"It's a lonely life, but you're used to it now, aren't you?" asked McDunn.

"Yes," I said. "You're a good talker, thank the Lord."

"Well, it's your turn on land tomorrow," he said, smiling, "to dance the ladies and drink gin."

"What do you think, McDunn, when I leave you out here alone?"

"On the mysteries of the sea." McDunn lit his pipe. It was a quarter past seven of a cold November evening, the heat on, the light switching its tail in two hundred directions, the Fog Horn bumbling in the high throat of the tower. There wasn't a town for a hundred miles down the coast, just a road which came lonely through dead country to the sea, with few cars on it, a stretch of two miles of cold water out to our rock, and rare few ships.

"The mysteries of the sea," said McDunn thoughtfully. "You

know, the ocean's the biggest damned snowflake ever? It rolls and swells a thousand shapes and colors, no two alike. Strange. One night, years ago, I was here alone, when all of the fish of the sea surfaced out there. Something made them swim in and lie in the bay, sort of trembling and staring up at the tower light going red, white, red, white across them so I could see their funny eyes. I turned cold. They were like a big peacock's tail, moving out there until midnight. Then, without so much as a sound, they slipped away, the million of them was gone. I kind of think maybe, in some sort of way, they came all those miles to worship. Strange. But think how the tower must look to them, standing seventy feet above the water, the God-light flashing out from it, and the tower declaring itself with a monster voice. They never came back, those fish, but don't you think for a while they thought they were in the Presence?"

I shivered. I looked out at the long gray lawn of the sea stretching away into nothing and nowhere.

"Oh, the sea's full." McDunn puffed his pipe nervously, blinking. He had been nervous all day and hadn't said why. "For all our engines and so-called submarines, it'll be ten thousand centuries before we set foot on the real bottom of the sunken lands, in the fairy kingdoms there, and know *real* terror. Think of it, it's still the year 300,000 Before Christ down under there. While we've paraded around with trumpets, lopping off each other's countries and heads, they have been living beneath the sea twelve miles deep and cold in a time as old as the beard of a comet."

"Yes, it's an old world."

"Come on. I got something special I been saving up to tell you."

We ascended the eighty steps, talking and taking our time. At the top, McDunn switched off the room lights so there'd be no reflection in the plate glass. The great eye of the light was humming, turning easily in its oiled socket. The Fog Horn was blowing steadily, once every fifteen seconds.

"Sounds like an animal, don't it?" McDunn nodded to himself. "A big lonely animal crying in the night. Sitting here on the edge of ten billion years calling out to the Deeps, I'm here, I'm here, I'm here. And the Deeps *do* answer, yes, they do. You been here now for three months, Johnny, so I better prepare you. About this time of year," he said, studying the murk and fog, "something comes to visit the lighthouse."

"The swarms of fish like you said?"

"No, this is something else. I've put off telling you because you might think I'm daft. But tonight's the latest I can put it off, for if my calendar's marked right from last year, tonight's the night it comes. I won't go into detail, you'll have to see it yourself. Just sit down there. If you want, tomorrow you can pack your duffel and take the motorboat in to land and get your car parked there at the dinghy pier on the cape and drive on back to some little inland town and keep your lights burning nights, I won't question or blame you. It's happened three years now, and this is the only time anyone's been here with me to verify it. You wait and watch."

Half an hour passed with only a few whispers between us. When we grew tired waiting, McDunn began describing some of his ideas to me. He had some theories about the Fog Horn itself.

"One day many years ago a man walked along and stood in the sound of the ocean on a cold sunless shore and said, 'We need a voice to call across the water, to warn ships; I'll make one. I'll make a voice like all of time and all of the fog that ever was; I'll make a voice that is like an empty bed beside you all night long, and like an empty house when you open the door, and like trees in autumn with no leaves. A sound like the birds flying south, crying, and a sound like November wind and the sea on the hard, cold shore. I'll make a sound that's so alone that no one can miss it, that whoever hears it will weep in their souls, and hearths will seem warmer, and being inside will seem better to all who hear it in the distant towns. I'll make me a sound and an apparatus and they'll call it a Fog Horn and whoever hears it will know the sadness of eternity and the briefness of life.'"

The Fog Horn blew.

"I made up that story," said McDunn quietly, "to try to

explain why this thing keeps coming back to the lighthouse every year. The Fog Horn calls it, I think, and it comes. . . ."

"But—" I said.

"Sssst!" said McDunn. "There!" He nodded out to the Deeps.

Something was swimming toward the lighthouse tower.

It was a cold night, as I have said; the high tower was cold, the light coming and going, and the Fog Horn calling and calling through the raveling mist. You couldn't see far and you couldn't see plain, but there was the deep sea moving on its way about the night earth, flat and quiet, the color of gray mud, and here were the two of us alone in the high tower, and there, far out at first, was a ripple, followed by a wave, a rising, a bubble, a bit of froth. And then, from the surface of the cold sea came a head, a large head, dark-colored, with immense eyes, and then a neck. And then—not a body—but more neck and more! The head rose a full forty feet above the water on a slender and beautiful dark neck. Only then did the body, like a little island of black coral and shells and crayfish, drip up from the subterranean. There was a flicker of tail. In all, from head to tip of tail, I estimated the monster at ninety or a hundred feet.

I don't know what I said. I said something.

"Steady, boy, steady," whispered McDunn.

"It's impossible!" I said.

"No, Johnny, *we're* impossible. *It's* like it always was ten million years ago. *It* hasn't changed. It's *us* and the land that've changed, become impossible. *Us!*"

It swam slowly and with a great dark majesty out in the icy waters, far away. The fog came and went about it, momentarily erasing its shape. One of the monster eyes caught and held and flashed back our immense light, red, white, red, white, like a disk held high and sending a message in primeval code. It was as silent as the fog through which it swam.

"It's a dinosaur of some sort!" I crouched down, holding to the stair rail.

"Yes, one of the tribe."

"But they died out!"

"No, only hid away in the Deeps. Deep, deep down in the deepest Deeps. Isn't *that* a word now, Johnny, a real word, it says so much: the Deeps. There's all the coldness and darkness and deepness in the world in a word like that."

"What'll we do?"

"Do? We got our job, we can't leave. Besides, we're safer here than in any boat trying to get to land. That thing's as big as a destroyer and almost as swift."

"But here, why does it come *here?*"

The next moment I had my answer.

The Fog Horn blew.

And the monster answered.

A cry came across a million years of water and mist. A cry so anguished and alone that it shuddered in my head and my body. The monster cried out at the tower. The Fog Horn blew. The monster roared again. The Fog Horn blew. The monster opened its great toothed mouth and the sound that came from it was the sound of the Fog Horn itself. Lonely and vast and far away. The sound of isolation, a viewless sea, a cold night, apartness. That was the sound.

"Now," whispered McDunn, "do you know why it comes here?"

I nodded.

"All year long, Johnny, that poor monster there lying far out, a thousand miles at sea, and twenty miles deep maybe, biding its time, perhaps it's a million years old, this one creature. Think of it, waiting a million years; could *you* wait that long? Maybe it's the last of its kind. I sort of think that's true. Anyway, here come men on land and build this lighthouse, five years ago. And set up their Fog Horn and sound it and sound it, out toward the place where you bury yourself in sleep and sea memories of a world where there were thousands like yourself, but now you're alone, all alone in a world not made for you, a world where you have to hide.

"But the sound of the Fog Horn comes and goes, comes and goes, and you stir from the muddy bottom of the Deeps, and your eyes open like the lenses of two-foot cameras and you move, slow, slow, for you have the ocean sea on your shoulders, heavy. But that Fog Horn comes through a thousand miles of water, faint and familiar, and the furnace in your belly stokes up, and you begin to rise, slow, slow. You feed yourself on great slakes of cod and minnow, on rivers of jellyfish, and you rise slow through the autumn months, through September when the fogs started, through October with more fog and the horn still calling you on, and then, late in November, after pressurizing yourself day by day, a few feet higher every hour, you are near the surface and still alive. You've got to go slow; if you surfaced all at once you'd explode. So it takes you all of three months to surface, and then a number of days to swim through the cold waters to the lighthouse. And there you are, out there, in the night, Johnny, the biggest damn monster in creation. And here's the lighthouse calling to you, with a long neck like your neck sticking way up out of the water, and a body like your body, and, most important of all, a voice like your voice. Do you understand now, Johnny, do you understand?"

The Fog Horn blew.

The monster answered.

I saw it all, I knew it all—the million years of waiting alone, for someone to come back who never came back. The million years of isolation at the bottom of the sea, the insanity of time there, while the skies cleared of reptile-birds, the swamps dried on the continental lands, the sloths and saber-tooths had their day and sank in tar pits, and men ran like white ants upon the hills.

The Fog Horn blew.

"Last year," said McDunn, "that creature swam round and round, round and round, all night. Not coming too near, puzzled, I'd say. Afraid, maybe. And a bit angry after coming all this way. But the next day, unexpectedly, the fog lifted, the sun came out fresh, the sky was as blue as a painting. And the monster swam off away from the heat and the silence and didn't come back. I suppose it's been brooding on it for a year now, thinking it over from every which way."

The monster was only a hundred yards off now, it and the Fog Horn crying at each other. As the lights hit them, the monster's eyes were fire and ice, fire and ice.

"That's life for you," said McDunn. "Someone always waiting for someone who never comes home. Always someone loving some thing more than that thing loves them. And after a while you want to destroy whatever that thing is, so it can't hurt you no more."

The monster was rushing at the lighthouse.

The Fog Horn blew.

"Let's see what happens," said McDunn.

He switched the Fog Horn off.

The ensuing minute of silence was so intense that we could hear our hearts pounding in the glassed area of the tower, could hear the slow greased turn of the light.

The monster stopped and froze. Its great lantern eyes blinked. Its mouth gaped. It gave a sort of rumble, like a volcano. It twitched its head this way and that, as if to seek the sounds now dwindled off into the fog. It peered at the lighthouse. It rumbled again. Then its eyes caught fire. It reared up, threshed the water, and rushed at the tower, its eyes filled with angry torment.

"McDunn!" I cried. "Switch on the horn!"

McDunn fumbled with the switch. But even as he flicked it on, the monster was rearing up. I had a glimpse of its gigantic paws, fishskin glittering in webs between the fingerlike projections, clawing at the tower. The huge eye on the right side of its anguished head glittered before me like a caldron into which I might drop, screaming. The tower shook. The Fog Horn cried; the monster cried. It seized the tower and gnashed at the glass, which shattered in upon us.

McDunn seized my arm. "Downstairs!"

The tower rocked, trembled, and started to give. The Fog Horn and the monster roared. We stumbled and half fell down the stairs. "Quick!"

We reached the bottom as the tower buckled down toward us. We ducked under the stairs into the small stone cellar. There were a thousand concussions as the rocks rained down; the Fog Horn stopped abruptly. The monster crashed upon the tower. The tower fell. We knelt together, McDunn and I, holding tight, while our world exploded.

Then it was over, and there was nothing but darkness and the wash of the sea on the raw stones.

That and the other sound.

"Listen," said McDunn quietly. "Listen."

We waited a moment. And then I began to hear it. First a great vacuumed sucking of air, and then the lament, the bewilderment, the loneliness of the great monster, folded over and upon us, above us, so that the sickening reek of its body filled the air, a stone's thickness away from our cellar. The monster gasped and cried. The tower was gone. The light was gone. The thing that had called to it across a million years was gone. And the monster was opening its mouth and sending out great sounds. The sounds of a Fog Horn, again and again. And ships far at sea, not finding the light, not seeing anything, but passing and hearing late that night, must've thought: There it is, the lonely sound, the Lonesome Bay horn. All's well. We've rounded the cape.

And so it went for the rest of that night.

The sun was hot and yellow the next afternoon when the rescuers came out to dig us from our stoned-under cellar.

"It fell apart, is all," said Mr. McDunn gravely. "We had a few bad knocks from the waves and it just crumbled." He pinched my arm.

There was nothing to see. The ocean was calm, the sky blue. The only thing was a great algaic stink from the green matter that covered the fallen tower stones and the shore rocks. Flies buzzed about. The ocean washed empty on the shore.

The next year they built a new lighthouse, but by that time I had a job in the little town and a wife and a good small warm house that glowed yellow on autumn nights, the doors locked, the chimney puffing smoke. As for McDunn, he was master of the new lighthouse, built to his own specifications, out of steel-reinforced concrete. "Just in case," he said.

The new lighthouse was ready in November. I drove down alone one evening late and parked my car and looked across the gray waters and listened to the new horn sounding, once, twice, three, four times a minute far out there, by itself.

The monster?

It never came back.

"It's gone away," said McDunn. "It's gone back to the Deeps. It's learned you can't love anything too much in this world. It's gone into the deepest Deeps to wait another million years. Ah, the poor thing! Waiting out there, and waiting out there, while man comes and goes on this pitiful little planet. Waiting and waiting."

I sat in my car, listening. I couldn't see the lighthouse or the light standing out in Lonesome Bay. I could only hear the Horn, the Horn, the Horn. It sounded like the monster calling.

I sat there wishing there was something I could say.

SHIRLEY JACKSON

Shirley Jackson was born in San Francisco in 1916 (she frequently gave her birth year as 1919, so as to appear younger than her husband, the critic Stanley Edgar Hyman). She was educated at the University of Rochester and at Syracuse University, where she met Hyman; they married in 1940. Jackson soon began publishing stories and sketches in *The New Yorker, Mademoiselle, Charm,* and other magazines; some of these stories—especially those about the four children she would bear—were gathered in the volumes *Life among the Savages* (1953) and *Raising Demons* (1957), and represent some of her most piquantly winsome work. Grimmer stories, probing the realms of supernatural and psychological horror, were collected in *The Lottery* (1949). The title story, which created a furor when published in *The New Yorker* for June 26, 1948, remains her most celebrated tale. Jackson moved to Bennington, Vermont, in 1945, where Hyman was a professor, and lived there for the remainder of her life.

Several of Jackson's novels broach the supernatural in varying degrees. *The Bird's Nest* (1954) is an account of split personality. *The Sundial* (1958) is a bizarre, misanthropic tale of a family that believes itself to be the last survivors on earth. *The Haunting of Hill House* (1959) is an imperishable haunted house tale, and was effectively filmed by Robert Wise as *The Haunting* (1963). *We Have*

Always Lived in the Castle (1962) is a grim tale of domestic isolation. Jackson was working on a novel, *Come Along with Me,* that might have been supernatural, but it remained unfinished at the time of her death in 1965; it appeared in the posthumous collection *Come Along with Me* (1968).

"A Visit" (first published in *New World Writing* no. 2, 1952 as "The Lovely House"; collected in *Come Along with Me*) is one of Jackson's subtlest tales of the supernatural and excels in delicacy of character portrayal. Loosely based upon a visit to her home by Dylan Thomas, it suggests that the visitor, Margaret, is unable to leave the house because her likeness has been engrafted into the tapestry being weaved by the mother of her friend Carla.

A VISIT

The house in itself was, even before anything had happened there, as lovely a thing as she had ever seen. Set among its lavish grounds, with a park and a river and a wooded hill surrounding it, and carefully planned and tended gardens close upon all sides, it lay upon the hills as though it were something too precious to be seen by everyone; Margaret's very coming there had been a product of such elaborate arrangement, and such letters to and fro, and such meetings and hopings and wishings, that when she alighted with Carla Montague at the doorway of Carla's home, she felt that she too had come home, to a place striven for and earned. Carla stopped before the doorway and stood for a minute, looking first behind her, at the vast reaching gardens and the green lawn going down to the river, and the soft hills beyond, and then at the perfect grace of the house, showing so clearly the long-boned structure within, the curving staircases and the arched doorways and the tall thin lines of steadying beams, all of it resting back against the hills, and up, past rows of windows and the flying lines of the roof, on, to the tower—Carla stopped, and looked, and smiled, and then turned and said, "Welcome, Margaret."

"It's a lovely house," Margaret said, and felt that she had much better have said nothing.

The doors were opened and Margaret, touching as she went the warm head of a stone faun beside her, passed inside. Carla, following, greeted the servants by name, and was welcomed with reserved pleasure; they stood for a minute on the rose and white tiled floor. "Again, welcome, Margaret," Carla said.

Far ahead of them the great stairway soared upward, held to the hall where they stood by only the slimmest of carved balustrades; on Margaret's left hand a tapestry moved softly as the door behind was closed. She could see the fine threads of the weave, and the light colors, but she could not have told the picture unless she went far away, perhaps as far away as the staircase, and looked at it from there; perhaps, she thought, from halfway up the stairway this great hall, and perhaps the whole house, is visible, as a complete body of story together, all joined and in sequence. Or perhaps I shall be allowed to move slowly from one thing to another, observing each, or would that take all the time of my visit?

"I never saw anything so lovely," she said to Carla, and Carla smiled.

"Come and meet my mama," Carla said.

They went through doors at the right, and Margaret, before she could see the light room she went into, was stricken with fear at meeting the owners of the house and the park and the river, and as she went beside Carla she kept her eyes down.

"Mama," said Carla, "this is Margaret, from school."

"Margaret," said Carla's mother, and smiled at Margaret kindly. "We are very glad you were able to come."

She was a tall lady wearing pale green and pale blue, and Margaret said as gracefully as she could, "Thank you, Mrs. Montague; I am very grateful for having been invited."

"Surely," said Mrs. Montague softly, "surely my daughter's friend Margaret from school should be welcome here; surely we should be grateful that she has come."

"Thank you, Mrs. Montague," Margaret said, not knowing how she was answering, but knowing that she was grateful.

When Mrs. Montague turned her kind eyes on her daughter, Margaret was at last able to look at the room where she stood next to her friend; it was a pale green and a pale blue long room with tall windows that looked out onto the lawn and the sky, and thin colored china ornaments on the mantel. Mrs. Montague had left her needlepoint when they came in and from where Margaret stood she could see the pale sweet pattern from the underside; all soft colors it was, melting into one another endlessly, and not finished. On the table nearby were books, and one large book of sketches that were most certainly Carla's; Carla's harp stood next to the windows, and beyond one window were marble steps outside, going shallowly down to a fountain, where water moved in the sunlight. Margaret thought of her own embroidery—a pair of slippers she was working for her friend—and knew that she should never be able to bring it into this room, where Mrs. Montague's long white hands rested on the needlepoint frame, soft as dust on the pale colors.

"Come," said Carla, taking Margaret's hand in her own. "Mama has said that I might show you some of the house."

They went out again into the hall, across the rose and white tiles which made a pattern too large to be seen from the floor, and through a doorway where tiny bronze fauns grinned at them from the carving. The first room that they went into was all gold, with gilt on the window frames and on the legs of the chairs and tables, and the small chairs standing on the yellow carpet were made of gold brocade with small gilded backs, and on the wall were more tapestries showing the house as it looked in the sunlight with even the trees around it shining, and these tapestries were let into the wall and edged with thin gilded frames.

"There is so much tapestry," Margaret said.

"In every room," Carla agreed. "Mama has embroidered all the hangings for her own room, the room where she writes her letters. The other tapestries were done by my grandmamas and my great-grandmamas and my great-great-grandmamas."

The next room was silver, and the small chairs were of silver brocade with narrow silvered backs, and the tapestries on the walls of this room were edged with silver frames and showed the house in moonlight, with the white light shining on the stones and the windows glittering.

"Who uses these rooms?" Margaret asked.

"No one," Carla said.

They passed then into a room where everything grew

smaller as they looked at it: the mirrors on both sides of the room showed the door opening and Margaret and Carla coming through, and then, reflected, a smaller door opening and a small Margaret and a smaller Carla coming through, and then, reflected again, a still smaller door and Margaret and Carla, and so on, endlessly, Margaret and Carla diminishing and reflecting. There was a table here and nesting under it another lesser table, and under that another one, and another under that one, and on the greatest table lay a carved wooden bowl holding within it another carved wooden bowl, and another within that, and another within that one. The tapestries in this room were of the house reflected in the lake, and the tapestries themselves were reflected, in and out, among the mirrors on the wall, with the house in the tapestries reflected in the lake.

This room frightened Margaret rather, because it was so difficult for her to tell what was in it and what was not, and how far in any direction she might easily move, and she backed out hastily, pushing Carla behind her. They turned from here into another doorway which led them out again into the great hall under the soaring staircase, and Carla said, "We had better go upstairs and see your room; we can see more of the house another time. We have *plenty* of time, after all," and she squeezed Margaret's hand joyfully.

They climbed the great staircase, and passed, in the hall upstairs, Carla's room, which was like the inside of a shell in pale colors, with lilacs on the table, and the fragrance of the lilacs followed them as they went down the halls.

The sound of their shoes on the polished floor was like rain, but the sun came in on them wherever they went. "Here," Carla said, opening a door, "is where we have breakfast when it is warm; here," opening another door, "is the passage to the room where Mama does her letters. And that—" nodding, "—is the stairway to the tower, and *here* is where we shall have dances when my brother comes home."

"A real tower?" Margaret said.

"And *here*," Carla said, "is the old schoolroom, and my brother and I studied here before he went away, and I stayed on alone studying here until it was time for me to come to school and meet *you*."

"Can we go up into the tower?" Margaret asked.

"Down here, at the end of the hall," Carla said, "is where all my grandpapas and my grandmamas and my great-great-grandpapas and grandmamas live." She opened the door to the long gallery, where pictures of tall old people in lace and pale waistcoats leaned down to stare at Margaret and Carla. And then, to a walk at the top of the house, where they leaned over and looked at the ground below and the tower above, and Margaret looked at the gray stone of the tower and wondered who lived there, and Carla pointed out where the river ran far below, far away, and said they should walk there tomorrow.

"When my brother comes," she said, "he will take us boating on the river."

In her room, unpacking her clothes, Margaret realized that her white dress was the only one possible for dinner, and thought that she would have to send home for more things; she had intended to wear her ordinary gray downstairs most evenings before Carla's brother came, but knew she could not when she saw Carla in light blue, with pearls around her neck. When Margaret and Carla came into the drawing room before dinner Mrs. Montague greeted them very kindly, and asked had Margaret seen the painted room, or the room with the tiles?

"We had no time to go near that part of the house at all," Carla said.

"After dinner, then," Mrs. Montague said, putting her arm affectionately around Margaret's shoulders, "we will go and see the painted room and the room with the tiles, because they are particular favorites of mine."

"Come and meet my papa," Carla said.

The door was just opening for Mr. Montague, and Margaret, who felt almost at ease now with Mrs. Montague, was frightened again of Mr. Montague, who spoke loudly and said, "So this is m'girl's friend from school? Lift up your head, girl, and let's have a look at you." When Margaret looked up blindly, and smiled weakly, he patted her cheek and said, "We shall have to make you look bolder before you leave us," and then he tapped his daughter on the shoulder and said she had grown to a monstrous fine girl.

They went in to dinner, and on the walls of the dining room were tapestries of the house in the seasons of the year, and the dinner service was white china with veins of gold running through it, as though it had been mined and not molded. The fish was one Margaret did not recognize, and Mr. Montague very generously insisted upon serving her himself without smiling at her ignorance. Carla and Margaret were each given a glassful of pale spicy wine.

"When my brother comes," Carla said to Margaret, "we will not dare be so quiet at table." She looked across the white cloth to Margaret, and then to her father at the head, to her mother at the foot, with the long table between them, and said, "My brother can make us laugh all the time."

"Your mother will not miss you for these summer months?" Mrs. Montague said to Margaret.

"She has my sisters, ma'am," Margaret said, "and I have been away at school for so long that she has learned to do without me."

"We mothers never learn to do without our daughters," Mrs. Montague said, and looked fondly at Carla. "Or our sons," she added with a sigh.

"When my brother comes," Carla said, "you will see what this house can be like with life in it."

"When does he come?" Margaret asked.

"One week," Mr. Montague said, "three days, and four hours."

When Mrs. Montague rose, Margaret and Carla followed her, and Mr. Montague rose gallantly to hold the door for them all.

That evening Carla and Margaret played and sang duets, although Carla said that their voices together were too thin to be appealing without a deeper voice accompanying, and that when her brother came they should have some splendid trios. Mrs. Montague complimented their singing, and Mr. Montague fell asleep in his chair.

Before they went upstairs Mrs. Montague reminded herself

of her promise to show Margaret the painted room and the room with the tiles, and so she and Margaret and Carla, holding their long dresses up away from the floor in front so that their skirts whispered behind them, went down a hall and through a passage and down another hall, and through a room filled with books and then through a painted door into a tiny octagonal room where each of the sides were paneled and painted, with pink and blue and green and gold small pictures of shepherds and nymphs, lambs and fauns, playing on the broad green lawns by the river, with the house standing lovely behind them. There was nothing else in the little room, because seemingly the paintings were furniture enough for one room, and Margaret felt surely that she could stay happily and watch the small painted people playing, without ever seeing anything more of the house. But Mrs. Montague led her on, into the room of the tiles, which was not exactly a room at all, but had one side all glass window looking out onto the same lawn of the pictures in the octagonal room. The tiles were set into the floor of this room, in tiny bright spots of color which showed, when you stood back and looked at them, that they were again a picture of the house, only now the same materials that made the house made the tiles, so that the tiny windows were tiles of glass, and the stones of the tower were chips of gray stone, and the bricks of the chimneys were chips of brick.

Beyond the tiles of the house Margaret, lifting her long skirt as she walked, so that she should not brush a chip of the tower out of place, stopped and said, "What is *this*?" And stood back to see, and then knelt down and said, "*What* is this?"

"Isn't she enchanting?" said Mrs. Montague, smiling at Margaret, "I've always loved her."

"I was wondering what Margaret would say when she saw it," said Carla, smiling also.

It was a curiously made picture of a girl's face, with blue chip eyes and a red chip mouth, staring blindly from the floor, with long light braids made of yellow stone chips going down evenly on either side of her round cheeks.

"She is pretty," said Margaret, stepping back to see her better. "What does it say underneath?"

She stepped back again, holding her head up and back to read the letters, pieced together with stone chips and set unevenly in the floor. "Here was Margaret," it said, "who died for love."

II

There was, of course, not time to do everything. Before Margaret had seen half the house, Carla's brother came home. Carla came running up the great staircase one afternoon calling, "Margaret, Margaret, he's come," and Margaret, running down to meet her, hugged her and said, "I'm so glad."

He had certainly come, and Margaret, entering the drawing room shyly behind Carla, saw Mrs. Montague with tears in her eyes and Mr. Montague standing straighter and prouder than before, and Carla said, "Brother, here is Margaret."

He was tall and haughty in uniform, and Margaret wished she had met him a little later, when she had perhaps been to her room again, and perhaps tucked up her hair. Next to him stood his friend, a captain, small and dark and bitter, and smiling bleakly upon the family assembled. Margaret smiled back timidly at them both, and stood behind Carla.

Everyone then spoke at once. Mrs. Montague said "We've missed you so," and Mr. Montague said "Glad to have you back, m'boy," and Carla said "We shall have such times—I've promised Margaret—" and Carla's brother said "So this is Margaret?" and the dark captain said "I've been wanting to come."

It seemed that they all spoke at once, every time; there would be a long waiting silence while all of them looked around with joy at being together, and then suddenly everyone would have found something to say. It was so at dinner. Mrs. Montague said "You're not eating enough," and "You used to be more fond of pomegranates," and Carla said "We're to go boating," and "We'll have a dance, won't we?" and "Margaret and I insist upon a picnic," and "I saved the river for my brother to show to Margaret." Mr. Montague puffed and laughed and passed the wine, and Margaret hardly dared lift her eyes. The black captain said "Never realized what an attractive old place it could be, after all," and Carla's brother said "There's much about the house I'd like to show Margaret."

After dinner they played charades, and even Mrs. Montague did Achilles with Mr. Montague, holding his heel and both of them laughing and glancing at Carla and Margaret and the captain. Carla's brother leaned on the back of Margaret's chair and once she looked up at him and said, "No one ever calls you by name. Do you actually have a name?"

"Paul," he said.

The next morning they walked on the lawn, Carla with the captain and Margaret with Paul. They stood by the lake, and Margaret looked at the pure reflection of the house and said, "It almost seems as though we could open a door and go in."

"There," said Paul, and he pointed with his stick at the front entrance, "there is where we shall enter, and it will swing open for us with an underwater crash."

"Margaret," said Carla, laughing, "you say odd things, sometimes. If you tried to go into *that* house, you'd be in the lake."

"Indeed, and not like it much, at all," the captain added.

"Or would you have the side door?" asked Paul, pointing with his stick.

"I think I prefer the front door," said Margaret.

"But you'd be drowned," Carla said. She took Margaret's arm as they started back toward the house, and said, "We'd make a scene for a tapestry right now, on the lawn before the house."

"Another tapestry?" said the captain, and grimaced.

They played croquet, and Paul hit Margaret's ball toward a wicket, and the captain accused her of cheating prettily. And they played word games in the evening, and Margaret and Paul won, and everyone said Margaret was so clever. And they walked endlessly on the lawns before the house, and looked into the still lake, and watched the reflection of the house in the water, and Margaret chose a room in the reflected house for her own, and Paul said she should have it.

"That's the room where Mama writes her letters," said Carla, looking strangely at Margaret.

"Not in our house in the lake," said Paul.

"And I suppose if you like it she would lend it to you while you stay," Carla said.

"Not at all," said Margaret amiably. "I think I should prefer the tower anyway."

"Have you seen the rose garden?" Carla asked.

"Let me take you there," said Paul.

Margaret started across the lawn with him, and Carla called to her, "Where are you off to now, Margaret?"

"Why, to the rose garden," Margaret called back, and Carla said, staring, "You are really very odd, sometimes, Margaret. And it's growing colder, far too cold to linger among the roses," and so Margaret and Paul turned back.

Mrs. Montague's needlepoint was coming on well. She had filled in most of the outlines of the house, and was setting in the windows. After the first small shock of surprise, Margaret no longer wondered that Mrs. Montague was able to set out the house so well without a pattern or a plan; she did it from memory and Margaret, realizing this for the first time, thought "How amazing," and then "But of course how else *would* she do it?"

To see a picture of the house, Mrs. Montague needed only to lift her eyes in any direction, but, more than that, she had of course never used any other model for her embroidery; she had of course learned the faces of the house better than the faces of her children. The dreamy life of the Montagues in the house was most clearly shown Margaret as she watched Mrs. Montague surely and capably building doors and windows, carvings and cornices, in her embroidered house, smiling tenderly across the room to where Carla and the captain bent over a book together, while her fingers almost of themselves turned the edge of a carving Margaret had forgotten or never known about until, leaning over the back of Mrs. Montague's chair, she saw it form itself under Mrs. Montague's hands.

The small thread of days and sunlight, then, that bound Margaret to the house, was woven here as she watched. And Carla, lifting her head to look over, might say, "Margaret, do come and look, here. Mother is always at her work, but my brother is rarely home."

They went for a picnic, Carla and the captain and Paul and Margaret, and Mrs. Montague waved to them from the doorway as they left, and Mr. Montague came to his study window and lifted his hand to them. They chose to go to the wooded hill beyond the house, although Carla was timid about going too far away—"I always like to be where I can see the roofs, at least," she said—and sat among the trees, on moss greener than Margaret had ever seen before, and spread out a white cloth and drank red wine.

It was a very proper forest, with neat trees and the green moss, and an occasional purple or yellow flower growing discreetly away from the path. There was no sense of brooding silence, as there sometimes is with trees about, and Margaret realized, looking up to see the sky clearly between the branches, that she had seen this forest in the tapestries in the breakfast room, with the house shining in the sunlight beyond.

"Doesn't the river come through here somewhere?" she asked, hearing, she thought, the sound of it through the trees. "I feel so comfortable here among these trees, so at home."

"It is possible," said Paul, "to take a boat from the lawn in front of the house and move without sound down the river, through the trees, past the fields and then, for some reason, around past the house again. The river, you see, goes almost around the house in a great circle. We are very proud of that."

"The river *is* nearby," said Carla. "It goes almost completely around the house."

"Margaret," said the captain. "You must not look rapt on a picnic unless you are contemplating nature."

"I was, as a matter of fact," said Margaret. "I was contemplating a caterpillar approaching Carla's foot."

"Will you come and look at the river?" said Paul, rising and holding his hand out to Margaret. "I think we can see much of its great circle from near here."

"Margaret," said Carla as Margaret stood up, "you are *always* wandering off."

"I'm coming right back," Margaret said, with a laugh. "It's only to look at the river."

"Don't be away long," Carla said. "We must be getting back before dark."

The river as it went through the trees was shadowed and cool, broadening out into pools where only the barest movement disturbed the ferns along its edge, and where small stones made it possible to step out and see the water all around, from a precarious island, and where without sound a leaf might be carried from the limits of sight to the limits of sight, moving swiftly but imperceptibly and turning a little as it went.

"Who lives in the tower, Paul?" asked Margaret, holding a fern and running it softly over the back of her hand. "I know someone lives there, because I saw someone moving at the window once."

"Not *lives* there," said Paul, amused. "Did you think we kept a political prisoner locked away?"

"I thought it might be the birds, at first," Margaret said, glad to be describing this to someone.

"No," said Paul, still amused. "There's an aunt, or a great-aunt, or perhaps even a great-great-great-aunt. She doesn't live there, at all, but goes there because she says she cannot *endure* the sight of tapestry." He laughed. "She has filled the tower with books, and a huge old cat, and she may practice alchemy there, for all anyone knows. The reason you've never seen her would be that she has one of her spells of hiding away. Sometimes she is downstairs daily."

"Will I ever meet her?" Margaret asked wonderingly.

"Perhaps," Paul said. "She might take it into her head to come down formally one night to dinner. Or she might wander carelessly up to you where you sat on the lawn, and introduce herself. Or you might never see her, at that."

"Suppose I went up to the tower?"

Paul glanced at her strangely. "I suppose you could, if you wanted to," he said. "*I've* been there."

"Margaret," Carla called through the woods. "Margaret, we shall be late if you do not give up brooding by the river."

All this time, almost daily, Margaret was seeing new places in the house: the fan room, where the most delicate filigree fans had been set into the walls with their fine ivory sticks painted in exquisite miniature; the small room where incredibly perfect wooden and glass and metal fruits and flowers and trees stood on glittering glass shelves, lined up against the windows. And daily she passed and repassed the door behind which lay the stairway to the tower, and almost daily she stepped carefully around the tiles on the floor which read "Here was Margaret, who died for love."

It was no longer possible, however, to put off going to the tower. It was no longer possible to pass the doorway several times a day and do no more than touch her hand secretly to the panels, or perhaps set her head against them and listen, to hear if there were footsteps up or down, or a voice calling her. It was not possible to pass the doorway once more, and so in the early morning Margaret set her hand firmly to the door and pulled it open, and it came easily, as though relieved that at last, after so many hints and insinuations, and so much waiting and such helpless despair, Margaret had finally come to open it.

The stairs beyond, gray stone and rough, were, Margaret thought, steep for an old lady's feet, but Margaret went up effortlessly, though timidly. The stairway turned around and around, going up to the tower, and Margaret followed, setting her feet carefully upon one step after another, and holding her hands against the warm stone wall on either side, looking forward and up, expecting to be seen or spoken to before she reached the top; perhaps, she thought once, the walls of the tower were transparent and she was clearly, ridiculously visible from the outside, and Mrs. Montague and Carla, on the lawn—if indeed they ever looked upward to the tower—might watch her and turn to one another with smiles, saying, "There is Margaret, going up to the tower at last," and, smiling, nod to one another.

The stairway ended, as she had not expected it would, in a heavy wooden door, which made Margaret, standing on the step below to find room to raise her hand and knock, seem smaller, and even standing at the top of the tower she felt that she was not really tall.

"Come in," said the great-aunt's voice, when Margaret had

knocked twice; the first knock had been received with an expectant silence, as though inside someone had said inaudibly, "Is that someone knocking at *this* door?" and then waited to be convinced by a second knock; and Margaret's knuckles hurt from the effort of knocking to be heard through a heavy wooden door. She opened the door awkwardly from below—how much easier this all would be, she thought, if I knew the way—went in, and said politely, before she looked around, "I'm Carla's friend. They said I might come up to the tower to see it, but of course if you would rather I went away I shall." She had planned to say this more gracefully, without such an implication that invitations to the tower were issued by the downstairs Montagues, but the long climb and her being out of breath forced her to say everything at once, and she had really no time for the sounding periods she had composed.

In any case the great-aunt said politely—she was sitting at the other side of the round room, against a window, and she was not very clearly visible—"I am amazed that they told you about me at all. However, since you are here I cannot pretend that I really object to having you; you may come in and sit down."

Margaret came obediently into the room and sat down on the stone bench which ran all the way around the tower room, under the windows which of course were on all sides and open to the winds, so that the movement of the air through the tower room was insistent and constant, making talk difficult and even distinguishing objects a matter of some effort.

As though it were necessary to establish her position in the house emphatically and immediately, the old lady said, with a gesture and a grin, "My tapestries," and waved at the windows. She seemed to be not older than a great-aunt, although perhaps too old for a mere aunt, but her voice was clearly able to carry through the sound of the wind in the tower room and she seemed compact and strong beside the window, not at all as though she might be dizzy from looking out, or tired from the stairs.

"May I look out the window?" Margaret asked, almost of the cat, which sat next to her and regarded her without friendship, but without, as yet, dislike.

"Certainly," said the great-aunt. "Look out the windows, by all means."

Margaret turned on the bench and leaned her arms on the wide stone ledge of the window, but she was disappointed. Although the tops of the trees did not reach halfway up the tower, she could see only branches and leaves below and no sign of the wide lawns or the roofs of the house or the curve of the river.

"I hoped I could see the way the river went, from here."

"The river doesn't *go* from here," said the old lady, and laughed.

"I mean," Margaret said, "they told me that the river went around in a curve, almost surrounding the house."

"Who told you?" said the old lady.

"Paul."

"I see," said the old lady. "*He's* back, is he?"

"He's been here for several days, but he's going away again soon."

"And what's *your* name?" asked the old lady, leaning forward.

"Margaret."

"I see," said the old lady again. "That's my name, too," she said.

Margaret thought that "How nice" would be an inappropriate reply to this, and something like "Is it?" or "Just imagine" or "What a coincidence" would certainly make her feel more foolish than she believed she really was, so she smiled uncertainly at the old lady and dismissed the notion of saying "What a lovely name."

"He should have come and gone sooner," the old lady went on, as though to herself. "Then we'd have it all behind us."

"Have all *what* behind us?" Margaret asked, although she felt that she was not really being included in the old lady's conversation with herself, a conversation that seemed—and probably was—part of a larger conversation which the old lady had with herself constantly and on larger subjects than the matter of Margaret's name, and which even Margaret, intruder as she was, and young, could not be allowed to interrupt for very long. "Have all *what* behind us?" Margaret asked insistently.

"I say," said the old lady, turning to look at Margaret, "he should have come and gone already, and we'd all be well out of it by now."

"I see," said Margaret. "Well, I don't think he's going to be here much longer. He's talking of going." In spite of herself, her voice trembled a little. In order to prove to the old lady that the trembling in her voice was imaginary, Margaret said almost defiantly, "It will be very lonely here after he has gone."

"We'll be well out of it, Margaret, you and I," the old lady said. "Stand away from the window, child, you'll be wet."

Margaret realized with this that the storm, which had—she knew now—been hanging over the house for long sunny days had broken, suddenly, and that the wind had grown louder and was bringing with it through the windows of the tower long stinging rain. There were drops on the cat's black fur, and Margaret felt the side of her face wet. "Do your windows close?" she asked. "If I could help you—?"

"*I* don't mind the rain," the old lady said. "It wouldn't be the first time it's rained around the tower."

"*I* don't mind it," Margaret said hastily, drawing away from the window. She realized that she was staring back at the cat, and added nervously, "Although, of course, getting wet is—" She hesitated and the cat stared back at her without expression. "I mean," she said apologetically, "some people don't *like* getting wet."

The cat deliberately turned its back on her and put its face closer to the window.

"What were you saying about Paul?" Margaret asked the old lady, feeling somehow that there might be a thin thread of reason tangling the old lady and the cat and the tower and the rain, and even, with abrupt clarity, defining Margaret herself and the strange hesitation which had caught at her here in the tower. "He's going away soon, you know."

"It would have been better if it were over with by now," the old lady said. "These things don't take really long, you know, and the sooner the better, *I* say."

"I suppose *that's* true," Margaret said intelligently.

"After all," said the old lady dreamily, with raindrops in her hair, "we don't always see ahead, into things that are going to happen."

Margaret was wondering how soon she might politely go back downstairs and dry herself off, and she meant to stay politely only so long as the old lady seemed to be talking, however remotely, about Paul. Also, the rain and the wind were coming through the window onto Margaret in great driving gusts, as though Margaret and the old lady and the books and the cat would be washed away, and the top of the tower cleaned of them.

"I *would* help you if I could," the old lady said earnestly to Margaret, raising her voice almost to a scream to be heard over the wind and the rain. She stood up to approach Margaret, and Margaret, thinking she was about to fall, reached out a hand to catch her. The cat stood up and spat, the rain came through the window in a great sweep, and Margaret, holding the old lady's hands, heard through the sounds of the wind the equal sounds of all the voices in the world, and they called to her saying, "Goodbye, goodbye," and "All is lost" and another voice saying, "I will always remember you," and still another called, "It is so dark." And, far away from the others, she could hear a voice calling, "Come back, come back." Then the old lady pulled her hands away from Margaret and the voices were gone. The cat shrank back and the old lady looked coldly at Margaret and said, "As I was saying, I would help you if I *could*."

"I'm so sorry," Margaret said weakly. "I thought you were going to fall."

"Goodbye," said the old lady.

III

At the ball Margaret wore a gown of thin blue lace that belonged to Carla, and yellow roses in her hair, and she carried one of the fans from the fan room, a daintily painted ivory thing which seemed indestructible, since she dropped it twice, and which had a tiny picture of the house painted on its ivory sticks, so that when the fan was closed the house was gone. Mrs. Montague had given it to her to carry, and had given Carla another, so that when Margaret and Carla passed one another dancing, or met by the punch bowl or in the halls, they said happily to one another, "Have you still got your fan? I gave mine to someone to hold for a minute; I showed mine to everyone. Are you still carrying your fan? I've got *mine.*"

Margaret danced with strangers and with Paul, and when she danced with Paul they danced away from the others, up and down the long gallery hung with pictures, in and out between the pillars which led to the great hall opening into the room of the tiles. Near them danced ladies in scarlet silk, and green satin, and white velvet, and Mrs. Montague, in black with diamonds at her throat and on her hands, stood at the top of the room and smiled at the dancers, or went on Mr. Montague's arm to greet guests who came laughingly in between the pillars looking eagerly and already moving in time to the music as they walked. One lady wore white feathers in her hair, curling down against her shoulder; another had a pink scarf over her arms, and it floated behind her as she danced. Paul was in his haughty uniform, and Carla wore red roses in her hair and danced with the captain.

"Are you really going tomorrow?" Margaret asked Paul once during the evening; she knew that he was, but somehow asking the question—which she had done several times before—established a communication between them, of his right to go and her right to wonder, which was sadly sweet to her.

"I *said* you might meet the great-aunt," said Paul, as though in answer; Margaret followed his glance, and saw the old lady of the tower. She was dressed in yellow satin, and looked very regal and proud as she moved through the crowd of dancers, drawing her skirt aside if any of them came too close to her. She was coming toward Margaret and Paul where they sat on small chairs against the wall, and when she came close enough she smiled, looking at Paul, and said to him, holding out her hands, "I am very glad to see you, my dear."

Then she smiled at Margaret and Margaret smiled back, thankful that the old lady held out no hands to her.

"Margaret told me you were here," the old lady said to Paul, "and I came down to see you once more."

"I'm happy that you did," Paul said. "I wanted to see you so much that I almost came to the tower."

They both laughed and Margaret, looking from one to the other of them, wondered at the strong resemblance between them. Margaret sat very straight and stiff on her narrow chair, with her blue lace skirt falling charmingly around her and her hands folded neatly in her lap, and listened to their talk. Paul had found the old lady a chair and they sat with their heads near together, looking at one another as they talked, and smiling.

"You look very fit," the old lady said. "Very fit indeed." She sighed.

"You look wonderfully well," Paul said.

"Oh, well," said the old lady. "I've aged. I've aged, I know it."

"So have I," said Paul.

"Not noticeably," said the old lady, shaking her head and regarding him soberly for a minute. "*You* never will, I suppose."

At that moment the captain came up and bowed in front of Margaret, and Margaret, hoping that Paul might notice, got up to dance with him.

"I saw you sitting there alone," said the captain, "and I seized the precise opportunity I have been awaiting all evening."

"Excellent military tactics," said Margaret, wondering if these remarks had not been made a thousand times before, at a thousand different balls.

"I could be a splendid tactician," said the captain gallantly, as though carrying on his share of the echoing conversation, the words spoken under so many glittering chandeliers, "if my objective were always so agreeable to me."

"I saw you dancing with Carla," said Margaret.

"Carla," he said, and made a small gesture that somehow showed Carla as infinitely less than Margaret. Margaret knew that she had seen him make the same gesture to Carla, probably with reference to Margaret. She laughed.

"I forget what I'm supposed to say now," she told him.

"You're supposed to say," he told her seriously, "'And do you really leave us so soon?'"

"And do you really leave us so soon?" said Margaret obediently.

"The sooner to return," he said, and tightened his arm around her waist. Margaret said, it being her turn, "We shall miss you very much."

"*I* shall miss *you*," he said, with a manly air of resignation.

They danced two waltzes, after which the captain escorted her handsomely back to the chair from which he had taken her, next to which Paul and the old lady continued in conversation, laughing and gesturing. The captain bowed to Margaret deeply, clicking his heels.

"May I leave you alone for a minute or so?" he asked. "I believe Carla is looking for me."

"I'm perfectly all right here," Margaret said. As the captain hurried away she turned to hear what Paul and the old lady were saying.

"I remember, I remember," said the old lady laughing, and she tapped Paul on the wrist with her fan. "I never imagined there would be a time when I should find it funny."

"But it *was* funny," said Paul.

"We were so young," the old lady said. "I can hardly remember."

She stood up abruptly, bowed to Margaret, and started back across the room among the dancers. Paul followed her as far as the doorway and then left her to come back to Margaret. When he sat down next to her he said, "So you met the old lady?"

"I went to the tower," Margaret said.

"She told me," he said absently, looking down at his gloves. "Well," he said finally, looking up with an air of cheerfulness. "Are they *never* going to play a waltz?"

Shortly before the sun came up over the river the next morning they sat at breakfast, Mr. and Mrs. Montague at the ends of the table, Carla and the captain, Margaret and Paul. The red roses in Carla's hair had faded and been thrown away, as had Margaret's yellow roses, but both Carla and Margaret still wore their ball gowns, which they had been wearing for so long that the soft richness of them seemed natural, as though they were to wear nothing else for an eternity in the house, and the gay confusion of helping one another dress, and admiring one another, and straightening the last folds to hang more gracefully, seemed all to have happened longer ago than memory, to be perhaps a dream that might never have happened at all, as perhaps the figures in the tapestries on the walls of the dining room might remember, secretly, an imagined process of dressing themselves and coming with laughter and light voices to sit on the lawn where they were woven. Margaret, looking at Carla, thought that she had never seen Carla so familiarly as in this soft white gown, with her hair dressed high on her head—had it really been curled and pinned that way? Or had it always, forever, been so?—and the fan in her hand—had she not always had that fan, held just so?—and when Carla turned her head slightly on her long neck she captured the air of one of the portraits in the long gallery. Paul and the captain were still somehow trim in their uniforms; they were leaving at sunrise.

"Must you really leave this morning?" Margaret whispered to Paul.

"You are all kind to stay up and say goodbye," said the captain, and he leaned forward to look down the table at Margaret, as though it were particularly kind of her.

"Every time my son leaves me," said Mrs. Montague, "it is as though it were the first time."

Abruptly, the captain turned to Mrs. Montague and said, "I noticed this morning that there was a bare patch on the grass before the door. Can it be restored?"

"I had not known," Mrs. Montague said, and she looked nervously at Mr. Montague, who put his hand quietly on the table and said, "We hope to keep the house in good repair so long as we are able."

"But the broken statue by the lake?" said the captain. "And the tear in the tapestry behind your head?"

"It is wrong of you to notice these things," Mrs. Montague said, gently.

"What can I do?" he said to her. "It is impossible not to notice these things. The fish are dying, for instance. There are no grapes in the arbor this year. The carpet is worn to thread near your embroidery frame," he bowed to Mrs. Montague, "and in the house itself—" bowing to Mr. Montague, "—there is a noticeable crack over the window of the conservatory, a crack in the solid stone. Can you repair that?"

Mr. Montague said weakly, "It is very wrong of you to notice these things. Have you neglected the sun, and the bright perfection of the drawing room? Have you been recently to the gallery of portraits? Have you walked on the green portions of the lawn, or only watched for the bare places?"

"The drawing room is shabby," said the captain softly. "The green brocade sofa is torn a little near the arm. The carpet has lost its luster. The gilt is chipped on four of the small chairs in the gold room, the silver paint scratched in the silver room. A tile is missing from the face of Margaret, who died for love, and in the great gallery the paint has faded slightly on the portrait of—" bowing to Mr. Montague, "—your great-great-great-grandfather, sir."

Mr. Montague and Mrs. Montague looked at one another, and then Mrs. Montague said, "Surely it is not necessary to reproach *us* for these things?"

The captain reddened and shook his head.

"My embroidery is very nearly finished," Mrs. Montague said. "I have only to put the figures into the foreground."

"*I* shall mend the brocade sofa," said Carla.

The captain glanced once around the table, and sighed. "I must pack," he said. "We cannot delay our duties even though we have offended lovely women." Mrs. Montague, turning coldly away from him, rose and left the table, with Carla and Margaret following.

Margaret went quickly to the tile room, where the white face of Margaret who died for love stared eternally into the sky beyond the broad window. There was indeed a tile missing

Shirley Jackson

from the wide white cheek, and the broken spot looked like a tear, Margaret thought; she kneeled down and touched the tile face quickly to be sure that it was not a tear.

Then she went slowly back through the lovely rooms, across the broad rose and white tiled hall, and into the drawing room, and stopped to close the tall doors behind her.

"There really is a tile missing," she said.

Paul turned and frowned; he was standing alone in the drawing room, tall and bright in his uniform, ready to leave. "You are mistaken," he said. "It is not possible that anything should be missing."

"I saw it."

"It is not *true*, you know," he said. He was walking quickly up and down the room, slapping his gloves on his wrist, glancing nervously, now and then, at the door, at the tall windows opening out onto the marble stairway. "The house is the same as ever," he said. "It does not change."

"But the worn carpet . . ." It was under his feet as he walked.

"Nonsense," he said violently. "Don't you think I'd know my own house? I care for it constantly, even when *they* forget; without this house I could not exist; do you think it would begin to crack while I am here?"

"How can you keep it from aging? Carpets *will* wear, you know, and unless they are replaced . . ."

"Replaced?" He stared as though she had said something evil. "What could replace anything in this house?" He touched Mrs. Montague's embroidery frame, softly. "All we can do is add to it."

There was a sound outside; it was the family coming down the great stairway to say goodbye. He turned quickly and listened, and it seemed to be the sound he had been expecting. "I will always remember you," he said to Margaret, hastily, and turned again toward the tall windows. "Goodbye."

"It is so dark," Margaret said, going beside him. "You will come back?"

"I will come back," he said sharply. "Goodbye." He stepped across the sill of the window onto the marble stairway outside;

he was black for a moment against the white marble, and Margaret stood still at the window watching him go down the steps and away through the gardens. "Lost, lost," she heard faintly, and, from far away, "all is lost."

She turned back to the room, and, avoiding the worn spot in the carpet and moving widely around Mrs. Montague's embroidery frame, she went to the great doors and opened them. Outside, in the hall with the rose and white tiled floor, Mr. and Mrs. Montague and Carla were standing with the captain.

"Son," Mrs. Montague was saying. "When will you be back?"

"Don't *fuss* at me," the captain said. "I'll be back when I can."

Carla stood silently, a little away. "Please be careful," she said, and, "Here's Margaret, come to say goodbye to you, brother."

"Don't linger, m'boy," said Mr. Montague. "Hard on the women."

"There are so many things Margaret and I planned for you while you were here," Carla said to her brother. "The time has been so short."

Margaret, standing beside Mrs. Montague, turned to Carla's brother (*and Paul; who was Paul?*) and said "Goodbye." He bowed to her and moved to go to the door with his father.

"It is hard to see him go," Mrs. Montague said. "And we do not know when he will come back." She put her hand gently on Margaret's shoulder. "We must show you more of the house," she said. "I saw you one day try the door of the ruined tower; have you seen the hall of flowers? Or the fountain room?"

"When my brother comes again," Carla said, "we shall have a musical evening, and perhaps he will take us boating on the river."

"And my visit?" asked Margaret smiling. "Surely there will be an end to my visit?"

Mrs. Montague, with one last look at the door from which Mr. Montague and the captain had gone, dropped her hand from Margaret's shoulder and said, "I must go to my embroidery. I have neglected it while my son was with us."

"You will not leave us before my brother comes again?" Carla asked Margaret.

"I have only to put the figures into the foreground," Mrs. Montague said, hesitating on her way to the drawing room. "I shall have you exactly if you sit on the lawn near the river."

"We shall be models of stillness," said Carla, laughing. "Margaret, will you come and sit beside me on the lawn?"

RICHARD MATHESON

Richard Burton Matheson was born in Allendale, New Jersey, in 1926. He served in the U.S. Army during World War II and subsequently gained a degree in journalism from the University of Missouri. He married Ruth Ann Woodson in 1952; one of their sons is the noted contemporary horror and science fiction writer Richard Christian Matheson. Matheson burst onto the horror scene in 1954 with two volumes, the novel *I Am Legend* and the story collection *Born of Man and Woman*. *I Am Legend* is one of the most inventive elaborations of the vampire myth since Bram Stoker's *Dracula*, portraying a future society in which a virus has transformed every human being, with one exception, into a vampire; it was filmed as *The Omega Man*. Matheson subsequently wrote *The Shrinking Man* (1956), filmed the next year as *The Incredible Shrinking Man* with his screenplay. Matheson did much work in film and television, writing many scripts for Rod Serling's *The Twilight Zone* and also for *Thriller* and other series. *A Stir of Echoes* (1958) is an effective novel about psychic powers.

In spite of the success of such novels as *Hell House* (1971)—a takeoff of Shirley Jackson's *The Haunting of Hill House*—and *What Dreams May Come* (1978), many critics believe that Matheson's best work is in the short story, especially in the five-volume series, *Shock!* (1961), *Shock II* (1964), *Shock III* (1966), *Shock Waves* (1970), and *Shock 4*

(1980). Matheson, along with Ray Bradbury, Fritz Leiber, and Charles Beaumont, is credited with bringing supernatural horror down to earth, eschewing the Gothic extravaganzas of Lovecraft for mundane, contemporary settings for greater immediacy of effect. The immense *Collected Stories* appeared in 1989.

"Long Distance Call" (first published in *Beyond Fantasy Fiction,* November 1953, and reprinted in *Shock!*) is typical of Matheson's work in utilizing a common utilitarian device—the telephone—to effect a novel treatment of the conventional supernatural theme of the reanimated dead.

LONG DISTANCE CALL

Just before the telephone rang, storm winds toppled the tree outside her window and jolted Miss Keene from dreaming sleep. She flung herself up with a gasp, her frail hands crumpling twists of sheet in either palm. Beneath her fleshless chest the heart jerked taut, the sluggish blood spurted. She sat in rigid muteness, her eyes staring at the night.

In another second, the telephone rang.

Who on earth? The question shaped unwittingly in her brain. Her thin hand faltered in the darkness, the fingers searching a moment and then Miss Elva Keene drew the cool receiver to her ear.

"Hello," she said.

Outside a cannon of thunder shook the night, twitching Miss Keene's crippled legs. *I've missed the voice,* she thought, *the thunder has blotted out the voice.*

"Hello," she said again.

There was no sound. Miss Keene waited in expectant lethargy. Then she repeated. "Hel-*lo,*" in a cracking voice. Outside the thunder crashed again.

Still no voice spoke, not even the sound of a phone being disconnected met her ears. Her wavering hand reached out and thumped down the receiver with an angry motion.

"Inconsideration," she muttered, thudding back on her pillow. Already her infirm back ached from the effort of sitting.

She forced out a weary breath. Now she'd have to suffer

through the whole tormenting process of going to sleep again—the composing of jaded muscles, the ignoring of abrasive pain in her legs, the endless, frustrating struggle to turn off the faucet in her brain and keep unwanted thoughts from dripping. Oh, well, it had to be done; Nurse Phillips insisted on proper rest. Elva Keene breathed slowly and deeply, drew the covers to her chin and labored hopefully for sleep.

In vain.

Her eyes opened and, turning her face to the window, she watched the storm move off on lightning legs. *Why can't I sleep,* she fretted, *why must I always lie here awake like this?*

She knew the answer without effort. When a life was dull, the smallest element added seemed unnaturally intriguing. And life for Miss Keene was the sorry pattern of lying flat or being propped on pillows, reading books which Nurse Phillips brought from the town library, getting nourishment, rest, medication, listening to her tiny radio—and waiting, *waiting* for something different to happen.

Like the telephone call that wasn't a call.

There hadn't even been the sound of a receiver replaced in its cradle. Miss Keene didn't understand that. Why would anyone call her exchange and then listen silently while she said, "Hello," over and over again? *Had* it actually been anyone calling?

What she should have done, she realized then, was to keep listening until the other person tired of the joke and put down the receiver. What she should have done was to speak out forcefully about the inconsideration of a prankish call to a crippled maiden lady in the middle of a stormy night. Then, if there had been someone listening, whoever it was would have been properly chastened by her angry words and . . .

"Well, of course."

She said it aloud in the darkness, punctuating the sentence with a cluck of somewhat relieved disgust. Of course, the telephone was out of order. Someone had tried to contact her, perhaps Nurse Phillips to see if she was all right. But the other end of the line had broken down in some way, allowing her phone to ring but no verbal communication to be made. Well, of course, that was the case.

Miss Keene nodded once and closed her eyes gently. Now to sleep, she thought. Far away, beyond the county, the storm cleared its murky throat. *I hope no one is worrying,* Elva Keene thought, *that would be too bad.*

She was thinking that when the telephone rang again.

There, she thought, *they are trying to reach me again.* She reached out hurriedly in the darkness, fumbled until she felt the receiver, then pulled it to her ear.

"Hello," said Miss Keene.

Silence.

Her throat contracted. She knew what was wrong, of course, but she didn't like it, no, not at all.

"Hello?" she said tentatively, not yet certain that she was wasting breath.

There was no reply. She waited a moment, then spoke a third time, a little impatiently now, loudly, her shrill voice ringing in the dark bedroom. *"Hello!"*

Nothing. Miss Keene had the sudden urge to fling the receiver away. She forced down that curious instinct—no, she must wait; wait and listen to hear if anyone hung up the phone on the other end of the line.

So she waited.

The bedroom was very quiet now, but Elva Keene kept straining to hear; either the sound of a receiver going down or the buzz which usually follows. Her chest rose and fell in delicate lurches, she closed her eyes in concentration, then opened them again and blinked at the darkness. There was no sound from the telephone; not a click, not a buzz, not a sound of someone putting down a receiver.

"Hello!" she cried suddenly, then pushed away the receiver.

She missed her target. The receiver dropped and thumped once on the rug. Miss Keene nervously clicked on the lamp, wincing as the leprous bulb light filled her eyes. Quickly, she lay on her side and tried to reach the silent, voiceless telephone.

But she couldn't stretch far enough and crippled legs prevented her from rising. Her throat tightened. My God, must she leave it there all night, silent and mystifying?

Remembering then, she reached out abruptly and pressed

the cradle arm. On the floor, the receiver clicked, then began to buzz normally. Elva Keene swallowed and drew in a shaking breath as she slumped back on her pillow.

She threw out hooks of reason then and pulled herself back from panic. *This is ridiculous,* she thought, *getting upset over such a trivial and easily explained incident. It was the storm, the night, the way in which I'd been shocked from sleep. (What was it that had awakened me?) All these things piled on the mountain of teeth-grinding monotony that's my life. Yes, it was bad, very bad.* But it wasn't the incident that was bad. It was her reaction to it.

Miss Elva Keene numbed herself to further premonitions. *I shall sleep now,* she ordered her body with a petulant shake. She lay very still and relaxed. From the floor she could hear the telephone buzzing like the drone of far-off bees. She ignored it.

Early the next morning, after Nurse Phillips had taken away the breakfast dishes, Elva Keene called the telephone company.

"This is Miss Elva," she told the operator.

"Oh, yes, Miss Elva," said the operator, a Miss Finch. "Can I help you?"

"Last night my telephone rang twice," said Elva Keene. "But when I answered it, no one spoke. And I didn't hear any receiver drop. I didn't even hear a dial tone—just silence."

"Well, I'll tell you, Miss Elva," said the cheery voice of Miss Finch, "that storm last night just about ruined half our service. We're being flooded with calls about knocked down lines and bad connections. I'd say you're pretty lucky your phone is working at all."

"Then you think it was probably a bad connection," prompted Miss Keene, "caused by the storm?"

"Oh yes, Miss Elva, that's all."

"Do you think it will happen again?"

"Oh, it *may,*" said Miss Finch. "It *may.* I really couldn't tell you, Miss Elva. But if it does happen again, you just call me and then I'll have one of our men check on it."

"All right," said Miss Elva. "Thank you, dear."

She lay on her pillows all morning in a relaxed torpor. *It gives one a satisfied feeling,* she thought, *to solve a mystery, slight as it is. It had been a terrible storm that caused the bad connection. And no wonder when it had even knocked down the ancient oak tree beside the house. That was the noise that had awakened me of course, and a pity it was that the dear tree had fallen. How it shaded the house in hot summer months. Oh, well, I suppose I should be grateful, she thought, that the tree fell across the road and not across the house.*

The day passed uneventfully, an amalgam of eating, reading Angela Thirkell and the mail (two throw-away advertisements and the light bill), plus brief chats with Nurse Phillips. Indeed, routine had set in so properly that when the telephone rang early that evening, she picked it up without even thinking.

"Hello," she said.

Silence.

It brought her back for a second. Then she called Nurse Phillips.

"What is it?" asked the portly woman as she trudged across the bedroom rug.

"This is what I was telling you about," said Elva Keene, holding out the receiver. "Listen."

Nurse Phillips took the receiver in her hand and pushed back gray locks with the earpiece. Her placid face remained placid. "There's nobody there," she observed.

"That's right," said Miss Keene. "That's right. Now you just listen and see if you can hear a receiver being put down. I'm sure you won't."

Nurse Phillips listened for a moment, then shook her head. "I don't hear anything," she said and hung up.

"Oh, wait!" Miss Keene said hurriedly. "Oh, well, it doesn't matter," she added, seeing it was already done. "If it happens too often, I'll just call Miss Finch and they'll have a repairman check on it."

"I see," Nurse Phillips said and went back to the living room.

Nurse Phillips left the house at eight, leaving on the bedside table, as usual, an apple, a cookie, a glass of water and the bottle of pills. She puffed up the pillows behind Miss Keene's fragile back, moved the radio and telephone a little closer to the bed, looked around complacently, then turned for the door, saying, "I'll see you tomorrow."

It was fifteen minutes later when the telephone rang. Miss Keene picked up the receiver quickly. She didn't bother saying hello this time—she just listened.

At first it was the same—an absolute silence. She listened a moment more, impatiently. Then, on the verge of replacing the receiver, she heard the sound. Her cheek twitched, she jerked the telephone back to her ear.

"Hello?" she asked tensely.

A murmuring, a dull humming, a rustling sound—what was it? Miss Keene shut her eyes tightly, listening hard, but she couldn't identify the sound; it was too soft, too undefined. It deviated from a sort of whining vibration . . . to an escape of air . . . to a bubbling sibilance. *It must be the sound of the connection,* she thought, *it must be the telephone itself making the noise. Perhaps a wire blowing in the wind somewhere, perhaps . . .*

She stopped thinking then. She stopped breathing. The sound had ceased. Once more, silence rang in her ears. She could feel the heartbeats stumbling in her chest again, the walls of her throat closing in. *Oh, this is ridiculous,* she told herself. *I've already been through this—it was the storm, the storm!*

She lay back on her pillows, the receiver pressed to her ear, nervous breaths faltering from her nostrils. She could feel unreasoning dread rise like a tide within her, despite all attempts at sane deduction. Her mind kept slipping off the glassy perch of reason; she kept falling deeper and deeper.

Now she shuddered violently as the sounds began again. They couldn't *possibly* be human sounds, she knew, and yet there was something about them, some inflection, some almost identifiable arrangement of . . .

Her lips shook and a whine began to hover in her throat. But she couldn't put down the telephone, she simply couldn't. The sounds held her hypnotized. Whether they were the rise and fall of the wind or the muttering of faulty mechanisms, she didn't know, but they would not let her go.

"Hello?" she murmured, shakily.

The sounds rose in volume. They rattled and shook in her brain.

"Hello!" she screamed.

"H-e-l-l-o," answered a voice on the telephone. Then Miss Keene fainted dead away.

"Are you certain it was someone saying *hello?*" Miss Finch asked Miss Elva over the telephone. "It might have been the connection, you know."

"I tell you it was a *man!*" a shaking Elva Keene cried. "It was the same man who kept listening to me say hello over and over and over again without answering me back. The same one who made terrible noises over the telephone!"

Miss Finch cleared her throat politely. "Well, I'll have a man check your line, Miss Elva, as soon as he can. Of course, the men are very busy now with all the repairs on storm wreckage, but as soon as it's possible . . ."

"And what am I going to do if this—this *person* calls again?"

"You just hang up on him, Miss Elva."

"But he keeps calling!"

"Well." Miss Finch's affability wavered. "Why don't you find out who he is, Miss Elva? If you can do that, why, we can take immediate action, you see and . . ."

After she'd hung up, Miss Keene lay against the pillows tensely, listening to Nurse Phillips sing husky love songs over the breakfast dishes. Miss Finch didn't believe her story, that was apparent. Miss Finch thought she was a nervous old woman falling prey to imagination. Well, Miss Finch would find out differently.

"I'll just keep calling her and calling her until she *does,*" she said irritably to Nurse Phillips just before afternoon nap.

"You just do that," said Nurse Phillips. "Now take your pill and lie down."

Miss Keene lay in grumpy silence, her vein-rutted hands knotted at her sides. It was ten after two and, except for the bubbling of Nurse Phillips's front-room snores, the house was silent in the October afternoon. *It makes me angry,* thought Elva

Keene, *that no one will take this seriously. Well*—her thin lips pressed together—*the next time the telephone rings I'll make sure that Nurse Phillips listens until she does hear something.*

Exactly then the phone rang.

Miss Keene felt a cold tremor lace down her body. Even in the daylight with sunbeams speckling her flowered coverlet, the strident ringing frightened her. She dug porcelain teeth into her lower lip to steady it. *Shall I answer it?* the question came and then, before she could even think to answer, her hand picked up the receiver. A deep ragged breath; she drew the phone slowly to her ear. She said, "Hello?"

The voice answered back, "Hello?"—hollow and inanimate.

"Who is this?" Miss Keene asked, trying to keep her throat clear.

"Hello?"

"Who's calling, please?"

"Hello?"

"Is anyone there!"

"Hello?"

"Please . . . !"

"Hello?"

Miss Keene jammed down the receiver and lay on her bed trembling violently, unable to catch her breath. *What is it,* begged her mind, *what in God's name is it?*

"Margaret!" she cried. *"Margaret!"*

In the front room she heard Nurse Phillips grunt abruptly and then start coughing.

"Margaret, please . . . !"

Elva Keene heard the large-bodied woman rise to her feet and trudge across the living room floor. *I must compose myself,* she told herself, fluttering hands to her fevered cheeks. *I must tell her exactly what happened, exactly.*

"What is it?" grumbled the nurse. "Does your stomach ache?"

Miss Keene's throat drew in tautly as she swallowed. "He just called again," she whispered.

"Who?"

"That man!"

"What man?"

"The one who keeps calling!" Miss Keene cried. "He keeps saying hello over and over again. That's all he says—hello, hello, hel . . ."

"Now stop this," Nurse Phillips scolded stolidly. "Lie back and . . ."

"I don't *want* to lie back!" she said frenziedly. "I want to know who this terrible person is who keeps frightening me!"

"Now don't work yourself into a state," warned Nurse Phillips. "You know how upset your stomach gets."

Miss Keene began to sob bitterly. "I'm afraid. I'm afraid of him. Why does he keep calling me?"

Nurse Phillips stood by the bed looking down in bovine inertia. "Now, what did Miss Finch tell you?" she said softly.

Miss Keene's shaking lips could not frame the answer.

"Did she tell you it was the connection?" the nurse soothed. "Did she?"

"But it isn't! It's a man, a *man!*"

Nurse Phillips expelled a patient breath. "If it's a man," she said, "then just hang up. You don't have to talk to him. Just hang up. Is that so hard to do?"

Miss Keene shut tear-bright eyes and forced her lips into a twitching line. In her mind the man's subdued and listless voice kept echoing. Over and over, the inflection never altering, the question never deferring to her replies—just repeating itself endlessly in doleful apathy. *Hello? Hello?* Making her shudder to the heart.

"Look," Nurse Phillips spoke.

She opened her eyes and saw the blurred image of the nurse putting the receiver down on the table.

"There," Nurse Phillips said, "nobody can call you now. You leave it that way. If you need anything all you have to do is dial. Now isn't that all right? Isn't it?"

Miss Keene looked bleakly at her nurse. Then, after a moment, she nodded once. Grudgingly.

She lay in the dark bedroom, the sound of the dial tone humming in her ear; keeping her awake. *Or am I just telling myself that?* she thought. *Is it really keeping me awake? Didn't I sleep that first night with the receiver off the hook? No, it wasn't the sound, it was something else.*

She closed her eyes obdurately. *I won't listen,* she told herself, *I just won't listen to it.* She drew in trembling breaths of the night. But the darkness would not fill her brain and blot away the sound.

Miss Keene felt around the bed until she found her jacket. She draped it over the receiver, swathing its black smoothness in woolly turns. Then she sank back again, stern breathed and taut. *I will sleep,* she demanded, *I will sleep.*

She heard it still.

Her body grew rigid and, abruptly, she unfolded the receiver from its thick wrappings and slammed it down angrily on the cradle. Silence filled the room with a delicious peace. Miss Keene fell back on the pillow with a feeble groan. *Now to sleep,* she thought.

The telephone rang.

Her breath snuffed off. The ringing seemed to permeate the darkness, surrounding her in a cloud of ear-lancing vibration. She reached out to put the receiver on the table again, then jerked her hand back with a gasp, realizing she would hear the man's voice again.

Her throat pulsed nervously. *What I'll do,* she planned, *what I'll do is take off the receiver very quickly—very quickly—and put it down, then push down on the arm and cut off the line. Yes, that's what I'll do!*

She tensed herself and spread her hand out cautiously until the ringing phone was under it. Then, breath held, she followed her plan, slashed off the ring, reached quickly for the cradle arm . . .

And stopped, frozen, as the man's voice reached out through darkness to her ears. "Where are you?" he asked. "I want to talk to you."

Claws of ice clamped down on Miss Keene's shuddering chest. She lay petrified, unable to cut off the sound of the man's dull, expressionless voice, asking, "Where are you? I want to talk to you."

A sound from Miss Keene's throat, thin and fluttering.

And the man said, "Where are you? I want to talk to you."

"No, no," sobbed Miss Keene.

"Where are you? I want . . ."

She pressed the cradle arm with taut white fingers. She held it down for five minutes before letting it go.

"I tell you I won't have it!"

Miss Keene's voice was a frayed ribbon of sound. She sat inflexibly on the bed, straining her frightened anger through the mouthpiece vents.

"You say you hang up on this man and he still calls?" Miss Finch inquired.

"I've *explained* all that!" Elva Keene burst out. "I had to leave the receiver off the phone all night so he wouldn't call. And the buzzing kept me awake. I didn't get a *wink* of sleep! Now, I want this line checked, do you hear me? I want you to stop this terrible thing!"

Her eyes were like hard, dark beads. The phone almost slipped from her palsied fingers.

"All right, Miss Elva," said the operator. "I'll send a man out today."

"Thank you, dear, thank you," Miss Keene said. "Will you call me when . . ."

Her voice stopped abruptly as a clicking sound started on the telephone.

"The line is busy," she announced.

The clicking stopped and she went on. "To repeat, will you let me know when you find out who this terrible person is?"

"Surely, Miss Elva, surely. And I'll have a man check your telephone this afternoon. You're at 127 Mill Lane, aren't you?"

"That's right, dear. You will see to it, won't you?"

"I promise faithfully, Miss Elva. First thing today."

"Thank you, dear," Miss Keene said, drawing in relieved breath.

There were no calls from the man all that morning, none that afternoon. Her tightness slowly began to loosen. She played a game of cribbage with Nurse Phillips and even managed a little laughter. It was comforting to know that the telephone company was working on it now. They'd soon catch that awful man and bring back her peace of mind.

But when two o'clock came, then three o'clock—and still no repairman at her house—Miss Keene began worrying again.

"What's the *matter* with that girl?" she said pettishly. "She promised me faithfully that a man would come this afternoon."

"He'll be here," Nurse Phillips said. "Be patient."

Four o'clock arrived and no man. Miss Keene would not play cribbage, read her book or listen to her radio. What had begun to loosen was tightening again, increasing minute by minute until five o'clock, when the telephone rang, her hand spurted out rigidly from the flaring sleeve of her bed jacket and clamped down like a claw on the receiver. *If the man speaks,* raced her mind, *if he speaks I'll scream until my heart stops.*

She pulled the receiver to her ear. "Hello?"

"Miss Elva, this is Miss Finch."

Her eyes closed and breath fluttered through her lips. "Yes?" she said.

"About those calls you say you've been receiving."

"Yes?" In her mind, Miss Finch's words cutting—"those calls you *say* you've been receiving."

"We sent a man out to trace them," continued Miss Finch. "I have his report here."

Miss Keene caught her breath. "Yes?"

"He couldn't find anything."

Elva Keene didn't speak. Her gray head lay motionless on the pillow, the receiver pressed to her ear.

"He says he traced the—the difficulty to a fallen wire on the edge of town."

"Fallen—wire?"

"Yes, Miss Elva." Miss Finch did not sound happy.

"You're telling me I didn't hear anything?"

Miss Finch's voice was firm. "There's no way anyone could have phoned you from that location," she said.

"I tell you a *man* called me!"

Miss Finch was silent and Miss Keene's fingers tightened convulsively on the receiver.

"There must be a phone there," she insisted. "There must be *some* way that man was able to call me!"

"Miss Elva, there's no one out there."

"Out where, *where?*"

The operator said, "Miss Elva, it's the cemetery."

In the black silence of her bedroom, a crippled maiden lady lay waiting. Her nurse would not remain for the night; her nurse had patted her and scolded her and ignored her.

She was waiting for a telephone call.

She could have disconnected the phone, but she had not the will. She lay there waiting, waiting, thinking.

Of the silence—of ears that had not heard, seeking to hear again. Of sounds bubbling and muttering—the first stumbling attempts at speech by one who had not spoken—how long? Of—*hello? hello?*—first greeting by one long silent. Of—*where are you?* Of (that which made her lie so rigidly) the clicking and the operator speaking her address. Of—

The telephone ringing.

A pause. Ringing. The rustle of a nightgown in the dark.

The ringing stopped.

Listening.

And the telephone slipping from white fingers, the eyes staring, the thin heartbeats slowly pulsing.

Outside, the cricket-rattling night.

Inside, the words still sounding in her brain—giving terrible meaning to the heavy, choking silence.

"Hello, Miss Elva. I'll be right over."

CHARLES BEAUMONT

Charles Beaumont—the pseudonym, and later the legally adopted name, of Charles Leroy Nutt—was born in Chicago in 1929. A high-school dropout, he served briefly in the U.S. Army before taking up a career in writing in the early 1950s. It was just at this time that the pulp magazines were dying out, and supernatural fiction—often disguised as mystery or suspense fiction—had to appear in the science fiction digest magazines or in mainstream magazines. Beaumont published widely in such digests as *Infinity Science Fiction* and such men's magazines as *Playboy* and *Rogue*. His first story collection, *The Hunger and Other Stories,* appeared in 1957, and several others—*Yonder: Stories of Fantasy and Science Fiction* (1958), *Night Ride and Other Journeys* (1960), *The Magic Man* (1965), and *The Edge* (1966)—appeared in rapid succession. Many of Beaumont's stories present a fusion of science fiction, fantasy, mystery, suspense, and the supernatural, so that genre classification of his work becomes difficult. Of his two novels, *Run from the Hunter* (1957; with John E. Tomerlin) is a crime thriller, and *The Intruder* (1959) is a mainstream novel of race relations in the South. Some of his best-known horror tales are "The Howling Man," a brilliant tale of the Devil, and "Black Country," which ingeniously fuses the supernatural with blues music.

Beaumont did much work in film and television, writing the screenplay (with Ben Hecht) to the film *Queen of Outer Space* and writing many scripts for Rod Serling's *The Twilight Zone*. These have now been collected in *The Twilight Zone Scripts of Charles Beaumont, Volume I* (2004), with more volumes to follow. Beaumont, afflicted with an extremely advanced case of Alzheimer's disease, died in 1967. His *Selected Stories* appeared in 1988.

"The Vanishing American" (first published in the *Magazine of Fantasy and Science Fiction*, August 1955, and collected in *The Hunger and Other Stories*) exhibits Beaumont's use of the supernatural as a metaphor for social and psychological trauma in the literal vanishment of a dispirited office worker.

THE VANISHING AMERICAN

He got the notion shortly after five o'clock; at least, a part of him did, a small part hidden down beneath all the conscious cells—*he* didn't get the notion until some time later. At exactly five p.m., the bell rang. At two minutes after, the chairs began to empty. There was the vast slamming of drawers, the straightening of rulers, the sound of bones snapping and mouths yawning and feet shuffling tiredly.

Mr. Minchell relaxed. He rubbed his hands together and relaxed and thought how nice it would be to get up and go home, like the others. But of course there was the tape, only three-quarters finished. He would have to stay.

He stretched and said good night to the people who filed past him. As usual, no one answered. When they had gone, he set his fingers pecking again over the keyboard. The *click-clicking* grew loud in the suddenly still office, but Mr. Minchell did not notice. He was lost in the work. Soon, he knew, it would be time for the totaling, and his pulse quickened at the thought of this.

He lit a cigarette. Heart tapping, he drew in smoke and released it.

He extended his right hand and rested his index and middle fingers on the metal bar marked TOTAL. A mile-long ribbon of paper lay gathered on the desk, strangely festive. He glanced at it, then at the manifest sheet. The figure 18037448 was circled in red. He pulled breath into his lungs, locked it there; then he closed his eyes and pressed the TOTAL bar.

There was a smooth low metallic grinding, followed by absolute silence.

Mr. Minchell opened one eye, dragged it from the ceiling on down to the adding machine.

He groaned, slightly.

The total read: 18037447.

"God." He stared at the figure and thought of the fifty-three pages of manifest, the three thousand separate rows of figures that would have to be checked again. "God."

The day was lost, now. Irretrievably. It was too late to do anything. Madge would have supper waiting, and F. J. didn't approve of overtime; also . . .

He looked at the total again. At the last two digits.

He sighed. Forty-seven. And thought, startled: Today, for the Lord's sake, is my birthday! Today I am forty—what?—forty-seven. And that explains the mistake, I suppose. Subconscious kind of thing . . .

Slowly he got up and looked around the deserted office.

Then he went to the dressing room and got his hat and his coat and put them on, carefully.

"Pushing fifty now . . ."

The outside hall was dark. Mr. Minchell walked softly to the elevator and punched the *Down* button. "Forty-seven," he said, aloud; then, almost immediately, the light turned red and the thick door slid back noisily. The elevator operator, a bird-thin, tan-fleshed girl, swiveled her head, looking up and down the hall. "Going down," she said.

"Yes," Mr. Minchell said, stepping forward.

"Going down." The girl clicked her tongue and muttered, "Damn kids." She gave the lattice gate a tired push and moved the smooth wooden-handled lever in its slot.

Odd, Mr. Minchell decided, was the word for this particular girl. He wished now that he had taken the stairs. Being alone with only one other person in an elevator had always made him nervous: now it made him very nervous. He felt the tension growing. When it became unbearable, he cleared his throat and said, "Long day."

The girl said nothing. She had a surly look, and she seemed to be humming something deep in her throat.

Mr. Minchell closed his eyes. In less than a minute—during which time he dreamed of the cables snarling, of the car being caught between floors, of himself trying to make small talk with the odd girl for six straight hours—he opened his eyes again and walked into the lobby, briskly.

The gate slammed.

He turned and started for the doorway. Then he paused, feeling a sharp increase in his heartbeat. A large, red-faced, magnificently groomed man of middle years stood directly beyond the glass, talking with another man.

Mr. Minchell pushed through the door, with effort. He's seen me now, he thought. If he asks any questions, though, or anything, I'll just say I didn't put it on the time card; that ought to make it all right . . .

He nodded and smiled at the large man. "Good night, Mr. Diemel."

The man looked up briefly, blinked, and returned to his conversation.

Mr. Minchell felt a burning come into his face. He hurried on down the street. Now the notion—though it was not even that yet, strictly: it was more a vague feeling—swam up from the bottom of his brain. He remembered that he had not spoken directly to F. J. Diemel for over ten years, beyond a "Good morning" . . .

Ice-cold shadows fell off the tall buildings, staining the streets, now. Crowds of shoppers moved along the pavement like juggernauts, exhaustedly, but with great determination. Mr. Minchell looked at them. They all had furtive appearances, it seemed to him suddenly, even the children, as if each was fleeing from some hideous crime. They hurried along, staring.

But not, Mr. Minchell noticed, at him. Through him, yes. Past him. As the elevator operator had done, and now F. J. And had anyone said good night?

He pulled up his coat collar and walked toward the drugstore, thinking. He was forty-seven years old. At the current life-expectancy rate, he might have another seventeen or eighteen years left. And then death.

If you're not dead already.

He paused and for some reason remembered a story he'd once read in a magazine. Something about a man who dies and whose ghost takes up his duties, or something; anyway, the man didn't know he was dead—that was it. And at the end of the story, he runs into his own corpse.

Which is pretty absurd: he glanced down at his body. Ghosts don't wear $36 suits, nor do they have trouble pushing doors open, nor do their corns ache like blazes, and what the devil is wrong with me today?

He shook his head.

It was the tape, of course, and the fact that it was his birthday. That was why his mind was behaving so foolishly.

He went into the drugstore. It was an immense place, packed with people. He walked to the cigar counter, trying not to feel intimidated, and reached into his pocket. A small man elbowed in front of him and called loudly: "Gimme coupla nickels, will you, Jack?" The clerk scowled and scooped the change out of his cash register. The small man scurried off. Others took his place. Mr. Minchell thrust his arm forward. "A pack of Luckies, please," he said. The clerk whipped his fingers around a pile of cellophaned packages and, looking elsewhere, droned: "Twenty-six." Mr. Minchell put his twenty-six-cents-exactly on the glass shelf. The clerk shoved the cigarettes toward the edge and picked up the money, deftly. Not once did he lift his eyes.

Mr. Minchell pocketed the Luckies and went back out of the store. He was perspiring now, slightly, despite the chill wind. The word "ridiculous" lodged in his mind and stayed there. Ridiculous, yes, for heaven's sake. Still, he thought—now just answer the question—isn't it true? Can you honestly say that that clerk saw you?

Or that anybody saw you today?

Swallowing dryly, he walked another two blocks, always in the direction of the subway, and went into a bar called the Chez When. One drink would not hurt, one small, stiff, steadying shot.

The bar was a gloomy place, and not very warm, but there was a good crowd. Mr. Minchell sat down on a stool and folded his hands. The bartender was talking animatedly with an old woman, laughing with boisterous good humor from time to time. Mr. Minchell waited. Minutes passed. The bartender looked up several times, but never made a move to indicate that he had seen a customer.

Mr. Minchell looked at his old gray overcoat, the humbly floraled tie, the cheap sharkskin suit-cloth, and became aware of the extent to which he detested this ensemble. He sat there and detested his clothes for a long time. Then he glanced around. The bartender was wiping a glass, slowly.

All right, the hell with you. I'll go somewhere else.

He slid off the stool. Just as he was about to turn he saw the mirrored wall, pink-tinted and curved. He stopped, peering. Then he almost ran out of the bar.

Cold wind went into his head.

Ridiculous. The mirror was curved, you jackass. How do you expect to see yourself in curved mirrors?

He walked past high buildings, and now past the library and stone lion he had once, long ago, named King Richard; and he did not look at the lion, because he'd always wanted to ride the lion, ever since he was a child, and he'd promised himself he would do that, but he never did.

He hurried on to the subway, took the stairs by twos, and clattered across the platform in time to board the express.

It roared and thundered. Mr. Minchell held onto the strap and kept himself from staring. No one watched him. No one even glanced at him when he pushed his way to the door and went out onto the empty platform.

He waited. Then the train was gone, and he was alone.

He walked up the stairs. It was fully night now, a soft, unshadowed darkness. He thought about the day and the strange things that were gouging into his mind and thought about all this as he turned down a familiar street which led to his familiar apartment.

The door opened.

His wife was in the kitchen, he could see. Her apron flashed across the arch, and back, and across. He called: "Madge, I'm home."

Madge did not answer. Her movements were regular. Jimmy was sitting at the table, drooling over a glass of pop, whispering to himself.

"I said—" Mr. Minchell began.

"Jimmy, get up and go to the bathroom, you hear? I've got your water drawn."

Jimmy promptly broke into tears. He jumped off the chair and ran past Mr. Minchell into the bedroom. The door slammed viciously.

"Madge."

Madge Minchell came into the room, tired and lined and heavy. Her eyes did not waver. She went into the bedroom, and there was a silence; then a sharp slapping noise, and a yelling.

Mr. Minchell walked to the bathroom, fighting down the small terror. He closed the door and locked it and wiped his forehead with a handkerchief. Ridiculous, he thought, and ridiculous and ridiculous. I am making something utterly foolish out of nothing. All I have to do is look in the mirror, and—

He held the handkerchief to his lips. It was difficult to breathe.

Then he knew that he was afraid, more so than ever before in a lifetime of being afraid.

Look at it this way, Minchell: why shouldn't *you vanish?*

"Young man, just you wait until your father gets here!"

He pushed the handkerchief against his mouth and leaned on the door and gasped.

"What do you mean, vanish?"

Go on, take a look. You'll see what I mean.

He tried to swallow, couldn't. Tried to wet his lips, found that they stayed dry.

"Lord—"

He slitted his eyes and walked to the shaving mirror and looked in.

His mouth fell open.

The mirror reflected nothing. It held nothing. It was dull and gray and empty.

Mr. Minchell stared at the glass, put out his hand, drew it back hastily.

He squinted. Inches away. There was a form now: vague, indistinct, featureless: but a form.

"Lord," he said. He understood why the elevator girl hadn't seen him, and why F. J. hadn't answered him, and why the clerk at the drugstore and the bartender and Madge . . .

"I'm not dead."

Of course you're not dead—not that way.

"—tan your hide, Jimmy Minchell, when he gets home."

Mr. Minchell suddenly wheeled and clicked the lock. He rushed out of the steam-filled bathroom, across the room, down the stairs, into the street, into the cool night.

A block from home he slowed to a walk.

Invisible! He said the word over and over, in a half-voice. He said it and tried to control the panic that pulled at his legs, and at his brain, and filled him.

Why?

A fat woman and a little girl passed by. Neither of them looked up. He started to call out and checked himself. No. That wouldn't do any good. There was no question about it now. He was invisible.

He walked on. As he did, forgotten things returned; they came and they left, too fast. He couldn't hold onto them. He could only watch, and remember. Himself as a youngster, reading: the Oz books, Tarzan, and Mr. Wells. Himself going to the University, wanting to teach, and meeting Madge; then not planning any more, and Madge changing, and all the dreams put away. For later. For the right time. And then Jimmy—little strange Jimmy, who ate filth and picked his nose and watched television, who never read books, never; Jimmy, his son, whom he would never understand . . .

He walked by the edge of the park now. Then on past the park, through a maze of familiar and unfamiliar neighborhoods. Walking, remembering, looking at the people and feeling pain because he knew that they could not see him, not now or ever again, because he had vanished. He walked and remembered and felt pain.

All the stagnant dreams came back. Fully. The trip to Italy he'd planned. The open sports car, bad weather be damned. The firsthand knowledge that would tell him whether he did or did not approve of bullfighting. The book . . .

Then something occurred to him. It occurred to Mr. Minchell that he had not just suddenly vanished, like that, after all. No; he had been vanishing gradually for a long while. Every time he said good morning to that bastard Diemel he got a little harder to see. Every time he put on this horrible suit he faded. The process of disappearing was set into action every time he brought his pay check home and turned it over to Madge, every time he kissed her, or listened to her vicious unending complaints, or decided against buying that novel, or punched the adding machine he hated so, or . . .

Certainly.

He had vanished for Diemel and the others in the office years ago. And for strangers right afterwards. Now even Madge and Jimmy couldn't see him. And he could barely see himself, even in a mirror.

It made terrible sense to him. *Why* shouldn't *you disappear?* Well, why, indeed? There wasn't any very good reason, actually. None. And this, in a nightmarish sort of a way, made it as brutally logical as a perfect tape.

Then he thought about going back to work tomorrow and the next day and the day after that. He'd have to, of course. He couldn't let Madge and Jimmy starve; and, besides, what else would he do? It wasn't as if anything important had changed. He'd go on punching the clock and saying good morning to people who didn't see him, and he'd run the tapes and come home beat, nothing altered, and some day he'd die and that would be that.

All at once he felt tired.

He sat down on a cement step and sighed. Distantly he realized that he had come to the library. He sat there, watching the people, feeling the tiredness seep through him, thickly.

Then he looked up.

Above him, black and regal against the sky, stood the huge

stone lion. Its mouth was open, and the great head was raised proudly.

Mr. Minchell smiled. King Richard. Memories scattered in his mind: old King Richard, well, my God, here we are.

He got to his feet. Fifty thousand times, at least, he had passed this spot, and every time he had experienced that instant of wild craving. Less so of late, but still, had it ever completely gone? He was amazed to find that now the childish desire was welling up again, stronger than ever before. Urgently.

He rubbed his cheek and stood there for several minutes. It's the most ridiculous thing in the world, he thought, and I must be going out of my mind, and that must explain everything. But, he inquired of himself, even so, why not?

After all, I'm invisible. No one can see me. Of course, it didn't have to be this way, not really. I don't know, he went on, I mean, I believed that I was doing the right thing. Would it have been right to go back to the University and the hell with Madge? I couldn't change that, could I? Could I have done anything about that, even if I'd known?

He nodded sadly.

All right, but don't make it any worse. Don't for God's sake *dwell* on it!

To his surprise, Mr. Minchell found that he was climbing up the concrete base of the statue. It ripped the breath from his lungs—and he saw that he could much more easily have gone up a few extra steps and simply stepped on—but there didn't seem anything else to do but just this, what he was doing. Once upright, he passed his hand over the statue's flank. The surface was incredibly sleek and cold, hard as a lion's muscles ought to be, and tawny.

He took a step backwards. Lord! Had there ever been such power? Such marvelous downright power and—majesty, as was here? From stone—no, indeed. It fooled a good many people, but it did not fool Mr. Minchell. He knew. This lion was no mere library decoration. It was an animal, of deadly cunning and fantastic strength and unbelievable ferocity. And it didn't move for the simple reason that it did not care to move. It was waiting. Some day it would see what it was waiting for, its enemy, coming down the street. Then look out, people!

He remembered the whole yarn now. Of everyone on Earth, only he, Henry Minchell knew the secret of the lion. And only he was allowed to sit astride this mighty back.

He stepped onto the tail, experimentally. He hesitated, gulped, and swung forward, swiftly, on up to the curved rump.

Trembling, he slid forward, until finally he was over the shoulders of the lion, just behind the raised head.

His breath came very fast.

He closed his eyes.

It was not long before he was breathing regularly again. Only now it was the hot, fetid air of the jungle that went into his nostrils. He felt the great muscles ripple beneath him and he listened to the fast crackle of crushed foliage, and he whispered:

"Easy, fellow."

The flying spears did not frighten him; he sat straight, smiling, with his fingers buried in the rich tawny mane of King Richard, while the wind tore at his hair . . .

Then, abruptly, he opened his eyes.

The city stretched before him, and the people, and the lights. He tried quite hard not to cry, because he knew that forty-seven-year-old men never cried, not even when they had vanished, but he couldn't help it. So he sat on the stone lion and lowered his head and cried.

He didn't hear the laughter at first.

When he did hear it, he thought that he was dreaming. But it was true: somebody was laughing.

He grasped one of the statue's ears for balance and leaned forward. He blinked. Below, some fifteen feet, there were people. Young people. Some of them with books. They were looking up and smiling and laughing.

Mr. Minchell wiped his eyes.

A slight horror came over him, and fell away. He leaned farther out.

One of the boys waved and shouted: "Ride him, Pop!"

Mr. Minchell almost toppled. Then, without understanding, without even trying to understand—merely knowing—he grinned widely, showing his teeth, which were his own and very white.

"You—see me?" he called.

The young people roared.

"You do!" Mr. Minchell's face seemed to melt upwards. He let out a yell and gave King Richard's shaggy stone mane an enormous hug.

Below, other people stopped in their walking and a small crowd began to form. Dozens of eyes peered sharply, quizzically.

A woman in gray furs giggled.

A thin man in a blue suit grunted something about these damned exhibitionists.

"You pipe down," another man said. "Guy wants to ride the goddamn lion it's his own business."

There were murmurings. The man who had said pipe down was small and he wore black-rimmed glasses. "I used to do it all the time." He turned to Mr. Minchell and cried: "How is it?"

Mr. Minchell grinned. Somehow, he realized, in some mysterious way, he had been given a second chance. And this time he knew what he would do with it. "Fine!" he shouted, and stood upon King Richard's back and sent his derby spinning out over the heads of the people. "Come on up!"

"Can't do it," the man said. "Got a date." There was a look of profound admiration in his eyes as he strode off. Away from the crowd he stopped and cupped his hands and cried: "I'll be seeing you!"

"That's right," Mr. Minchell said, feeling the cold new wind on his face. "You'll be seeing me."

Later, when he was good and ready, he got down off the lion.

T. E. D. KLEIN

Theodore Donald Klein (the E. in his name does not stand for anything) was born in 1947. Exhibiting an early interest in supernatural fiction, he attended Brown University and wrote an honors thesis (1969) on the influence of the Irish writer Lord Dunsany on H. P. Lovecraft. In the 1970s he produced several notable tales of supernatural horror, some published in small-press magazines and others appearing in anthologies; among them were "Petey" (1979), a story of monstrous horror in rural Connecticut; "Children of the Kingdom" (1980), a chilling tale of terrors on the underside of New York City; "Black Man with a Horn" (1980), a tale utilizing Lovecraft's Cthulhu Mythos; and "Nadelman's God" (1985), a tale fusing cosmicism and psychological horror. These four tales were gathered in a landmark volume, *Dark Gods* (1985). A year previously, Klein published *The Ceremonies,* an immense expansion of what remains his best-known tale, "The Events at Poroth Farm," and drawing upon Klein's sensitive reading of Lovecraft, Arthur Machen, Algernon Blackwood, and other supernatural writers.

Klein edited *Rod Serling's The Twilight Zone Magazine* from its inception in 1981 until 1986, making it the flagship publication in its field. He has since written relatively little: a second novel has been in gestation for two decades, while only a few short stories have appeared in magazines and anthologies. Some of his later works include "Ladder" (1990), another tale of cosmic horror, and several supernatural stories for younger readers. Klein has also written engagingly about horror fiction in such works as *Raising Goosebumps for Fun and Profit* (1988). In spite of his small output, Klein remains a leading figure in the field and one of the masters of the modern horror tale.

"The Events at Poroth Farm" (*From Beyond the Dark Gateway*, December 1972) is a dense, complex work of horror in rural New Jersey and well utilizes Klein's exhaustive reading of previous horror literature. Klein has revised the tale on several occasions; the text used here derives from his latest revision, in a volume of his uncollected tales, *Reassuring Tales* (2007).

THE EVENTS AT POROTH FARM

As soon as the phone stops ringing, I'll begin this affidavit. Lord, it's hot in here. Perhaps I should open a window. . . .

Thirteen rings. It has a sense of humor.

I suppose that ought to be comforting.

Somehow I'm not comforted. If it feels free to indulge in these teasing, tormenting little games, so much the worse for me.

The summer is over now, but this room is like an oven. My shirt is already drenched, and this pen feels slippery in my hand. In a moment or two the little drop of sweat that's collecting above my eyebrow is going to splash onto this page.

Just the same, I'll keep that window closed. Outside, through the dusty panes of glass, I can see a boy in red spectacles sauntering toward the courthouse steps. Perhaps there's a telephone booth in back. . . .

A sense of humor—that's one quality I never noticed in it. I saw only a deadly seriousness and, of course, an intelligence that grew at terrifying speed, malevolent and inhuman. If it now feels itself safe enough to toy with me before doing whatever it intends to do, so much the worse for me. So much the worse, perhaps, for us all.

I hope I'm wrong. Though my name is Jeremy, derived from Jeremiah, I'd hate to be a prophet in the wilderness. I'd much rather be a harmless crank.

But I believe we're in for trouble.

I'm a long way from the wilderness now, of course. Though perhaps not far enough to save me. . . . I'm writing this affidavit in room 2-K of the Union Hotel, overlooking Main Street in Flemington, New Jersey, twenty miles south of Gilead. Directly across the street, hippies lounging on its steps, stands the county courthouse where Bruno Hauptmann was tried back in 1935. (Did they ever find the body of that child?) Hauptmann undoubtedly walked down those very steps, now lined with teenagers savoring their last week of summer vacation. Where that boy in the red spectacles sits sucking on his cigarette—did the killer once halt there, police and reporters around him, and contemplate his imminent execution?

For several days now I have been afraid to leave this room.

I have perhaps been staring too often at that ordinary-looking boy on the steps. He sits there every day. The red spectacles conceal his eyes; it's impossible to tell where he's looking.

I know he's looking at me.

But it would be foolish of me to waste time worrying about executions when I have these notes to transcribe. It won't take long, and then, perhaps, I'll sneak outside to mail them—and leave New Jersey forever. I remain, despite all that's happened, an optimist. What was it my namesake said? "Thou art my hope in the day of evil."

There *is*, surprisingly, some real wilderness left in New Jersey, assuming one wants to be a prophet. The hills to the west, spreading from the southern swamplands to the Delaware and beyond to Pennsylvania, provide shelter for deer, pheasant, even an occasional bear—and hide hamlets never visited by outsiders: pockets of ignorance, some of them, citadels of ancient superstition utterly cut off from news of New York and the rest of the state, religious communities where customs haven't changed appreciably since the days of their settlement a century or more ago.

It seems incredible that villages so isolated can exist today on the very doorstep of the world's largest metropolis—villages with nothing to offer the outsider, and hence never visited, except by the occasional hunter who stumbles on them unwittingly. Yet as you speed down one of the state highways, consider how few of the cars slow down for the local roads. It is easy to pass the little towns without even a glance at the signs; and if there are no signs . . . ? And consider, too, how seldom the local traffic turns off onto the narrow roads that emerge without warning from the woods. And when those untraveled side roads lead into others still deeper in wilderness; and when those in turn give way to dirt roads, deserted for weeks on end. . . . It is not hard to see how tiny rural communities can exist less than an hour from major cities, virtually unaware of one another's existence.

Television, of course, will link the two—unless, as is often the case, the elders of the community choose to see this distraction as the Devil's tool and proscribe it. Telephones put these outcast settlements in touch with their neighbors—unless they choose to ignore their neighbors. And so in the course of years they are . . . forgotten.

New Yorkers were amazed when in the winter of 1968 the *Times* "discovered" a religious community near New Providence that had existed in its present form since the late 1800s—less than forty miles from Times Square. Agricultural work was performed entirely by hand, women still wore long dresses with high collars, and town worship was held every evening.

I, too, was amazed. I'd seldom traveled west of the Hudson and still thought of New Jersey as some dismal extension of the Newark slums, ruled by gangsters, foggy with swamp gases and industrial waste, a gray land that had surrendered to the city.

Only later did I learn of the rural New Jersey, and of towns whose solitary general stores double as post offices, with one or two gas pumps standing in front. And later still I learned of Baptistown and Quakertown, their old religions surviving unchanged, and of towns like Lebanon, Landsdown, and West Portal, close to Route 22 and civilization but heavy with secrets city folk never dreamed of: Mt. Airy, with its network of hidden caverns, and Mt. Olive, bordering the infamous Budd Lake; Middle Valley, sheltered by dark cliffs, subject of the recent archaeological debate chronicled in *Natural History*, where the wanderer may still find grotesque relics of pagan worship and, some say, may still hear the chants that echo from the cliffs on certain nights; and towns with names like Zion and Zaraphath and Gilead, forgotten communities of bearded men and black-robed women, walled hamlets too small or obscure for most maps of the state. This was the wilderness into which I traveled, weary of Manhattan's interminable din; and it was outside Gilead where, until the tragedies, I chose to make my home for three months.

Among the silliest of literary conventions is the "town that won't talk"—the Bavarian village where peasants turn away from tourists' queries about "the castle" and silently cross themselves, the New England harbor town where fishermen feign ignorance and cast "furtive glances" at the traveler. In actuality, I have found, country people love to talk to the stranger, provided he shows a sincere interest in their anecdotes. Storekeepers will interrupt their activity at the cash register to tell you their theories on a recent murder; farmers will readily spin tales of buried bones and of a haunted house down the road. Rural townspeople are not so reticent as the writers would have us believe.

Gilead, isolated though it is behind its oak forests and ruined walls, is no exception. The inhabitants regard all outsiders with an initial suspicion, but let one demonstrate a respect for their traditional reserve and they will prove friendly enough. They don't favor modern fashions or flashy automobiles, but they can hardly be described as hostile, although that was my original impression.

When asked about the terrible events at Poroth Farm, they will prove more than willing to talk. They will tell you of bad crops and polluted well water, of emotional depression leading to a fatal argument. In short, they will describe a conventional rural murder, and will even volunteer their opinions on the killer's present whereabouts.

But you will learn almost nothing from them—or almost nothing that is true. They don't know what really happened. I do. I was there.

I had come to spend the summer with Sarr Poroth and his wife. I needed a place where I could do a lot of reading without distraction, and Poroth's farm, secluded as it was even from the village of Gilead three miles down the dirt road, appeared the perfect spot for my studies.

I had seen the Poroths' advertisement in the *Hunterdon County Democrat* on a trip west through Princeton last spring. They advertised for a summer or long-term tenant to live in one of the outbuildings behind the farmhouse. As I soon learned, the building was a long low cinderblock affair, unpleasantly suggestive of army barracks but clean, new, and cool in the sun; by the start of summer ivy sprouted from the walls and disguised the ugly gray brick. Originally intended to house chickens, it had in fact remained empty for several years until the farm's original owner, a Mr. Baber, sold out last fall to the Poroths, who immediately saw that with the installation of dividing walls, linoleum floors, and other improvements the building might serve as a source of income. I was to be their first tenant.

The Poroths, Sarr and Deborah, were in their early thirties, only slightly older than I, although anyone who met them might have believed the age difference to be greater; their relative solemnity and the drabness of their clothing added years to their appearance, and so did their hair styles: Deborah, though possessing a beautiful length of black hair, wound it all in a tight bun behind her neck, pulling the hair back from her face with a severity which looked almost painful, and Sarr maintained a thin fringe of black beard that circled from ears to chin in the manner of the Pennsylvania Dutch, who leave their hair shaggy but refuse to grow moustaches lest they resemble the military class they've traditionally despised. Both man and wife were hardworking, grave of expression, and pale despite the time spent laboring in the sun—a pallor accentuated by the inky blackness of their hair. I imagine this unhealthy aspect was due, in part, to the considerable amount of inbreeding that went on in the area, the Poroths themselves being, I believe, third cousins. On first meeting, one might have taken them for brother and sister, two gravely devout children aged in the wilderness.

And yet there was a difference between them—and, too, a

difference that set them both in contrast to others of their sect. The Poroths were, as far as I could determine, members of a tiny Mennonitic order outwardly related to the Amish, though doctrinal differences were apparently rather profound. It was this order that made up the large part of the community known as Gilead.

I sometimes think the only reason they allowed an infidel like me to live on their property (for my religion was among the first things they inquired about) was because of my name; Sarr was very partial to Jeremiah, and the motto of his order was, "Stand ye in the ways, and see, and ask for the old paths, where is the good way, and walk therein." (VI:16)

Having been raised in no particular religion except a universal skepticism, I began the summer with a hesitancy to bring up the topic in conversation, and so I learned comparatively little about the Poroths' beliefs. Only toward the end of my stay did I begin to thumb through the Bible in odd moments and take to quoting jeremiads. That was, I suppose, Sarr's influence.

I was able to learn, nonetheless, that for all their conservative aura the Poroths were considered, in effect, young liberals by most of Gilead. Sarr had a bachelor's degree in religious studies from Rutgers, and Deborah had attended a nearby community college for two years, unusual for women of the sect. Too, they had only recently taken to farming, having spent the first year of their marriage near New Brunswick, where Sarr had hoped to find a teaching position and, when the job situation proved hopeless, had worked as a sort of handyman/carpenter. While most inhabitants of Gilead had never left the farm, the Poroths were coming to it late—their families had been merchants for several generations—and so were relatively inexperienced.

The inexperience showed. The farm comprised some ninety acres, but most of that was forest, or fields of weeds too thick and high to walk through. Across the back yard, close to my rooms, ran a small, nameless stream nearly choked with green scum. A large cornfield to the north lay fallow, but Sarr was planning to seed it this year, using borrowed equipment.

His wife spent much of her time indoors, for though she maintained a small vegetable garden, she preferred keeping house and looking after the Poroths' great love, their seven cats.

As if to symbolize their broad-mindedness, the Poroths owned a television set, very rare in Gilead; in light of what was to come, however, it is unfortunate they lacked a telephone. (Apparently the set had been received as a wedding present from Deborah's parents, but the monthly expense of a telephone was simply too great.) Otherwise, though, the little farmhouse was "modern" in that it had a working bathroom and gas heat. That they had advertised in the local newspaper was considered scandalous by some of the order's more orthodox members, and indeed a mere subscription to that innocuous weekly had at one time been regarded as a breach of religious conduct.

Though outwardly similar, both of them tall and pale, the Poroths were actually so different as to embody the maxim that "opposites attract." It was that carefully nurtured reserve that deceived one at first meeting, for in truth Deborah was far more talkative, friendly, and energetic than her husband. Sarr was moody, distant, silent most of the time, with a voice so low that one had trouble following him in conversation. Sitting as stonily as one of his cats, never moving, never speaking, perennially inscrutable, he tended to frighten visitors to the farm until they learned that he was not really sitting in judgment on them; his reserve was not born of surliness but of shyness.

Where Sarr was catlike, his wife hid beneath the formality of her order the bubbly personality of a kitten. Given the smallest encouragement—say, a family visit—she would plunge into animated conversation, gesticulating, laughing easily, hugging whatever cat was nearby or shouting to guests across the room. When drinking—for both of them enjoyed liquor and, curiously, it was not forbidden by their faith—their innate differences were magnified: Deborah would forget the restraints placed upon women in the order and would eventually dominate the conversation, while her husband would seem to grow increasingly withdrawn and morose.

Women in the region tended to be submissive to the men,

and certainly the important decisions in the Poroths' lives were made by Sarr. Yet I really cannot say who was the stronger of the two. Only once did I ever see them quarrel. . . .

Perhaps the best way to tell it is by setting down portions of the journal I kept this summer. Not every entry, of course. Mere excerpts. Just enough to make this affidavit comprehensible to anyone unfamiliar with the incidents at Poroth Farm.

The journal was the only writing I did all summer; my primary reason for keeping it was to record the books I'd read each day, as well as to examine my reactions to relative solitude over a long period of time. All the rest of my energies (as you will no doubt gather from the notes below) were spent reading, in preparation for a course I plan to teach at Trenton State this fall. Or *planned,* I should say, because I don't expect to be anywhere around here come fall.

Where will I be? Perhaps that depends on what's beneath those rose-tinted spectacles.

The course was to cover the Gothic tradition from Shakespeare to Faulkner, from *Hamlet* to *Absalom, Absalom!* (And why not view the former as Gothic, with its ghost on the battlements and concern for lost inheritance?) To make the move to Gilead, I'd rented a car for a few days and had stuffed it full of books— only a few of which I ever got to read. But then, I couldn't have known. . . .

How pleasant things were, at the beginning.

JUNE 4

Unpacking day. Spent all morning putting up screens, and a good thing I did. Night now, and a million moths tapping at the windows. One of them as big as a small bird—white—largest I've ever seen. What kind of caterpillar must it have been? I hope the damned things don't push through the screens.

Had to kill literally hundreds of spiders before moving my stuff in. The Poroths finished doing the inside of this building only a couple of months ago, and already it's infested. Arachnidae—hate the bastards. Why? We'll take that one up with Sigmund someday. Daydreams of Revenge of the Spiders. Writhing body covered with a frenzy of hairy brown legs. "Egad, man, that face! That bloody, torn face! And the missing eyes! It looks like—no! Jeremy!" Killing spiders is supposed to bring bad luck. (Insidious Sierra Club propaganda masquerading as folk myth?) But can't sleep if there's anything crawling around . . . so what the hell?

Supper with the Poroths. Began to eat, then heard Sarr saying grace. Apologies—but things like that don't embarrass me as much as they used to. (Is that because I'm nearing thirty?)

Chatted about crops, insects, humidity. (Very damp area—band of purplish mildew already around bottom of walls out here.) Sarr told of plans to someday build a larger house when Deborah has a baby, three or four years from now. He wants to build it out of stone. Then he shut up, and I had to keep the conversation going. (Hate eating in silence—animal sounds of mastication, bubbling stomachs.) Deborah joked about cats being her surrogate children. All seven of them hanging around my legs, rubbing against ankles. My nose began running and my eyes itched. Goddamned allergy. Must remember to start treatments this fall, when I get to Trenton. Deborah sympathetic, Sarr merely watching; she told me my eyes were bloodshot, offered antihistamine. Told them I was glad they at least believe in modern medicine—I'd been afraid she'd offer herbs or mud or something. Sarr said some of the locals still use "snake oil." Asked him how snakes were killed, quoting line from *Vathek:* "The oil of the serpents I have pinched to death will be a pretty present." We discussed wisdom of pinching snakes. Apparently there's a copperhead out back, near the brook. . . .

The meal was good—lamb and noodles. Not bad for twenty dollars a week, since I detest cooking. Spice cake for dessert, home-made, of course. Deborah is a good cook. Handsome woman, too.

Still light when I left their kitchen. Fireflies already on the lawn—I've never seen so many. Knelt and watched them a while, listening to the crickets. Think I'll like it here.

Took nearly an hour to arrange my books the way I wanted

T. E. D. Klein

them. Alphabetical order by authors? No, chronological. . . .
But anthologies mess that system up, so back to authors. Why
am I so neurotic about my books?

Anyway, they look nice there on the shelves.

Sat up tonight finishing *The Mysteries of Udolpho*. Figure it's
best to get the long ones out of the way first. Radcliffe's unfortunate penchant for explaining away all her ghosts and appari-
tions really a mistake and a bore. All in all, not exactly the most
fascinating reading, though a good study in Romanticism.
Montoni the typical Byronic hero/villain. But can't demand
students read *Udolpho*—too long. In fact, had to keep remind-
ing myself to slow down, have patience with the book. Tried to
put myself in frame of mind of 1794 reader with plenty of time
on his hands. It works, too—I do have plenty of time out here,
and already I can feel myself beginning to unwind. What New
York does to people. . . .

It's almost two a.m. now, and I'm about ready to turn in.
Too bad there's no bathroom in this building—I hate pissing
outside at night. God knows what's crawling up your ankles. . . .
But it's hardly worth stumbling through the darkness to the
farmhouse, and maybe waking up Sarr and Deborah. The
nights out here are really pitch-black.

. . . Felt vulnerable, standing there against the night. But
what made me even uneasier was the view I got of this building.
The lamp on the desk casts the only light for miles, and as I
stood outside looking into this room, I could see dozens of
flying shapes making right for the screens. When you're inside
here it's as if you're in a display case—the whole night can
see you, but all you can see is darkness. I wish this room didn't
have windows on three of the walls—though that does let in the
breeze. And I wish the woods weren't so close to my windows by
the bed. I suppose privacy is what I wanted—but feel a little un-
protected out here.

Those moths are still batting themselves against the
screens, but as far as I can see the only things that have gotten
in are a few gnats flying around this lamp. The crickets sound
good—you sure don't hear them in the city. Frogs are croaking
in the brook.

My nose is only now beginning to clear up. Those god-damned cats. I'll walk to town tomorrow. Must remember to buy some Contac. Even though the cats are all outside during the day, that farmhouse is full of their scent. But I don't expect to be spending that much time inside the house anyway; this allergy will keep me away from the TV and out here with the books.

Just saw an unpleasantly large spider scurry across the floor near the foot of my bed. Vanished behind the footlocker. Must remember to buy some insect spray.

JUNE 11

Hot today, but at night comes a chill. The dampness of this place seems to magnify temperature. Sat outside most of the day finishing the Maturin book, *Melmoth the Wanderer,* and feeling vaguely guilty each time I heard Sarr or Deborah working out there in the field. Well, I've paid for my reading time, so I guess I'm entitled to enjoy it. Though some of these old Gothics are a bit hard to enjoy. The trouble with *Melmoth* is that it wants you to hate. You're especially supposed to hate the Catholics. No doubt its picture of the Inquisition is accurate, but all a book like this can do is put you in an unconstructive rage. Those vicious characters have been dead for centuries, and there's no way to punish them. Still, it's a nice, cynical book for those who like atrocity scenes—starving prisoners forced to eat their girlfriends. And narratives within narratives within narratives within narratives. I may assign some sections to my class. . . .

Just before dinner, in need of a break, read a story by Arthur Machen. Welsh writer, turn of the century, though think the story's set somewhere in England: old house in the hills, dark woods with secret paths and hidden streams. God, what an experience! I was a little confused by the framing device and all its high-flown talk of "cosmic evil," but the sections from the young girl's notebook were . . . staggering. That air of paganism, the malevolent little faces peeping from the shadows, and those rites she can't dare talk about. . . . It's called "The White

People," and it must be the most persuasive horror tale ever written.

Afterward, strolling toward the house, I was moved to climb the old tree in the side yard—the Poroths had already gone in to get dinner ready—and stood upright on a great heavy branch near the middle, making strange gestures and faces that no one could see. Can't see exactly what it was I did, or why. It was getting dark—fireflies below me and a mist rising off the field. I must have looked like a madman's shadow as I made signs to the woods and the moon.

Lamb tonight, and damned good. I may find myself getting fat. Offered, again, to wash the dishes, but apparently Deborah feels that's her role, and I don't care to dissuade her. So talked a while with Sarr about his cats—the usual subject of conversation, especially because, now that summer's coming, they're bringing in dead things every night. Field mice, moles, shrews, birds, even a little garter snake. They don't eat them, just lay them out on the porch for the Poroths to see—sort of an offering, I guess. Sarr tosses the bodies in the garbage can, which, as a result, smells indescribably foul. Deborah wants to put bells around their necks; she hates mice but feels sorry for the birds. When she finished the dishes, she and Sarr sat down to watch one of their godawful TV programs, so I came out here to read.

Spent the usual ten minutes going over this room, spray can in hand, looking for spiders to kill. Found a couple of little ones, then spent some time spraying bugs that were hanging on the screens hoping to get in. Watched a lot of long-legged things curl up and die. . . . Tended not to kill the moths, unless they were making too much of a racket banging against the screen; I can tolerate them okay, but it's only fireflies I really like. I always feel a little sorry when I kill one by mistake and see it hold that cold glow too long. (That's how you know they're dead: the dead ones don't wink. They just keep their light on till it fades away.)

The insecticide I'm using is made right here in New Jersey, by the Ortho Chemical Company. The label on the can says, "warning. For Outdoor Use Only." That's why I bought it—figured it's the most powerful brand available.

Sat in bed reading Algernon Blackwood's witch/cat story, "Ancient Sorceries" (nowhere near as good as Machen, or as his own tale "The Willows"), and it made me think of those seven cats. The Poroths have around a dozen names for each one of them, which seems a little ridiculous since the creatures barely respond to even one name. Sasha, for example, the orange one, is also known as Butch, which comes from Bouche, mouth. And that's short for Eddie La Bouche, so he's also called Ed or Eddie—which in turn comes from some friend's mispronunciation of the cat's original name, Itty, short for Itty Bitty Kitty, which, apparently, he once was. And Zoë, the cutest of the kittens, is also called Bozo and Bisbo. Let's see, how many others can I remember? (I'm just learning to tell some of them apart.) Felix, or "Flixie," was originally called Paleface, and Phaedra, his mother, is sometimes known as Phuddy, short for Phuddy Duddy.

Come to think of it, the only cat that hasn't got multiple names is Bwada, Sarr's cat. (All the others were acquired after he married Deborah, but Bwada was his pet years before.) She's the oldest of the cats, and the meanest. Fat and sleek, with fine gray fur darker than silver gray, lighter than charcoal. She's the only cat that's ever bitten anyone—Deborah, as well as friends of the Poroths—and after seeing the way she snarls at the other cats when they get in her way, I decided to keep my distance. Fortunately she's scared of me and retreats whenever I approach. I think being spayed is what's messed her up and given her an evil disposition.

Sounds are drifting from the farmhouse. I can vaguely make out a psalm of some kind. It's late, past eleven, and I guess the Poroths have turned off the TV and are singing their evening devotions. . . .

And now all is silence. They've gone to bed. I'm not very tired yet, so I guess I'll stay up a while and read some—

Something odd just happened. I've never heard anything like it. While writing for the past half hour I've been aware, if half-consciously, of the crickets. Their regular chirping can be pretty soothing, like the sound of a well-tuned machine. But just a few seconds ago they seemed to miss a beat. They'd been singing along steadily, ever since the moon came up, and all of a sudden they just *stopped* for a beat—and then they began again, only they were out of rhythm for a moment or two, as if a hand had jarred the record or there'd been some kind of momentary break in the natural flow. . . .

They sound normal enough now, though. Think I'll go back to *Otranto* and let that put me to sleep. It may be the foundation of the English Gothics, but I can't imagine anyone actually reading it for pleasure. I wonder how many pages I'll be able to get through before I drop off. . . .

JUNE 12

Slept late this morning, and then, disinclined to read Walpole on such a sunny day, took a walk. Followed the little brook that runs past my building. There's still a lot of that greenish scum clogging one part of it, and if we don't have some rain soon I expect it will get worse. But the water clears up considerably when it runs past the cornfield and through the woods.

Passed Sarr out in the field—he yelled to watch out for the copperhead, which put a pall on my enthusiasm for exploration. . . . But as it happened I never ran into any snakes, and have a fair idea I'd survive even if bitten. Walked around half a mile into the woods, branches snapping in my face. Made an effort to avoid walking into the little yellow caterpillars that hang from every tree. At one point I had to get my feet wet, because the trail that runs alongside the brook disappeared and the undergrowth was thick. Ducked under a low arch made by decaying branches and vines, my sneakers sloshing in the water. Found that as the brook runs west it forms a small circular pool with banks of wet sand, surrounded by tall oaks, their roots thrust into the water. Lots of animal tracks in the sand—deer, I believe, and what may be a fox or perhaps some farmer's dog. Obviously a watering place. Waded into the center of the pool—it only came up a little past my ankles—but didn't stand there long because it started looking like rain.

The weather remained nasty all day, but no rain has come yet. Cloudy now, though; can't see any stars.

Finished *Otranto,* began *The Monk.* So far so good—rather dirty, really. Not for today, of course, but I can imagine the sensation it must have caused back at the end of the eighteenth century.

Had a good time at dinner tonight, since Sarr had walked into town and brought back some wine. (Medical note: I seem to be less allergic to cats when mildly intoxicated.) We sat around the kitchen afterward playing poker for matchsticks—very sinful indulgence, I understand; Sarr and Deborah told me, quite seriously, that they'd have to say some extra prayers tonight by way of apology to the Lord.

Theological considerations aside, though, we all had a good time and Deborah managed to clean us both out. Women's intuition, she says. I'm sure she must have it—she's the type. Enjoy being around her, and not always so happy to trek back outside, through the high grass, the night dew, the things in the soil. . . . I've got to remember, though, that they're a couple, I'm the single one, and I mustn't intrude too long. So left them tonight at eleven—or actually a little after that, since their clock is slightly out of kilter. They have this huge grandfather-type clock, a wedding present from Sarr's parents, that has supposedly been keeping perfect time for a century or more. You can hear its ticking all over the house when everything else is still. Deborah said that last night, just as they were going to bed, the clock seemed to slow down a little, then gave a couple of faster beats and started in as before. Sarr, who's pretty good with mechanical things, examined it, but said he saw nothing wrong. Well, I guess everything's got to wear out a bit, after years and years.

Back to *The Monk.* May Brother Ambrosio bring me pleasant dreams.

JUNE 13

Read a little in the morning, loafed during the afternoon. At 4:30 watched *The Thief of Baghdad*—ruined on TV and portions omitted, but still a great film. Deborah puttered around the kitchen, and Sarr spent most of the day outside. Before dinner I went out back with a scissors and cut away a lot of ivy that has tried to grow through the windows of my building. The little shoots fasten onto the screens and really cling.

Beef with rice tonight, and apple pie for dessert. Great. I stayed inside the house after dinner to watch the late news with the Poroths. The announcer mentioned that today was Friday the thirteenth, and I nearly gasped. I'd known, on some dim automatic level, that it was the thirteenth, if only from keeping this journal; but I hadn't had the faintest idea it was Friday. That's how much I've lost track of time out here; day drifts into day, and every one but Sunday seems completely interchangeable. Not a bad feeling, really, though at certain moments this isolation makes me feel somewhat adrift. I'd been so used to living by the clock and the calendar. . . .

We tried to figure out if anything unlucky happened to any of us today. About the only incident we could come up with was Sarr's getting bitten by some animal a cat had left on the porch. The cats had been sitting by the front door waiting to be let in for their dinner, and when Sarr came in from the field he was greeted with the usual assortment of dead mice and moles. As he always did, he began gingerly picking the bodies up by the tails and tossing them into the garbage can, meanwhile scolding the cats for being such natural-born killers. There was one body, he told us, that looked different from the others he'd seen: rather like a large shrew, only the mouth was somehow askew, almost as if it were vertical instead of horizontal, with a row of little yellow teeth exposed. He figured that, whatever it was, the cats had pretty well mauled it, which probably accounted for its unusual appearance; it was quite tattered and bloody by this time.

In any case, he'd bent down to pick it up, and the thing had bitten him on the thumb. Apparently it had just been feigning death, like an opossum, because as soon as he yelled and dropped it the thing sped off into the grass, with Bwada and the rest in hot pursuit. Deborah had been afraid of rabies—always a real danger around here, rare though it is—but apparently the bite hadn't even pierced the skin. Just a nip, really. Hardly a Friday-the-thirteenth tragedy.

Lying in bed now, listening to sounds in the woods. The trees come really close to my windows on one side, and there's always some kind of sound coming from the underbrush in addition to the tapping at the screens. A million creatures out there, after all—most of them insects and spiders, a colony of frogs in the swampy part of the woods, and perhaps even skunks and raccoons. Depending on your mood, you can either ignore the sounds and just go to sleep or—as I'm doing now—remain awake listening to them. When I lie here thinking about what's out there, I feel more protected with the light off. So I guess I'll put away this writing. . . .

JUNE 15

Something really weird happened today. I still keep trying to figure it out.

Sarr and Deborah were gone almost all day; Sunday worship is, I assume, the center of their religious activity. They walked into Gilead early in the morning and didn't return until after four. They'd left, in fact, before I woke up. Last night they'd asked me if I'd like to come along, but I got the impression they'd invited me mainly to be polite, so I declined. I wouldn't want to make them uncomfortable during services, but perhaps someday I'll accompany them anyway, since I'm curious to see a fundamentalist church in action.

In any case, I was left to share the farm with the Poroths' seven cats and the four hens they'd bought last week. From my window I could see Bwada and Phaedra chasing after something near the barn; lately they'd taken to stalking grasshoppers. As I do every morning, I went into the farmhouse kitchen and made myself some breakfast, leafing through one of the Poroths' religious magazines, and then returned to my rooms out back for some serious reading. I picked up *Dracula* again, which I'd started yesterday, but the soppy Victorian sentimentality began to annoy me; the book had begun so well, on such a frightening note—Jonathan Harker trapped in that Carpathian castle, inevitably the prey of its terrible owner—that when Stoker switched the locale to England and his main characters to women, he simply couldn't sustain that initial tension.

With the Poroths gone I felt a little lonely and bored, something I hadn't felt out here yet. Though I'd brought shelves of books to entertain me, I felt restless and wished I owned a car. I'd have gone for a drive; surely there must be plenty of places worth exploring. As things stood, though, I had nothing to do except watch television or take a walk.

I followed the stream again into the woods and eventually came to the circular pool. There were some new animal tracks in the wet sand, and, ringed by oaks, the place was very beautiful, but still I felt bored. Again I waded into the center of the water and looked up at the sky through the trees. Feeling myself alone, I began to make some of the odd signs with face and hands that I had that evening in the tree—but I felt that these movements had been unaccountably robbed of their power. Standing there up to my ankles in water, I felt foolish.

Worse than that, upon leaving it I found a red-brown leech clinging to my right ankle. It wasn't large and I was able to scrape it off with a stone, but it left me with a little round bite that oozed blood, and a feeling of—how shall I put it?—physical helplessness. I felt that the woods had somehow become hostile to me and, more important, would forever remain hostile. Something had passed.

I followed the stream back to the farm, and there I found Bwada, lying on her side near some rocks along its bank. Her legs were stretched out as if she were running, and her eyes were wide and astonished-looking. Flies were crawling over them.

She couldn't have been dead for long, since I'd see her only a few hours before, but she was already stiff. There was foam around her jaws. I couldn't tell what had happened to her until I turned her over with a stick and saw, on the side that had lain against the ground, a gaping red hole that opened like some new orifice. The skin around it was folded back in little triangular flaps, exposing the pink flesh beneath. I backed off in disgust, but I could see even from several feet away that the hole had been made *from the inside.*

I can't say that I was very upset at Bwada's death, because

I'd always hated her. What did upset me, though, was the manner of it—I can't figure out what could have done that to her. I vaguely remember reading about a kind of slug that, when eaten by a bird, will bore its way out through the bird's stomach. . . . But I'd never heard of something like this happening with a cat. And even more peculiar, how could—

Well, anyway, I saw the body and thought, Good riddance. But I didn't know what to do with it. Looking back, of course, I wish I'd buried it right there. . . . But I didn't want to go near it again. I considered walking into town and trying to find the Poroths, because I knew their cats were like children to them, even Bwada, and that they'd want to know right away. But I really didn't feel like running around Gilead asking strange people where the Poroths were—or, worse yet, stumbling into some forbidding-looking church in the middle of a ceremony.

Finally I made up my mind to simply leave the body there and pretend I'd never seen it. Let Sarr discover it himself. I didn't want to have to tell him when he got home that his pet had been killed; I prefer to avoid unpleasantness. Besides, I felt strangely guilty, the way one often does after someone else's misfortune.

So I spent the rest of the afternoon reading in my room, slogging through the Stoker. I wasn't in the best mood to concentrate. Sarr and Deborah got back after four—they shouted hello and went into the house. When Deborah called me for dinner, they still hadn't come outside.

All the cats except Bwada were inside having their evening meal when I entered the kitchen, and Sarr asked me if I'd seen her during the day. I lied and said I hadn't. Deborah suggested that occasionally Bwada ignored the supper call because, unlike the other cats, she sometimes ate what she killed. "Maybe she's just full," said Deborah, and laughed. That rattled me a bit, but I had to stick to my lie.

Sarr seemed more concerned than Deborah, and when he told her he intended to search for the cat after dinner (it would still be light), I readily offered my help. I figured I could lead him to the spot where the body lay. . . .

And then, in the middle of our dinner, came that scratching at the door. Sarr got up and opened it. Bwada walked in.

T. E. D. Klein

Now I knew she was dead. She was *stiff* dead. That wound in her side had been unmistakable, and now it was only . . . a reddish swelling. Hairless. Luckily the Poroths didn't notice my shock; they were busy fussing over her, seeing what was wrong. "Look, she's hurt herself," said Deborah. "She's bumped into something." The animal didn't walk well, and there was a clumsiness in the way she held herself. When Sarr put her down after examining the swelling, she slipped when she tried to walk away.

The Poroths concluded that she had run into a rock or some other object and had badly bruised herself; they believe her lack of coordination is due to the shock, or perhaps to a pinching of the nerves. That sounds logical enough. Sarr told me before I came out here for the night that if she's worse tomorrow, he'll take her to the local vet, even though he'll have trouble paying for treatment. I immediately offered to lend him money, or even pay for the visit myself, because I desperately wanted to hear a doctor's opinion.

My own conclusion is really not that different from Sarr's. I tend to think now that maybe, just maybe, I was wrong in thinking the cat dead. I'm no scientist—maybe what I mistook for rigor mortis was some kind of fit. Maybe she really did run into something sharp, and then went into some kind of shock . . . whose effect hasn't yet worn off. Is this possible?

But I could swear that hole came from inside her.

I couldn't continue dinner and told the Poroths my stomach hurt, which was partly true. We all watched Bwada stumble around the kitchen floor, ignoring the food Deborah put before her as if it weren't there. Her movements were stiff, tentative, like a newborn animal still unsure how to move its muscles. I guess that's the result of her fit.

When I left the house tonight, a little while ago, she was huddled in the corner staring at me. Deborah was crooning over her, but the cat was staring at me.

Killed a monster of a spider behind my suitcase tonight. That Ortho spray really does a job. When Sarr was in here a few days ago he said the room smelled of spray, but I guess my allergy's too bad for me to smell it.

I enjoy watching the zoo outside my screens. Put my face close and stare the bugs eye to eye. Zap the ones whose faces I don't like with my spray can.

Tried to read more of the Stoker—but one thing keeps bothering me. The way that cat stared at me. Deborah was brushing its back, Sarr fiddling with his pipe, and that cat just stared at me and never blinked. I stared back, said, "Hey, Sarr? Look at Bwada. That damned cat's not blinking." And just as he looked up, it blinked. Heavily.

Hope we can go to the vet tomorrow, because I want to ask him whether cats can impale themselves on a rock or a stick, and if such an accident might cause a fit of some kind that would make them rigid.

Cold night. Sheets are damp and the blanket itches. Wind from the woods—ought to feel good in the summer, but it doesn't feel like summer. That damned cat didn't blink till I mentioned it. Almost as if it understood me.

JUNE 17

. . . Swelling on her side's all healed now. Hair growing back over it. She walks fine, has a great appetite, shows affection to the Poroths. Sarr says her recovery demonstrates how the Lord watches over animals—affirms his faith. Says if he'd taken her to a vet he'd just have been throwing away money.

Read some LeFanu. "Green Tea," about the phantom monkey with eyes that glow, and "The Familiar," about the little staring man who drives the hero mad. Not the smartest choices right now, the way I feel, because for all the time that fat gray cat purrs over the Poroths, it just stares at me. And snarls. I suppose the accident may have addled its brain a bit. I mean, if spaying can change a cat's personality, certainly a goring on a rock might.

Spent a lot of time in the sun today. The flies made it pretty hard to concentrate on the stories, but figured I'd get a suntan. I probably have a good tan now (hard to tell, because the mirror in here is small and the light dim), but suddenly it occurs to me that I'm not going to be seeing anyone for a long time anyway, except the Poroths, so what the hell do I care how I look?

Can hear them singing their nightly prayers now. A rather comforting sound, I must admit, even if I can't share the sentiments.

Petting Felix today—my favorite of the cats, real charm—came away with a tick on my arm which I didn't discover till taking a shower before dinner. As a result, I can still feel imaginary ticks crawling up and down my back. Damned cat.

JUNE 21

. . . Coming along well with the Victorian stuff. Zipped through "The Uninhabited House" and "Monsieur Maurice," both very literate, sophisticated. Deep into the terrible suffering of "The Amber Witch," poor priest and daughter near starvation, when Deborah called me in for dinner. Roast beef, with salad made from garden lettuce. Quite good. And Deborah was wearing one of the few sleeveless dresses I've seen on her. So she has a body after all. . . .

A rainy night. Hung around the house for a while reading in their living room while Sarr whittled and Deborah crocheted. Rain sounded better from in there than it does out here where it's not so cozy.

At eleven we turned on the news, cats purring around us, Sarr with Zoë on his lap, Deborah petting Phaedra, me sniffling. . . . Halfway through the wrap-up I pointed to Bwada, curled up at my feet, and said, "Look at her. You'd think she was watching the news with us." Deborah laughed and leaned over to scratch Bwada behind the ears. As she did so, Bwada turned to look at me.

The rain is letting up slightly. I can still hear the dripping from the trees, leaf to leaf to the dead leaves lining the forest floor; it will probably continue on and off all night. Occasionally I think I hear thrashings in one of the oaks near the barn, but then the sound turns into the falling of the rain.

Mildew higher on the walls of this place. Glad my books are

on shelves off the ground. So damp in here my envelopes are ruined—glue moistened, sealing them all shut. Stamps that had been in my wallet are stuck to the dollar bills. At night my sheets are clammy and cold, but each morning I wake up sweating.

Finished "The Amber Witch," really fine. Would that all lives had such happy endings.

JUNE 22

Rain continued through most of the morning. After the Poroths returned from church (looking, with their black clothes and large old-fashioned umbrellas, like figures out of Edward Gorey), I passed some time indoors helping them prepare strips of molding for the upstairs study. Worked out in the tool shed, one of the old wooden outbuildings. I measured, Sarr sawed, Deborah sanded. All in all, hardly felt useful, but I was in the mood for companionship.

While they were busy, I sat staring out the window. The day had finally cleared. There's a narrow cement walk running from the shed to the main house, and, as was their habit, Minnie and Felix, two of the kittens, were crouched in the middle of it taking in the late afternoon sun. Suddenly Bwada appeared on the house's front porch and began slinking along the cement path in our direction, tail swishing from side to side. When she neared the kittens she gave a snarl—I could see her mouth working—and they leaped to their feet, bristling, and ran off into the grass.

Called this to Poroths' attention. They said, in effect, Yes, we know, she's always been nasty to the kittens, probably because she never had any of her own. And besides, she's getting older.

When I turned back to the window, Bwada was gone. Asked the Poroths if they didn't think she'd gotten worse lately. Realized that, in speaking, I'd unconsciously dropped my voice, as if someone might be listening through the chinks in the floorboards.

Deborah conceded that, yes, the cat is behaving worse these days toward the others. And not just toward the kittens, as before. Butch, the adult orange male, seems particularly afraid of her. . . .

Later, good Sunday dinner—chicken breast, rice, slice of rhubarb pie—and came back here.

Yet now am a little irritated at the Poroths. Will have to tell them when I see them tomorrow morning. They claim they never come into these rooms, respect privacy of a tenant, etc. etc., but one of them must have been in here, because I've just noticed my can of insect spray is missing. I don't mind their borrowing it, but I like to have it by my bed on nights like this. Went over room looking for spiders, just in case; had a fat copy of *American Scholar* in my hand to crush them (only thing it's good for). But found nothing.

Tried to read some *Walden* as a break from all the horror stuff, but found my eyes too irritated, watery. Keep scratching them as I write this. Nose pretty clogged, too—the damned allergy's worse tonight. Probably because of the dampness. Expect I'll have trouble getting to sleep.

JUNE 24

Slept very late this morning because the noise from the woods kept me up late last night. (Come to think of it, the Poroths' praying was unusually loud as well, but that wasn't what bothered me.) I'd been in the middle of writing in this journal—some thoughts on A. E. Coppard—when it came. I immediately stopped writing and shut off the light.

At first it sounded like something in the woods near my room—an animal? a child? I couldn't tell, but smaller than a man—shuffling through the dead leaves, kicking them around as if it didn't care who heard it. There was a snapping of branches and, every so often, a silence and then a bump, as if it were hopping over fallen logs. I stood in the dark listening to it, then crept to the window and looked out. Thought I noticed some bushes moving, back there in the undergrowth, but it may have been the wind.

The sound grew farther away. Whatever it was must have been walking directly out into the deepest part of the woods, where the ground gets swampy and treacherous, because, very faintly, I could hear the sucking sounds of feet slogging through the mud.

I stood by the window for almost an hour, occasionally hearing what I thought were movements off there in the swamp, but finally all was quiet except for the crickets and the frogs. I had no intention of going out there with my flashlight in search of the intruder—that's only for guys in the movies—and I wondered if I should call Sarr. But by this time the noise had stopped and whatever it was had obviously moved on. Besides, I tend to think he'd have been angry if I'd awakened him and Deborah just because some stray dog had wandered near the farm. I recalled how annoyed he'd been earlier that day when— maybe not all that tactfully—I'd asked him what he'd done with my bug spray. (Will walk to town later and pick up a a new one. Still can't figure out where I misplaced mine.)

I went over to the windows on the other side and watched the moonlight on the barn for a while; my nose probably looked crosshatched from pressing against the screen. In contrast to the woods, the grass looked peaceful under the full moon. Then I lay in bed, but had a hard time falling asleep. Just as I was getting relaxed the sounds started again. High-pitched wails and caterwauls, from deep within the woods. Even after thinking about it all today, I still don't know whether the noise was human or animal. There were no actual words, of that I'm certain, but nevertheless there was the impression of *singing*. In a crazy, tuneless kind of way the sound seemed to carry the same solemn rhythm as the Poroths' prayers earlier that night.

The noise only lasted a minute or two, but I lay awake till the sky began to get lighter. Probably should have read a little more Coppard, but was reluctant to turn on the lamp.

. . . Slept all morning and, in the afternoon, followed the road in the opposite direction from Gilead, seeking anything of interest. But the road just gets muddier and muddier till it disappears altogether by the ruins of an old homestead—rocks and cement covered with moss—and it looked so much like poison ivy around there that I didn't want to risk tramping through it.

At dinner (pork chops, home-grown stringbeans, and pudding—quite good), mentioned the noise of last night. Sarr acted very concerned and went to his room to look up something in one of his books; Deborah and I discussed the matter at some length and concluded that the shuffling sounds weren't necessarily related to the wailing. The former were almost definitely those of a dog—dozens in the area, and they love to prowl around at night, exploring, hunting coons—and as for the wailing . . . well, it's hard to say. She thinks it may have been an owl or whippoorwill, while I suspect it may have been that same stray dog. I've heard the howl of wolves and I've heard hounds baying at the moon, and both have the same element of, I suppose, *worship* in them that these did.

Sarr came back downstairs and said he couldn't find what he'd been looking for. Said that when he moved into this farm he'd had "a fit of piety" and had burned a lot of old books he'd found in the attic; now he wishes he hadn't.

Looked up something on my own after leaving the Poroths. *Field Guide to Mammals* lists both red and gray foxes and, believe it or not, coyotes as surviving here in New Jersey. No wolves left, though—but the guide might be wrong.

Then, on a silly impulse, opened another reference book, Barbara Byfield's *Glass Harmonica*. Sure enough, my hunch was right: looked up June twenty-third, and it said, "St. John's Eve. Sabbats likely."

I'll stick to the natural explanation. Still, I'm glad Mrs. Byfield lists nothing for tonight; I'd like to get some sleep. There is, of course, a beautiful full moon—werewolf weather, as Maria Ouspenskaya might have said. But then, there are no wolves left in New Jersey. . . .

(Which reminds me, really must read some Marryat and Endore. But only after *Northanger Abbey;* my course always comes first.)

JUNE 25

. . . After returning from town, the farm looked very lonely. Wish they had a library in Gilead with more than religious tracts. Or a stand that sold the *Times*. (Though it's strange how, after a week or two, you no longer miss it.)

Overheated from walk—am I getting out of shape? Or is it just the hot weather? Took a cold shower. When I opened the bathroom door I accidentally let Bwada out—I'd wondered why the chair was propped against it. She raced into the kitchen, pushed open the screen door by herself, and I had no chance to catch her. (Wouldn't have attempted to anyway; her claws are wicked.) I apologized later when Deborah came in from the fields. She said Bwada had become vicious toward the other cats and that Sarr had confined her to the bathroom as punishment. The first time he'd shut her in there, Deborah said, the cat had gotten out; apparently she's smart enough to turn the doorknob by swatting at it a few times. Hence the chair.

Sarr came in carrying Bwada, both obviously out of temper. He'd seen a streak of orange running through the field toward him, followed by a gray blur. Butch had stopped at his feet and Bwada had pounced on him, but before she could do any damage Sarr had grabbed her around the neck and carried her back here. He'd been bitten once and scratched a lot on his hands, but not badly; maybe the cat still likes him best. He threw her back in the bathroom and shoved the chair against the door, then sat down and asked Deborah to join him in some silent prayer. I thumbed uneasily through a religious magazine till they were done, and we sat down to dinner.

I apologized again, but he said he wasn't mad at me, that the Devil had gotten into his cat. It was obvious he meant that quite literally. During dinner (omelet—the hens have been laying well) we heard a grating sound from the bathroom, and Sarr ran in to find her almost out the window; somehow she must have been strong enough to slide the sash up partway. She seemed so placid, though, when Sarr pulled her down from the sill—he'd been expecting another fight—that he let her out into the kitchen. At this she simply curled up near the stove and went to sleep; I guess she'd worked off her rage for the day. The other cats gave her a wide berth, though.

Watched a couple of hours of television with the Poroths. They may have gone to college, but the shows they find interesting . . . God! I'm ashamed of myself for sitting there like a cretin in front of that box. I won't even mention what we watched, lest history record the true abysmality of my tastes.

And yet I find that the TV draws us closer, as if we were having an adventure together. Shared experience, really. Like knowing the same people or going to the same school.

But there's a lot of duplicity in those Poroths—and I don't mean just religious hypocrisy, either. Came out here after watching the news, and though I hate to accuse anyone of spying on me, there's no doubt that Sarr or Deborah has been inside this room today. I began tonight's entry with great irritation because I found my desk in disarray; this journal wasn't even put back in the right drawer. I keep all my pens on one side, all my pencils on another, ink and erasers in the middle, etc., and when I sat down tonight I saw that everything was out of place. Thank God I haven't included anything too personal in here. . . . What I assume happened was that Deborah came in to wash the mildew off the walls—she's mentioned doing so several times, and she knew I'd be in town part of the day—and got sidetracked into reading this, thinking it must be some kind of secret diary. (I'm sure she was disappointed to find that it's merely a literary journal, with nothing about her in it.)

What bugs me is the difficulty of broaching the subject. I can't just walk in and charge Deborah with being a sneak—Sarr is moody enough as it is—and even if I hint at "someone messing up my desk," they'll know what I mean and perhaps get angry. Whenever possible I prefer to avoid unpleasantness. I guess the best thing to do is simply hide this book under my mattress from now on and say nothing. If it happens again, though, I'll definitely move out of here.

. . . I've been reading some *Northanger Abbey*. Really quite witty, as all her stuff is, but it's obvious the mock-Gothic bit isn't central to the story. I'd thought it was going to be a real parody. . . . Love stories always tend to bore me, and normally I'd be asleep right now, but my damned nose is so clogged tonight that it's hard to breathe when I lie back. Usually being out here clears it up. I've used this goddamned inhaler a dozen times in the past hour, but within a few minutes I sneeze and have to use it again. Wish Deborah'd gotten around to cleaning off the mildew instead of wasting her time looking in here for True Confessions and deep dark secrets. . . .

Think I hear something moving outside. Best to shut off my light.

JUNE 30

Slept late. Read some Shirley Jackson stories over breakfast, but got so turned off at her view of humanity that I switched to old Aleister Crowley, who at least keeps a sunny disposition. For her, people in the country are callous and vicious, those in the city are callous and vicious, husbands are (of course) callous and vicious, and children are merely sadistic. The only ones with feelings are her put-upon middle-aged heroines, with whom she obviously identifies. I guess if she didn't write so well the stories wouldn't sting so.

Inspired by Crowley, walked back to the pool in the woods. Had visions of climbing a tree, swinging on vines, anything to commemorate his exploits. . . . Saw something dead floating in the center of the pool and ran back to the farm. Copperhead? Caterpillar? It had somehow opened up. . . .

Joined Sarr chopping stakes for tomatoes. Could hear his ax all over the farm. He told me Bwada hadn't come home last night, and no sign of her this morning. Good riddance, as far as I'm concerned. Helped him chop some stakes while he was busy peeling off bark. That ax can get heavy fast! My arm hurt after three lousy stakes, and Sarr had already chopped fifteen or sixteen. Must start exercising. But I'll wait till my arm's less tired. . . .

JULY 2

Unpleasant day. Two a.m. now and still can't relax.

Sarr woke me up this morning—stood at my window calling "Jeremy . . . Jeremy . . ." over and over very quietly. He had something in his hand which, through the screen, I first took for a farm implement; then I saw it was a rifle. He said he wanted me to help him. With what? I asked.

"A burial."

Last night, after he and Deborah had gone to bed, they'd heard the kitchen door open and someone enter the house. They both assumed it was me, come to use the bathroom—but then they heard the cats screaming. Sarr ran down and switched on the light in time to see Bwada on top of Butch, claws in his side, fangs buried in his neck. From the way he described it, sounds almost sexual in reverse. Butch had stopped struggling, and Minnie, the orange kitten, was already dead. The door was partly open, and when Bwada saw Sarr, she ran out.

Sarr and Deborah hadn't followed her; they'd spent the night praying over the bodies of Minnie and Butch. I *thought* I'd heard their voices late last night, but that's all I heard, probably because I'd been playing my radio. (Something I rarely do— you can't hear noises from the woods with it on.)

Poroths took deaths the way they'd take the death of a child. Regular little funeral service over by the unused pasture. (Hard to say if Sarr and Deborah were dressed in mourning, since that's the way they always dress.) Must admit I didn't feel particularly involved—my allergy's never permitted me to take much interest in the cats, though I'm fond of Felix—but I tried to act concerned: when Sarr asked, appropriately, "Is there no balm in Gilead? Is there no physician there?" (Jeremiah VIII:22), I nodded gravely. Read passages out of Deborah's Bible (Sarr seemed to know them all by heart), said amen when they did, knelt when they knelt, and tried to comfort Deborah when she cried. Asked her if cats could go to heaven, received a tearful "Of course." But Sarr added that Bwada would burn in hell.

What concerned me, apparently a lot more than it did either of them, was how the damned thing could get into the house. Sarr gave me this stupid, earnest answer: "She was always a smart cat." Like an outlaw's mother, still proud of her baby. . . .

Yet he and I looked all over the land for her so he could

kill her. Barns, tool shed, old stables, garbage dump, etc. He called her and pleaded with her, swore to me she hadn't always been like this.

We could hardly check every tree on the farm—unfortunately—and the woods are a perfect hiding place, even for animals larger than a cat. So naturally we found no trace of her. We did try, though; we even walked up the road as far as the ruined homestead.

But for all that, we could have stayed much closer to home.

We returned for dinner, and I stopped at my room to change clothes. My door was open. Nothing inside was ruined, everything was in its place, everything as it should be—except the bed. The sheets were in tatters right down to the mattress, and the pillow had been ripped to shreds. Feathers were all over the floor. There were even claw marks on my blanket.

At dinner the Poroths demanded they be allowed to pay for the damage—nonsense, I said, they have enough to worry about—and Sarr suggested I sleep downstairs in their living room. "No need for that," I told him, "I've got lots more sheets." But he said no, he didn't mean that: he meant for my own protection. He believes the thing is particularly inimical, for some reason, toward me.

It seemed so absurd at the time. . . . I mean, nothing but a big fat gray cat. But now, sitting out here, a few feathers still scattered on the floor around my bed, I wish I were back inside the house. I did give in to Sarr when he insisted I take his ax with me. . . . But what I'd rather have is simply a room without windows.

I don't think I want to go to sleep tonight, which is one reason I'm continuing to write this. Just sit up all night on my new bedsheets, my back against the Poroths' pillow, leaning against the wall behind me, the ax beside me on the bed, this journal on my lap. . . . The thing is, I'm rather tired out from all the walking I did today. Not used to that much exercise.

I'm pathetically aware of every sound. At least once every five minutes some snapping of a branch or rustling of leaves makes me jump.

"Thou art my hope in the day of evil." At least that's what the man said. . . .

JULY 3

Woke up this morning with the journal and the ax cradled in my arms. What awakened me was the trouble I had breathing—nose all clogged, gasping for breath. Down the center of one of my screens, facing the woods, was a huge slash. . . .

JULY 15

Pleasant day, St. Swithin's Day—and yet, my birthday. Thirty years old, lordy lordy lordy. Today I am a man. First dull thoughts on waking: "Damnation. Thirty today." But another voice inside me, smaller but more sensible, spat contemptuously at such an artificial way of charting time. "Ah, don't give it another thought," it said. "You've still got plenty of time to fool around." Advice I took to heart.

Weather today? Actually, somewhat nasty. And thus the weather for the next forty days, since "If rain on St. Swithin's Day, forsooth, no summer drouthe," or something like that. My birthday predicts the weather. It's even mentioned in *The Glass Harmonica.*

As one must, took a critical self-assessment. First area for improvement: flabby body. Second? Less bookish, perhaps? Nonsense—I'm satisfied with the progress I've made. "And seekest thou great things for thyself? Seek them not." (Jeremiah XLV:5) So I simply did what I remembered from the RCAF exercise series and got good and winded. Flexed my stringy muscles in the shower, certain I'll be a Human Dynamo by the end of the summer. Simply a matter of willpower.

Was so ambitious I trimmed the ivy around my windows again. It's begun to block the light, and someday I may not be able to get out the door.

Read Ruthven Todd's *Lost Traveller*. Merely the narrative of a dream turned to nightmare, and illogical as hell. Wish, too, that there'd been more than merely a few hints of sex. On the whole, rather unpleasant; that gruesome ending is so inevitable. . . . Took me much of the afternoon. Then came upon an incredible essay by Lafcadio Hearn, something entitled "Gaki," detailing the curious Japanese belief that insects are really demons or the ghosts of evil men. Uncomfortably convincing!

Dinner late because Deborah, bless her, was baking me a cake. Had time to walk into town and phone parents. Happy birthday, happy birthday. Both voiced first worry—mustn't I be getting bored out here? Assured them I still had plenty of books and did not grow tired of reading.

"But it's so . . . *secluded* out there," Mom said. "Don't you get lonely?"

Ah, she hadn't reckoned on the inner resources of a man of thirty. Was tempted to quote *Walden*—"Why should I feel lonely? Is not our planet in the Milky Way?"—but refrained. How can I get lonely, I asked, when there's still so much to read? Besides, there are the Poroths to talk to.

Then the kicker: Dad wanted to know about the cat. Last time I'd spoken to them it had sounded like a very real danger. "Are you still sleeping inside the farmhouse, I hope?"

No, I told him, really, I only had to do that for a few days, while it was prowling around at night. Yes, it had killed some chickens—a hen every night, in fact. But there were only four of them, and then it stopped. We haven't had a sign of it in more than a week. (I didn't tell him that it had left the hens uneaten, dead in the nest. No need to upset him further.)

"But what it did to your sheets . . ." he went on. "If you'd been sleeping . . . Such savagery."

Yes, that was unfortunate, but there's been no trouble since. Honest. It was only an animal, after all, just a housecat gone a little wild. It posed the same kind of threat as (I was going to say, logically, a wildcat; but for Mom said) a nasty little dog. Like Mrs. Miller's bull terrier. Besides, it's probably miles and miles away by now. Or dead.

They offered to drive out with packages of food, magazines, a portable TV, but I made it clear I needed nothing. Getting too fat, actually.

Still light when I got back. Deborah had finished the cake, Sarr brought up some wine from the cellar, and we had a nice little celebration. The two of them being over thirty, they were happy to welcome me to the fold.

It's nice out here. The wine has relaxed me and I keep yawning. It was good to talk to Mom and Dad again. Just as long as I don't dream of *The Lost Traveller*, I'll be content. And happier still if I don't dream at all. . . .

JULY 30

Well, Bwada is dead—this time for sure. We'll bury her tomorrow. Deborah was hurt, just how badly I can't say, but she managed to fight Bwada off. Tough woman, though she seems a little shaken. And with good reason.

It happened this way: Sarr and I were in the tool shed after dinner, building more shelves for the upstairs study. Though the fireflies were out, there was still a little daylight left. Deborah had gone up to bed after doing the dishes; she's been tired a lot lately, falls asleep early every night while watching TV with Sarr. He thinks it may be something in the well water.

It had begun to get dark, but we were still working. Sarr dropped a box of nails, and while we were picking them up, he thought he heard a scream. Since I hadn't heard anything, he shrugged and was about to start sawing again when—fortunately—he changed his mind and ran off to the house. I followed him as far as the porch, not sure whether to go upstairs, until I heard him pounding on their bedroom door and calling Deborah's name. As I ran up the stairs I heard her say, "Wait, don't come in. I'll unlock the door . . . soon." Her voice was extremely hoarse, practically a croaking. We heard her rummaging in the closet—finding her bathrobe, I suppose—and then she opened the door.

She looked absolutely white. Her long hair was in tangles and her robe buttoned incorrectly. Around her neck she had wrapped a towel, but we could see patches of blood soaking through it. Sarr helped her over to the bed, shouting at me to bring up some bandages from the bathroom.

When I returned Deborah was lying in bed, still pressing the towel to her throat. I asked Sarr what had happened; it almost looked as if the woman had tried suicide.

He didn't say anything, just pointed to the floor on the other side of the bed. I stepped around for a look. A crumpled gray shape was lying there, half covered by the bedclothes. It was Bwada, a wicked-looking wound in her side. On the floor next to her lay one of the Poroths' old black umbrellas—the thing that Deborah had used to kill her.

She told us she'd been asleep when she felt something crawl heavily over her face. It had been like a bad dream. She'd tried to sit up, and suddenly Bwada was at her throat, digging in. Luckily she'd had the strength to tear the animal off and dash to the closet, where the first weapon at hand was the umbrella. Just as the cat sprang at her again, Deborah said, she'd raised the weapon and lunged. Amazing; how many women, I wonder, would have had such presence of mind? The rest sounds incredible to me, but it's probably the sort of crazy thing that happens in moments like this: somehow the cat had impaled itself on the umbrella.

Her voice, as she spoke, was barely more than a whisper. Sarr had to persuade her to remove the towel from her throat; she kept protesting that she wasn't hurt that badly, that the towel had stopped the bleeding. Sure enough, when Sarr finally lifted the cloth from her neck, the wounds proved relatively small, the slash marks already clotting. Thank God that thing didn't really get its teeth in. . . .

My guess—only a guess—is that it had been weakened from days of living in the woods. (It was obviously incapable of feeding itself adequately, as I think was proved by its failure to eat the hens it had killed.) While Sarr dressed Deborah's wounds, I pulled back the bedclothes and took a closer look at the animal's body. The fur was matted and patchy. Odd that an umbrella could make a puncture like that, ringed by flaps of skin, the flesh seeming to push outward. Deborah must have had the extraordinary good luck to have jabbed the animal precisely in its old wound, which had reopened. Naturally I didn't mention this to Sarr.

He made dinner for us tonight—soup, actually, because he thought that was best for Deborah. Her voice sounded so bad he told her not to strain it any more by talking, at which she nodded and smiled. We both had to help her downstairs, as she was clearly weak from shock.

In the morning Sarr will have the doctor out. He'll have to examine the cat, too, to check for rabies, so we put the body in the freezer to preserve it as well as possible. Afterward we'll bury it.

Deborah seemed okay when I left. Sarr was reading through some medical books, and she was just lying on the living room couch gazing at her husband with a look of purest gratitude—not moving, not saying anything, not even blinking.

I feel quite relieved. God knows how many nights I've lain here thinking every sound I heard was Bwada. I'll feel more relieved, of course, when that demon's safely underground; but I think I can say, at the risk of being melodramatic, that the reign of terror is over.

Hmm, I'm still a little hungry—used to more than soup for dinner. These daily push-ups burn up energy. I'll probably dream of hamburgers and chocolate layer cakes.

JULY 31

. . . The doctor collected scrapings from Bwada's teeth and scolded us for doing a poor job of preserving the body. Said storing it in the freezer was a sensible idea, but that we should have done so sooner, since it was already decomposing. The dampness, I imagine, must act fast on dead flesh.

He pronounced Deborah in excellent condition—the marks on her throat are, remarkably, almost healed—but he said her reflexes were a little off. Sarr invited him to stay for the burial, but he declined—and quite emphatically, at that. He's not a member of their order, doesn't live in the area, and apparently doesn't get along that well with the people of Gilead, most of whom mistrust modern science. (Not that the old geezer sounded very representative of modern science. When I asked him for some good exercises, he recommended "chopping wood and running down deer.")

Standing under the heavy clouds, Sarr looked like a revivalist minister. His sermon was from Jeremiah XXII:19—"He shall be buried with the burial of an ass." The burial took place far from the graves of Bwada's two victims, and closer to the woods. We sang one song, Deborah just mouthing the words (still mustn't strain throat muscles). Sarr solemnly asked the Lord to look mercifully upon all His creatures, and I muttered an "amen." Then we walked back to the house, Deborah leaning on Sarr's arm; she's still a little stiff.

It was gray the rest of the day, and I sat in my room reading *The King in Yellow*—or rather, Chambers' collection of the same name. One look at the *real* book, so Chambers would claim, and I might not live to see the morrow, at least through the eyes of a sane man. (That single gimmick—masterful, I admit—seems to be his sole inspiration.)

I was disappointed that dinner was again made by Sarr; Deborah was upstairs resting, he said. He sounded concerned, felt there were things wrong with her the doctor had overlooked. We ate our meal in silence, and I came back here immediately after washing the dishes. Feel very drowsy and, for some reason, also rather depressed. It may be the gloomy weather—we are, after all, just animals, more affected by the sun and the seasons than we like to admit. More likely it was the absence of Deborah tonight. Hope she feels better.

Note: The freezer still smells of the cat's body; opened it tonight and got a strong whiff of decay.

AUGUST 1

Writing this, breaking habit, in early morning. Went to bed last night just after finishing the entry above, but was awakened around two by sounds coming from the woods. Wailing, deeper than before, followed by a low, guttural monologue. No words, at least that I could distinguish. If toads could talk . . . For some reason I fell asleep before the sounds ended, so I don't know what followed.

Could very well have been an owl of some kind, and later a large bullfrog. But I quote, without comment, from *The Glass Harmonica*: "July 31: Lammas Eve. Sabbats likely."

Little energy to write tonight, and even less to write about. (Come to think of it, I slept most of the day: woke up at eleven, later took an afternoon nap. Alas, senile at thirty!) Too tired to shave, and haven't had the energy to clean this place, either; thinking about work is easier than doing it. The ivy's beginning to cover the windows again, and the mildew's been climbing steadily up the walls. It's like a dark green band that keeps widening. Soon it will reach my books. . . .

Speaking of which, note: opened M. R. James at lunch today—*Ghost Stories of an Antiquary*—and a silverfish slithered out. Omen?

Played a little game with myself this evening—

I just had one hell of a shock. While writing the above I heard a soft tapping, like nervous fingers drumming on a table, and discovered an enormous spider, biggest of the summer, crawling only a few inches from my ankle. It must have been living behind this desk. . . .

When you can hear a spider walk across the floor, you *know* it's time to keep your socks on. Thank God for insecticide.

Oh, yeah, that game—the What If game. I probably play it too often. (Vain attempt to enlarge realm of the possible? Heighten my own sensitivity? Or merely work myself into an icy sweat?) I pose unpleasant questions for myself and consider the consequences, e.g., what if this glorified chicken coop is sinking into quicksand? (Wouldn't be at all surprised.) What if the Poroths are tired of me? What if I woke up inside my own coffin?

What if I never see New York again?

What if some horror stories aren't really fiction? If Machen sometimes told the truth? If there *are* White People, malevolent little faces peering out of the moonlight? Whispers in the grass? Poisonous things in the woods? Perfect hate and evil in the world?

Enough of this foolishness. Time for bed.

AUGUST 9

. . . Read some Hawthorne in the morning and, over lunch, reread this week's *Hunterdon County Democrat* for the dozenth time. Sarr and Deborah were working somewhere in the fields, and I felt I ought to get some physical activity myself; but the thought of starting my exercises again after more than a week's laziness just seemed too unpleasant. . . . I took a walk down the road, but only as far as a smashed-up cement culvert half buried in the woods. I was bored, but Gilead just seemed too far away.

Was going to cut the ivy away from my windows when I got back, but decided the place looks more artistic covered in vines. Rationalization?

Chatted with Poroths about politics. The World Situation, a little cosmology, blah blah blah. Dinner wasn't very good, probably because I'd been looking forward to it all day. The lamb was underdone and the beans were cold. Still, I'm always the gentleman, and was almost pleased when Deborah agreed to my offer to do the dishes. I've been doing them a lot lately.

I didn't have much interest in reading tonight and would have been up for some television, but Sarr's recently gotten into one of his religious kicks and began mumbling prayers to himself immediately after dinner. (Deborah, more human, wanted to watch the TV news. She seems to have an insatiable curiosity about world events, yet she claims the isolation here appeals to her.) Absorbed in his chanting, Sarr made me uncomfortable—I didn't like his face—and so after doing the dishes, I left.

I've been listening to the radio for the last hour or so. . . . I recall days when I'd have gotten uptight at having wasted an hour—but out here I've lost all track of time. Feel adrift—a little disconcerting, but healthy, I'm sure.

. . . Shut the radio off a moment ago, and now realize my room is filled with crickets. Up close their sound is hardly pleasant—cross between a radiator and a tea-kettle, very shrill. They'd been sounding off all night, but I'd thought it was interference on the radio.

Now I notice them; they're all over the room. A couple of dozen, I should think. Hate to kill them, really—they're one of the few insects I can stand, along with ladybugs and fireflies. But they make such a racket!

Wonder how they got in. . . .

AUGUST 14

Played with Felix all morning—mainly watching him chase insects, climb trees, doze in the sun. Spectator sport. After lunch went back to my room to look up something in Lovecraft and discovered my books were out of order. (Saki, for example, was filed under "S," whereas—whether out of fastidiousness or pedantry—I've always preferred to file him as "Munro.") This is definitely one of the Poroths' doing. I'm pissed they didn't mention coming in here, but also a little surprised they'd have any interest in this stuff.

Arranged them correctly again, then sat down to reread Lovecraft's essay on "Supernatural Horror in Literature." It upset me to see how little I've actually read, how far I still have to go. So many obscure authors, so many books I've never come across. . . . Left me feeling depressed and tired, so I took a nap for the rest of the afternoon.

Over dinner—vegetable omelet, rather tasteless—Deborah continued to question us on current events. It's getting to be like junior high school, with daily newspaper quizzes. . . . Don't know how she got started on this, or why the sudden interest, but it obviously annoys the hell out of Sarr.

Sarr used to be a sucker for her little-girl pleadings—I remember how he used to carry her upstairs, becoming pathetically tender, the moment she'd say, "Oh, honey, I'm so tired"—but now he just becomes angry. Often he goes off morose and alone to pray, and the only time he laughs is when he watches television.

Tonight, thank God, he was in a mood to forgo the prayers, and so after dinner we all watched a lot of offensively ignorant programs. I was disturbed to find myself laughing along with the canned laughter, but I have to admit the TV helps us get along better together. Came back here after the news.

Not very tired, having slept so much of the afternoon, so began to read John Christopher's *The Possessors;* but good though it was, my mind began to wander to all the books I *haven't* yet read, and I got so depressed I turned on the radio. Find it takes my mind off things.

AUGUST 19

Slept long into the morning, then walked down to the brook, scratching groggily. Deborah was kneeling by the water, lost, it seemed, in daydream, and I was embarrassed because I'd come upon her talking to herself. We exchanged a few insincere words and she went back toward the house.

Sat by some rocks, throwing blades of grass into the water. The sun on my head felt almost painful, as if my brain were growing too large for my skull. I turned and looked at the farmhouse. In the distance it looked like a picture at the other end of a large room, the grass for a carpet, the ceiling the sky. Deborah was stroking a cat, then seemed to grow angry when it struggled from her arms; I could hear the screen door slam as she went into the kitchen, but the sound reached me so long after the visual image that the whole scene struck me as, somehow, fake. I gazed up at the maples behind me, and they seemed trees out of a cheap postcard, the kind in which paint is thinly dabbed over a black-and-white photograph; if you look closely you can see that the green in the trees is not merely in the leaves, but rather floats as a vapor over leaves, branches, parts of the sky. . . . The trees behind me seemed the productions of a poor painter, the color and shape not quite meshing. Parts of the sky were green, and pieces of the green seemed to float away from my vision. No matter how hard I tried, I couldn't follow them.

Far down the stream I could see something small and kicking, a black beetle, legs in the air, borne swiftly along in the current. Then it was gone.

Thumbed through the Bible while I ate my lunch—mostly cookies. By late afternoon I was playing word games while I lay on the grass near my room. The shrill twitter of the birds, I would say, the birds singing in the sun. . . . And inexorably I'd continue with the sun dying in the moonlight, the moonlight falling on the floor, the floor sagging to the cellar, the cellar filling with water, the water seeping into the ground, the ground twisting into smoke, the smoke staining the sky, the sky burning in the sun, the sun dying in the moonlight, the moonlight falling on the floor . . . —melancholy progressions that held my mind like a whirlpool.

Sarr woke me for dinner; I had dozed off, and my clothes were damp from the grass. As we walked up to the house together he whispered that, earlier in the day, he'd come upon his wife bending over me, peering into my sleeping face. "Her eyes were wide," he said. "Like Bwada's." I said I didn't understand why he was telling me this.

"Because," he recited in a whisper, gripping my arm, "the heart is deceitful above all things, and desperately wicked: who can know it?"

I recognized that. Jeremiah XVII:9.

Dinner was especially uncomfortable; the two of them sat picking at their food, occasionally raising their eyes to one another like children in a staring contest. I longed for the conversations of our early days, inconsequential though they must have been, and wondered where things had gone wrong.

The meal was dry and unappetizing, but the dessert looked

delicious—chocolate mousse, made from an old family recipe. Deborah had served it earlier in the summer and knew both Sarr and I loved it. This time, however, she gave none to herself, explaining that she had to watch her weight.

"Then we'll not eat any!" Sarr shouted, and with that he snatched my dish from in front of me, grabbed his own, and hurled them both against the wall, where they splattered like mudballs.

Deborah was very still; she said nothing, just sat there watching us. Thank heaven, she didn't look particularly afraid of this madman, I was happy to see—but *I* was. He may have read my thoughts, because as I got up from my seat, he said much more gently, in the soft voice normal to him, "Sorry, Jeremy. I know you hate scenes. We'll pray for each other, all right?"

"Are you okay?" I asked Deborah, with more bravado than I felt. "I'm going out now, but I'll stay if you think you'll need me for anything." She stared at me with a slight smile and shook her head. I raised my eyebrows and nodded toward her husband, and she shrugged.

"Things will work out," she said. I could hear Sarr laughing as I shut the door.

When I snapped on the light out here I took off my shirt and stood in front of the little mirror. It had been nearly a week since I'd showered, and I'd become used to the smell of my body. My hair had wound itself into greasy brown curls, my beard was at least two weeks old, and my eyes . . . well, the eyes that stared back at me looked like those of an old man. The whites were turning yellow, like old teeth. I looked at my chest and arms, flabby at thirty, and I thought of the frightening alterations in my friend Sarr, and I knew I'd have to get out of here.

Just glanced at my watch. It's now quite late: two-thirty. I've been packing my things.

AUGUST 20

I woke about an hour ago and continued packing. Lots of books to put away, but I'm just about done. It's not even nine a.m. yet, much earlier than I normally get up; but I guess the thought of leaving here fills me with energy.

The first thing I saw on rising was a garden spider whose body was as big as some of the mice the cats have killed. It was sitting on the ivy that grows over my window sill—fortunately on the other side of the screen. Apparently it had had good hunting all summer, preying on the insects that live in the leaves. Concluding that nothing so big and fearsome has a right to live, I held the spray can against the screen and doused the creature with poison. It struggled halfway up the screen, then stopped, arched its legs, and dropped backwards into the ivy.

I plan to walk into town this morning and telephone the office in Flemington where I rented my car. If they can have one ready today I'll hitch there to pick it up; otherwise I'll spend tonight here and pick it up tomorrow. I'll be leaving a little early in the season, but the Poroths already have my month's rent, so they shouldn't be too offended.

And anyway, how could I be expected to stick around here with all that nonsense going on, never knowing when my room might be ransacked, having to put up with Sarr's insane suspicions and Deborah's moodiness?

Before I go into town, though, I really must shave and shower for the good people of Gilead. I've been sitting inside here waiting for some sign the Poroths are up, but as yet—it's almost nine—I've heard nothing. I wouldn't care to barge in on them while they're still having breakfast or, worse, just getting up. . . . So I'll just wait here by the window till I see them.

. . . Ten o'clock now, and they still haven't come out. Perhaps they're having a talk. . . . I'll give them half an hour more, then I'm going in.

Here my journal ends. Until today, almost a week later, I have not cared to set down any of the events that followed. But here in the temporary safety of this hotel room, protected by a heavy brass travel-lock I had sent up from the hardware store down the street, watched over by the good people of Flemington— and perhaps by something not good—I can continue my narrative.

The first thing I noticed as I approached the house was that the shades were drawn, even in the kitchen. Had they decided to sleep late this morning? I wondered. Throughout my thirty years I have come to associate drawn shades with a foul smell, the smell of a sickroom, of shamefaced poverty and food gone bad, of people lying too long beneath blankets; but I was not ready for the stench of decay that met me when I opened the kitchen door and stepped into the darkness. Something had died in that room—and not recently.

At the moment the smell first hit, four little shapes scrambled across the linoleum toward me and out into the daylight. The Poroths' cats.

By the other wall a lump of shadow moved; a pale face caught light penetrating the shades. Sarr's voice, its habitual softness exaggerated to a whisper: "Jeremy. I thought you were still asleep."

"Can I—"

"No. Don't turn on the light." He got to his feet, a black form towering against the window. Fiddling nervously with the kitchen door—the tin doorknob, the rubber bands stored around it, the fringe at the bottom of the drawn window shade—I opened it wider and let in more sunlight. It fell on the dark thing at his feet, over which he had been crouching: Deborah, the flesh at her throat torn and wrinkled like the skin of an old apple.

Her clothing lay in a heap beside her. She appeared long dead. The eyes were shriveled, sunken into sockets black as a skull's.

I think I may have staggered at that moment, because he came toward me. His steady, unblinking gaze looked so sincere—but *why was he smiling?* "I'll make you understand," he was saying, or something like that; even now I feel my face twisting into horror as I try to write of him. "I had to kill her. . . ."

"You—"

"She tried to kill me," he went on, silencing all questions. "The same thing that possessed Bwada . . . possessed her."

My hand played behind my back with the bottom of the window shade. "But her throat—"

"That happened a long time ago. Bwada did it. I had nothing to do with . . . that part." Suddenly his voice rose. "Don't you understand? She tried to stab me with the bread knife." He turned, stooped over, and, clumsy in the darkness, began feeling about him on the floor. "Where is that thing?" he was mumbling. "I'll show you. . . ." As he crossed a beam of sunlight, something gleamed like a silver handle on the back of his shirt.

Thinking, perhaps, to help him search, I pulled gently on the window shade, then released it; it snapped upward like a gunshot, flooding the room with light. From deep within the center of his back protruded the dull wooden haft of the bread knife, buried almost completely but for an inch or two of gleaming steel.

He must have heard my intake of breath—that sight chills me even today, the grisly absurdity of the thing—he must have heard me, because immediately he stood, his back to me, and reached up behind himself toward the knife, his arm stretching in vain, his fingers curling around nothing. The blade had been planted in a spot he couldn't reach.

He turned towards me and shrugged in embarrassment, a child caught in a foolish error. "Oh, yeah," he said, grinning at his own weakness, "I forgot it was there."

Suddenly he thrust his face into mine, fixing me in a gaze that never wavered, his eyes wide as if with candor. "It's easy for us to forget things," he explained—and then, still smiling, still watching, volunteered that last trivial piece of information, that final message whose words released me from inaction and left me free to dash from the room, to sprint in panic down the road to town, pursued by what had once been the farmer Sarr Poroth.

It serves no purpose here to dwell on my flight down that twisting dirt road, breathing in such deep gasps that I was soon moaning with every breath; how, with my enemy racing behind me, not even winded, his steps never flagging, I veered into the woods; how I finally lost him, perhaps from the inexperience of whatever thing now controlled his body, and was able to make my way back to the road, only to come upon him again as he rounded a bend; his laughter as he followed me, and how it continued long after I had evaded him a second time; and how, after hiding until nightfall in the old cement culvert, I ran the rest of the way in pitch-darkness, stumbling in the ruts, torn by vines, nearly blinding myself when I ran into a low branch, until I arrived in Gilead filthy, exhausted, and nearly incoherent.

Suffice it to say that my escape was largely a matter of luck, a physical wreck fleeing something oblivious to pain or fatigue; but that, beyond mere luck, I had been impelled by an almost ecstatic sense of dread produced by his last words to me, that last communication from an alien face smiling inches from my own, and which I chose to take as his final warning:

"Sometimes we forget to blink."

You can read the rest in the newspapers. The *Hunterdon County Democrat* covered most of the story, though its man wrote it up as merely another lunatic wife-slaying, the result of loneliness, religious mania, and a mysteriously tainted well. (Traces of insecticide were found, among other things, in the water.) The *Somerset Reporter* took a different slant, implying that I had been the third member of an erotic triangle and that Sarr had murdered his wife in a fit of jealousy.

Needless to say, I was by this time past caring what was written about me. I was too haunted by visions of that lonely, abandoned farmhouse, the wails of its hungry cats, and by the sight of Deborah's corpse, discovered by the police, protruding from that hastily dug grave beyond the cornfield.

Accompanied by state troopers, I returned to my ivy-covered outbuilding. A bread knife had been plunged deep into its door, splintering the wood on the other side. The blood on it was Sarr's.

My journal had been hidden under my mattress and so was untouched, but (I look at them now, piled in cardboard boxes beside my suitcase) my precious books had been hurled about the room, their bindings slashed. My summer is over, and now I sit inside here all day listening to the radio, waiting for the next report. Sarr—or his corpse—has not been found.

I should think the evidence was clear enough to corroborate my story, but I suppose I should have expected the reception it received from the police. They didn't laugh at my theory of "possession"—not to my face, anyway—but they ignored it in obvious embarrassment. Some see a nice young bookworm gone slightly deranged after contact with a murderer; others believe my story to be the desperate fabrication of an adulterer trying to avoid the blame for Deborah's death.

I can understand their reluctance to accept my explanation of the events, for it's one that goes a little beyond the "natural," a little beyond the scientific considerations of motive, *modus operandi,* and fingerprints. But I find it quite unnerving that at least one official—an assistant district attorney, I think, though I'm afraid I'm rather ignorant of these matters—believes I am guilty of murder.

There has, of course, been no arrest. Still, I've been given the time-honored admonition against leaving town.

The theory proposing my own complicity in the events is, I must admit, rather ingenious—and so carefully worked out that it will surely gain more adherents than my own. This public official is going to try to prove that I killed poor Deborah in a fit of passion and, immediately afterward, disposed of Sarr. He points out that their marriage had been an observably happy one until I arrived, a disturbing influence from the city. My motive, he says, was simple lust—unrequited, to be sure— aggravated by boredom. The heat, the insects, and, most of all, the oppressive loneliness—all constituted an environment alien to any I'd been accustomed to, and all worked to unhinge my reason.

I have no cause for fear, however, because this affidavit will certainly establish my innocence. Surely no one can ignore the evidence of my journal (though I can imagine someone of implacable hostility maintaining that I wrote the journal not at the farm but here in the Union Hotel, this very week).

What galls me is not the suspicions of a few detectives, but the predicament their suspicions place me in. Quite simply, *I cannot run away.* I am compelled to remain locked up in this room, potential prey to whatever the thing that was Sarr Poroth has now become—the thing that was once a cat, and once a woman, and once . . . what? A large white moth? A serpent? A shrewlike thing with wicked teeth?

A police chief? A president? A boy with eyes of blood that sits beneath my window?

Lord, who will believe me?

It was that night that started it all, I'm convinced of it now. The night I made those strange signs in the tree. The night the crickets missed a beat.

I'm not a philosopher, and I can supply no ready explanation for why this new evil has been released into the world. I'm only a poor scholar, a bookworm, and I must content myself with mumbling a few phrases that keep running through my mind, phrases out of books read long ago when such abstractions meant, at most, a pleasant shudder. I am haunted by scraps from the myth of Pandora, and by a semantic discussion I once read comparing "unnatural" and "supernatural."

And something about "a tiny rent in the fabric of the universe. . . ."

Just large enough to let something in. Something not of nature, and hard to kill. Something with its own obscure purpose.

Ironically, the police may be right. Perhaps it was my visit to Gilead that brought about the deaths. Perhaps I had a hand in letting loose the force that, to date, has snuffed out the lives of four hens, three cats, and at least two people—but will hardly be content to stop there.

I've just checked. He hasn't moved from the steps of the courthouse; and even when I look out my window, the rose spectacles never waver. Who knows where the eyes beneath them point? Who knows if they remember to blink?

Lord, this heat is sweltering. My shirt is sticking to my skin, and droplets of sweat are rolling down my face and dripping onto this page, making the ink run.

My hand is tired from writing, and I think it's time to end this affidavit.

If, as I now believe possible, I inadvertently called down evil from the sky and began the events at Poroth Farm, my death will only be fitting. And after my death, many more. We are all, I'm afraid, in danger. Please, then, forgive this prophet of doom, old at thirty, his last jeremiad: "The harvest is past, the summer is ended, and we are not saved."

STEPHEN KING

Stephen Edwin King was born in Portland, Maine, in 1947 and has spent nearly his entire life in his native state. He graduated from the University of Maine at Orono in 1970 and the next year married Tabitha Jane Spruce. He began publishing short stories of supernatural horror in magazines in the late 1960s. His first novel, *Carrie,* appeared in 1974; when it was made into a spectacularly popular film the next year, King's career as a bestseller was launched. Since that time, nearly every one of his novels has achieved bestseller status and has been adapted for film or television, including *The Shining* (1977; filmed by Stanley Kubrick), *The Dead Zone* (1979), *Firestarter* (1980), *Christine* (1983), *Pet Sematary* (1983), *It* (1986), *Misery* (1987), and many others. King also wrote six novels, ranging from suspense to science fiction, under the pseudonym Richard Bachman, some of which represent his most effective work. He has also written a fusion of the Western with the supernatural tale in a seven-volume series, *The Dark Tower* (1982–2004).

Although he has become the most popular author of supernatural fiction in the twentieth century, in his later years King has increasingly departed from the supernatural and written work of a more mainstream character. This tendency began with four novellas published as *Different Seasons* (1982), and has continued with such works as *Gerald's Game* (1992), *Dolores Claiborne* (1993), and *Hearts in Atlantis* (1999). He has written two fantasy novels in collaboration with Peter Straub, *The Talisman* (1984) and *Black House* (2002). King, although criticized by some for unoriginality in the use of supernatural tropes and for occasionally slipshod or verbose writing, received a National Book Award in 2003 for "distinguished contributions to American letters."

King's early short stories were collected in *Night Shift* (1978). One tale in that volume, "Night Surf" (first published in *Cavalier,* August 1974), cleverly fuses the supernatural with the science fiction tale in its account of a flu that has decimated humanity. Other short stories can be found in *Skeleton Crew* (1985) and *Nightmares and Dreamscapes* (1993).

NIGHT SURF

After the guy was dead and the smell of his burning flesh was off the air, we all went back down to the beach. Corey had his radio, one of those suitcase-sized transistor jobs that take about forty batteries and also make and play tapes. You couldn't say the sound reproduction was great, but it sure was loud. Corey had been well-to-do before A6, but stuff like that didn't matter anymore. Even his big radio/tape-player was hardly more than a nice-looking hunk of junk. There were only two radio stations left on the air that we could get. One was WKDM in Portsmouth—some backwoods deejay who had gone nutty-religious. He'd play a Perry Como record, say a prayer, bawl, play a Johnny Ray record, read from Psalms (complete with each "selah," just like James Dean in *East of Eden*), then bawl some more. Happy-time stuff like that. One day he sang "Bringing in the Sheaves" in a cracked, moldy voice that sent Needles and me into hysterics.

The Massachusetts station was better, but we could only get it at night. It was a bunch of kids. I guess they took over the transmitting facilities of WRKO or WBZ after everybody left or died. They only gave gag call letters, like WDOPE or KUNT or WA6 or stuff like that. Really funny, you know—you could die laughing. That was the one we were listening to on the way back to the beach. I was holding hands with Susie; Kelly and Joan were ahead of us, and Needles was already over the brow of the point and out of sight. Corey was bringing up the rear, swinging his radio. The Stones were singing "Angie."

"Do you *love* me?" Susie was asking. "That's all I want to know, do you *love* me?" Susie needed constant reassurance. I was her teddy bear.

"No," I said. She was getting fat, and if she lived long enough, which wasn't likely, she would get really flabby. She was already mouthy.

"You're rotten," she said, and put a hand to her face. Her lacquered fingernails twinkled dimly with the half-moon that had risen about an hour ago.

"Are you going to cry again?"

"Shut up!" She sounded like she was going to cry again, all right.

We came over the ridge and I paused. I always have to pause. Before A6, this had been a public beach. Tourists, picnickers, runny-nosed kids and fat baggy grandmothers with sunburned elbows. Candy wrappers and popsicle sticks in the sand, all the beautiful people necking on their beach blankets, intermingled stench of exhaust from the parking lot, seaweed, and Coppertone oil.

But now all the dirt and all the crap was gone. The ocean had eaten it, all of it, as casually as you might eat a handful of Cracker Jacks. There were no people to come back and dirty it again. Just us, and we weren't enough to make much mess. We loved the beach too, I guess—hadn't we just offered it a kind of sacrifice? Even Susie, little bitch Susie with her fat ass and her cranberry bellbottoms.

The sand was white and duned, marked only by the high-tide line—twisted skein of seaweed, kelp, hunks of driftwood. The moonlight stitched inky crescent-shaped shadows and folds across everything. The deserted lifeguard tower stood white and skeletal some fifty yards from the bathhouse, pointing toward the sky like a finger bone.

And the surf, the night surf, throwing up great bursts of foam, breaking against the headlands for as far as we could see in endless attacks. Maybe that water had been halfway to England the night before.

"'Angie,' by the Stones," the cracked voice on Corey's radio said. "I'm sureya dug that one, a blast from the past that's a golden gas, straight from the grooveyard, a platta that mattas. I'm Bobby. This was supposed to be Fred's night, but Fred got the flu. He's all swelled up." Susie giggled then, with the first tears still on her eyelashes. I started toward the beach a little faster to keep her quiet.

"Wait up!" Corey called. "Bernie? Hey, Bernie, wait up!"

The guy on the radio was reading some dirty limericks, and a girl in the background asked him where did he put the beer. He said something back, but by that time we were on the beach. I looked back to see how Corey was doing. He was coming down on his backside, as usual, and he looked so ludicrous I felt a little sorry for him.

"Run with me," I said to Susie.

"Why?"

I slapped her on the can and she squealed. "Just because it feels good to run."

We ran. She fell behind, panting like a horse and calling for me to slow down, but I put her out of my head. The wind rushed past my ears and blew the hair off my forehead. I could smell the salt in the air, sharp and tart. The surf pounded. The waves were like foamed black glass. I kicked off my rubber sandals and pounded across the sand barefoot, not minding the sharp digs of an occasional shell. My blood roared.

And then there was the lean-to with Needles already inside and Kelly and Joan standing beside it, holding hands and looking at the water. I did a forward roll, feeling sand go down the back of my shirt, and fetched up against Kelly's legs. He fell on top of me and rubbed my face in the sand while Joan laughed.

We got up and grinned at each other. Susie had given up running and was plodding toward us. Corey had almost caught up to her.

"Some fire," Kelly said.

"Do you think he came all the way from New York, like he said?" Joan asked.

"I don't know." I couldn't see that it mattered anyway. He had been behind the wheel of a big Lincoln when we found him, semi-conscious and raving. His head was bloated to the size of a football and his neck looked like a sausage. He had Captain Trips and not far to go, either. So we took him up to the Point that overlooks the beach and burned him. He said his name was Alvin Sackheim. He kept calling for his grandmother. He thought Susie was his grandmother. This struck her funny, God knows why. The strangest things strike Susie funny.

It was Corey's idea to burn him up, but it started off as a joke. He had read all those books about witchcraft and black magic at college, and he kept leering at us in the dark beside Alvin Sackheim's Lincoln and telling us that if we made a sacrifice to the dark gods, maybe the spirits would keep protecting us against A6.

Of course none of us really believed that bullshit, but the talk got more and more serious. It was a new thing to do, and finally we went ahead and did it. We tied him to the observation gadget up there—you put a dime in it and on a clear day you can see all the way to Portland Headlight. We tied him with our belts, and then we went rooting around for dry brush and hunks of driftwood like kids playing a new kind of hide-and-seek. All the time we were doing it Alvin Sackheim just sort of leaned there and mumbled to his grandmother. Susie's eyes got very bright and she was breathing fast. It was really turning her on. When we were down in the ravine on the other side of the outcrop she leaned against me and kissed me. She was wearing too much lipstick and it was like kissing a greasy plate.

I pushed her away and that was when she started pouting.

We went back up, all of us, and piled dead branches and twigs up to Alvin Sackheim's waist. Needles lit the pyre with his Zippo, and it went up fast. At the end, just before his hair caught on fire, the guy began to scream. There was a smell just like sweet Chinese pork.

"Got a cigarette, Bernie?" Needles asked.

"There's about fifty cartons right behind you."

He grinned and slapped a mosquito that was probing his arm. "Don't want to move."

I gave him a smoke and sat down. Susie and I met Needles in Portland. He was sitting on the curb in front of the State Theater, playing Leadbelly tunes on a big old Gibson guitar he had looted someplace. The sound had echoed up and down Congress Street as if he were playing in a concert hall.

Susie stopped in front of us, still out of breath. "You're rotten, Bernie."

"Come on, Sue. Turn the record over. That side stinks."

"Bastard. Stupid, unfeeling son of a bitch. *Creep!*"

"Go away," I said, "or I'll black your eye, Susie. See if I don't."

She started to cry again. She was really good at it. Corey came up and tried to put an arm around her. She elbowed him in the crotch and he spit in her face.

"I'll *kill* you!" She came at him, screaming and weeping, making propellers with her hands. Corey backed off, almost fell, then turned tail and ran. Susie followed him, hurling hysterical obscenities. Needles put back his head and laughed. The sound of Corey's radio came back to us faintly over the surf.

Kelly and Joan had wandered off. I could see them down by the edge of the water, walking with their arms around each other's waist. They looked like an ad in a travel agent's window— *Fly to Beautiful St. Lorca.* It was all right. They had a good thing.

"Bernie?"

"What?" I sat and smoked and thought about Needles flipping back the top of his Zippo, spinning the wheel, making fire with flint and steel like a caveman.

"I've got it," Needles said.

"Yeah?" I looked at him. "Are you sure?"

"Sure I am. My head aches. My stomach aches. Hurts to piss."

"May it's just Hong Kong flu. Susie had Hong Kong flu. She wanted a Bible." I laughed. That had been while we were still at the University, about a week before they closed it down for good, a month before they started carrying bodies away in dump trucks and burying them in mass graves with payloaders.

"Look." He lit a match and held it under the angle of his jaw. I could see the first triangular smudges, the first swelling. It was A6, all right.

"Okay," I said.

"I don't feel so bad," he said. "In my mind, I mean. You, though. You think about it a lot. I can tell."

"No I don't." A lie.

"Sure you do. Like that guy tonight. You're thinking about that, too. We probably did him a favor, when you get right down to it. I don't think he even knew it was happening."

"He knew."

He shrugged and turned on his side. "It doesn't matter."

We smoked and I watched the surf come in and go out. Needles had Captain Trips. That made everything real all over again. It was late August already, and in a couple of weeks the first chill of fall would be creeping in. Time to move inside someplace. Winter. Dead by Christmas, maybe, all of us. In somebody's front room with Corey's expensive radio/tape-player on top of a bookcase full of Reader's Digest Condensed Books and the weak winter sun lying on the rug in meaningless windowpane patterns.

The vision was clear enough to make me shudder. Nobody should think about winter in August. It's like a goose walking over your grave.

Needles laughed. "See? You *do* think about it."

What could I say? I stood up. "Going to look for Susie."

"Maybe we're the last people on earth, Bernie. Did you ever think of that?" In the faint moonlight he already looked half dead, with circles under his eyes and pallid, unmoving fingers like pencils.

I walked down to the water and looked out across it. There was nothing to see but the restless, moving humps of the waves, topped by delicate curls of foam. The thunder of the breakers was tremendous down here, bigger than the world. Like standing inside a thunderstorm. I closed my eyes and rocked on my bare feet. The sand was cold and damp and packed. And if we were the last people on earth, so what? This would go on as long as there was a moon to pull the water.

Susie and Corey were up the beach. Susie was riding him as if he were a bucking bronc, pounding his head into the running boil of the water. Corey was flailing and splashing. They were both soaked. I walked down and pushed her off with my foot. Corey splashed away on all fours, spluttering and whoofing.

"I *hate you!*" Susie screamed at me. Her mouth was a dark grinning crescent. It looked like the entrance to a fun house. When I was a kid my mother used to take us kids to Harrison State Park and there was a fun house with a big clown face on the front, and you walked in through the mouth.

"Come on, Susie. Up, Fido." I held out my hand. She took it doubtfully and stood up. There was damp sand clotted on her blouse and skin.

"You didn't have to push me, Bernie. You don't ever—"

"Come on." She wasn't like a jukebox; you never had to put in a dime and she never came unplugged.

We walked up the beach toward the main concession. The man who ran the place had had a small overhead apartment. There was a bed. She didn't really deserve a bed, but Needles was right about that. It didn't matter. No one was really scoring the game anymore.

The stairs went up the side of the building, but I paused for just a minute to look in the broken window at the dusty wares inside that no one had cared enough about to loot—stacks of sweatshirts ("Anson Beach" and a picture of sky and waves printed on the front), glittering bracelets that would green the wrist on the second day, bright junk earrings, beachballs, dirty greeting cards, badly painted ceramic madonnas, plastic vomit (*So realistic! Try it on your wife!*), Fourth of July sparklers for a Fourth that never was, beach towels with a voluptuous girl in a bikini standing amid the names of a hundred famous resort areas, pennants (*Souvenir of Anson Beach and Park*), balloons, bathing suits. There was a snack bar up front with a big sign saying TRY OUR CLAM CAKE SPECIAL.

I used to come to Anson Beach a lot when I was still in high school. That was seven years before A6, and I was going with a girl named Maureen. She was a big girl. She had a pink checked bathing suit. I used to tell her it looked like a tablecloth. We had walked along the boardwalk in front of this place, barefoot, the boards hot and sandy beneath our heels. We had never tried the clam cake special.

"What are you looking at?"

"Nothing. Come on."

I had sweaty, ugly dreams about Alvin Sackheim. He was propped behind the wheel of his shiny yellow Lincoln, talking about his grandmother. He was nothing but a bloated, blackened head and a charred skeleton. He smelled burnt. He talked on and on, and after a while I couldn't make out a single word. I woke up breathing hard.

Susie was sprawled across my thighs, pale and bloated. My watch said 3:50, but it had stopped. It was still dark out. The surf pounded and smashed. High tide. Make it 4:15. Light soon. I got out of bed and went to the doorway. The sea breeze felt fine against my hot body. In spite of it all I didn't want to die.

I went over in the corner and grabbed a beer. There were three or four cases of Bud stacked against the wall. It was warm, because there was no electricity. I don't mind warm beer like some people do, though. It just foams a little more. Beer is beer. I went back out on the landing and sat down and pulled the ring tab and drank up.

So here we were, with the whole human race wiped out, not by atomic weapons or bio-warfare or pollution or anything *grand* like that. *Just the flu.* I'd like to put down a huge plaque somewhere, in the Bonneville Salt Flats, maybe. Bronze Square. Three miles on a side. And in big raised letters it would say, for the benefit of any landing aliens: JUST THE FLU.

I tossed the beer can over the side. It landed with a hollow clank on the cement walk that went around the building. The lean-to was a dark triangle on the sand. I wondered if Needles was awake. I wondered if I would be.

"Bernie?"

She was standing in the doorway wearing one of my shirts. I hate that. She sweats like a pig.

"You don't like me much anymore, do you, Bernie?"

I didn't say anything. There were times when I could still feel sorry for everything. She didn't deserve me any more than I deserved her.

"Can I sit down with you?"

"I doubt if it would be wide enough for both of us."

She made a choked hiccupping noise and started to go back inside.

"Needles has got A6," I said.

She stopped and looked at me. Her face was very still. "Don't joke, Bernie."

I lit a cigarette.

"He can't! He had—"

"Yes, he had A2. Hong Kong flu. Just like you and me and Corey and Kelly and Joan."

"But that would mean he isn't—"

"Immune."

"Yes. Then we could get it."

"Maybe he lied when he said he had A2. So we'd take him along with us that time," I said.

Relief spilled across her face. "Sure, that's it. I would have lied if it had been me. Nobody likes to be alone, do they?" She hesitated. "Coming back to bed?"

"Not just now."

She went inside. I didn't have to tell her that A2 was no guarantee against A6. She knew that. She had just blocked it out. I sat and watched the surf. It was really up. Years ago, Anson had been the only halfway decent surfing spot in the state. The Point was a dark, jutting hump against the sky. I thought I could see the upright that was the observation post, but it probably was just imagination. Sometimes Kelly took Joan up to the point. I didn't think they were up there tonight.

I put my face in my hands and clutched it, feeling the skin, its grain and texture. It was all narrowing so swiftly, and it was all so mean—there was no dignity in it.

The surf coming in, coming in, coming in. Limitless. Clean and deep. We had come here in the summer, Maureen and I, the summer after high school, the summer before college and reality and A6 coming out of Southeast Asia and covering the world like a pall, July, we had eaten pizza and listened to her radio, I had put oil on her back, she had put oil on mine, the air had been hot, the sand bright, the sun like a burning glass.

DENNIS ETCHISON

Dennis William Etchison was born in Stockton, California, in 1943, and has spent all of his life in his native state. Etchison made his first professional sale while still in high school, and during the time he attended Los Angeles State College and UCLA he continued to sell short stories in the horror and science fiction fields. After two pseudonymous novels in the 1960s, his first official books were novelizations of the films *The Fog* (1980), *Halloween II* (1981), *Halloween III* (1982), and *Videodrome* (1983), the last three published under the pseudonym Jack Martin. In 1982 his first short story collection, *The Dark Country*, appeared, establishing Etchison as one of the leading literary figures in the realm of supernatural horror. Other collections, including *Red Dreams* (1986), *The Blood Kiss* (1988), *The Death Artist* (2000), and *Talking in the Dark* (2001), have followed, revealing Etchison's skill at mingling tropes from horror, fantasy, and science fiction; in particular, such tales as "The Dead Line," "It Only Comes Out at Night," and "The Last Reel" exhibit Etchison's deftness in such supernatural motifs as the vampire and the zombie and in the depiction of the California milieu that renders him a local color writer of note.

Etchison has been less successful in the novel form. His first novel, *Darkside* (1986), is an able treatment of the nihilism of modern teenage culture, but *Shadowman* (1993),

California Gothic (1995), and *Double Edge* (1997) are only occasionally effective. Etchison is also an accomplished editor, having assembled the three-volume series *Masters of Darkness* (1986–91), in which leading contemporary horror writers have chosen their own favorite stories, as well as *Cutting Edge* (1986), *MetaHorror* (1992), and *The Museum of Horrors* (2001). Several of these volumes contain introductions featuring Etchison's pungent comments on the current state of the horror and science fiction fields.

"The Late Shift" (first published in Kirby McCauley's groundbreaking anthology, *Dark Forces* [1980], and collected in *The Dark Country*) demonstrates Etchison's skill at evoking horror from the most mundane elements of daily life, by the utilization of a subtle and evocative prose style reminiscent of such other California writers as James M. Cain or Raymond Chandler.

THE LATE SHIFT

They were driving back from a midnight screening of *The Texas Chainsaw Massacre* ("Who will survive and what will be left of them?") when one of them decided they should make the Stop 'N Start Market on the way home. Macklin couldn't be sure later who said it first, and it didn't really matter, for there was the all-night logo, its bright colors cutting through the fog before they had reached 26th Street, and as soon as he saw it Macklin moved over close to the curb and began coasting toward the only sign of life anywhere in town at a quarter to two in the morning.

They passed through the electric eye at the door, rubbing their faces in the sudden cold light. Macklin peeled off toward the news rack, feeling like a newborn before the LeBoyer Method. He reached into a row of well-thumbed magazines, but they were all chopper, custom car, detective and stroke books, as far as he could see.

"Please, please, sorry, thank you," the night clerk was saying.

"No, no," said a woman's voice, "can't you hear? I want that box, *that* one."

"Please, please," said the night man again.

Macklin glanced up.

A couple of guys were waiting in line behind her, next to the styrofoam ice chests. One of them cleared his throat and moved his feet.

The woman was trying to give back a small, oblong carton,

but the clerk didn't seem to understand. He picked up the box, turned to the shelf, back to her again.

Then Macklin saw what it was: a package of one dozen prophylactics from behind the counter, back where they kept the cough syrup and airplane glue and film. That was all she wanted—a pack of Polaroid SX-70 Land Film.

Macklin wandered to the back of the store.

"How's it coming, Whitey?"

"I got the Beer Nuts," said Whitey, "and the Jiffy Pop, but I can't find any Olde English 800." He rummaged through the refrigerated case.

"Then get Schlitz Malt Liquor," said Macklin. "That ought to do the job." He jerked his head at the counter. "Hey, did you catch that action up there?"

"What's that?"

Two more guys hurried in, heading for the wine display. "Never mind. Look, why don't you just take this stuff up there and get a place in line? I'll find us some Schlitz or something. Go on, they won't sell it to us after two o'clock."

He finally found a six-pack hidden behind some bottles, then picked up a quart of milk and a half-dozen eggs. When he got to the counter, the woman had already given up and gone home. The next man in line asked for cigarettes and beef jerky. Somehow the clerk managed to ring it up; the electronic register and UPC Code lines helped him a lot.

"Did you get a load of that one?" said Whitey. "Well, I'll be gonged. Old Juano's sure hit the skids, huh? The pits. They should have stood him in an aquarium."

"Who?"

"Juano. It *is* him, right? Take another look." Whitey pretended to study the ceiling.

Macklin stared at the clerk. Slicked-back hair, dyed and greasy and parted in the middle, a phony Hitler moustache, thrift-shop clothes that didn't fit. And his skin didn't look right somehow, like he was wearing makeup over a face that hadn't seen the light of day in ages. But Whitey was right. It was Juano. He had waited on Macklin too many times at that little Mexican restaurant over in East L.A., Mama Something's. Yes, that was it, Mama Carnita's on Whittier Boulevard. Macklin and his friends, including Whitey, had eaten there maybe fifty or a hundred times, back when they were taking classes at Cal State. It was Juano for sure.

Whitey set his things on the counter. "How's it going, man?" he said.

"Thank you," said Juano.

Macklin laid out the rest and reached for his money. The milk made a lumpy sound when he let go of it. He gave the carton a shake. "Forget this," he said. "It's gone sour." Then, "Haven't seen you around, old buddy. Juano, wasn't it?"

"Sorry. Sorry," said Juano. He sounded dazed, like a sleepwalker.

Whitey wouldn't give up. "Hey, they still make that good *menudo* over there?" He dug in his jeans for change. "God, I could eat about a gallon of it right now, I bet."

They were both waiting. The seconds ticked by. A radio in the store was playing an old 60s song. *Light My Fire*, Macklin thought. The Doors. "You remember me, don't you? Jim Macklin." He held out his hand. "And my trusted Indian companion, Whitey? He used to come in there with me on Tuesdays and Thursdays."

The clerk dragged his feet to the register, then turned back, turned again. His eyes were half-closed. "Sorry," he said. "Sorry. Please."

Macklin tossed down the bills, and Whitey counted his coins and slapped them onto the countertop. "Thanks," said Whitey, his upper lip curling back. He hooked a thumb in the direction of the door. "Come on. This place gives me the creeps."

As he left, Macklin caught a whiff of Juano or whoever he was. The scent was sickeningly sweet, like a gilded lily. His hair? Macklin felt a cold draft blow through his chest, and shuddered; the air conditioning, he thought.

At the door, Whitey spun around and glared.

"So what," said Macklin. "Let's go."

"What time does Tube City here close?"

"Never. Forget it." He touched his friend's arm.

"The hell I will," said Whitey. "I'm coming back when they change fucking shifts. About six o'clock, right? I'm going to be standing right there in the parking lot when he walks out. That son of a bitch still owes me twenty bucks."

"Please," muttered the man behind the counter, his eyes fixed on nothing. "Please. Sorry. Thank you."

The call came around ten. At first he thought it was a gag; he propped his eyelids up and peeked around the apartment, half-expecting to find Whitey still there, curled up asleep among the loaded ashtrays and pinched beer cans. But it was no joke.

"Okay, okay, I'll be right there," he grumbled, not yet comprehending, and hung up the phone.

St. John's Hospital on 14th. In the lobby, families milled about, dressed as if on their way to church, watching the elevators and waiting obediently for the clock to signal the start of visiting hours. Business hours, thought Macklin. He got the room number from the desk and went on up.

A police officer stood stiffly in the hall, taking notes on an accident report form. Macklin got the story from him and from an irritatingly healthy-looking doctor—the official story—and found himself, against his will, believing in it. In some of it.

His friend had been in an accident, sometime after dawn. His friend's car, the old VW, had gone over an embankment, not far from the Arroyo Seco. His friend had been found near the wreckage, covered with blood and reeking of alcohol. His friend had been drunk.

"Let's see here now. Any living relatives?" asked the officer. "All we could get out of him was your name. He was in a pretty bad state of shock, they tell me."

"No relatives," said Macklin. "Maybe back on the reservation. I don't know. I'm not even sure where the—"

A long, angry rumble of thunder sounded outside the windows. A steely light reflected off the clouds and filtered into the corridor. It mixed with the fluorescents in the ceiling, rendering the hospital interior a hard-edged, silvery gray. The faces of the policeman and the passing nurses took on a shaded, unnatural cast.

It made no sense. Whitey couldn't have been that drunk when he left Macklin's apartment. Of course he did not actually remember his friend leaving. But Whitey was going to the Stop 'N Start if he was going anywhere, not halfway across the county to—where? Arroyo Seco? It was crazy.

"Did you say there was liquor in the car?"

"Afraid so. We found an empty fifth of Jack Daniel's wedged between the seats."

But Macklin knew he didn't keep anything hard at his place, and neither did Whitey, he was sure. Where was he supposed to have gotten it, with every liquor counter in the state shut down for the night?

And then it hit him. Whitey never, but never drank sour mash whiskey. In fact, Whitey never drank anything stronger than beer, anytime, anyplace. Because he couldn't. It was supposed to have something to do with his liver, as it did with other Amerinds. He just didn't have the right enzymes.

Macklin waited for the uniforms and coats to move away, then ducked inside.

"Whitey," he said slowly.

For there he was, set up against firm pillows, the upper torso and most of the hand bandaged. The arms were bare, except for an ID bracelet and an odd pattern of zigzag lines from wrist to shoulder. The lines seemed to have been painted by an unsteady hand, using a pale gray dye of some kind.

"Call me by my name," said Whitey groggily. "It's White Feather."

He was probably shot full of painkillers. But at least he was okay. Wasn't he? "So what's with the war paint, old buddy?"

"I saw the Death Angel last night."

Macklin faltered. "I—I hear you're getting out of here real soon," he tried. "You know, you almost had me worried there. But I reckon you're just not ready for the bone orchard yet."

"Did you hear what I said?"

"What? Uh, yeah. Yes." What had they shot him up with?

Macklin cleared his throat and met his friend's eyes, which were focused beyond him. "What was it, a dream?"

"A dream," said Whitey. The eyes were glazed, burned out.

What happened? Whitey, he thought. Whitey. "You put that war paint on yourself?" he said gently.

"It's pHisoHex," said Whitey, "mixed with lead pencil. I put it on, the nurse washes it off, I put it on again."

"I see." He didn't, but went on. "So tell me what happened, partner. I couldn't get much out of the doctor."

The mouth smiled humorlessly, the lips cracking back from the teeth. "It was Juano," said Whitey. He started to laugh bitterly. He touched his ribs and stopped himself.

Macklin nodded, trying to get the drift. "Did you tell that to the cop out there?"

"Sure. Cops always believe a drunken Indian. Didn't you know that?"

"Look. I'll take care of Juano. Don't worry."

Whitey laughed suddenly in a high voice that Macklin had never heard before. "*He-he-he!* What are you going to do, kill him?"

"I don't know," he said, trying to think in spite of the clattering in the hall.

"They make a living from death, you know," said Whitey.

Just then a nurse swept into the room, pulling a cart behind her.

"How did you get in here?" she demanded.

"I'm just having a conversation with my friend here."

"Well, you'll have to leave. He's scheduled for surgery this afternoon."

"Do you know about the Trial of the Dead?" asked Whitey.

"Shh, now," said the nurse. "You can talk to your friend as long as you want to, later."

"I want to know," said Whitey, as she prepared a syringe.

"What is it we want to know, now?" she said, preoccupied. "What dead? Where?"

"Where?" repeated Whitey. "Why, here, of course. The dead are here. Aren't they." It was a statement. "Tell me something. What do you do with them?"

"Now what nonsense . . . ?" The nurse swabbed his arm, clucking at the ritual lines on the skin.

"I'm asking you a question," said Whitey.

"Look, I'll be outside," said Macklin, "okay?"

"This is for you, too," said Whitey. "I want you to hear. Now if you'll just tell us, Miss Nurse. What do you do with the people who die in here?"

"Would you please—"

"I can't hear you." Whitey drew his arm away from her.

She sighed. "We take them downstairs. Really, this is most . . ."

But Whitey kept looking at her, nailing her with those expressionless eyes.

"Oh, the remains are tagged and kept in cold storage," she said, humoring him. "Until arrangements can be made with the family for services. There now, can we—?"

"But what happens? Between the time they become 'remains' and the services? How long is that? A couple of days? Three?"

She lost patience and plunged the needle into the arm.

"Listen," said Macklin, "I'll be around if you need me. And hey, buddy," he added, "we're going to have everything all set up for you when this is over. You'll see. A party, I swear. I can go and get them to send up a TV right now, at least."

"Like a bicycle for a fish," said Whitey.

Macklin attempted a laugh. "You take it easy, now."

And then he heard it again, that high, strange voice. *"He-he-he! ta munka sni kun."*

Macklin needed suddenly to be out of there.

"Jim?"

"What?"

"I was wrong about something last night."

"Yeah?"

"Sure was. That place wasn't Tube City. This is. *He-he-he!*"

That's funny, thought Macklin, like an open grave. He walked out. The last thing he saw was the nurse bending over Whitey, drawing her syringe of blood like an old-fashioned phlebotomist.

. . .

All he could find out that afternoon was that the operation wasn't critical, and there would be additional X-rays, tests and a period of "observation," though when pressed for details the hospital remained predictably vague no matter how he put the questions.

Instead of killing time, he made for the Stop 'N Start.

He stood around until the store was more or less empty, then approached the counter. The manager, whom Macklin knew slightly, was working the register himself.

Raphael stonewalled Macklin at the first mention of Juano; his beady eyes receded into glacial ignorance. No, the night man was named Dom or Don; he mumbled so that Macklin couldn't be sure. No, Don (or Dom) had been working here for six, seven months; no, no, no.

Until Macklin came up with the magic word: police.

After a few minutes of bobbing and weaving, it started to come out. Raphe sounded almost scared, yet relieved to be able to talk about it to someone, even to Macklin.

"They bring me these guys, my friend," whispered Raphe. "I don't got nothing to do with it, believe me.

"The way it seems to me, it's company policy for all the stores, not just me. Sometimes they call and say to lay off my regular boy, you know, on the graveyard shift. 'Specially when there's been a lot of holdups. Hell, that's right by me. I don't want Dom shot up. He's my best man!

"See, I put the hours down on Dom's pay so it comes out right with the taxes, but he has to kick it back. It don't even go on his check. Then the district office, they got to pay the outfit that supplies these guys, only they don't give 'em the regular wage. I don't know if they're wetbacks or what. I hear they only get maybe $1.25 an hour, or at least the outfit that brings 'em in does, so the office is making money. You know how many stores, how many shifts that adds up to?

"Myself, I'm damn glad they only use 'em after dark, late, when things can get hairy for an all-night man. It's the way they look. But you already seen one, this Juano-Whatever. So you know. Right? You know something else, my friend? They *all* look messed up.".

Macklin noticed goose bumps forming on Raphe's arms.

"But I don't personally know nothing about it."

They, thought Macklin, poised outside the Stop 'N Start. Sure enough, like clockwork They had brought Juano to work at midnight. Right on schedule. With raw, burning eyes he had watched Them do something to Juano's shirt front and then point him at the door and let go. What did They do, wind him up? But They would be back. Macklin was sure of that. They, whoever They were. The Paranoid They.

Well, he was sure as hell going to find out who They were now.

He popped another Dexamyl and swallowed dry until it stayed down.

Threats didn't work any better than questions with Juano himself. Macklin had had to learn that the hard way. The guy was so sublimely creepy it was all he could do to swivel back and forth between register and counter, slithering a hyaline hand over the change machine in the face of the most outraged customers, like Macklin, giving out with only the same pathetic, wheezing *please, please, sorry, thank you,* like a stretched cassette tape on its last loop.

Which had sent Macklin back to the car with exactly no options, nothing to do that might jar the nightmare loose except to pound the steering wheel and curse and dream redder and redder dreams of revenge. He had burned rubber between the parking lot and Sweeney Todd's Pub, turning over two pints of John Courage and a shot of Irish whiskey before he could think clearly enough to waste another dime calling the hospital, or even to look at his watch.

At six o'clock They would be back for Juano. And then. He would. Find out.

Two or three hours in the all-night movie theatre downtown, merging with the shadows on the tattered screen. The popcorn girl wiping stains off her uniform. The ticket girl staring through him, and again when he left. Something about her. He tried to think. Something about the people who work night owl shifts anywhere. He remembered faces down the years. It didn't matter what they looked like. The nightwalkers, insomniacs, addicts, those without the money for a cheap hotel, they would always come back to the only game in town. They had no choice. It didn't matter that the ticket girl was messed up. It didn't matter that Juano was messed up. Why should it?

A blue van glided into the lot.

The Stop 'N Start sign dimmed, paling against the coming morning. The van braked. A man in rumpled clothes climbed out. There was a second figure in the front seat. The driver unlocked the back doors, silencing the birds that were gathering in the trees. The he entered the store.

Macklin watched. Juano was led out. The a.m. relief man stood by shaking his head.

Macklin hesitated. He wanted Juano, but what could he do now? What the hell had he been waiting for, exactly? There was still something else, something else . . . It was like the glimpse of a shape under a sheet in a busy corridor. You didn't know what it was at first, but it was there; you knew what it might be, but you couldn't be sure, not until you got close and stayed next to it long enough to be able to read its true form.

The driver helped Juano into the van. He locked the doors, started the engine and drove away.

Macklin, his lights out, followed.

He stayed with the van as it snaked a path across the city, nearer and nearer the foothills. The sides were unmarked, but he figured it must operate like one of those minibus porta-maid services he had seen leaving Malibu and Bel-Air late in the afternoon, or like the loads of kids trucked in to push magazine subscriptions and phony charities in the neighborhoods near where he lived.

The sky was still black, beginning to turn slate close to the horizon. Once they passed a garbage collector already on his rounds. Macklin kept his distance.

They led him finally to a street that dead-ended at a

construction site. Macklin idled by the corner, then saw the van turn back.

He let them pass, cruised to the end and made a slow turn.

Then he saw the van returning.

He pretended to park. He looked up.

They had stopped the van crosswise in front of him, blocking his passage.

The man in rumpled clothes jumped out and opened Macklin's door.

Macklin started to get out but was pushed back.

"You think you're a big enough man to be trailing people around?"

Macklin tried to penetrate the beam of the flashlight. "I saw my old friend Juano get into your truck," he began. "Didn't get a chance to talk to him. Thought I might as well follow him home and see what he's been up to."

The other man got out of the front seat of the van. He was younger, delicate-boned. He stood on one side, listening.

"I saw him get in," said Macklin, "back at the Stop 'N Start on Pico?" He groped under the seat for the tire iron. "I was driving by and—"

"Get out."

"What?"

"We saw you. Out of the car."

He shrugged and swung his legs around, lifting the iron behind him as he stood.

The younger man motioned with his head and the driver yanked Macklin forward by the shirt, kicking the door closed on Macklin's arm at the same time. He let out a yell as the tire iron clanged to the pavement.

"Another accident?" suggested the younger man.

"Too messy, after the one yesterday. Come on, pal, you're going to get to see your friend."

Macklin hunched over in pain. One of them jerked his bad arm up and he screamed. Over it all he felt a needle jab him high, in the armpit, and then he was falling.

The van was bumping along on the freeway when he came

out of it. With his good hand he pawed his face, trying to clear his vision. His other arm didn't hurt, but it wouldn't move when he wanted it to.

He was sprawled on his back. He felt a wheel humming under him, below the tirewell. And there were the others. They were sitting up. One was Juano.

He was aware of a stink, sickeningly sweet, with an overlay he remembered from his high school lab days but couldn't quite place. It sliced into his nostrils.

He didn't recognize the others. Pasty faces. Heads thrown forward, arms distended strangely with the wrists jutting out from the coat sleeves.

"Give me a hand," he said, not really expecting it.

He strained to sit up. He could make out the backs of two heads in the cab, on the other side of the grid.

He dropped his voice to a whisper. "Hey. Can you guys understand me?"

"Let us rest," someone said weakly.

He rose too quickly and his equilibrium failed. He had been shot up with something strong enough to knock him out, but it was probably the Dexamyl that had kept his mind from leaving his body completely. The van yawed, descending an off ramp, and he began to drift. He heard voices. They slipped in and out of his consciousness like fish in darkness, moving between his ears in blurred levels he could not always identify.

"There's still room at the cross." That was the younger, small-boned man, he was almost sure.

"Oh, I've been interested in Jesus for a long time, but I never could get a handle on him . . ."

"Well, beware the wrath to come. You really should, you know."

He put his head back and became one with a dark dream. There was something he wanted to remember. He did not want to remember it. He turned his mind to doggerel, to the old song. *The time to hesitate is through,* he thought. *No time to wallow in the mire. Try now we can only lose / And our love become a funeral pyre.* The van bumped to a halt. His head bounced off steel.

The door opened. He watched it. It seemed to take forever.

Through slitted eyes: a man in a uniform that barely fit, hobbling his way to the back of the van, supported by the two of them. A line of gasoline pumps and a sign that read we never close—never undersold. The letters breathed. Before they let go of him, the one with rumpled clothes unbuttoned the attendant's shirt and stabbed a hypodermic into the chest, close to the heart and next to a strap that ran under the arms. The needle darted and flashed dully in the wan morning light.

"This one needs a booster," said the driver, or maybe it was the other one. Their voices ran together. "Just make sure you don't give him the same stuff you gave old Juano's sweetheart there. I want them to walk in on their own hind legs." "You think I want to carry 'em?" "We've done it before, brother. Yesterday, for instance." At that Macklin let his eyelids down the rest of the way, and then he was drifting again.

The wheels drummed under him.

"How much longer?" "Soon now. Soon."

These voices weak, like a folding and unfolding of paper.

Brakes grabbed. The doors opened again. A thin light played over Macklin's lids, forcing them up.

He had another moment of clarity; they were becoming more frequent now. He blinked and felt pain. This time the van was parked between low hills. Two men in Western costumes passed by, one of them leading a horse. The driver stopped a group of figures in togas. He seemed to be asking for directions.

Behind them, a castle lay in ruins. Part of a castle. And over to the side Macklin identified a church steeple, the corner of a turn-of-the-century street, a mock-up of a rocket launching pad and an old brick schoolhouse. Under the flat sky they receded into intersections of angles and vistas which teetered almost imperceptibly, ready to topple.

The driver and the other one set a stretcher on the tailgate. On the litter was a long, crumpled shape, sheeted and encased in a plastic bag. They sloughed it inside and started to secure the doors.

"You got the pacemaker back, I hope." "Stunt director said it's in the body bag." "It better be. Or it's our ass in a sling. Your ass. How'd he get so racked up, anyway?" "Ran him over a cliff in a sports car. Or no, maybe this one was the head-on they staged for, you know, that new cop series. That's what they want now, realism. Good thing he's a cremation—ain't no way Kelly or Dee's gonna get this one pretty again by tomorrow." "That's why, man. That's why they picked him. Ashes don't need makeup."

The van started up.

"Going home," someone said weakly.

"Yes . . ."

Macklin was awake now. Crouching by the bag, he scanned the faces, Juano's and the others'. The eyes were staring, fixed on a point as untouchable as the thinnest of plasma membranes, and quite unreadable.

He crawled over next to the one from the self-service gas station. The shirt hung open like folds of skin. He saw the silver box strapped to the flabby chest, directly over the heart. Pacemaker? he thought wildly.

He knelt and put his ear to the box.

He heard a humming, like an electric wristwatch.

What for? To keep the blood pumping just enough so the tissues don't rigor mortis and decay? For God's sake, for how much longer?

He remembered Whitey and the nurse. *"What happens? Between the time they become 'remains' and the services? How long is that? A couple of days? Three?"*

A wave of nausea broke inside him. When he gazed at them again the faces were wavering, because his eyes were filled with tears.

"Where are we?" he asked.

"I wish you could be here," said the gas station attendant.

"And where is that?"

"We have all been here before," said another voice.

"Going home," said another.

Yes, he thought, understanding. Soon you will have your rest; soon you will no longer be objects, commodities. You will be honored and grieved for and your personhood given back, and then you will at last rest in peace. It is not for nothing that you have labored so long and so patiently. You will see, all of you. Soon.

He wanted to tell them, but he couldn't. He hoped they already knew.

The van lurched and slowed. The hand brake ratcheted.

He lay down and closed his eyes.

He heard the door creak back.

"Let's go."

The driver began to herd the bodies out. There was the sound of heavy, dragging feet, and from outside the smell of fresh-cut grass and roses.

"What about this one?" said the driver, kicking Macklin's shoe.

"Oh, he'll do his forty-eight-hours' service, don't worry. It's called utilizing your resources."

"Tell me about it. When do we get the Indian?"

"Soon as St. John's certificates him. He's overdue. The crash was sloppy."

"This one won't be. But first Dee'll want him to talk, what he knows and who he told. Two doggers in two days is too much. Then we'll probably run him back to his car and do it. And phone it in, so St. John's gets him. Even if it's DOA. Clean as hammered shit. Grab the other end."

He felt the body bag sliding against his leg. Grunting, they hauled it out and hefted it toward—where?

He opened his eyes. He hesitated only a second, to take a deep breath.

Then he was out of the van and running.

Gravel kicked up under his feet. He heard curses and metal slamming. He just kept his head down and his legs pumping. Once he twisted around and saw a man scurrying after him. The driver paused by the mortuary building and shouted. But Macklin kept moving.

He stayed on the path as long as he dared. It led him past mossy trees and bird-stained statues. Then he jumped and cut across a carpet of matted leaves and into a glade. He passed a gate that spelled DRY LAWN CEMETERY in old iron, kept running until he spotted a break in the fence where it sloped by the edge of the grounds. He tore through huge, dusty ivy and skidded down, down. And then he was on a sidewalk.

Cars revved at a wide intersection, impatient to get to work. He heard coughing and footsteps, but it was only a bus stop at the middle of the block. The air brakes of a commuter special hissed and squealed. A clutch of grim people rose from the bench and filed aboard like sleepwalkers.

He ran for it, but the doors flapped shut and the bus roared on.

More people at the corner, stepping blindly between each other. He hurried and merged with them.

Dry cleaners, laundromat, hamburger stand, parking lot, gas station, all closed. But there was a telephone at the gas station.

He ran against the light. He sealed the booth behind him and nearly collapsed against the glass.

He rattled money into the phone, dialed Operator and called for the police.

The air was close in the booth. He smelled hair tonic. Sweat swelled out of his pores and glazed his skin. Somewhere a radio was playing.

A sergeant punched onto the line. Macklin yelled for them to come and get him. Where was he? He looked around frantically, but there were no street signs. Only a newspaper rack chained to a post. NONE OF THE DEAD HAS BEEN IDENTIFIED, read the headline.

His throat tightened, his voice racing. "None of the dead has been identified," he said, practically babbling.

Silence.

So he went ahead, pouring it out about a van and a hospital and a man in rumpled clothes who shot guys up with some kind of super-adrenaline and electric pacemakers and nightclerks and crash tests. He struggled to get it all out before it was too late. A part of him heard what he was saying and wondered if he had lost his mind.

"Who will bury them?" he cried. "What kind of monsters—"

The line clicked off.

He hung onto the phone. His eyes were swimming with

sweat. He was aware of his heart and counted the beats, while the moisture from his breath condensed on the glass.

He dropped another coin into the box.

"Good morning, St. John's, may I help you?"

He couldn't remember the room number. He described the man, the accident, the date. Sixth floor, yes, that was right. He kept talking until she got it.

There was a pause. Hold.

He waited.

"Sir?"

He didn't say anything. It was as if he had no words left.

"I'm terribly sorry . . ."

He felt the blood drain from him. His fingers were cold and numb.

". . . But I'm afraid the surgery wasn't successful. The party did not recover. If you wish I'll connect you with—"

"The party's name was White Feather," he said mechanically. The receiver fell and dangled, swinging like the pendulum of a clock.

He braced his legs against the sides of the booth. After what seemed like a very long time he found himself reaching reflexively for his cigarettes. He took one from the crushed pack, straightened it and hung it on his lips.

On the other side of the frosted glass, featureless shapes lumbered by on the boulevard. He watched them for a while.

He picked up a book of matches from the floor, lit two together and held them close to the glass. The flame burned a clear spot through the moisture.

Try to set the night on fire, he thought stupidly, repeating the words until they and any others he could think of lost meaning.

The fire started to burn his fingers. He hardly felt it. He ignited the matchbook cover, too, turning it over and over. He wondered if there was anything else that would burn, anything and everything. He squeezed his eyelids together. When he opened them, he was looking down at his own clothing.

He peered out through the clear spot in the glass.

Outside, the outline fuzzy and distorted but quite unmistakable, was a blue van. It was waiting at the curb.

THOMAS LIGOTTI

Thomas Ligotti was born in Detroit in 1953. While working for Gale Research Company, he began publishing his short fiction in small-press magazines such as *Nyctalops, Eldritch Tales,* and *Fantasy Tales,* and his first volume, *Songs of a Dead Dreamer,* was published in 1986 with little fanfare by Silver Scarab Press, although it contained an enthusiastic introduction by British supernaturalist Ramsey Campbell. But Ligotti's reputation slowly grew by word-of-mouth, and in 1989 his first volume was republished in an expanded edition in England. Since then, Ligotti has issued further volumes of short stories, including *Grimscribe: His Lives and Works* (1991), *Noctuary* (1994), and *My Work Is Not Yet Done* (2002). *The Nightmare Factory* (1996) is an omnibus of his first three collections.

Ligotti, although influenced by Edgar Allan Poe, H. P. Lovecraft, and other writers of the American supernatural tradition, has developed a highly original and distinctive approach to the field, fusing psychological and supernatural tropes to create a nightmarish world of terror in which almost anything can occur. His subject matter is bolstered by an idiosyncratic and occasionally difficult and obscure style that seeks to destroy the distinction between the real and the imaginary. Ligotti has professed that he cannot write horror novels and that the supernatural is in fact incapable of being cogently expressed in the novel form; accordingly, in spite of the fact that the title story of *My Work Is Not Yet Done* is a novella of more than thirty thousand words, Ligotti has adhered to short fiction, passing up the possibility of broader popular recognition and seemingly content with the admiration of a small band of cognoscenti. Ligotti has also written provocatively about the horror story, both in interviews and in such essays as "The Consolations of Horror" (1989). He now lives in Florida.

"Vastarien" (first published in *Crypt of Cthulhu*, St. John's Eve 1987, and included in *Songs of a Dead Dreamer*, 1989) is representative of Ligotti's eccentric work in its elaboration of H. P. Lovecraft's concept of the "forbidden book" that can lead to death or madness.

VASTARIEN

Within the blackness of his sleep a few lights began to glow like candles in a cloistered cell. Their illumination was unsteady and dim, issuing from no definite source. Nonetheless, he now discovered many shapes beneath the shadows: tall buildings whose rooftops nodded groundward, wide buildings whose facades seemed to follow the curve of a street, dark buildings whose windows and doorways tilted like badly hung paintings. And even if he found himself unable to fix his own location in this scene, he knew where his dreams had delivered him once more.

Even as the warped structures multiplied in his vision, crowding the lost distance, he possessed a sense of intimacy with each of them, a peculiar knowledge of the spaces within them and of the streets which coiled themselves around their mass. Once again he knew the depths of their foundations, where an obscure life seemed to establish itself, a secret civilization of echoes flourishing among groaning walls. Yet upon his probing more extensively into such interiors, certain difficulties presented themselves: stairways that wandered off-course into useless places; caged elevators that urged unwanted stops on their passengers; then ladders ascending into a maze of shafts and conduits, the dark valves and arteries of a petrified and monstrous organism.

And he knew that every corner of this corroded world was prolific with choices, even if they had to be made blindly in a place where clear consequences and a hierarchy of possibilities were lacking. For there might be a room whose shabby and soundless decor exudes a desolate serenity which at first attracts the visitor, who then discovers certain figures enveloped in plush furniture, figures that do not move or speak but only stare; and, concluding that these weary mannikins have exercised a bizarre indulgence in repose, the visitor must ponder the alternatives: to linger or to leave?

Eluding the claustral enchantments of such rooms, his gaze now roamed the streets of this dream. He scanned the altitudes beyond the high sloping roofs: there the stars seemed to be no more than silvery cinders which showered up from the mouths of great chimneys and clung to something dark and dense looming above, something that closed in upon each black horizon. It appeared to him that certain high towers nearly breached this sagging blackness, stretching themselves nightward to attain the farthest possible remove from the world below. And toward the peak of one of the highest towers he spied vague silhouettes that moved hectically in a bright window, twisting and leaning upon the glass like shadow-puppets in the fever of some mad dispute.

Through the mazy streets his vision slowly glided, as if carried along by a sluggish draft. Darkened windows reflected the beams of stars and streetlamps; lighted windows, however dim their glow, betrayed strange scenes which were left behind long before their full mystery could overwhelm the dreaming traveller. He wandered into thoroughfares more remote, soaring past cluttered gardens and crooked gates, drifting alongside an expansive wall that seemed to border an abyss, and floating over bridges that arched above the black purling waters of canals.

Near a certain street corner, a place of supernatural clarity and stillness, he saw two figures standing beneath the crystalline glaze of a lamp ensconced high upon a wall of carved stone. Their shadows were perfect columns of blackness upon the livid pavement; their faces were a pair of faded masks concealing profound schemes. And they seemed to have lives of their own, with no awareness of their dreaming observer, who wished only to live with these specters and know *their* dreams, to remain in this place where everything was transfixed in the order of the unreal.

Never again, it seemed, could he be forced to abandon this realm of beautiful shadows.

Victor Keirion awoke with a brief convulsion of his limbs, as if he had been chaotically scrambling to break his fall from an imaginary height. For a moment he held his eyes closed, hoping to preserve the dissipating euphoria of the dream. Finally he blinked once or twice. Moonlight through a curtainless window allowed him the image of his outstretched arms and his somewhat twisted hands. Releasing his awkward hold on the edge of the sheeted mattress, he rolled onto his back. Then he groped around until his fingers found the cord dangling from the light above the bed. A small, barely furnished room appeared.

He pushed himself up and reached toward the painted metal nightstand. Through the spaces between his fingers he saw the pale gray binding of a book and some of the dark letters tooled upon its cover: V, S, R, N. Suddenly he withdrew his hand without touching the book, for the magical intoxication of the dream had died, and he feared that he would not be able to revive it.

Freeing himself from the coarse bedcovers, he sat at the edge of the mattress, elbows resting on his legs and hands loosely folded. His hair and eyes were pale, his complexion rather grayish, suggesting the color of certain clouds or that of long confinement. The single window in the room was only a few steps away, but he kept himself from approaching it, from even glancing in its direction. He knew exactly what he would see at that time of night: tall buildings, wide buildings, dark buildings, a scattering of stars and lights, and some lethargic movement in the streets below.

In so many ways the city outside the window was a semblance of that other place, which now seemed impossibly far off and inaccessible. But the likeness was evident only to his inner vision, only in the recollected images he formed when his eyes were closed or out of focus. It would be difficult to conceive of a creature for whom *this* world—its bare form seen with open eyes—represented a coveted paradise.

Now standing before the window, his hands tearing into the pockets of a papery bathrobe, he saw that something was missing from the view, some crucial property that was denied to the stars above and the streets below, some unearthly essence needed to save them. The word *unearthly* reverberated in the room. In that place and at that hour, the paradoxical absence, the missing quality, became clear to him: it was the element of the unreal.

For Victor Keirion belonged to that wretched sect of souls who believe that the only value of this world lies in its power—at certain times—to suggest another world. Nevertheless, the place he now surveyed through the high window could never be anything but the most gauzy phantom of that other place, nothing save a shadowy mimic of the anatomy of that great dream. And although there were indeed times when one might be deceived, isolated moments when a gift for disguise triumphs, the impersonation could never be perfect or lasting. No true challenge to the rich unreality of Vastarien, where every shape suggested a thousand others, every sound disseminated everlasting echoes, every word founded a world. No horror, no joy was the equal of the abysmally vibrant sensations known in this place that was elsewhere, this spellbinding retreat where all experiences were interwoven to compose fantastic textures of feeling, a fine and dark tracery of limitless patterns. For everything in the unreal points to the infinite, and everything in Vastarien was unreal, unbounded by the tangible lie of existing. Even its most humble aspects proclaimed this truth: what door, he wondered, in any other world could imply the abundant and strange possibilities that belonged to the entrancing doors in the dream?

Then, as he focused his eyes upon a distant part of the city, he recalled a particular door, one of the least suggestive objects he had ever confronted, intimating little of what lay beyond.

It was a rectangle of smudged glass within another rectangle of scuffed wood, a battered thing lodged within a brick wall at the bottom of a stairway leading down from a crumbling street. And it pushed easily inward, merely a delicate formality between the underground shop and the outside world. Inside was an open room vaguely circular in shape, unusual in seeming more like the lobby of an old hotel than a bookstore. The circumference of the room was composed of crowded bookshelves whose separate sections were joined to one another to create an irregular polygon of eleven sides, with a long desk standing where a twelfth would have been. Beyond the desk stood a few more bookshelves arranged in aisles, their monotonous length leading into shadows. At the furthest point from this end of the shop, he began his circuit of the shelves, which appeared so promising in their array of old and ruddy bindings, like remnants of some fabulous autumn.

Very soon, however, the promise was betrayed and the mystique of the Librairie de Grimoires, in accord with his expectations, was stripped away to reveal, in his eyes, a side-show of charlatanry. For this disillusionment he had only himself to blame. Moreover, he could barely articulate the nature of the discrepancy between what he had hoped to find and what he actually found in such places. Aside from this hope, there was little basis for his belief that there existed some other arcana, one of a different kind altogether from that proffered by the books before him, all of which were sodden with an obscene reality, falsely hermetic ventures which consisted of circling the same absurd landscape. The other worlds portrayed in these books inevitably served as annexes of this one; they were impostors of the authentic unreality which was the only realm of redemption, however gruesome it might appear. And it was this *terminal* landscape that he sought, not those rituals of the "way" that never arrives, heavens or hells that are mere pretexts for circumnavigating the real and revelling in it. For he dreamed of strange volumes that turned away from all earthly light to become lost in their own nightmares, pages that preached a nocturnal salvation, a liturgy of shadows, catechism of phantoms. His absolute: to dwell among the ruins of reality.

And it seemed to surpass all probability that there existed no precedent for this dream, no elaboration of this vision into a word, a delirious bible that would be the blight of all others—a scripture that would begin in apocalypse and lead its disciple to the wreck of all creation.

He had, in fact, come upon passages in certain books that approached this ideal, hinting to the reader—almost admonishing him—that the page before his eyes was about to offer a view from the abyss and cast a wavering light on desolate hallucinations. *To become the wind in the dead of winter,* so might begin an enticing verse of dreams. But soon the bemazed visionary would falter, retracting the promised scene of a shadow kingdom at the end of all entity, perhaps offering an apologetics for this lapse into the unreal. The work would then once more take up the universal theme, disclosing its true purpose in belaboring the most futile and profane of all ambitions: power, with knowledge as its drudge. The vision of a disastrous enlightenment, of a catastrophic illumination, was conjured up in passing and then cast aside. What remained was invariably a metaphysics as systematically trivial and debased as the physical laws it purported to transcend, a manual outlining the path to some hypothetical state of absolute glory. What remained *lost* was the revelation that nothing ever known has ended in glory; that all which ends does so in exhaustion, in confusion, and debris.

Nevertheless, a book that contained even a false gesture toward his truly eccentric absolute might indeed serve his purpose. Directing the attention of a bookseller to selected contents of such books, he would say: "I have an interest in a certain subject area, perhaps you will see . . . that is, I wonder, do you know of other, what should I say, *sources* that you would be able to recommend for my. . . ."

Occasionally he was referred to another bookseller or to the owner of a private collection. And ultimately he would be forced to realize that he had been grotesquely misunderstood when he found himself on the fringe of a society devoted to some strictly demonic enterprise.

The very bookshop in which he was now browsing represented only the most recent digression in a search without progress.

But he had learned to be cautious and would try to waste as little time as possible in discovering if there was anything hidden for him here. Certainly not on the shelves which presently surrounded him.

"Have you seen our friend?" asked a nearby voice, startling him somewhat. Victor Keirion turned to face the stranger. The man was rather small and wore a black overcoat; his hair was also black and fell loosely across his forehead. Besides his general appearance, there was also something about his presence that made one think of a crow, a scavenging creature in wait. "Has he come out of his hole?" the man asked, gesturing toward the empty desk and the dark area behind it.

"I'm sorry, I haven't seen anyone," Keirion replied. "I only now noticed you."

"I can't help being quiet. Look at these little feet," the man said, pointing to a highly polished pair of black shoes. Without thinking, Keirion looked down; then, feeling duped, he looked up again at the smiling stranger.

"You look very bored," said the human crow.

"I'm sorry?"

"Never mind. I can see that I'm bothering you." Then the man walked away, his coat flapping slightly, and began browsing some distant bookshelves. "I've never seen you in here before," he said from across the room.

"I've never been in here before," Keirion answered.

"Have you ever read this?" the stranger asked, pulling down a book and holding up its wordless black cover.

"Never," Keirion replied without so much as glancing at the book. Somehow this seemed the best action to take with this character, who appeared to be foreign in some indefinable way, intangibly alien.

"Well, you must be looking for something special," continued the other man, replacing the black book on its shelf. "And I know what that's like, when you're looking for something very special. Have you ever heard of a book, an extremely special book, that is not . . . yes, that is not *about* something, but actually is that something?"

For the first time the obnoxious stranger had managed to

intrigue Keirion rather than annoy him. "That sounds . . . ," he started to say, but then the other man exclaimed:

"There he is, there he is. Excuse me."

It seemed that the proprietor—that mutual friend—had finally made his appearance and was now standing behind the desk, looking toward his two customers. "My friend," said the crow-man as he stepped with outstretched hand over to the smoothly bald and softly fat gentleman. The two of them briefly shook hands; they whispered for a few moments. Then the crow-man was invited behind the desk, and—led by the heavy, unsmiling bookseller—made his way into the darkness at the back of the shop. In a distant corner of that darkness the brilliant rectangle of a doorway suddenly flashed into outline, admitting through its frame a large, two-headed shadow.

Left alone among the worthless volumes of that shop, Victor Keirion felt the sad frustration of the uninvited, the abandoned. More than ever he had become infected with hopes and curiosities of an indeterminable kind. And he soon found it impossible to remain outside that radiant little room the other two had entered, and on whose threshold he presently stood in silence.

The room was a cramped bibliographic cubicle within which stood another cubicle formed by free-standing bookcases, creating four very narrow aisleways in the space between them. From the doorway he could not see how the inner cubicle might be entered, but he heard the voices of the others whispering within. Stepping quietly, he began making his way along the perimeter of the room, his eyes voraciously scanning a wealth of odd-looking volumes.

Immediately he sensed that something of a special nature awaited his discovery, and the evidence for this intuition began to build. Each book that he examined served as a clue in this delirious investigation, a cryptic sign which engaged his powers of interpretation and imparted the faith to proceed. Many of the works were written in foreign languages he did not read; some appeared to be composed in ciphers based on familiar characters and others seemed to be transcribed in a wholly artificial cryptography. But in every one of these books he found an oblique guidance, some feature of more or less indirect significance: a strangeness in the typeface, pages and bindings of uncommon texture, abstract diagrams suggesting no orthodox ritual or occult system. Even greater anticipation was inspired by certain illustrated plates, mysterious drawings and engravings that depicted scenes and situations unlike anything he could name. And such works as *Cynothoglys* or *The Noctuary of Tine* conveyed schemes so bizarre, so remote from known texts and treatises of the esoteric tradition, that he felt assured of the sense of his quest.

The whispering grew louder, though no more distinct, as he edged around a corner of that inner cubicle and anxiously noted the opening at its far end. At the same time he was distracted, for no apparent reason, by a small grayish volume leaning within a gap between larger and more garish tomes. The little book had been set upon the highest shelf, making it necessary for him to stretch himself, as if on an upright torture rack, to reach it. Trying not to give away his presence by the sounds of his pain, he finally secured the ashen-colored object—as pale as his own coloring—between the tips of his first two fingers. Mutely he strained to slide it quietly from its place; this act accomplished, he slowly shrunk down to his original stature and looked into the book's brittle pages.

It seemed to be a chronicle of strange dreams. Yet somehow the passages he examined were less a recollection of unruled visions than a tangible incarnation of them, not mere rhetoric but the thing itself. The use of language in the book was arrantly unnatural and the book's author unknown. Indeed, the text conveyed the impression of speaking for itself and speaking only to itself, the words flowing together like shadows that were cast by no forms outside the book. But although this volume appeared to be composed in a vernacular of mysteries, its words did inspire a sure understanding and created in their reader a visceral apprehension of the world they described, existing inseparable from it. Could this truly be the invocation of Vastarien, that improbable world to which those gnarled letters on the front of the book alluded? And was it a world at all? Rather the unreal essence of one, all natural elements purged by an occult process of extraction, all days distilled into dreams and nights into nightmares. Each passage he entered in the book both enchanted and appalled him with images and incidents so freakish and chaotic that his usual sense of these terms disintegrated along with everything else. Rampant oddity seemed to be the rule of the realm; imperfection became the source of the miraculous—wonders of deformity and marvels of miscreation. There was horror, undoubtedly. But it was a horror uncompromised by any feeling of lost joy or thwarted redemption; rather, it was a deliverance by damnation. And if Vastarien was a nightmare, it was a nightmare transformed in spirit by the utter absence of refuge: nightmare made normal.

"I'm sorry, I didn't see that you had drifted in here," said the bookseller in a high thin voice. He had just emerged from the inner chamber of the room and was standing with arms folded across his wide chest. "Please don't touch anything. And may I take that from you?" The right arm of the bookseller reached out, then returned to its former place when the man with the pale eyes did not relinquish the merchandise.

"I think I would like to purchase it," said Keirion. "I'm sure I would, if. . . ."

"Of course, if the price is reasonable," finished the bookseller. "But who knows, you might not be able to understand how valuable these books can be. That one . . . ," he said, removing a little pad and pencil from inside his jacket and scribbling briefly. He ripped off the top sheet and held it up for the would-be buyer to see, then confidently put away all writing materials, as if that would be the end of it.

"But there must be some latitude for bargaining," Keirion protested.

"I'm afraid not," answered the bookseller. "Not with something that is the only one of its kind, as are many of these volumes. Yet that one book you are holding, that single copy. . . ."

A hand touched the bookseller's shoulder and seemed to switch off his voice. Then the crow-man stepped into the aisleway, his eyes fixed upon the object under discussion, and asked: "Don't you find that the book is somewhat . . . difficult?"

"Difficult," repeated Keirion. "I'm not sure. . . . If you mean that the language is strange, I would have to agree, but—"

"No," interjected the bookseller, "that's not what he means at all."

"Excuse us a moment," said the crow-man.

Then both men went back into the inner room, where they whispered for some time. When the whispering ceased, the bookseller came forth and announced that there had been a mistake. The book, while something of a curiosity, was worth a good deal less than the price earlier quoted. The revised evaluation, while still costly, was nevertheless within the means of this particular buyer, who agreed at once to pay it.

Thus began Victor Keirion's preoccupation with a certain book and a certain hallucinated world, though to make a distinction between these two phenomena ultimately seemed an error: the book, indeed, did not merely describe that strange world but, in some obscure fashion, was a true composition of the thing itself, its very form incarnate.

Each day thereafter he studied the hypnotic episodes of the little book; each night, as he dreamed, he carried out shapeless expeditions into its fantastic topography. To all appearances it seemed he had discovered the summit or abyss of the unreal, that paradise of exhaustion, confusion, and debris where reality ends and where one may dwell among its ruins. And it was not long before he found it necessary to revisit that twelve-sided shop, intending to question the obese bookseller on the subject of the book and unintentionally learning the truth of how it came to be sold.

When he arrived at the bookstore, sometime in the middle of a grayish afternoon, Victor Keirion was surprised to find that the door, which had opened so freely on his previous visit, was now firmly locked. It would not even rattle in its frame when he nervously pushed and pulled on the handle. Since the interior of the store was lighted, he took a coin from his pocket and began tapping on the glass. Finally, someone came forward from the shadows of the back room.

"Closed," the bookseller pantomimed on the other side of the glass.

"But. . . ." Keirion argued, pointing to his wristwatch.

"Nevertheless," the wide man shouted. Then, after scrutinizing the disappointed patron, the bookseller unlocked the door and opened it far enough to carry on a brief conversation. "And what is it I can do for you. I'm closed, so you'll have to come some other time if—"

"I only wanted to ask you something. Do you remember the book that I bought from you not long ago, the one—"

"Yes, I remember," replied the bookseller, as if quite prepared for the question. "And let me say that I was quite impressed, as of course was . . . the other man."

"Impressed?" Keirion repeated.

"Flabbergasted is more the word in his case," continued the bookseller. "He said to me, 'The book has found its reader,' and what could I do but agree with him?"

"I'm afraid I don't understand," said Keirion.

The bookseller blinked and said nothing. After a few moments he reluctantly explained: "I was hoping that by now you would understand. He hasn't contacted you? The man who was in here that day?"

"No, why should he?"

The bookseller blinked again and said: "Well, I suppose there's no reason you need to stand out there. It's getting very cold, don't you feel it?" Then he closed the door and pulled Keirion a little to one side of it, whispering: "There's just one thing I would like to tell you. I made no mistake that day about the price of that book. And it was the price—in full—which was paid by the other man, don't ask me anything else about him. That price, of course, minus the small amount that you yourself contributed. I didn't cheat anyone, least of all *him*. He would have been happy to pay even more to get that book into your hands. And although I'm not exactly sure of his reasons, I think you should know that."

"But why didn't he simply purchase the book for himself?" asked Keirion.

The bookseller seemed confused. "It was of no use to him. Perhaps it would have been better if you hadn't given yourself away when he asked you about the book. How much you knew."

"But I don't know anything, apart from what I've read in the book itself. I came here to find—"

"—Nothing, I'm afraid. You're the one who should be telling me, very impressive. But I'm not asking, don't misunderstand. And there's nothing more I can tell you, since I've already violated every precept of discretion. This is such an exceptional case, though. Very impressive, if in fact you are the reader of that book."

Realizing that, at best, he had been led into a dialogue of mystification, and possibly one of lies, Victor Keirion had no regrets when the bookseller held the door open for him to leave.

But before very many days, and especially nights, had passed he learned why the bookseller had been so impressed with him, and why the crowlike stranger had been so generous: the bestower of the book who was blind to its mysteries. In the course of those days, those nights, he learned that the stranger had given only so that he might possess the thing he could gain in no other way, that he was reading the book with borrowed eyes and stealing its secrets from the soul of its rightful reader. At last it became clear what was happening to him throughout those strange nights of dreaming.

On each of those nights the shapes of Vastarien slowly pushed through the obscurity of his sleep, a vast landscape emerging from its own profound slumber and drifting forth from a place without name or dimension. And as the crooked monuments became manifest once again, they seemed to expand and soar high above him, drawing his vision toward them. Progressively the scene acquired nuance and articulation; steadily the creation became dense and intricate within its black womb: the streets were sinuous entrails winding through the dark body, and each edifice was the jutting bone of a skeleton hung with a thin musculature of shadows.

But just as his vision reached out to embrace fully the mysterious and jagged form of the dream, it all appeared to pull away, abandoning him on the edge of a dreamless void. The landscape was receding, shrinking into the distance. Now all he could see was a single street bordered by two converging rows of buildings. And at the opposite end of that street, rising up taller than the buildings themselves, stood a great figure in silhouette. This looming colossus made no movement or sound but firmly dominated the horizon where the single remaining street seemed to end. From this position the towering shadow was absorbing all other shapes into its own, which gradually was gaining in stature as the landscape withdrew and diminished. And the outline of this titanic figure appeared to be that of a man, yet it was also that of a dark and devouring bird.

Although for several nights Victor Keirion managed to awake before the scavenger had thoroughly consumed what was not its own, there was no assurance that he would always be able to do so and that the dream would not pass into the hands of another. Ultimately, he conceived and executed the act that was necessary to keep possession of the dream he had coveted for so long.

Vastarien, he whispered as he stood in the shadows and moonlight of that bare little room, where a massive metal door prevented his escape. Within that door a small square of thick glass was implanted so that he might be watched by day and by night. And there was an unbending web of heavy wire covering the window which overlooked the city that was *not* Vastarien. *Never,* chanted a voice which might have been his own. Then more insistently: *never, never, never. . . .*

When the door was opened and some men in uniforms entered the room, they found Victor Keirion screaming to the raucous limits of his voice and trying to scale the thick metal mesh veiling the window, as if he were dragging himself along some unlikely route of liberation. Of course, they pulled him to the floor; they stretched him out upon the bed, where his wrists and ankles were tightly strapped. Then through the doorway strode a nurse who carried slender syringe crowned with a silvery needle.

During the injection he continued to scream words which everyone in the room had heard before, each outburst developing the theme of his unjust confinement: how the man he had murdered was using him in a horrible way, a way impossible to explain or make credible. The man could not read the book—there, *that* book—and was stealing the dreams which the book had spawned. *Stealing my dreams,* he mumbled softly as the drug began to take effect. *Stealing my. . . .*

The group remained around the bed for a few moments, silently staring at its restrained occupant. Then one of them pointed to the book and initiated a conversation now familiar to them all.

"What should we do with it? It's been taken away enough times already, but then there's always another that appears."

"And there's no point to it. Look at these pages—nothing, nothing written anywhere."

"So why does he sit reading them for hours? He does nothing else."

"I think it's time we told someone in authority."

"Of course, we could do that, but what exactly would we say? That a certain inmate should be forbidden from reading a certain book? That he becomes violent?"

"And then they'll ask why we can't keep the book away from him or him from the book? What should we say to that?"

"There would be nothing we could say. Can you imagine what lunatics we would seem? As soon as we opened our mouths, that would be it for all of us."

"And when someone asks what the book means to him, or even what its name is . . . what would be our answer?"

As if in response to this question, a few shapeless groans arose from the criminally insane creature who was bound to the bed. But no one could understand the meaning of the word or words that he uttered, least of all himself. For he was now far from his own words, buried deep within the dreams of a place where everything was transfixed in the order of the unreal; and whence, it truly seemed, he would never return.

KARL EDWARD WAGNER

Karl Edward Wagner was born in Knoxville, Tennessee, in 1945. He was trained as a psychiatrist before abandoning that career for writing and editing. Initially influenced by the sword-and-sorcery tales of Robert E. Howard, Wagner produced several novels and stories centering around the figure of Kane, a prehistoric hero (loosely modeled on the biblical Cain) who uses both his mind and his muscles to overcome his enemies. Wagner also wrote a novel utilizing Howard's heroes Bran Mak Morn (*Legion from the Shadows*, 1976) and Conan (*The Road of Kings*, 1979). In 1980 he took over the editorship of the series *The Year's Best Horror Stories*, and his diligence in unearthing worthy stories from small-press and other obscure publications earned him well-deserved respect.

In addition, Wagner wrote numerous short stories of fantasy, science fiction, and the supernatural set in the contemporary world. His most celebrated tale, "Sticks" (1974), is largely a pastiche of H. P. Lovecraft and was meant as an homage to the celebrated fantasy artist Lee Brown Coye. His supernatural tales are gathered in *In a Lonely Place* (1983), *Why Not You and I?* (1987), and *Unthreatened by the Morning Light* (1989). These stories range from tributes to such writers as Ambrose Bierce and Robert W. Chambers to tormented tales of medical horror, drug addiction, and sexual aberration. Along with David A.

Drake (his collaborator on the science fiction novel *Killer* [1986], set in ancient Rome) and Jim Groce, Wagner founded a specialty press, Carcosa, that issued four volumes from 1973 to 1981. Wagner, beset by alcoholism and other ailments, died unexpectedly in 1994. A posthumous volume of stories, *Exorcisms and Ecstasies,* appeared in 1997. His final volume of *The Year's Best Horror Stories* was published in 1994, after which the series was canceled.

"Endless Night" (first published in *The Architecture of Fear,* edited by Kathryn Cramer and Peter D. Pautz [1987], and collected in *Exorcisms and Ecstasies*) is a prose-poetic narrative in which dream and reality are inextricably confused.

ENDLESS NIGHT

I runne to death, and death meets me as fast,
And all my pleasures are like yesterday;
—John Donne, *Holy Sonnet I*

The dream landscape always stretched out the same. It had become as familiar as the neighborhood yards of his childhood, as the condo-blighted streets of his middle years. Dreams had to have some basis in reality—or so his therapists had tried to reassure him. If this one did, it was of some unrecognized reality.

They stood upon the edge of the swamp, although somehow he understood that this had once been a river, and then a lake, as all became stagnant and began to sink. The bridge was a relic, stretched out before them to the island—on the far shore—beyond. It was a suspension bridge, from a period which he could not identify with certainty, but suspected was of the early 1930s judging by the Art Deco pylons. It seemed ludicrously narrow and wholly inappropriate for its task. As the waters had risen, or the land mass had sunk, its roadway, ridged and as gap-toothed as a railway trestle, had settled into the water's surface—so that midway across one must slosh through ankle-deep water, feeling beneath the scum for the solid segments of roadway. Spanish moss festooned the fraying cables; green lichens fringed the greener verdigris of bronze faces staring out from the rotting concrete pylons. Inscriptions, no doubt explaining their importance, were blurred beyond legibility.

It was always a breathless relief to reach the upward-sloping paving of the far end, scramble toward the deserted shoreline beyond. His chest would be aching by then, as though the warm, damp air he tried to suck into his lungs were devoid of sustenance. There were ripples in the water, not caused by any current, and while he had never seen anything within the tepid depths, he knew it was essential not to linger in crossing.

His companion or guide—he sometimes thought of her as his muse—always seemed to know the way, so he followed her. Usually she was blonde. Her bangs obscured her eyes, and he only had an impression of her face in profile—thin, with straight nose and sharp chin. He sensed that her cheekbones would be pronounced, her eyes large and watchful and widely spaced. She was barefoot. Sometimes she tugged up her skirt to hold its hem above the water, more often she was wearing only a long T-shirt over what he assumed was a swimsuit. He realized that he knew her, but he could never remember her name.

He supposed he looked like himself. The waters gave back no reflection.

It—the building—dominated the shoreline beyond. From the other side he often thought of it as an office building, possibly some sort of apartment complex. He was certain then that he could see lights shining from its many-tiered windows. It appeared to have been constructed of some salmon-hued brick, or perhaps the color was another illusion of the declining sun. It was squat, as broad as its dozen-or-more stories of height, and so polyhedral as to seem almost round. Its architecture impressed him as featureless—stark walls and windows, Bauhaus utilitarian. Either its creator had lacked any imagination or else had sacrificed external form to unguessable function.

The features of the shoreline never impressed themselves upon his memory. There was a rising land, vague blotches of trees, undergrowth. The road dragged slowly upward toward the building. Trees overhung from either side, reaching toward one another, garlanded with hanging vines and moss— darkening skies a leaden ribbon overhead. The pavement was cracked and broken—calling to mind orphaned segments of a WPA-era two-lane highway, bypassed alongside stretches of the interstate, left to decompose into the wounded earth. Its surface was swept clean. Not disused; rather, seldom used.

Perhaps too frequently used.

If there were other structures near the building, he never noticed them. Perhaps there were none; perhaps they were simply inconsequential in comparison. Sometimes he thought of an immense office building raised out of the wilderness of an industrial park or a vast stadium born of the leveled wasteland of urban renewal, left alone and alien in a region where the *genius loci* ultimately reconquered. A barren space, encroached upon by that which was beyond, surrounded the building—sometimes grass-latticed pavement (parking lot?), sometimes a scorched and eroded barrier of weeds (ground zero?).

Desolation, not wholly dead.

Abandoned, not entirely forgotten.

The lights in the windows, which he was certain he had seen from across the water, never shone as they entered.

There was a wire fence, sometimes: barbed wire leaning from its summit, or maybe insulated balls of brown ceramic nestling high-voltage lines. No matter. All was rusted, corroded, sagging like the skeletal remains that rotted at its base. When there was a fence at all.

If there was a fence, gaps pierced the wire barrier like the rotted lace of a corpse's mantilla. Sometimes the gate lay in wreckage beneath its graffitied arch: Abandon Hope. Joy Through Work. War Is Peace. Ask Not.

My Honor Is Loyalty.

One of his dreams is a fantasy of Nazis.

He knows that they are Nazis because they are all wearing jack boots and black uniforms, SS insignia and swastika armbands, monocles and Luger pistols. And there are men in slouch-brim hats and leather overcoats, all wearing thick glasses—Gestapo, they have to be. White-clad surgeons with button-up-the-back surplices, each one resembling Lionel Atwill, suck glowing fluids into improbable hypodermics, send tentative spurts pulsing from their needles.

Monocles and thick-lensed spectacles and glass-hard blue eyes peer downward. Their faces are distorted and hideous—as if he, or they, someone, is viewing this perspective through a magnifying glass. The men in black uniforms are goose-stepping and Heil-Hitlering in geometric patterns behind the grinning misshapen faces of the doctors.

The stairway is of endless black marble, polished to a mirror-sheen, giving back no reflection. The SS officers, alike as a thousand black-uniformed puppets, are goose-stepping in orderly, powerful ranks down the polished stairway. Toward them, up the stairway, a thousand blonde and blue-eyed Valkyries, sequin-pantied and brass-brassiered, flaxen locks bleached and bobbed and marcelled, are marching in rhythm—a Rockette chorus line of Lorelei.

> *Wir werden weiter marschieren,*
> *wenn alles in Sherben fällt,*
> *denn heute gehört uns Deutschland*
> *und morgen die ganze Welt!*

Needles plunge downward.

Inward.

Distancing.

Der Führer leans and peers inward. He wipes the needles with his tongue and snorts piggishly. *Our final revenge,* Hitler promises, in a language he seems to understand. The dancers merge upon the stairway, form a thousand black-and-white swastikas as they twist their flesh together into DNA coils.

Sieg Heil!

Someday.

A thousand bombs burn a thousand coupled moths into a thousand flames.

A thousand, less one.

Distance.

While he hated and feared all of his fantasies, he usually hated and feared this one worst of all. When he peered through the windows of the building, he saw rows of smokestacks belching uncounted souls into the recoiling sky.

But often there was no fence. Only a main entrance.

A Grand Entrance. Glass and aluminum and tile. Uncorroded, but obscured by thin dust. A receptionist's desk. A lobby of precisely arranged furniture: art moderne or coldly functional—nonetheless serving no function in the sterile emptiness.

No one to greet him, to verify an appointment, to ask for plastic cards and indecipherable streams of numbers. He always thought of this as some sort of hospital, possibly abandoned in the panic of some unleashed plague virus.

He always avoided the lifts. (Shouldn't he think of them as elevators?) Instead he followed her through the deserted (were they ever occupied?) hallways and up the hollow stairwell that gave back no echo to their steps.

There is another fantasy that he cannot will away.

He is conscious of his body in this fantasy, but no more able to control his body than to control his fantasy.

He is small—a child, he believes, looking at the boyish arms and legs that are restrained to the rails of the hospital bed, and examining the muted tenderness in the faces of the white-clad suppliants who insert the needles and apply the electrodes to his flesh.

Electric current makes a nova of his brain. Thoughts and memories scatter like a deck of cards thrown against the sudden wind. Drugs hold his raped flesh half-alert against the torture. Smokestacks spew forth a thousand dreams. All must be arranged in a New Order.

A thousand cards dance in changing patterns across his vision. Each card has a face, false as a waxen mask. His body strains against the leather cuffs; his scream is taken by a soggy wad of tape on a wooden paddle.

The cards are telling him something, something very essential. He does not have time to read their message.

I'm not a fortune-teller! he screams at the shifting patterns of cards. The wadded tape steals his protests.

The rape is over. They are wheeling him away.

The cards filter down from their enhanced freedom, falling like snowflakes in a dying dream.

And then he counts them all.

All are there. And in their former order.

Order must be maintained.

The Old Order is stronger.

But he knows—almost for certain—that he has never been a patient in any hospital. Ever.

His health is perfect. All too perfect.

She always led him through the maze within—upward, onward, forward. The Eternal Female/Feminine Spirit-Force. Goethe's personal expression of the ultimate truth of human existence—describing a power that transcended and revoked an informed commitment to damnation—translated awkwardly into pretentious nonsense in English. He remembered that he had never read Goethe, could not understand a word of German.

His therapists said it was a reaction to his adoption in infancy as a German war orphan by an American family. The assertive and anonymous woman represented his natural mother, whom he had never known. But his birth certificate proved that he had been born to unexceptional middle-class American parents in Cleveland, Ohio.

And his memories of them were as faded and unreal as time-leached color slides. Memories fade before light, and into night.

False memories. Reality a sudden celluloid illusion.

Lightning rips the night.

Doctor! It's alive!

Another fantasy evokes (or is invoked by, say his therapists) visions of *Macbeth,* of scary campfire stories, of old films scratched and eroded from too many showings. His (disremembered) parents (probably) only allowed him to partake of the first, but Shakespeare knew well the dark side of dreams.

Sometimes he is on a desolate stretch of moor, damp and furred with tangles of heather. (He supposes it is heather, remembering *Macbeth.*) Or perhaps he is on a high mountain, with barren rocks thrusting above dark forest. (He insists that

he has never read *Faust,* but admits to having seen *Fantasia.*)
Occasionally he stands naked within a circle of standing stones,
huge beneath the empty sky. (He confesses to having read an
article about Stonehenge.) And in this same Gothic context, he
has another such fantasy, and he never speaks of its imperfectly
remembered fragments to anyone—not to lovers, therapists,
priests, or his other futile confidants.

It is, again (to generalize), a fantasy in which he is again the
observer. Passive, certainly. Helpless, to be sure. But the restraints hold a promise of power to be feared, of potential to be
unleashed.

Hooded figures surround him, center upon his awareness.
Their cloaks are sometimes dark and featureless, sometimes
fantastically embroidered and colored. He never sees their faces.

He never sees himself, although he senses he stands naked
and vulnerable before them.

He is there. In their midst. *They* see him.

It is all that matters.

They reach/search/take/give/violate/empower.

There is no word in English.

His therapists tell him this is a homosexual rape fantasy.

There is no word in any language.

There is only the power.

The stairway climbed inexorably as she led him upward into
the building. Returning—and they always returned, he knew
now—the descent would be far more intolerable, for he would
have his thoughts to carry with him.

A stairwell door: very commonplace usually (a Hilton or a
Hyatt?), but sometimes of iron-bound oak, or maybe no more
than a curtain. No admonition. No advice. On your own. He
would have welcomed *Fire Exit Only* or *Please Knock.*

She always opened the door—some atavistic urge of mas-
culine courtesy always surfaced, but he was never fast enough
or certain enough—and she held it for him, waiting and
demanding.

Beyond, there was always the same corridor, circling and

enclosing the building. If there were any significance to the level upon which they had emerged, it was unknown to him. She might know, but he never asked her. It terrified him that she might know.

There is innocence, if not guiltlessness, in randomness.

He decided to look upon the new reality beyond the darkened windows of the corridor. She was impatient, but she could not deny him this delay, this respite.

Outside the building he saw stretches of untilled farmland, curiously demarcated by wild hedgerows and stuttering walls of toppled stone. He moved to the next window and saw only a green expanse of pasture, its grassy limitlessness ridged by memories of ancient fields and villages.

He paused here, until she caught at his arm, pulled him away. The next window—only a glimpse—overlooked a city that he was given no time to recognize, had he been able to do so through the knowledge of the fire that consumed it.

There were doors along the other side of the corridor. He pretended that some might open upon empty apartments, that others led to vacant offices. Sometimes there were curtained recesses that suggested confessionals, perhaps secluding some agent of a higher power—although he had certainly never been a Catholic, and such religion that he recalled only underscored the futility of redemption.

She drew aside a curtain, beckoned him to enter.

He moved past her, took his seat.

Not a confessional. He had known that. He always knew where she would lead him.

The building was only a façade, changing as his memory decayed and fragmented, recognizing only one reality in a dream-state that had consumed its dreamer.

A stadium. A coliseum. An arena.

Whatever its external form, it inescapably remained unchanged in its function.

This time the building's interior was a circular arena, dirt-floored and ringed by many tiers of wooden bleachers. The wooden benches were warped and weathered silver-gray. Any paint had long since peeled away, leaving splinters and rot. The building was only a shell, hollow as a whitened skull, encircled by derelict rows of twisted benches and sagging wooden scaffolding.

The seats were all empty. The seats had been empty, surely, for many years.

He sensed a lingering echo of "Take Me Out to the Ball Game" played on a steam calliope. Before his time. Casey at the bat. This was Muddville. Years after. Still no joy.

He desperately wished for another reality, but he knew it would always end the same. The presentations might be random, might have some unknowable significance. What mattered was that he knew where he really was and why he was here.

Whether he wanted to be here was of no consequence.

She suggested, as always. *The woman at the bank who wouldn't approve the car loan. Send for her.*

She was only doing her job.

But you hated her in that moment. And you remember that hatred.

Involuntarily, he thought of her.

The numberless windows of the building's exterior pulsed with light.

A window opened.

Power, not light, sent through. And returned.

And the woman was in the arena. Huddled in the dirt, too confused to sense fear.

The unseen crowd murmured in anticipation.

He stared down at the woman, concentrating, channeling the power within his brain.

She screamed, as invisible flames consumed her being. Her scream was still an echo when her ashes drifted to the ground.

He looked for movement among the bleachers. Whatever watched from there remained hidden.

Another, she urged him.

He tried to think of those who had created him, this time to send for them. But the arena remained empty. Those he hated above all others were long beyond the vengeance of even his power.

Forget them. There are others.

But I don't hate them.

If not now, then soon you will. There is an entire world to hate.

And, he understood, too many nights to come.

> Some are Born to sweet delight,
> Some are Born to Endless Night.
> —William Blake, *Auguries of Innocence*

NORMAN PARTRIDGE

Norman Partridge was born in 1958. As a youth growing up in California, Partridge absorbed horror and fantasy through several media—oral tales from his father, books by Robert Bloch and Ray Bradbury, and films and television. All these elements are found in Partridge's work. He began publishing short stories in the small press in the 1980s, and his first story collection, *Mr. Fox and Other Feral Tales* (1992), won the Bram Stoker award from the Horror Writers Association. This was followed by the novel *Slippin' into Darkness* (1994), a powerful and moving nonsupernatural account of the effect of a woman's suicide upon the members of a gang who had raped her in high school. The collection *Bad Intentions* (1996) contains additional tales that fuse such pop-culture elements as B-movies, rock-and-roll, and hot rods with the supernatural. In that same year, Partridge coedited (with Martin H. Greenberg) *It Came from the Drive-In!*, an anthology of horror tales written in homage of the drive-in movie. After writing two crime novels, *Saguaro Riptide* (1997) and *The Ten-Ounce Siesta* (1998), Partridge published the novel *Wildest Dreams* (1998), a dark and gruesome novel about a bounty hunter and his sorcerer father. He has also written a novel in James O'Barr's graphic novel series The Crow, *Wicked Prayer* (2000); it was filmed in 2005. Partridge is at work on an expansion of his story "Frankenstein '59" (in *It Came from the Drive-In!*) into a novel.

Partridge, who lives in California and works in a library, has gathered his best tales in *The Man with the Barbed-Wire Fists* (2001); it includes such specimens as the vampire story "Do Not Hasten to Bid Me Adieu"; "In Beauty, Like the Night," a zombie tale; and "The Bars on Satan's Jailhouse," which melds the theme of lycanthropy with the Western.

"The Hollow Man" (first published in *Grue Magazine,* Fall 1991) is a subtle and ambiguous tale that appears to be told from the point of view of a wendigo, a mythical air elemental believed to haunt the forests of Canada.

THE HOLLOW MAN

Four. Yes, that's how many there were. Come to my home. Come to my home in the hills. Come in the middle of feast, when the skin had been peeled back and I was ready to sup. Interrupting, disrupting. Stealing the comfortable bloat of a full belly, the black scent of clean bones burning dry on glowing embers. Four.

Yes. That's how many there were. I watched them through the stretched-skin window, saw them standing cold in the snow with their guns at their sides.

The hollow man saw them too. He heard the ice dogs bark and raised his sunken face, peering at the men through the blue-veined window. He gasped, expectant, and I had to draw my claws from their fleshy sheaths and jab deep into his blackened muscles to keep him from saying words that weren't mine. Outside, they shouted, *Hullo! Hullo in the cabin!* and the hollow man sprang for the door. I jumped on his back and tugged the metal rings pinned into his neck. He jerked and whirled away from the latch, but I was left with the sickening sound of his hopeful moans.

Once again, control was mine, but not like before. The hollow man was full of strength that he hadn't possessed in weeks, and the feast was ruined.

They had ruined it.

"Hullo! We're tired and need food!"

The hollow man strained forward, his fingers groping for the door latch. My scaled legs flexed hard around his middle. His sweaty stomach sizzled and he cried at the heat of me. A rib snapped. Another. He sank backward and, with a dry flutter of wings, I pulled him away from the window, back into the dark.

"Could we share your fire? It's so damn cold!"

"We'd give you money, but we ain't got any. There ain't a nickel in a thousand miles of here . . ."

Small screams tore the hollow man's beaten lips. There was blood. I cursed the waste and twisted a handful of metal rings. He sank to his knees and quieted.

"We'll leave our guns. We don't mean no harm!"

I jerked one ring, then another. I cooed against the hollow man's skinless shoulder and made him pick up his rifle. When he had it loaded, cocked, and aimed through a slot in the door, I whispered in his ear and made him laugh.

And then I screamed out at them, "You dirty bastards! You stay away! You ain't comin' in here!"

Gunshots exploded. We only got one of them, not clean but bad enough. The others pulled him into the forest, where the dense trees muffled his screams and kept us from getting another clear shot.

The rifle clattered to the floor, smoking faintly, smelling good. We walked to the window. I jingled his neck rings and the hollow man squinted through the tangle of veins, to the spot where a red streak was freezing in the snow.

I made the hollow man smile.

So four. Still four, when night came and moonlight dripped like melting wax over the snow-capped ridges to the west. Four to make me forget the one nearly drained. Four to make me impatient while soft time crept toward the leaden hour, grain by grain, breath by breath . . .

The hour descended. I twisted rings and plucked black muscles, and the hollow man fed the fire and barred the door. I released him and he huddled in a corner, exhausted.

I rose through the chimney and thrust myself away from

the cabin. My wings fought the biting wind as I climbed high, searching the black forest below. I soared the length of a high mountain glacier and dove away, banking back toward the heart of the valley. Shadows that stretched forever, and then, deep in a jagged ravine that stabbed at a river, a sputtered glimmer of orange. A campfire.

So bold. So typical of their kind. I extended my wings and drifted down like a bat, coming to rest in the branches of a giant redwood. Its live green stench nearly made me retch. Huddling in my wings for warmth, I clawed through the bark with a wish to make the ancient monster scream. The tree quivered against the icy wind. Grinning, satisfied, I looked down.

Two strong, but different. One weak. One as good as dead.

Three.

Grizzly sat in silence, his black face as motionless as a tombstone. Instantly, I liked him best. Mammoth, wrapped in a bristling grizzly coat he looked even bigger, almost as big as a grizzly. He sat by the fire, staring at his reflection in a gleaming ax blade. He made me anxious. He could last for months.

Across from Grizzly, Redbeard turned a pot and boiled coffee. He straightened his fox-head cap and stroked his beard, clearing it of ice. I didn't like him. His milky squint was too much like my own. But any fool could see that he hated Grizzly, and that made me smile.

Away from them both, crouching under a tree with the whimpering ice dogs, Rabbit wept through swollen eyes. He dug deep in his plastic coat and produced a crucifix. I almost laughed out loud.

And in a tent, wrapped in sweat-damp wool and expensive eiderdown that couldn't keep him warm anymore, still clinging to life, was the dead man, who didn't matter.

But maybe I could make him matter.

And then there would only be two.

When the clouds came, when they suffocated the unblinking moon and brought sleep to the camp, I swept down to the dying fire and rolled comfortably in the crab-colored coals. The hush of the river crept over me as I decided what to do.

To make three into two.

Three men, and the dead man. Two tents: Grizzly and Redbeard in one, Rabbit and the dead man in the other. Easy. No worries, except for the dogs. (For ice dogs are wise. Their beast hearts hide simple secrets . . .)

The packed snow sizzled beneath my feet as I crept toward Rabbit's tent. The dead man's face pressed against one corner of the tent, molding his swollen features in yellow plastic. Each rattling breath gently puffed the thin material away from his face, and each weak gasp slowly drew it back. It was a steady, pleasant sound. I concentrated on it until it was mine.

No time for metal rings. No time for naked muscle and feast. Slowly, I reached out and took hold of Rabbit's mind, digging deep until I found his darkest nightmare. I pulled it loose and let it breathe. At first it frightened him, but I tugged its midnight corners straight and banished its monsters, and soon Rabbit was full of bliss, awake without even knowing it.

I circled the tent and pushed against the other side. The dead man rolled across, cold against the warmth of Rabbit's unbridled nightmare.

"Jesus, you're freezin', Charlie," whispered Rabbit as he moved closer. "But don't worry. I'll keep you warm, buddy. I've gotta keep you warm."

But in the safety of his nightmare, that wasn't what Rabbit wanted at all.

I waited in the tree until Grizzly found them the next morning, wrapped together in the dead man's bag. He shot Rabbit in the head and left him for the ice dogs.

Redbeard buried the dead man in a silky snowdrift.

That day was nothing. Grizzly and Redbeard sat at the edge of the clearing and wasted their only chance. Grizzly stared hungrily at the cabin, seeing only what I wanted him to see. Thick, safe walls. A puffing chimney. A home. But Redbeard, damned Redbeard, wise with fear and full of caution, sensed other things. The dead man's fevered rattle whispering through the trees. An ice dog gnawing a fresh, gristly bone. And bear traps, rusty with blood.

Redbeard rose and walked away. Soon Grizzly followed.

And then there was only the hollow man, rocking gently in his chair. The soles of his boots buffed the splintery floor and his legs swung back and forth, back and forth.

Two. Now two, as the second night was born, a silent twin to the first. Only two, as again I twisted rings and plucked muscles and put the hollow man to sleep. Just two, as my wings beat the night and I flew once more from the sooty chimney to the ravine that stabbed a river.

There they sat, as before, grizzly and fox. And there I watched, waiting, with nothing left to do but listen for the sweet arrival of the leaden hour.

Grizzly chopped wood and fed the fire. Redbeard positioned blackened pots and watched them boil. Both planned silently while they ate, and afterwards their mute desperation grew, knotting their minds into coils of anger. Grizzly charged the dying embers with whole branches and did not smile until the flames leaped wildly. The heat slapped at Redbeard in waves, harsh against the pleasant brandy-warmth that swam in his gut and slowed his racing thoughts.

"Tomorrow mornin'," blurted Redbeard, "we're gettin' away from here. I'm not dealin' with no crazy hermit."

Grizzly stared at his ax-blade reflection and smiled. "We're gonna kill us a crazy hermit," he said. "Tomorrow mornin'."

Soon the old words came, taut and cold, and then Grizzly sprang through the leaping flames, his black coat billowing, and Redbeard's fox-head cap flew from his head as he whirled around. Ax rang against knife. A white fist tore open a black lip, and the teeth below ripped into a pale knuckle. Knife split ebony cheek. Blood hissed through the flames and sizzled against burning embers. A sharp crack as the ax sank home in a tangle of ribs. Redbeard coughed a misty breath past Grizzly's ear, and the bigger man spun the smaller around, freed his ax, and watched his opponent stumble into the fire.

I laughed above the crackling roar. The ice dogs scattered into the forest, barking, wild with fear and the sour smell of death.

· · ·

So Grizzly had survived. He stood still, his singed coat smoking, his cut cheek oozing blood. His mind was empty—there was no remorse, only a feeling that he was the strongest, he was the best.

Knowing that, I flew home happy.

There was not much in the cabin that I could use. I found only a single whalebone needle, yellow with age, and no thread at all. I watched the veined window as I searched impatiently for a substitute, and at last I discovered a spool of fishing line in a rusty metal box. Humming, I went about my work. First I drew strips of the hollow man's pallid skin over his shrunken shoulder muscles, fastening them along his backbone with a cross stitch. Then I bunched the flabby tissue at the base of his skull and made the final secret passes with my needle.

Now he was nothing. I tore the metal rings out of his neck and the hollow man twitched as if shocked.

A bullet ripped through the cabin door. "I'm gonna get you, you bastard," cried Grizzly, his voice loud but worn. "You hear me? I'm gonna *get* you!"

The hollow man sprang from the rocker; his withered legs betrayed him and he fell to the floor. I balanced on the back of the chair and hissed at him, spreading my wings in mock menace. With a laughable scream, he flung himself at the door.

Grizzly must have been confused by the hollow man's ravings, for he didn't fire again until the fool was nearly upon him. An instant of pain, another of relief, and the hollow man crumpled, finished.

And then Grizzly just sat in the snow, his eyes fixed on the open cabin door. I watched him from a corner of the veined window, afraid to move. He took out his ax and stared at his reflection in the glistening blade. After a time Grizzly pocketed the ax, and then he pulled his great coat around him, disappearing into its bristling black folds.

In the afternoon I grew fearful. While the redwoods stretched their heavy shadows over the cabin, Grizzly rose and followed the waning sun up a slight ridge. He cleaned his gun.

He even slept for a few moments. Then he slapped his numb face awake and rubbed snow over his sliced cheek.

Grizzly came home.

I hid above the doorway. Grizzly sighed as he crossed the threshold, and I bit back my laughter. The door swung shut. Grizzly stooped and tossed a thick log onto the dying embers. He grinned as it crackled aflame.

I pushed off hard and dove from the ceiling. My claws ripped through grizzly hide and then into human hide. Grizzly bucked awfully, even tried to smash me against the hearth, but the heat only gave me power and as my legs burned into his stomach Grizzly screamed. I drove my claws into a shivering bulge of muscle and brought him to his knees.

The metal rings came next. I pinned them into his neck: one, two, three, four.

After I had supped, I sat the hollow man in the rocker and whispered to him as we looked through the veined window. A storm was rising in the west. We watched it come for a long time. Soon, a fresh dusting of snow covered the husk of man lying out on the ridge.

I told Grizzly that he had been my favorite. I told him that he would last a long time.

DAVID J. SCHOW

David J. Schow was born in Marburg, West Germany, in 1955, a German orphan who was adopted by American parents and brought to the United States at an early age. Settling in Los Angeles, Schow began writing in the late 1970s. He was the reputed coiner of the term splatterpunk, devised to denote a no-holds-barred approach to horror fiction, utilizing elements from popular culture (especially rock-and-roll music and slasher films) to underscore the violence and sterility of modern life. Although many avowed splatterpunk writers rendered themselves absurd by over-the-top grisliness with little aesthetic justification, Schow distinguished himself by his vivid, metaphor-laden prose and an underlying seriousness in his depictions of gruesome physical horror.

Schow's first novel, *The Kill Riff* (1988), is a nonsupernatural account of a psychotic man who seeks revenge upon a rock band for the death of his daughter during a rock concert. In 1990, Schow published three scintillating volumes: the short story collections *Seeing Red* and *Lost Angels* and the novel *The Shaft*. *Seeing Red* contains some of his best supernatural work (notably the story "Red Light," an account of "psychic vampirism" similar to Fritz Leiber's "The Girl with the Hungry Eyes"); *Lost Angels* is a collection of loosely linked novellas; *The Shaft*, set in Chicago, is perhaps one of the finest modern examples of the haunted house motif, as a dreary tenement is the setting for a hideous creature dwelling in a ventilation shaft. Schow's later stories appear in the collections *Black Leather Required* (1994), *Crypt Orchids* (1998), and *Eye* (2001). He has written several screenplays for film and television and several novelizations of television scripts under the pseudonym Stephen Grave. He has also written *The Outer Limits Companion* (1999) and edited the anthology *Silver Scream* (1988), a volume of horror tales about movies.

"Last Call for the Sons of Shock" (first published in *Black Leather Required*) is typical of Schow's scintillating mix of supernaturalism, B-movie references, and low farce.

LAST CALL FOR THE SONS OF SHOCK

Blank Frank notches down the Cramps, keeping an eye on the blue LED bars of the equalizer. He likes the light.

"Creature from the Black Leather Lagoon" calms.

The club is called Un/Dead. The sound system is from the guts of the old Tropicana, LA's altar of mud wrestling, foxy boxing, and the cocktease unto physical pain. It specs are for metal, loud, lots of it. The punch of the subwoofers is a lot like getting jabbed in the sternum by a big velvet piston.

Blank Frank likes the power. Whenever he thinks of getting physical, he thinks of the Vise Grip.

He perches a case of Stoli on one big shoulder and tucks another of Beam under his arm. After this he is done replenishing the bar. To survive the weekend crush, you've gotta arm. Blank Frank can lug a five-case stack without using a dolly. He has to duck to clear the lintel. The passage back to the phones and bathrooms is tricked out to resemble a bank vault door, with tumblers and cranks. It is up past six-six. Not enough for Blank Frank, who still has to stoop.

Two hours till doors open.

Blank Frank enjoys his quiet time. He has not forgotten the date. He grins at the movie poster framed next to the backbar register. He scored it at a Hollywood memorabilia shop for an obscene price even though he got a professional discount. He had it mounted on foamcore to flatten the creases. He does not permit dust to accrete on the glass. The poster is duotone, with lurid lettering. His first feature film. Every so often some Un/Dead patron with cash to burn will make an exorbitant offer to buy it. Blank Frank always says no with a smile . . . and usually sports a drink on the house for those who ask.

He nudges the volume back up for Bauhaus, doing "Bela Lugosi's Dead," extended mix.

The staff sticks to coffee and iced tea. Blank Frank prefers a nonalcoholic concoction of his own device, which he has christened a Blind Hermit. He rustles up one, now, in a chromium blender, one hand idly on his plasma globe. Michelle gave it to him about four years back, when they first became affordably popular. Touch the exterior and the purple veins of electricity follow your fingertips. Knobs permit you to fiddle with density and amplitude, letting you master the power, feel like Tesla showing off.

Blank Frank likes the writhing electricity.

By now he carries many tattoos. But the one on the back of his left hand—the hand toying with the globe—is his favorite: a stylized planet Earth, with a tiny propellered aircraft circling it. It is old enough that the cobalt-colored dermal ink has begun to blur.

Blank Frank has been utterly bald for three decades. A tiny wisp of hair issues from his occipital. He keeps it in a neat braid, clipped to six inches. It is dead white. Sometimes, when he drinks, the braid darkens briefly. He doesn't know why.

Michelle used to be a stripper, before management got busted, the club got sold, and Un/Dead was born of the ashes. She likes being a waitress and she likes Blank Frank. She calls him "big guy." Half the regulars think Blank Frank and Michelle have something steamy going. They don't. But the fantasy detours them around a lot of potential problems, especially on weekend nights. Blank Frank has learned that people often need fantasies to *seem* superficially true, whether they really are or not.

Blank Frank dusts. If only the bikers could see him now, being dainty and attentive. Puttering.

Blank Frank rarely has to play bouncer whenever some booze-fueled trouble sets to brewing inside Un/Dead. Mostly, he just strolls up behind the perp and waits for him or her to turn around and apologize. Blank Frank's muscle duties generally consist of just *looming.*

If not, he thinks with a smile, there's always the Vise Grip.

The video monitor shows a Red Top taxicab parking outside the employee entrance. Blank Frank is pleased. This arrival coincides exactly with his finish-up on the bartop, which now gleams like onyx. He taps up the slide pot controlling the mike volume on the door's security system. There will come three knocks.

Blank Frank likes all this gadgetry. Cameras and shotgun mikes, amps and strobes and strong, clean alternating current to web it all in concert with maestro surety. Blank Frank loves the switches and toggles and running lights. But most of all, he loves the power.

Tap-tap-tap. Precisely. Always three knocks.

"Good," he says to himself, drawing out the vowel. As he hastens to the door, the song ends and the club fills with the empowered hiss of electrified dead air.

Out by limo. In by cab. One of those eternally bedamned scheduling glitches.

The Count overtips the cabbie because his habit is to deal only in round sums. He never takes . . . change. The Count has never paid taxes. He has cleared forty-three million large in the past year, most of it safely banked in boullion, out-of-country, after overhead and laundering.

The Count raps smartly with his umbrella on the service door of Un/Dead. Blank Frank never makes him knock twice.

It is a pleasure to see Blank Frank's face overloading the tiny security window; his huge form filling the threshold. The Count enjoys Blank Frank despite his limitations when it comes to social intercourse. It is relaxing to appreciate Blank Frank's condition-less loyalty, the innate tidal pull of honor and raw justice that seems programmed into the big fellow. Soothing, it is, to sit and drink and chat lightweight chat with him, in the autopilot way normals told their normal acquaintances where they'd gone and what they'd done since their last visit. Venomless niceties.

None of the buildings in Los Angeles have been standing as long as the Count and Blank Frank have been alive.

Alive. Now there's a word that begs a few new comprehensive, enumerated definitions in the dictionary. Scholars could quibble, but the Count and Blank Frank and Larry were definitely alive. As in "living"—*especially* Larry. Robots, zombis and the walking dead in general could never get misty about such traditions as this threesome's annual conclaves at Un/Dead.

The Count's face is mappy, the wrinkles in his flesh, rice-paper fine. Not creases of age, but tributaries of usage, like the creeks and streams of palmistry. His pallor, as always, tends toward blue. He wears dark shades with faceted, lozenge-shaped lenses of apache tear; mineral crystal stained bloody-black. Behind them, his eyes, bright blue like a husky's. He forever maintains his hair wet and backswept, what Larry has called his "renegade opera conductor coif." Dramatic threads of pure cobalt-black streak backward from the snow-white crown and temples. His lips are as thin and bloodless as two slices of smoked liver. His diet does not render him robustly sanguine; it merely sustains him, these days. It bores him.

Before Blank Frank can get the door open, the Count fires up a handrolled cigarette of coca paste and drags the milky smoke deep. It mingles with the dope already loitering in his metabolism and perks him to.

The cab hisses away into the wet night. Rain on the way.

Blank Frank is holding the door for him, grandly, playing butler.

The Count's brow is overcast. "Have you forgotten so soon, my friend?" Only a ghost of his old, marble-mouthed, middle-Euro accent lingers. It is a trait that the Count has fought for long years to master, and he is justly proud that his English is intelligible. Occasionally, someone asks if he is from Canada.

Blank Frank pulls the exaggerated face of a child committing a big boo-boo. "Oops, sorry." He clears his throat. "Will you come in?"

Equally theatrically, the Count nods and walks several thousand worth of Armani double-breasted into the cool, dim retreat of the bar. It is *nicer* when you're invited, anyway.

"Larry?" says the Count.

"Not yet," says Blank Frank. "You know Larry—tardy is his twin. There's real-time and Larry time. Celebrities *expect* you to expect them to be late." He points toward the backbar clock, as if that explains everything.

The Count can see perfectly in the dark, even with his murky glasses. As he strips them, Blank Frank notices the silver crucifix dangling from his left earlobe, upside-down.

"You into metal?"

"I like the ornamentation," says the Count. "I was never too big on jewelry; greedy people try to dig you up and steal it if they know you're wearing it; just ask Larry. The sort of people who would come to thieve from the dead in the middle of the night are not the class one would choose for friendly diversion."

Blank Frank conducts the Count to three highback Victorian chairs he has dragged in from the lounge and positioned around a cocktail table. The grouping is directly beneath a pinlight spot, intentionally theatrical.

"Impressive." The Count's gaze flickers toward the bar. Blank Frank is way ahead of him.

The Count sits, continuing: "I once knew a woman who was beleaguered by a devastating allergy to cats. And this was a person who felt some deep emotional communion with that species. Then one day, poof! She no longer sneezed; her eyes no longer watered. She could stop taking medications that made her drowsy. She had forced herself to be around cats so much that her body chemistry adapted. The allergy receded." He fingers the silver cross hanging from his ear, a double threat, once upon a time. "I wear this as a reminder of how the body can triumph. Better living through chemistry."

"It was the same with me and fire." Blank Frank hands over a very potent mixed drink called a Gangbang. The Count sips, then presses his eyelids contentedly shut. Like a cat. The drink must be industrial strength. Controlled substances are the Count's lifeblood.

Blank Frank watches as the Count sucks out another long, deep, soul-drowning draught. "You know Larry's going to ask again, whether you're still doing . . . what you're doing."

"I brook no apologia or excuses." Nevertheless, Blank Frank sees him straighten in his chair, almost defensively. "I could say that you provide the same service in this place." With an outswept hand, he indicts the bar. If nothing else remains recognizable, the Count's gesticulations remain grandiose; physical exclamation points.

"It's legal. Food. Drink. Some smoke."

"Oh, yes, there's the rub." The Count pinches the bridge of his nose. He consumes commercial decongestants ceaselessly. Blank Frank expects him to pop a few pills, but instead the Count lays out a scoop of toot inside his mandarin pinky fingernail, which is lacquered ebony, elongated, a talon. Capacious. Blank Frank knows from experience that the hair and nails continue growing long after death. The Count inhales the equivalent of a pretty good dinner at Spago. Cappucino included.

"There is no place in the world I have not lived," says the Count. "Even the Arctic. The Australian outback. The Kenyan sedge. Siberia. I walk unharmed through fire-fight zones, through sectors of strife. You learn so much when you observe people at war. I've survived holocausts, conflagration, even a low-yield one-megaton test, once, just to see if I could do it. Sue me; I was high. But wherever I venture, whatever phylum of human beings I encounter, they all have one thing in common."

"The red stuff." Blank Frank half-jests; he dislikes it when the mood grows too grim.

"No. It is their need to be narcotized." The Count will not be swerved. "With television. Sex. Coffee. Power. Fast cars and sado-games. Emotional encumbrances. More than anything else, with *chemicals.* All drugs are like instant coffee. The fast purchase of a feeling. You *buy* the feeling, instead of earning it. You want to relax, go up or go down, get strong or get stupid?

You simply swallow or snort or inject, and the world changes because of you. The most lucrative commercial enterprises are those with the most undeniable core simplicity; just look at prostitution. Blood, bodies, armaments, position—all commodities. Human beings want so *much* out of life."

The Count smiles, sips. He knows that the end of life is only the beginning. Today is the first day of the rest of your death.

"I do apologize, my old friend, for coming on so aggressively. I've rationalized my calling, you see, to the point where it is a speech of lists; I make my case with demographics. Rarely do I find anyone who cares to suffer the speech."

"You've been rehearsing." Blank Frank recognizes the bold streak the Count gets in his voice when declaiming. Blank Frank has himself been jammed with so many hypos in the past few centuries that he has run out of free veins. He has sampled the Count's root canal quality coke; it made him irritable and sneezy. The only drugs that still seem to work on him unfailingly are extremely powerful sedatives in large, near-toxic dosages. And those never last long. "Tell me. The drugs. Do they have any effect on *you?*"

He sees the Count pondering how much honesty is too much. Then the tiny, knowing smile flits past again, a wraith between old comrades.

"I employ various palliatives. I'll tell you the absolute truth: Mostly it is an affectation, something to occupy my hands. Human habits—vices, for that matter—go a long way toward putting my customers at ease when I am closing negotiations."

"Now you're thinking like a merchant," says Blank Frank. "No royalty left in you?"

"A figurehead gig." The Count frowns. "Over whom, my good friend, would I hold illimitable dominion? Rock stars. Thrill junkies. Corporate monsters. No percentage in flaunting your lineage there. No. I occupy my time much as a fashion designer does. I concentrate on next season's line. I brought cocaine out of its Vin Mariani limbo and helped repopularize it in the Eighties. Then crank, then crack, then ice. Designer dope. You've heard of Ecstasy. You haven't heard of Chrome yet. Or Amp. But you will."

Suddenly a loud booming rattles the big main door, as though the entire DEA is hazarding a spot raid. Blank Frank and the Count are both twisted around in surprise. Blank Frank catches a glimpse of the enormous Browning Hi-Power holstered in the Count's left armpit.

It's probably just for the image, Blank Frank reminds himself.

The commotion sounds as though some absolute lunatic is kicking the door and baying at the moon. Blank Frank hurries over, his pulse relaxing as his pace quickens.

It has to be Larry.

"Gah-DAMN it's peachy to see ya, ya big dead dimwit!" Larry is a foot shorter than Blank Frank. Nonetheless, he bounds in, pounces, and suffocates his amigo is a big wolfy bear hug.

Larry is almost too much to take in with a single pair of eyes.

His skintight red Spandex tights are festooned with spangles and fringe that snake, at knee level, into golden cowboy boots. Glittering spurs on the boots. An embossed belt buckle the size of the grille on a Rolls. Larry is into ornaments, including a feathered earring with a skull of sterling, about a hundred metalzoid bracelets, and a three-finger rap ring of slush-cast 24K that spells out *AWOO*. His massive, pumped chest fairly bursts from a bright silver Daytona racing jacket, snapped at the waist but not zippered, so the world can see his collarless muscle tee in neon scarlet, featuring his caricature in yellow. Fiery letters on the shirt scream about THE REAL WOLF MAN. Larry is wearing his Ray-Bans at night and jingles a lot whenever he walks.

"Where's old Bat Man? Yo! I *see* you skulking in the dark!" Larry whacks Blank Frank on the bicep, then lopes to catch the Count. With the Count, it is always a normal handshake—dry, firm, businesslike. "Off thy bunnage, fang-dude; the party has *arriiiived!!*"

"Nothing like having a real celebrity in our midst," says Blank Frank. "But jeez—what the hell is this *'Real'* Wolf Man crap?"

Larry grimaces as if from a gas pain, showing teeth. "A slight little ole matter of copyrights, trademarks, eminent domain . . . and some fuckstick who *registered* himself with the World Wrestling Federation as 'The Wolfman.' Turns out to be a guy I bit, my ownself, a couple of decades ago. So I have to be 'The Real.' We did a tag-team thing, last Wrestlemania. But we can't think of a good team name."

"Runts of the Litter," opines the Count. Droll.

"Hellpups," says Blank Frank.

"Fuck ya both extremely much." Larry grins his trademark grin. Still showing teeth. He snaps off his shades and scans Un/Dead. "What's to quaff in this pit? Hell, what *town* is this, anywho?"

"On tour?" Blank Frank plays host.

"Yep. Gotta kick Jake the Snake's ass in Atlanta next Friday. Gonna strangle him with Damien, if the python'll put up with it. Wouldn't want to hurt him for real but might have old Jake pissing blood for a day, if you know what I mean."

Blank Frank grins; he knows what Larry means. He makes a fist with his left hand, then squeezes his left wrist tightly with his right hand. "Vise Grip him."

Larry is the inventor of the Vise Grip, second only to the Sleeper Hold in wrestling infamy. The Vise Grip has done Blank Frank a few favors with rowdies in the past. Larry owns the move, and is entitled to wax proud.

"I mean pissing *pure* blood!" Larry enthuses.

"Ecch," says the Count. "Please."

"Sorry, oh cloakless one. Hey! Remember that brewery, made about three commercials with the Beer Wolf before *that* campaign croaked and ate dirt? That was me!"

Blank Frank hoists his Blind Hermit. "Here's to the Beer Wolf, then. Long may he howl."

"Prost," says the Count.

"Fuckin A." Larry downs his entire mugful of draft in one slam-dunk. He belches, wipes foam from his mouth and lets go with a lupine *yee-hah.*

The Count dabs his lips with a cocktail napkin.

Blank Frank watches Larry do his thing and a stiff chaser of memory quenches his brain. That snout, the bicuspids, and those beady, ball-bearing eyes will always give Larry away. His eyebrows run together; that was supposed to be a classic clue in the good old days. Otherwise Larry is not so hirsute. In human form, at least. The hair on his forearms is very fine tan down. Pumping iron and beating up people for a living has bulked out his shoulders. He usually wears his shirts open-necked. T-shirts, he tears the throats out. He is all piston-muscles and zero flab. He is able to squeeze a full beer can in one fist and pop the top with a gunshot bang. His hands are callused and wily. The pentagram on his right palm is barely visible. It has faded, like Blank Frank's tattoo.

"Cool," Larry says of the Count's crucifix.

"Aren't *you* wearing a touch as well?" The Count points at Larry's skull earring. "Or is it the light?"

Larry's fingers touch the silver. "Yeah. Guilty. Guess we haven't had to fret that movieland spunk for quite apiece, now."

"I had fun." Blank Frank exhibits his tat. "It was good."

"Goood," Larry and the Count say together, funning their friend.

All three envision the tiny plane in growly flight, circling a black and white world, forever.

"How long have you *had* that?" Larry is already on his second mug, foaming at the mouth.

Blank Frank's pupils widen, filling with his skin illustration. He does not remember.

"At least forty years ago," says the Count. "They'd changed the logo by the time he'd committed to getting the tattoo."

"Maybe that was why I did it." Blank Frank is still a bit lost. He touches the tattoo as though it will lead to a swirl dissolve and an expository flashback.

"Hey, we *saved* that fuckin studio from bankruptcy." Larry bristles. "Us and A&C."

"They were shown the door, too." To this day, the Count is understandably piqued about the copyright snafu involving the use of his image. He sees his face everywhere, and does not rate compensation. This abrades his business instinct for the jugular. He understands too well why there must be a Real Wolf

Man. "Bud and Lou and you and me and the big guy all went out with the dishwater of the Second World War."

"*I* was at Lou's funeral," says Larry. "You were lurking the Carpathians." He turned to Blank Frank. "And *you* didn't even know about it."

"I loved Lou," says Blank Frank. "Did I ever tell you the story of how I popped him by accident on the set of—"

"*Yes.*" The Count and Larry speak in unison. This breaks the tension of remembrance tainted by the unfeeling court intrigue of studios. Recall the people, not the things.

Blank Frank tries to remember some of the others. He returns to the bar to rinse his glass. The plasma globe zizzes and snaps calmly, a man-made tempest inside clear glass.

"I heard ole Ace got himself a job at the Museum of Natural History." Larry refers to Ace Bandage; he has nicknames like this for everybody.

"The Prince," the Count corrects, "still guards the Princess. She's on display in the Egyptology section. The Prince cut a deal with museum security. He prowls the graveyard shift; guards the bone rooms. They've got him on a diet of synthetic tana leaves. It calmed him down. Like methadone."

"A night watchman gig," says Larry, obviously thinking of the low pay scale. But what in hell would the Prince need human coin for, anyway? "Hard to picture."

"Try looking in a mirror, yourself," says the Count.

Larry blows a raspberry. "Jealous."

It is very easy for Blank Frank to visualize the Prince, gliding through the silent, cavernous corridors in the wee hours. The museum is, after all, just one giant tomb.

Larry is fairly certain ole Fish Face—another nickname— escaped from a mad scientist in San Francisco and butterfly-stroked south, probably to wind up in bayou country. He and Larry had shared a solid mammal-to-amphibian simpatico. He and Larry had been the most physically violent of the old crew. Larry still entertains the notion of talking his scaly pal into doing a bout for pay-per-view. He has never been able to work out the logistics of a steel fishtank match, however.

"Griffin?" says the Count.

"Who can say?" Blank Frank shrugs. "He could be standing right here and we wouldn't know it unless he started singing 'Nuts in May.'"

"He was a misanthrope," says Larry. "His crazy kid, too. That's what using drugs will get you."

This last is a veiled stab at the Count's calling. The Count expects this from Larry, and stays venomless. The last thing he wants this evening is a conflict over the morality of substance use.

"I dream, sometimes, of those days," says Blank Frank. "Then I see the films again. The dreams are literalized. It's scary."

"Before *this* century," says the Count, "I never had to worry that anyone would stockpile my past." Of the three, he is the most paranoid where personal privacy is concerned.

"You're a romantic." Larry will only toss an accusation like this in special company. "It was important to a lot of people that we *be* monsters. You can't deny what's nailed down there in black and white. There was a time when the world *needed* monsters like that."

They each considered their current occupations, and found that they did indeed still fit into the world.

"Nobody's gonna pester you now," Larry presses on. "Don't bother to revise your past—today, your past is public record, and waiting to contradict you. We did our jobs. How many people become mythologically legendary for just doing their jobs?"

"Mythologically legendary?" mimics the Count. "You'll grow hair on your hands from using all those big words."

"Bite this." Larry offers the unilateral peace symbol.

"No, thank you; I've already dined. But I have brought something for you. For both of you."

Blank Frank and Larry both notice the Count is now speaking as though a big Mitchell camera is grinding away, somewhere just beyond the grasp of sight. He produces a small pair of wrapped gifts, and hands them over.

Larry wastes no time ripping into his. "Weighs a ton."

Nestled in styro popcorn is a wolf's head—savage, streamlined, smiling. The gracile canine neck is socketed.

"It's from the walking stick," says the Count. "All that was left."

"No kidding." Larry's voice grows small for the first time that evening. The wolf's head seems to gain weight in his grasp. Two beats of his powerful heart later, his eyes seem a bit wet.

Blank Frank's gift is much smaller and lighter.

"You were a conundrum," says the Count. He enjoys playing emcee. "So many choices, yet never easy to buy for. Some soil from Transylvania? Water from Loch Ness? A chunk of some appropriate ruined castle?"

What Blank Frank unwraps is a ring. Old gold, worn smooth of its subtler filigree. A small ruby set in the grip of a talon. He holds it to the light.

"As nearly as I could discover, that ring once belonged to a man named Ernst Volmer Klumpf."

"Whoa," says Larry. Weird name.

Blank Frank puzzles it. He holds it toward the Count, like a lens.

"Klumpf died a long time ago," says the Count. "Died and was buried. Then he was disinterred. Then a few of his choicer parts were recycled by a skillful surgeon of our mutual acquaintance."

Blank Frank stops looking so blank.

"In fact, part of Ernst Volmer Klumpf is still walking around today . . . tending bar for his friends, among other things."

The new expression on Blank Frank's pleases the Count. The ring just barely squeezes onto the big guy's left pinky—his smallest finger.

Larry, to avoid choking up, decides to make noise. Showing off, he vaults the bartop and draws his own refill. "This calls for a toast." He hoists his beer high, slopping the head. "To dead friends. Meaning us."

The Count pops several capsules from an ornate tin and washes them down with the last of his Gangbang. Blank Frank murders his Blind Hermit.

"Don't even think of the bill," says Blank Frank, who knows of the Count's habit of paying for everything. The Count smiles and nods graciously. In his mind, the critical thing is to keep the tab straight. Blank Frank pats the Count on the shoulder, hale and brotherly, since Larry is out of reach. The Count dislikes physical contact but permits this because it is, after all, Blank Frank.

"Shit man, we could make our own comeback sequel, with all the talent in this room," Larry says. "Maybe hook up with some of those new guys. Do a monster rally."

It could happen. They all look significantly at each other. A brief stink of guilt, of culpability, like a sneaky fart in a dimly lit chamber.

Make that dimly-lit *torture dungeon*, thinks Blank Frank, who never forgets the importance of staying in character.

Blank Frank thinks about sequels. About how studios had once jerked their marionette strings, compelling them to come lurching back for more, again and again, adding monsters when the brew ran weak, until they had all been bled dry of revenue potential and dumped at a bus stop to commence the long deathwatch that had made them nostalgia.

It was like living death, in its way.

And these gatherings, year upon year, had become sequels in their own right.

The realization is depressing. It sort of breaks the back of the evening for Blank Frank. He stands friendly and remains as chatty as he ever gets. But the emotion has soured.

Larry chugs so much that he has grown a touch bombed. The Count's chemicals intermix and buzz; he seems to sink into the depths of his coat, his chin ever-closer to the butt of the gun he carries. Larry drinks deep, then howls. The Count plugs one ear with a finger on his free hand. "I wish he wouldn't *do* that," he says in a proscenium-arch *sotto voce* that indicates his annoyance is mostly token.

When Larry tries to hurdle the bar again, moving exaggeratedly as he almost always does, he manages to plant his big wrestler's elbow right into the glass on Blank Frank's framed movie poster. It dents inward with a sharp crack, cobwebbing into a snap puzzle of fracture curves. Larry swears, instantly chagrined. Then, lamely, he offers to pay for the damage.

The Count, not unexpectedly, counter-offers to buy the poster, now that it's damaged.

Blank Frank shakes his massive square head at both of his friends. So many years, among them. "It's just glass. I can replace it. It wouldn't be the first time."

The thought that he has done this before depresses him further. He sees the reflection of his face, divided into staggered components in the broken glass, and past that, the lurid illustration. Him then. Him now.

Blank Frank touches his face as though it is someone else's. His fingernails have always been black. Now they are merely fashionable.

Larry remains embarrassed about the accidental damage and the Count begins spot-checking his Rolex every five minutes or so, as though he is pressing the envelope on an urgent appointment. Something has spoiled the whole mood of their reunion, and Blank Frank is angry that he can't quite pinpoint the cause. When he is angry, his temper froths quickly.

The Count is the first to rise. Decorum is all. Larry tries one more time to apologize. Blank Frank stays cordial, but is overpowered by the sudden strong need to get them the hell out of Un/Dead.

The Count bows stiffly. His limo manifests precisely on schedule. Larry gives Blank Frank a hug. His arms can reach all the way 'round.

"Au revoir," says the Count.

"Stay dangerous," says Larry.

Blank Frank closes and locks the service door. He monitors, via the tiny security window, the silent, gliding departure of the Count's limousine, the fading of Larry's spangles into the night.

Still half an hour till opening. The action at Un/Dead doesn't really crank until midnight anyway, so there's very little chance that some bystander will get hurt.

Blank Frank bumps up the volume and taps his club boot. A eulogy with a beat. He loves Larry and the Count in his massive, broad, uncompromisingly loyal way, and hopes they will understand his actions. He hopes that his two closest friends are perceptive enough, in the years to come, to know that he is not crazy.

Not crazy, and certainly not a monster.

While the music plays, he fetches two economy-sized plastic bottles of lantern kerosene, which he ploshes liberally around the bar, saturating the old wood trim. Arsonists call such flammable liquids "accelerator."

In the scripts, it was always an overturned lantern, or a flung torch from a mob of villagers, that touched off the conclusive inferno. Mansions, mad labs, even stone fortresses not only burned, but blew up, eliminating all phyla of menacing monsters until they were needed anew.

Dark threads snake through the tiny warrior braid at the base of Blank Frank's skull. All those Blind Hermits, don't you know.

The purple electricity arcs to meet his finger and trails after it loyally. He unplugs the plasma globe and cradles it beneath one giant forearm.

The movie poster, he leaves hanging in its violated frame.

He snaps the sulphur match with a black thumbnail. Ignition craters and blackens the head, eating it with a sharp hiss. Un/Dead's PA throbs to the bass line of "D.O.A." Phosphorus tinges the unmoving air. The match fires orange to yellow to steady blue-white. Its flamepoint reflects from Blank Frank's large black pupils. He can see himself, as if by candlelight, fragmented by broken picture glass. The past. In his grasp is the plasma globe, unblemished, pristine, awaiting a new charge of energy. The future.

He recalls his past experiences with fire, all of them. Burn down the monster. He drops the match into the thin pool of accelerator glistening on the bartop and the flame grows, quietly.

By striking the match, he has just purchased a feeling, as the Count would no doubt observe.

The Monster blunderingly topples a rack of beakers, a modern-day sorcerer's brew of flammables and caustics . . .

Never has he precipitated the end on purpose. Never, except in the first sequel. *We belong dead.* He was making a point.

The movie poster stays behind, in its smashed frame. That will be the price paid. Sacrifice something valuable.

More convincing, that way. He is staying dangerous.

Good.

And Blank Frank does, in fact, feel better.

Light springs, hard reddish-white now, behind him as he makes his exit and locks the door of Un/Dead. The night is cool by contrast, near foggy. Condensation mists the plasma globe as he strolls away, pausing once beneath a streetlamp to appreciate the ring on his little finger. He doesn't need to eat, to sleep.

Uninjured by the cataclysm, the Monster stumbles, grunting, away from the village and into the forest . . .

But this time, thinks Blank Frank, the old Monster knows where he's going.

He'll miss Michelle and the rest of the club staff. But he must move on, because he is not like them. He has all the time he'll ever need, and friends who will be around forever . . .

Un/Dead blazes. The night swallows him.

Blank Frank likes the power.

JOYCE CAROL OATES

Joyce Carol Oates was born in Millerport, New York, in 1938. She received a B.A. in English from Syracuse University and an M.A. from the University of Wisconsin. In 1962 she married Raymond J. Smith, settling in Detroit. There she wrote the novel *them* (1969), a searing study of the race riots plaguing the city. Between 1968 and 1978, Oates taught at the University of Windsor in Canada; from 1978 onward, she has taught creative writing at Princeton University, where she is now the Roger S. Berlind Distinguished Professor of the Humanities. Oates, one of the most prolific of contemporary American writers, has received many awards for her work, including the National Book Award and the Commonwealth Award for Distinguished Service in Literature.

The supernatural has been a pervasive theme in much of Oates's work as novelist and short story writer. A series of four novels, *Bellefleur* (1980), *A Bloodsmoor Romance* (1982), *Mysteries of Winterthurn* (1984), and *My Heart Laid Bare* (1998), applies the Gothic mode to American history and culture. *Bellefleur* features seven generations of grotesque characters, including a vampire, a mad scientist, and a mass murderer, dwelling in a haunted mansion. Much of Oates's horror work is nonsupernatural, as in the novel *Black Water* (1992), the short novel *Beasts* (2001), and the novel *The Tattooed Girl* (2003).

Oates has also utilized supernatural horror in many of her short stories. *Haunted: Tales of the Grotesque* (1994) contains the highest proportion of horror tales, but several of her other collections include one or more specimens. Oates has compiled the anthology *American Gothic Tales* (1996), the introduction to which elucidates her theory of supernatural writing. She has also edited *Tales of H. P. Lovecraft* (1997).

"Demon," a short story first published in the small-press chapbook *Demon and Other Tales* (1996), is a gripping and ambiguous horror tale in which the supernatural may or may not come into play.

DEMON

Demon-child. Kicked in the womb so his mother doubled over in pain. Nursing tugged and tore at her young breasts. Wailed through the night. Puked, shat. Refused to eat. *No he was loving, mad with love.* Of Mama. (Though fearful of Da.) Curling burrowing pushing his head into Mama's arms, against Mama's warm fleshy body. Starving for love, food. Starving for what he could not know yet to name: *God's grace, salvation.*

Sign of Satan: flamey-red ugly-pimply birthmark snake-shaped. On his underjaw, coiled below his ear. Almost you can't see it. A little boy he's teased by neighbor girls, hulking, big girls with titties and laughing-wet eyes. *Demon! demon! Lookit, sign of the demon!*

Those years passing in a fever-dream. Or maybe never passed. Mama prayed over him, hugged and slapped. Shook his skinny shoulders so his head flew. The minister prayed over him *Deliver us from evil* and he was good, he *was* delivered from evil. Except at school his eyes misting over, couldn't see the blackboard. Sullen and nasty-mouthed the teacher called him. Not like the other children.

If not like *the other children,* then like *who? what?*

Those years. As in a stalled city bus, exhaust pouring out the rear. The stink of it everywhere. Your hair, eyes. Clothes. Same view through the same fly-specked windows. Year after year the battered-tin diner, the vacant lot high with weeds and rubble and the path worn through it slantwise where children ran shouting above the river. Broken pavement littered like confetti from a parade long past.

Or maybe it was the edge of something vast, infinite. You could never come to the end of. Wavering and blinding in blasts of light. *Desert,* maybe. *Red Desert* where demons dance, swirl in the hot winds. Never seen a *desert* except pictures, a name on a map. And in his head.

Demon-child they whispered of him. But no, he was loving, mad with love. Too small, too short. Stunted legs. His head too big for his spindly shoulders. His strange waxy-pale moon-shaped face, almond eyes beautiful in shadowed sockets, small wet mouth perpetually sucking inward. As if to keep the bad words, words of filth and damnation, safely inside.

The sign of Satan coiled on his underjaw began to fade. Like his adolescent skin eruptions. Blood drawn gradually back into tissue, capillaries.

Not a demon-child but a pure good anxious loving child someone betrayed by squeezing him from her womb before he was ready.

Not a demon-child but for years he rode wild thunderous razor-hooved black stallions by night and by day. Furious galloping on sidewalks, in asphalt playgrounds. Through the school corridors trampling all in his way. Furious tearing hooves, froth-flecked nostrils, bared teeth. God's wrath, the black stallion rearing, whinnying. *I destroy all in my path. Beware!*

Not a demon-child but he'd torched the school, rows of stores, woodframe houses in the neighborhood. How many times the smelly bed where Mama and Da hid from him. And no one knew.

This January morning bright and windy and he's staring at the face floating in a mirror. Dirty mirror in a public lavatory, Trailways Bus Station. Where at last the demon has been released. For it is the New Year. The shifting of the earth's axis. For to be away from what is familiar, like walking on a sharp-slanted floor, allows *something other* in. Or the *something other* has been inside you all along and until now you do not know.

In his right eyeball a speck of dirt? dust? blood?

Scared, he knows right away. Knows even before he sees:

sign of Satan. In the yellowish-white of his eyeball. Not the coiled little snake but the five-sided star: *pentagram.*

He knows, he's been warned. Five-sided star: *pentagram.*

It's there, in his eye. Tries to rub it out with his fist.

Backs away terrified and gagging and he's running out of the fluorescent-bright lavatory and through the bus station where eyes trail after him curious, bemused, pitying, annoyed. He's a familiar sight here though no one knows his name. Runs home, about three miles. His mother knows there's trouble, has he lied about taking his medicine? hiding the pill under his tongue? Yes but God knows you can't oversee every minute with one like him. Yes but your love wears thin like the lead backing of a cheap mirror corroding the glass. Yes but you have prayed, you have prayed and prayed and cursed the words echoing not upward to God but downward as in an empty well.

Twenty-six years old, shaved head glinting blue. Luminous shining eyes women in the street call beautiful. In the neighborhood he's known by his first name. Sweet guy but strange, excitable. A habit of twitching his shoulders like he's shrugging free of somebody's grip.

Fast as you run somebody runs faster!

In the house that's a semi-detached rowhouse on Mill Street he's not listening to his angry mother asking why is he home so early, has a job in a building supply yard so why isn't he there? Pushes past the old woman and into the bathroom, shuts the door and there in the mirror oh God it's there: the five-sided star, *pentagram.* Sign of Satan. Embedded deep in his right eyeball, just below the dilated iris.

No! no! God help!

Goes wild rubs with both fists, pokes with fingers. He's weeping, shouting. Beats at himself, fists and nails. His sister now pounding on the door what is it? what's wrong? and Mama's voice loud and frightened. *It's happened,* he thinks. His first clear thought. *Happened.* Like a stone sinking so calm. Because hasn't he always known the prayers did no good, on your knees bowing your head inviting Jesus into your heart does no good. The sign of the demon would return, absorbed into his blood but must one day re-emerge.

Pushes past the women and in the kitchen paws through the drawer scattering cutlery that falls to the floor, bounces and clatters and there's the big carving knife in his hand, his hand shuts about it like fate. Pushes past the women now in reverse where they've followed him into the kitchen knocks his one-hundred-eighty-pound older sister aside with his elbow as lightly as he lifts bags of gravel, armloads of bricks. Hasn't he prayed Our Father to be a machine many times. A machine does not feel, a machine does not think. A machine does not hurt. A machine does not starve for love. A machine does not starve for what it does not know to name: *salvation.*

Back then inside the bathroom, slamming the door against the screaming women, and locking it. Gibbering to himself, *Away Satan! Away Satan! God help!* With a hand strangely steely as if practiced wielding the point of the knife, boldly inserting and twisting into the accursed eyeball. And no pain—only a burning cleansing roaring sensation as of a blast of fire. Out pops the eyeball, and out the sign of Satan. But connected by tissue, nerves. It's elastic so he's pulling, fingers now slippery-excited with blood. He's sawing with the sharp blade of the steak knife. Cuts the eyeball free, like Mama squeezing baby out of her belly into this pig trough of sin and filth, and no turning back till Jesus calls you home.

He drops the eyeball into the toilet, flushes the toilet fast.

Before Satan can intervene.

One of those antiquated toilets where water swirls about the stained bowl, wheezes and yammers to itself, sighs, grumbles, finally swallows like it's doing you a favor. And the sign of the demon is gone.

One eyesocket empty and fresh-bleeding he's on his knees praying *Thank you God! thank you God!* weeping as angels in radiant garments with faces of blinding brightness reach down to embrace him not minding his red-slippery mask of a face. Now he's one of them himself, now he will float into the sky where, some wind-blustery January morning, you'll see him, or a face like his, in a furious cloud.

CAITLÍN R. KIERNAN

Caitlín Rebekah Kiernan was born in 1964 in Skerries, Ireland, but came to the United States as a child, shortly after the death of her father. Her family lived in several locales in the South before settling in Birmingham, Alabama; in spite of her birth in Ireland, Kiernan now identifies herself as a Southern author and draws upon the heritage of Southern culture in much of her work. After receiving a degree in vertebrate paleontology from the University of Colorado, Kiernan returned to Birmingham to work at the Red Mountain Museum. She has published several scientific papers in such journals as the *Journal of Paleontology* and the *Journal of Vertebrate Paleontology,* and her scientific background is an essential component in several of her novels and tales.

Kiernan began publishing short stories in the 1990s, and they have now been gathered into five volumes: *Candles for Elizabeth* (1998), *Tales of Pain and Wonder* (2000), *Wrong Things* (2001; with Poppy Z. Brite), *From Weird and Distant Shores* (2002), and *To Charles Fort, with Love* (2005). Her work came to the attention of Neil Gaiman, who commissioned her to do much of the writing for *The Dreaming,* a successor to Gaiman's successful graphic novel *The Sandman;* Kiernan scripted *The Dreaming* from 1997 to 2001. Her first novel, *Silk* (1998), fuses supernatural and psychological horror in its account of the demons that emerge from a young woman's memories of her father's abusive treatment of her; it won the International Horror Guild award for best first novel. *Threshold* (2001), a cosmic novel that draws upon *Beowulf,* Algernon Blackwood, and others, won the IHG award for best novel. *Low Red Moon* (2003) is another cosmic novel; *The Five of Cups* (2003) is a vampire novel; *Murder of Angels* (2004) is a sequel to *Silk,* while *The Dry Salvages* (2004) is a dark science fiction novel. *Alabaster* (2006) is her latest story collection.

"In the Water Works (Birmingham, Alabama 1888)," first published in *Tales of Pain and Wonder,* effectively utilizes both Kiernan's knowledge of science and her sense of place in its evocative account of an ambiguous monster lurking in a tunnel in Birmingham.

IN THE WATER WORKS
(BIRMINGHAM, ALABAMA 1888)

Red Mountain, weathered tip end of Appalachia's long and scabby spine, this last ambitious foothill before the land slumps finally down to black-belt prairies so flat they've never imagined even these humble altitudes. And as if Nature hasn't done her best already, as if wind and rain and frost haven't whittled aeons away to expose the limestone and iron-ore bones, Modern Industry has joined in the effort, scraping away the stingy soil and so whenever it rains, the falling sky turns the ground to sea slime again, primordial mire the color of a butchery to give this place its name, rustdark mud that sticks stubborn to Henry Matthews' hobnailed boots as he wanders over and between the spoil piles heaped outside the opening to the Water Works tunnel.

Scarecrow tall and thin, young Mr. Henry S. Matthews, lately of some place far enough north to do nothing to better the reputation of a man who is neither married nor church-going, who teaches geography and math at the new Powell School on Sixth Avenue North and spends the remainder of his time with an assortment of books and rocks and pickled bugs. The sudden rumble of thunder somewhere down in the valley, then, and he moves too fast, careless as he turns to see, almost losing his footing as the wet stones slip and tilt beneath his feet.

"You best watch yourself up there, Professor," one of the workmen shouts, and there's laughter from the black hole in the mountain's side. Henry offers a perfunctory nod in the general direction of the tunnel, squints through the haze of light October rain and dust and coal smoke at the rough grid of the little city laid out north of the mountain; barely seventeen years since John Morris and the Elyton Land Company put pen to ink, ink to paper, and incorporated Birmingham, drawing a city from a hasty scatter of ironworks and mining camps. Seventeen years, and he wonders for a moment what this place was like before white men and their machines, before axes and the dividing paths of railroad tracks.

The thunder rolls and echoes no answer he can understand, and Henry looks back to the jumbled ground, the split and broken slabs of shale at his feet. The rain has washed away the thick dust of the excavations, making it easier for him to spot the shells and tracks of sea creatures preserved in the stone. Only a few weeks since he sent a large crate of fossils south to the State Geological Survey in Tuscaloosa, and already a small museum's worth of new specimens line the walls of his cramped room, sit beneath his bed and compete with his clothing for closet space, with his books for the shelves. An antediluvian seashore in hardened bits and pieces, and just last week he found the perfectly preserved carapace of a trilobite almost the length of his hand.

A whistle blows, shrill steam blat, and a few more men file out of the tunnel to eat their lunches in the listless rain. Henry reaches into a pocket of his waistcoat for the silver watch his mother gave him the year he left for college, wondering how a Saturday morning could slip by so fast; the clockblack hands at one and twelve, and he's suddenly aware of the tugging weight of his knapsack, the emptiness in his belly, hours now since breakfast but there's a boiled egg wrapped in waxed paper and a tin of sardines in his overcoat. The autumn sky growls again, and he snaps his watch closed and begins to pick his way cautiously down the spoil towards the other men.

Henry Matthews taps the brown shell of his hard-boiled egg against a piece of limestone, crack, crack, crack, soft white insides exposed, and he glances up at the steelgray sky overhead; the rain has stopped, stopped again, stopped for now, and crystalwet drops cling to the browngoldred leaves of the few hickory and hackberry trees still standing near the entrance of the tunnel. He sits with the miners, the foreman, the hard men who spend dawn to dusk in the shaft, shadowy days breaking stone and hauling it back into the sunlight. Henry suspects that the men tolerate his presence as a sort of diversion, a curiosity to interrupt the monotony of their days. This thin Yankee dude, this odd bird who picks about the spoil like there might be gold or silver when everyone knows there isn't anything worth beans going to come out of the mountain except the purplered ore, and that's more like something you have to be careful not to trip over than try to find.

Sometimes they joke, and sometimes they ask questions, their interest or suspicion piqued by his diligence, perhaps. "What you lookin' for anyways, Mister?" and he'll open his knapsack and show them a particularly clear imprint of a snail's whorled shell or the mineralized honeycomb of a coral head. Raised eyebrows and heads nodding, and maybe then someone will ask, "So, them's things what got buried in Noah's flood?" and Henry doubts any of these men have even heard of Lyell or Darwin or Cuvier, have any grasp of the marvelous advancement that science has made the last hundred years concerning the meaning of fossils and the progression of geological epochs. So he's always politic, aware that the wrong answer might get him exiled from the diggings. And, genuinely wishing that he had time to explain the wonders of his artefacts to these men, Henry only shrugs and smiles for them. "Well, actually, some of them are even a bit older than that," or a simple and noncommittal "Mmmmm," and usually that's enough to satisfy.

But today is different and the men are quiet, each one eating his cold potatoes or dried meat, staring silent at muddy boots and lunch pails, the mining-car track leading back inside the tunnel, and no one asks him anything. Henry looks up once from his sardines and catches one of the men watching him. He smiles, and the man frowns and looks quickly away. When the whistle blows again, the men rise slowly, moving with a reluctance that's plain enough to see, back towards the waiting tunnel. Henry wipes his fingers on his handkerchief, fish oil stains on white linen, is shouldering his knapsack, retrieving his geologist's hammer, when someone says his name, "Mr. Matthews?" voice low, almost whispered, and he looks up into the foreman's hazelbrown eyes.

"Yes, Mr. Wallace? Is there something I can do for you today?" and Warren Wallace looks away, nervous glance to his men for a moment that seems a lot longer to Henry who's anxious to get back to his collecting.

"You know all this geology business pretty good, don't you, Mr. Matthews? All about these rocks and such?" and Henry shrugs, nods his head, "Yes sir, I suppose that I do. I had a course or two—"

"Then maybe you could take a look at somethin' for me sometime," the foreman says, interrupting, looking back at Henry, and there are deep lines around his eyes, worry or lack of sleep, both maybe. The foreman spits a shitbrown streak of tobacco at the ground and shakes his head. "It probably ain't nothing, but I might want you to take a look at it sometime."

"Yes. Certainly," Henry says, "Anytime you'd like," but Warren Wallace is already walking away from him, following his men towards the entrance of the tunnel, shouting orders, and "Be careful up there, Mr. Matthews," he says, spoken without turning around, and Henry replies that he always is, but thanks for the concern anyway, and he goes back to the spoil piles.

Fifteen minutes later it's raining again, harder now, a cold and stinging rain from the north and wind that gusts and swirls dead leaves like drifting ash.

May 1887 when the Birmingham Water Works Company entered into a contract with Judge A. O. Lane, Mayor and Alderman, and plans were drawn to bring water from the distant Cahaba River north across Shades Valley to the thirsty citizens of the city. But Red Mountain standing there in the way, standing guard or simply unable to move, and its slopes too steep for gravity to carry the water over the top, so the long tunnel dreamed up by engineers, the particular brainchild of one Mr. W. A. Merkel, first chief engineer of the Cahaba Station. A two thousand, two hundred foot bore straight through the sedimentary heart of the obstacle, tons of stone blasted free with gelignite and nitro, pickaxes and sledge hammers and the sweat of men and mules. The promise of not less than five million gallons of fresh water a day, and in this bright age of invention and innovation it's a small job for determined men, moving mountains, coring them like ripe and crimson apples.

A week later, and Henry Matthews is again picking over the spoil heaps, a cool and sunny October day crisp as cider, an autumnsoft breeze that smells of dry and burning leaves, and his spirits are high, three or four exceptional trilobites from the hard limestone already and a single, disc-shaped test of some specie of echinodermia he's never encountered before, almost as big as a silver dollar. He stoops to get a better look at a promising slab when someone calls his name, and he looks up, mildly annoyed at the intrusion. Foreman Wallace is standing nearby, scratching at his thick black beard, and he points at Henry with one finger.

"How's the fishin', Professor?" he asks, and it takes Henry a moment to get the joke; he doesn't laugh, but a belated smile, finally, and then the foreman is crossing the uneven stones towards him.

"No complaints," Henry says and produces the largest of the trilobites for the foreman's inspection. Warren Wallace holds the oystergray chunk of limestone close and squints at the small dark *Cryptolithus* outstretched on the rock.

"Well," the foreman says and rubs at his beard again, wrinkles his thick eyebrows and stares back at Henry Matthews. "Ain't that some pumpkins. And this little bug used to be alive? Crawlin' around in the ocean?"

"Yes," Henry replies, and he points to the trilobite's bulbous glabellum and the pair of large compound eyes to either side. "This end was its head," he says. "And this was the tail," as his fingertip moves to the fan-shaped lobe at the other end of the creature. Warren Wallace glances back at the fossil once more before he returns it to Henry.

"Now, Professor, you tell me if you ever seen anything like this here," and the foreman produces a small bottle from his shirt pocket, apothecary bottle Henry thinks at first, and then no, not medicine, nitroglycerine. Warren Wallace passes the stoppered bottle to the schoolteacher, and, for a moment, Henry Matthews stares silently at the black thing trapped inside.

"Where did this come from?" he asks, trying not to show his surprise but wide eyes still on the bottle, unable to look away from the thing coiling and uncoiling in its eight-ounce glass prison.

"From the tunnel," the foreman replies, spits tobacco juice and glances over his shoulder at the gaping hole in the mountain. "About five hundred feet in, just a little ways past where the limerock goes to sandstone. That's where we hit the fissure."

Henry Matthews turns the bottle in his hand, and the thing inside uncoils, stretches chitinous segments, an inch, two inches, almost three, before it snaps back into a legless ball that glimmers iridescent in the afternoon sun.

"Ugly little bastard, ain't it?" the foreman says and spits again. "But you *ain't* never seen nothin' like it before, have you?" And Henry shakes his head, no, never, and now he wants to look away, doesn't like the way the thing in the bottle is making him feel. But it's stretched itself out again, and he can see tiny fibers like hairs or minute spines protruding between the segments.

"Can you show me?" he asks, realizes that he's almost whispering now, library or classroom whisper like maybe he's afraid someone will overhear, like this should be secret.

"Where it came from, will you take me there?"

"Yeah. I was hopin' you'd ask," the foreman says and rubs his beard. "But let me tell you, Professor, you ain't seen nothin' yet." And after Warren Wallace has taken the bottle back, returned it to his shirt pocket so that Henry doesn't have to look at the black thing anymore, the two men begin the climb down the spoil piles to the entrance of the tunnel.

A few feet past the entrance, fifteen, twenty, and the foreman stops, stands talking to a fat man with a pry bar while Henry looks back at the bright day framed in raw limestone and bracing timbers, blinking as his eyes slowly adjust to the gloom.

"Yeah," the fat man says, "Yeah," and Warren Wallace asks him another question. It's cooler in the tunnel, in the dark, and the air smells like rock dust and burning carbide and another smell tucked somewhere underneath, unhealthy smell like a wet cellar or rotting vegetables that makes Henry wrinkle his nose. "Yeah, I seen him before," the fat man with the pry bar says, wary reply to the foreman's question and a distrustful glance towards Henry Matthews.

"I want him to have a look at your arm, Jake, that's all," and Henry turns his back on the light, turns to face the foreman and the fat man. "*He* ain't no doctor," the fat man says. "And I already seen Doc Joe, anyways."

"He's right," Henry says, confused now, no idea what this man's arm and the thing in the jar might have to do with one another, blinking at Wallace through the dancing whiteyellow afterimages of the sunlight outside. "I haven't had any medical training to speak of, certainly nothing formal."

"Yeah?" the foreman says, and he sighs loudly, exasperation or disappointment, spits on the tunnel floor, tobacco juice on rusted steel rails. "C'mon then, Professor," and he hands a miner's helmet to Henry, lifts a lantern off an iron hook set into the rock wall. "Follow me, and don't touch anything. Some of these beams ain't as sturdy as they look."

The fat man watches them, massages his left forearm protectively when the schoolteacher steps past him, and now Henry can hear the sounds of digging somewhere in the darkness far ahead of them. Relentless clank and clatter of steel against stone, and the lantern throws long shadows across the rough limestone walls; fresh wound, these walls, this abscess hollowed into the world's thin skin. And such morbid thoughts as alien to Henry Matthews as the perpetual night of this place, and so he tells himself it's just the sight of the odd and squirming thing in the bottle, that and the natural uneasiness of someone who's never been underground before.

"You're wonderin' what Jake Isabell's arm has to do with that damned worm, ain't you?" the foreman asks, his voice too loud in the narrow tunnel even though he's almost whispering. And "Yes," Henry replies, "Yes, I was, as a matter of fact."

"It bit him a couple of days ago. Jesus, make him sick as a dyin' dog, too. But that's all. It bit him."

And "Oh," Henry says, unsure what else he should say and beginning to wish he was back out in the sun looking for his trilobites and mollusks with the high Octoberblue sky hung far, far overhead. "How deep are we now?" he asks, and the foreman stops and looks up at the low ceiling of the tunnel, rubs his beard. "Not very, not yet . . . hundred and twenty, maybe hundred and thirty feet." And then he reaches up and touches the ceiling a couple of inches above his head.

"You know how old these rocks are, Professor?" and Henry nods, tries too hard to sound calm when he answers the foreman.

"These layers of limestone here . . . well, they're probably part of the Lower Silurian system, some of the oldest with traces of living creatures found in them," and he pauses, realizes that he's sweating despite the cool and damp of the tunnel, wishes again he'd declined the foreman's invitation into the mountain. "But surely hundreds of thousands, perhaps *millions* of years old," he says.

"Damn," the foreman says and spits again. "Now that's somethin' to think about, ain't it, Professor? I mean, these rocks sittin' here all that time, not seein' the light of day all that time, and then *we* come along with our picks and dynamite—"

"Yes sir," Henry Matthews says and wipes the sweat from his face with his handkerchief. "It is, indeed," but Warren Wallace is moving again, dragging the little pool of lantern light along with him, and Henry has to hurry to catch up, almost smacks his forehead on the low, uneven ceiling. Another three hundred feet or so and they've reached the point where the gray limestone is overlain by beds of punky reddish sandstone, the bottom of the Red Mountain formation; lifeblood of the city locked away in these strata, clotthick veins of hematite for the coke ovens and blast furnaces dotting the valley below. "Not much farther," the foreman says. "We're almost there."

The wet, rotten smell stronger now, and glistening rivulets meander down the walls, runoff seeping down through the rocks above them, rain filtered through dead leaves and soil, through a hundred or a thousand cracks in the stone. Henry imagines patches of pale and rubbery mushrooms, perhaps more exotic fungi, growing in the dark. He wipes his face again and this time keeps the handkerchief to his nose, but the thick and rotten smell seeps up his nostrils, anyway. *If an odor alone could drown a man,* he thinks, is about to say something about the stench to Warren Wallace when the foreman stops, holds his lantern close to the wall, and Henry can see the big sheets of corrugated tin propped against the west side of the tunnel.

"At first I thought we'd hit an old mine shaft," he says, motions towards the tin with the lantern, causing their shadows to sway and contort along the damp tunnel. "Folks been diggin' holes in this mountain since the forties to get at the ore. So that's what I thought, at first."

"But you've changed your mind?" Henry asks, words muffled by the useless handkerchief pressed to his face.

"Right now, Professor, I'm a whole lot more interested in what *you* think," and then Wallace pulls back a big section of the tin, lets it fall loud to the floor, tin clamor against the steel rails at his feet. Henry gags, bilehot rush from his gut and the distant taste of breakfast in the back of his mouth. "Jesus," he hisses, not wanting to be sick in front of the foreman, and the schoolteacher leans against the tunnel wall for support, presses his left palm against moss-slick stone, stone gone soft as the damprough hide of some vast amphibian.

"Sorry. Guess I should'a warned you about the stink," and Warren Wallace frowns, grim face like Greek tragedy, and takes a step back from the hole in the wall of the tunnel, hole within a hole, and now Henry's eyes are watering so badly he can hardly see. "Merkel had us plowin' through here full chisel until we hit that thing. Now it's all I can do to keep my men workin'."

"Can't exactly blame them," Henry wheezes and gags again, spits at the tunnel floor, but the taste of the smell clings to his tongue, coats it like a mouthful of cold bacon grease. The foreman gestures for him to come closer, close enough he can peer down into the gap in the rock and Henry knows that's the last thing he wants to do. But he loathes that irrational fear, fear of the unknown that keeps men ignorant, keeps men down, and all his life gone to the purging of that instinctual dread, first from himself and then his students. And so Henry Matthews holds his breath against the stench and steps over the mining car tracks, glances once at Warren Wallace, and to see a strong man so afraid and hardly any effort into hiding it is enough to get him to the crumbling edge of the hole.

And that's the best word, hole, a wide crevice in the wall of the tunnel maybe four feet across and dropping suddenly away into darkness past the reach of the lantern, running west into more blackness but pinching closed near the tunnel's ceiling. A natural fault, he thinks at first, evidence of the great and ancient forces that must have raised these mountains up, and the smell could be almost anything. Perhaps this shaft opens somewhere on the surface, a treacherous, unnoticed pit in the woods overhead, and from time to time an unfortunate animal might fall, might lie broken and rotting in the murk below, food for devouring mold and insects. And the thing in the jar is probably nothing more or less than the larvae of some large beetle new to entomology or perhaps only the hitherto unknown pupa of a familiar specie.

"Take the lantern," Warren Wallace says, then, handing the kerosene lamp to the schoolteacher. "Hold it right inside there, but don't lean too far in, mind you," and Henry feels the foreman's hand on his shoulder, weight and strength meant to be reassuring.

"Hold it out over the hole," he says, "and look down."

Henry Matthews does as he's told, already half-convinced of his clever induction and preparing himself for the unpleasant (but perfectly ordinary) sight of a badly decomposed raccoon or opossum, maybe even a deer carcass at the bottom and the maggots, maybe more of the big black things that supposedly bit Mr. Isabell's arm. He exhales, a little dizzy from holding his breath, then gasps in another lung full of the rancid air rising up from the pit. One hand braced against the tunnel wall, and leans as far out as he dares, a foot, maybe two, the flickering yellow light washing down and down, and he almost cries out at the unexpected sight of his own reflection staring back up at him from the surface of a narrow subterranean pool.

"It's flooded," he says, half to himself, half to the foreman, and Warren Wallace murmurs a reply, yeah, it's flooded, and something else that Henry doesn't quite catch. He's watching the water, ten feet down to the surface at the most, water as smooth and black as polished obsidian.

"Now look at the *walls*, Professor, where they meet the water," and he does, positions the lantern for a better view, and maybe just a little braver now, a little more curious, so he's leaning farther out, the foreman's hand still holding him back.

At first he doesn't see anything, angle a little less than ninety degrees where black rock meets blacker water, and then he does see something and thinks it must be the roots of some plant growing in the pool, or, more likely, running down from the forest above to find this hidden moisture. Gnarled roots as big around as his arm, twisted wood knotted back upon itself.

But one of them moves, then, abrupt twitch as it rolls away from the others, and Henry Matthews realizes that they're *all* moving now, each tendril creeping slow across the slick face of the crevice like blind and roaming fingers, searching. "My God," he whispers. "My God in Heaven," starts to pull away from the hole, but the foreman's hand holds him fast. "No. Not yet," Warren Wallace says calmly, and "Watch them for just another second, Professor."

And one of the tendrils has pulled free of the rest, rises silently from the water like a charmed cobra. Henry can see that it's turning towards him, already six or seven feet of it suspended above the dark water, but it's still coming. The water dripping off it very, very loud, impossible drip, drip, drip like a drumbeat in his ears, like his own racing heart, and then he notices the constant movement on the underside of the thing and knows at once what he's seeing. The worm thing in Wallace's bottle, coiling and uncoiling, and here are a thousand of them, restless polyps sprouting from this greater appendage, row upon writhing row, and now it's risen high enough that the thing is right in front of him, shimmering in the lantern light, a living question mark scant feet from Henry Matthew's face.

And later, lying awake in his room or walking at night along Twentieth Street, or broad daylight and staring up towards the mountain from the windows of his classroom, this is the part that he'll struggle to recall: Warren Wallace pulling him suddenly backwards, away from the hole as tendril struck, the lantern falling from his hand, tumbling into the hole, and maybe he heard it hit the water, heard it splash at the same moment he tumbled backwards into the dark, tripped on the rails and landed hard. And the foreman cursing, the sounds of him hastily working to cover the hole in the tunnel wall again, and lastly, the dullwet *thunk,* meatmallet thud again and again from the other side of the tin barrier.

Minutes later that seem like days, and the schoolteacher and the foreman sit alone together in the small and crooked shed near the tunnel, sloppy excuse for an office, a table and two stools, blueprints and a rusty stovepipe winding up towards the ceiling. Coal soot and the sicklysweet smell of Wallace's chewing tobacco. Henry Matthews sits on one of the stools, a hot cup of coffee in his hand, black coffee with a dash of whiskey from a bottle the foreman keeps in a box of tools under the table. And Warren Wallace sits across from him, staring down at his own cup, watching the steam rising from the coffee.

"I won't even try," Henry starts, stops, stares at the dirt floor and then begins again. "I *can't* tell you what that was, what it is. I don't think anyone could, Mr. Wallace."

"Yeah," the foreman says, shakes his head slow and sips at his coffee. Then, "I just wanted you to see it, Professor, before we bring in a fellow to brick up that hole next week. I wanted someone with some education to see it, so someone besides me and my men would know what was down there."

And for a while neither of them says anything else, and there's only the rattle and clatter of a locomotive passing by a little farther up the mountain, hauling its load of ore along the loop of the L. & N. Mineral Railroad. In the quiet left when the train has gone, the foreman clears his throat and, "You know what 'hematite' means?"

"From the Latin," Henry answers. "It means 'blood stone,'" and he takes a bitter, bourbon-tainted sip of his own coffee.

"Yeah," the foreman says. "I looked that up in a dictionary. Blood stone."

"What are you getting at?" Henry asks, watching the foreman, and Wallace looks a lot older than he ever realized before, deep lines and wrinkles, patches of gray in his dark beard. The foreman reaches beneath the table, lifts something wrapped in burlap and sets it in front of Henry Matthews.

"Just that maybe we ain't the only thing in the world that's got a use for that iron ore," he says and pulls the burlap back, revealing a large chunk of hematite. Granular rock the exact color of dried blood, and the foreman doesn't have to point out the deep pockmarks in the surface of the rock, row after row, each no bigger around than a man's finger, no bigger around than the writhing black thing in Warren Wallace's nitroglycerine bottle.

The chill and tinderdry end of November: Mr. W. A. Merkel's tunnel finished on schedule, and the Water Works began laying the two big pipes, forty-two and thirty inches round, that would eventually bring clean drinking water all the way from the new Cahaba Pumping Station. Henry Matthews never went back to the spoil heaps outside the tunnel, never saw Warren Wallace again; the last crate of his Silurian specimens shipped away to Tuscaloosa, and his attentions, his curiosity, shifted instead to the great Warrior coal field north of Birmingham, the smoke-gray shales and cinnamon sandstones laid down in steamy Carboniferous swamps uncounted ages after the silt and mud, the ancient reefs and tropical lagoons that finally became the strata of Red Mountain, were buried deep and pressed into stone.

But the foreman's pitted chunk of hematite kept in a locked strongbox in one undusted corner of Henry's room, and wrapped in cheesecloth and excelsior, nestled next to the stone and floating in cloudy preserving alcohol, the thing in the bottle. Kept like an unlucky souvenir or memento of a nightmare, and late nights when he awoke coldsweating and mouth too dry to speak, these were things to take out, to hold, something undeniable to look at by candle or kerosene light. A proof against madness, or a distraction from other memories, blurred, uncertain recollection of what he saw in that last moment before he fell, as the lantern tumbled towards the oilblack water and the darker shape moving just beneath its mirrored surface.

> All would be well.
> All would be heavenly—
> If the damned would only stay damned.
> —Charles Fort (1919)

SOURCES

Washington Irving: "The Adventure of the German Student"
First publication: *Tales of a Traveller* (London: John Murray, 1824).
Text: Washington Irving, *Tales of a Traveller,* ed. Judith Giblin Haig (The Complete Works of Washington Irving) (Boston: Twayne, 1987).

Nathaniel Hawthorne: "Edward Randolph's Portrait"
First publication: *United States Magazine and Democratic Review* (July 1838).
First collection: *Twice-Told Tales,* revised edition (Boston: James Munroe, 1842).
Text: Nathaniel Hawthorne, *Twice-Told Tales* (The Works of Nathaniel Hawthorne, Standard Library Edition) (Boston: Houghton Mifflin, 1883).

Edgar Allan Poe: "The Fall of the House of Usher"
First publication: *Burton's Gentleman's Magazine* (September 1839).
First collection: *Tales of the Grotesque and Arabesque* (Philadelphia: Lea & Blanchard, 1840).
Text: Edgar Allan Poe, *The Complete Works of Edgar Allan Poe,* ed. James A. Harrison (New York: Thomas Y. Crowell Co., 1902), Volume 3.

Fitz-James O'Brien: "What Was It?"
First publication: *Harper's Magazine* (March 1859).
First collection: *The Poems and Stories of Fitz-James O'Brien,* ed. William Winter (Boston: J. R. Osgood, 1881).

Text: Fitz-James O'Brien, *Collected Stories of Fitz-James O'Brien,* ed. Edward J. O'Brien (New York: Albert & Charles Boni, 1925).

Ambrose Bierce: "The Death of Halpin Frayser"
First publication: *Wave* (December 19, 1891).
First collection: *Can Such Things Be?* (New York: Cassell, 1893).
Text: Ambrose Bierce, *The Collected Works of Ambrose Bierce* (New York & Washington: Neale Publishing Co., 1909–12), Volume 3 (1910).

Robert W. Chambers: "The Yellow Sign"
First publication: Robert W. Chambers, *The King in Yellow* (New York: F. Tennyson Neely, 1895).
Text: *The King in Yellow* (New York: F. Tennyson Neely, 1895).

Henry James: "The Real Right Thing"
First publication: *Collier's Weekly* (December 16, 1899).
First collection: *The Soft Side* (New York: Macmillan, 1900).
Text: Henry James, *The Ghostly Tales of Henry James,* ed. Leon Edel (New Brunswick, NJ: Rutgers University Press, 1949).

H. P. Lovecraft: "The Call of Cthulhu"
First publication: *Weird Tales* (February 1928).
First collection: *The Outsider and Others,* ed. August Derleth and Donald Wandrei (Sauk City, WI: Arkham House, 1939).
Text: H. P. Lovecraft, *The Dunwich Horror and Others,* ed. S. T. Joshi (Sauk City, WI: Arkham House, 1984).

Clark Ashton Smith: "The Vaults of Yoh-Vombis"
First publication: *Weird Tales* (May 1932).
First collection: *Out of Space and Time* (Sauk City, WI: Arkham House, 1942).
Text: Clark Ashton Smith, *The Vaults of Yoh-Vombis,* ed. Steve Behrends, *The Unexpurgated Clark Ashton Smith* (West Warwick, RI: Necronomicon Press, 1988).

Robert E. Howard: "Old Garfield's Heart"
First publication: *Weird Tales* (December 1933).

First collection: *The Dark Man and Others* (Sauk City, WI: Arkham House, 1963).

Text: Robert E. Howard, *The Black Stranger and Other American Tales* (Lincoln: University of Nebraska Press, 2005).

Robert Bloch: "Black Bargain"
First publication: *Weird Tales* (May 1942).
First collection: *Flowers from the Moon and Other Lunacies,* ed. Robert M. Price (Sauk City, WI: Arkham House, 1998).
Text: *Flowers from the Moon and Other Lunacies* (Sauk City, WI: Arkham House, 1998).

August Derleth: "The Lonesome Place"
First publication: *Famous Fantastic Mysteries* (February 1948).
First collection: *Lonesome Places* (Sauk City, WI: Arkham House, 1962).
Text: *Lonesome Places* (Sauk City, WI: Arkham House, 1962).

Fritz Leiber: "The Girl with the Hungry Eyes"
First publication: *The Girl with the Hungry Eyes,* ed. Donald A. Wollheim (New York: Avon, 1949).
First collection: *The Secret Songs* (London: Rupert Hart-Davis, 1968).
Text: Fritz Leiber, *Horrible Imaginings,* ed. John Pelan (Seattle: Midnight House, 2004).

Ray Bradbury: "The Fog Horn"
First publication: *Saturday Evening Post* (June 23, 1951).
First collection: *The Golden Apples of the Sun* (Garden City, NY: Doubleday, 1953).
Text: Ray Bradbury, *The Stories of Ray Bradbury* (New York: Knopf, 1980).

Shirley Jackson: "A Visit"
First publication: *New World Writing* no. 2 (1952) (As "The Lovely House").
First collection: *Come Along with Me,* ed. Stanley Edgar Hyman (New York: Viking Press, 1968).
Text: *New World Writing* no. 2 (1952).

Richard Matheson: "Long Distance Call"

First publication: *Beyond Fantasy Fiction* (November 1953).

First collection: *Shock!* (New York: Dell, 1961).

Text: Richard Matheson, *Collected Stories* (Santa Cruz, CA: Scream / Press, 1989).

Charles Beaumont: "The Vanishing American"

First publication: *Magazine of Fantasy and Science Fiction* (August 1955).

First collection: *The Hunger and Other Stories* (New York: Putnam, 1957).

Text: Charles Beaumont, *Selected Stories*, ed. Roger Anker (Arlington Heights, IL: Dark Harvest, 1988).

T. E. D. Klein: "The Events at Poroth Farm"

First publication: *From Beyond the Dark Gateway* (December 1972).

First collection: *The Events at Poroth Farm* (West Warwick, RI: Necronomicon Press, 1990).

Text: *Reassuring Tales* (Burton, MI: Subterranean Press, 2007).

Stephen King: "Night Surf"

First publication: *Cavalier* (August 1974).

First collection: *Night Shift* (Garden City, NY: Doubleday, 1978).

Text: *Night Shift* (Garden City, NY: Doubleday, 1978).

Dennis Etchison: "The Late Shift"

First publication: *Dark Forces*, ed. Kirby McCauley (New York: Viking, 1980).

First collection: *The Dark Country* (Santa Cruz, CA: Scream/Press, 1982).

Text: Dennis Etchison, *Talking in the Dark: Selected Stories* (Lancaster, PA: Stealth Press, 2001).

Thomas Ligotti: "Vastarien"

First publication: *Crypt of Cthulhu* (St. John's Eve 1987).

First collection: *Songs of a Dead Dreamer*, revised edition (London: Robinson, 1989).

Text: *Songs of a Dead Dreamer,* revised edition (London: Robinson, 1989).

Karl Edward Wagner: "Endless Night"
First publication: *The Architecture of Fear,* ed. Kathryn Cramer and Peter D. Pautz (New York: Arbor House, 1987).
First collection: *Unthreatened by the Morning Light* (Eugene, OR: Pulphouse, 1989).
Text: Karl Edward Wagner, *Exorcisms and Ecstasies,* ed. Stephen Jones (Minneapolis, MN: Fedogan & Bremer, 1997).

Norman Partridge: "The Hollow Man"
First publication: *Grue Magazine* (Fall 1991).
First collection: *The Man with the Barbed-Wire Fists* (San Francisco: Night Shade Books, 2001).
Text: *The Man with the Barbed-Wire Fists* (San Francisco: Night Shade Books, 2001).

David J. Schow: "Last Call for the Sons of Shock"
First publication: David J. Schow, *Black Leather Required* (Shingletown, CA: Mark V. Ziesing, 1994).
Text: *Black Leather Required* (Shingletown, CA: Mark V. Ziesing, 1994).

Joyce Carol Oates: "Demon"
First publication: Joyce Carol Oates, *Demon and Other Tales* (West Warwick, RI: Necronomicon Press, 1996).
Text: *Demon and Other Tales* (West Warwick, RI: Necronomicon Press, 1996).

Caitlín R. Kiernan: "In the Water Works (Birmingham, Alabama 1888)"
First publication: Caitlín R. Kiernan, *Tales of Pain and Wonder* (Springfield, PA: Gauntlet Press, 2000).
Text: Caitlín R. Kiernan, *To Charles Fort, with Love* (Burton, MI: Subterranean Press, 2005).